RETRIBUTION

RETRIBUTION

T. WILLIAM

Charleston, SC
www.PalmettoPublishing.com

Retribution
Copyright © 2021 by T. William

Hardcover ISBN: 978-1-68515-307-6
Paperback ISBN: 978-1-68515-308-3
eBook ISBN: 978-1-68515-309-0

First Edition
First Printing

DEDICATION

There are certain people who are so afraid of losing that they are labeled workaholics. They will spend dozens of hours in preparation for a thirty minute hearing where they will try to impress a judge; and they will spend countless hours in preparation for days in a courtroom trying to impress a jury.

I am referring to those lawyers who would never think of misleading a judge; and whose word can always be trusted by opposing counsel. They are courtroom warriors who try multiple jury trials year after year, yet still have problems controlling their nerves while waiting for a verdict.

They are trial lawyers who feel equally comfortable representing a plaintiff or a defendant because they believe in the Seventh Amendment and an American's right to a trial by their peers.

This book is dedicated to those lawyers. Civil trial lawyers!

RET·RI·BU·TION (RE-TRE-'BYU-SHEN), N.:
   1. THE ACT OF GETTING EVEN;
   2. REVENGE

CHAPTER 1

THEY WERE NOT SURE if they had been caught. Anyway, it was exciting for her.

They had just finished having sex, if you want to call it that, for the third night in a row. It was Wednesday and Rick had been off for the weekend, but they had been together the Thursday and Friday before. Actually, Thursday was the first time, and they had done "it" twice that day and once the next.

Cora Smallwood was sure she was in love this time and this time was different. S. Richard Taggart was a professional man. He was a psychologist with an MS degree from Macon University—a good liberal arts school in Georgia. He told her he was working on his doctorate part time at the University of Florida. He told her that he loved her, too, and would prove it when she got out. He could teach her how to fly, and they could go off for long holidays. There was nobody else but her, he had repeatedly lied. He denied having a wife and never mentioned his two children.

The phone rang and Rick answered it. "I'll be right there. She couldn't sleep and needed to talk. She's still fragile, you know."

———

Carol Robertson did know. She was the head nurse for the closed psychiatric wing of the never-too-crowded Greenview Psychiatric Hospital. It was contained in a building just next to the large and overcrowded General Hospital of Gainesville. The grounds were kept nice, and the facility was housed in a two-story L- shaped building. The closed wing, or "unit" as it was sometimes called, was on the second floor, a portion of which was for children and adolescents only. The open wings were on the first and second floors.

Carol had been on duty two weeks ago when Cora had been transferred back from the open unit only hours before she was to be released to go home. She had also been on duty almost one month earlier when the patient was initially admitted.

Cora had been a transfer patient from a small hospital near Starke. She had overdosed on one of her several prescription drugs and was taken there by her brother, Richard. They had pumped her stomach and got her stable, but the small hospital wasn't equipped to handle psychiatric patients.

That same night she had been processed into the closed unit of Greenview, where her every move was supposed to be monitored. An orderly would help her to the toilet; help her bathe; and take her to and from her meals. A nurse would administer all medications following the strict orders of a medical doctor-- usually a psychiatrist.

A psychologist like Rick Taggart could not prescribe medicine, but was assigned to conduct therapy in both the open and closed units. Patients in the closed unit were totally dependent on the hospital staff. Cora liked being dependent on Rick.

After the first three days, her progress had been exceptional and she had been moved to the open unit. There, she could do anything within reason. Her meals were taken in the cafeteria. The rec room was available for pool, TV and a constant game of checkers. Telephone to call out, but no laptop, smartphones or computers. There were group sessions twice a day and private therapy—one-on-one talks—three times a week.

Cora had met Rick at the group sessions. She was one of eight patients in the group led by him. At first she had been shy but not withdrawn. Within four days she was a full participant and was eager to help "bring out" some of the others.

He was great, she thought. No, wonderful. He not only helped her but the others loved him too. At least most of the others.

One woman, younger than Cora, rudely refused to attend his group. Her name was Heather, and she ranted and raved. Cora remembered hearing that Heather was uncontrollable and eventually discharged back to her family. She also heard it had been Heather's third admission to the same hospital. Who knows where else she had been kicked out?

Cora really began to look forward to the private counseling. They could talk about anything. He wasn't shocked to learn that she had been in and out of hospitals every couple of years since she was fourteen. Nor that she had her first child when she was seventeen, but gave into her family's wishes and put it up for adoption. They told her the baby was a boy, but she really could not remember seeing him.

Cora let Rick know she was now thirty-two and had never been married. Her thirteen-year-old daughter lived with her sister's family, all of whom she hated. By the age of thirty, she had agreed to three abortions but refused to have her tubes tied.

Rick didn't mind. He never scolded her. He was nice, and he made her feel good with his compliments. To him, she was attractive and sweet. He told her so.

———

Two days before she was to be released, Rick told her that she would go home soon. There would be no more private sessions—just group therapy. However, if she ever just needed to talk, he would be around. Cora let him know that he was the best friend she had. The best thing that had ever happened to her was meeting Rick. That was the same day she wore a bathrobe to the private session. Wore panties but purposefully left off her bra.

Patients were allowed to wear regular clothes in the open unit if the clothes were clean. Bathrobes were not exactly regular, but she told Rick that she had not had time to dress after her shower. Cora noticed that Rick noticed. She caught him peering between the flaps at her relatively large breasts. She knew he would but didn't let him know that she knew he was looking.

The patient had the looks that some men find attractive. Even without makeup, Cora's face was pretty to some. She was slightly overweight, but her breasts were large enough to make her figure look good. She was always clean and took at least four showers a day. She didn't have that crusty odor that most of the other patients had.

Cora stood up and walked around the private room used only for therapy. Rick remained seated but followed her with his eyes as they continued to talk about the intended release. She stopped in front of him, uncomfortably close. He was looking up at her face when she stepped within inches. He was tempted to put his arms around her. Definitely aroused. He had been aroused by his patients before, but this time he refused to take the opportunity.

Instead, he stood and reported that the fifty minutes were up. Then he turned and walked to his right in order to physically remove himself from the awkward position.

Back in her semi-private room, Cora could not decide what had happened. Had she teased him? Was she really in love? Had she gone too far?

It really didn't matter, she concluded. In two days she would be out and would probably never see Rick again. She wasn't sure what she would have done had he accepted her unspoken invitation. Now that was over.

They saw each other in group the next day and the next. She wasn't quite as open, but still she had made progress. It was time for her to go home.

Cora would be released between 4:00 and 5:00 p.m. It was now 10:00 a.m. Her roommate had been released the day before and another had yet to be assigned. Using the "in-house" phone in the rec room, she called Rick and asked if he would come by for a talk before she left.

Of course, he should say no. She was obviously becoming infatuated with her therapist. Still, a short talk would be okay. It would lift her spirits. Since she was leaving anyway, he agreed to see her in her room at one o'clock.

Rick kept the appointment and was happy to see she was dressed appropriately when he arrived. Her few things were gathered. She was wearing Levi's, not too tight, and a cotton sleeveless sweater. She was wearing no socks with her white Keds. No jewelry. No makeup. Although she had on no perfume, he noticed that she smelled fresh and clean as usual.

He knew that the doors to patients' rooms were never to be completely closed when staff entered. So he purposely left it open at least one foot.

Cora had prepared. They could not be seen from the hall if they were positioned at the northeast corner of the room by the window. A chair had been purposely placed there, and it was the obvious place for the psychologist to sit. He did.

She initiated the small talk, but for her time was of the essence. She needed to know if there was a chance that she would ever see him again.

Looks were not important to her. Rick was about fifty, with greying but mostly black hair. He slicked it back. He was about five foot, eleven inches—two inches taller than Cora. Liked to wear collared T-shirts with khakis or blue jeans. His shoulders were not broad, and he was not overweight. She could overlook the fact that his fingernails were seldom clean. His hands looked like those of somebody who liked to work on cars. Or was it the airplane that everybody in the group knew about?

For the first time, she asked if he was married. For some reason that Rick did not understand, he said, "No, I was once but have been divorced for years."

"Children?"

He hesitated before saying, "Nope. I wasn't lucky." It did not bother him to deny having a wife. His conscience hurt when he denied his children.

"Do you like children?"

"Of course."

"Maybe you can meet my Renee. She's thirteen. I wish you could meet her. You've been so helpful to me. Maybe you could teach us how to get along without the interference from Regina. She's my sister, you know."

"I know." Then he added, not knowing why, "I would like to meet your daughter." He thought again. "Will she be coming today when your family picks you up?"

"What family? My brother will probably pick me up. Maybe my mother will come too. I doubt it. Daddy is the only one who ever loved me, but he's too old to come. Regina's not about to see me here, and Renee's staying with her right now."

Rick wondered what had caused such a long answer to such an easy question. There was a pause, and he was thinking what to say next. For some reason he felt uncomfortable.

Cora knew she was wasting too much time. She had to keep the conversation going. She stood from the corner of the bed that was assigned to her next would-be roommate.

As she walked toward the northeast corner of the room near the window, she said, "My brother's name is Richard too. We call him that, 'Richard,' not 'Rick,' like you. We're very close. Have been since we were teenagers. Will you kiss me goodbye, Richard?"

He was startled and began to stand as she put her arms around his neck. He put his arms around her waist, still amazed at his robotic reaction to what was going on.

She pecked his lips, and when he did not resist, she put her lips over his.

She could feel his warm tongue in her mouth. She could now feel him.

When the sun came from behind a cloud, Rick became aware that all that was happening was happening right in front of the window. They could be seen, if anybody was looking. He pushed away and looked out. Nobody was outside. They had not been caught.

As the head nurse, Carol Robertson, adjusted the shade of the window of an inside room in the closed wing, she wondered who she had just witnessed kissing passionately before the window of room 214. She wasn't trying to snoop, but the design of the building made everything that occurred in front of the windows of the open wing obvious.

The open unit was not *that* open. Visiting hours were not until three o'clock, but she convinced herself the view had not been clear. Head Nurse Robertson had to make a decision now. She decided not to mention what she should not have seen.

"Rick, can we see each other when I'm out?"

"Maybe. I have to leave now. Private counseling for Mr. Ross." He stammered. "Listen, Cora, that was a mistake. I'll try to see you when you check out."

"Can you see me before I check out?"

"I don't think so," he said while leaving the room.

Rick thought of how stupid he had been. He muttered, "She'll leave now. It won't happen again. Thank God she's leaving. What's wrong with me? Nobody would ever believe me again, even if she is crazy."

He could not get the events off his mind as he walked toward the private room for a private session with Edward Ross.

"Mr. Taggart!"

Rick turned in response to the call from the orderly's desk. "Mr. Taggart, you're wanted on the phone."

"Take a message, Don."

"She says it's important."

"Who?"

"Cora Smallwood. I'll ask her what she wants."

"No.... No. I'll take it in here," Rick said while pointing toward his small office.

Rick took the offensive. "Look Cora, I'm sorry, but I have work."

"I know, with Mr. Ross. Rick, will you see me when you're finished with him? I'll wait."

He knew he had to cut it off here and now. "No. I can't see you again today. I just found out that I will be assisting—what am I explaining for? No, Cora, I can't," he said firmly.

"How about tomorrow after I get home? Will you see me tomorrow?" She was begging, and she knew it.

It had to stop. "Cora, after you leave here, I can't see you anymore."

She hung up without saying goodbye.

Cora went to the bathroom and broke the razor out of her BIC. She raked it across her left wrist and walked out into the hallway, where she was certain she would attract attention. Don saw it first as the blood seemed to be pouring and forming a pool on the mock-tile floor. She slid down the wall and sat crying beside her room. She drew her knees up to her chest while locking her fingers in front of her calves. The blood was gushing down her ankle and into her left shoe, and she noticed the stain spread into the fibers of her Keds.

The crying caused the commotion that she had expected, or at least hoped for. Everybody seemed to join her in the hall at the same time. As she was placed on a stretcher, she could see Edward Ross pointing at her and saying something to Rick.

"They must be talking about me," she mused. "Rick knows. He knows I'll be staying now. He knows I love him and he loves me. Why else would he have kissed me?"

———

"The cut was not so bad. She's lucky," reported the emergency room doctor to Regina Baker, Cora's sister.

The wounds were bloody but not deep—just as Cora intended. Before midnight she was back in Greenview Psychiatric. Back in the closed unit, where she could depend on the staff. Where she would see S. Richard Taggart, psychologist.

She had not been processed out. She would have weeks with Rick.

Rick did not want to see her again. She was vulnerable, and so was he. The choice wasn't his. Cora was his patient so long as he worked there.

For the first couple of days, neither talked about the in-hospital events of the past. Cora was too drugged up. Rick did not want to.

When the bandages were removed from her wrist, it was obvious that the scar would be light. Maybe disappear. No tendons cut. There would be no permanent problem.

———

Cora's new roommate in the closed unit was at least eighty. She never talked, and that was okay with Cora. Mildred was out of the room most of the time and mostly asleep when she was not.

On the fourth night, nearly five weeks after Cora was initially admitted to Greenview, Mildred began to moan. This would not have been so unusual for the patients in the closed wing (nor the open wing for that matter), but Mildred had never made a sound. Cora could see the old lady by the night-light that was always on; and by the hall light that came through the door, which was always open at least twelve inches. She stared at the wrinkled face for fifteen minutes without trying to comfort her. Then the noise stopped. Mildred's eyes opened wide. Her breathing stopped. She was dead.

Cora tried to scream, but there was no sound. It was sometime between 2:00 and 3:00 a.m. before Mildred was found by the night nurse who was bringing medicine. Her body was quietly removed from room 223 after the paperwork was completed. Everybody was careful not to wake Cora, who slept not a wink that night.

The following day Rick met with Cora in the small room designed for private sessions in the closed wing. She had bathed twice that day. He noticed the dark rings under her eyes and told her so. She started to sob and told Rick what she had witnessed the night before.

The psychologist knew she needed comforting, and he hugged her. Cora put her face in his chest. Looked up and saw him looking at her.

"I love you," she said.

"I know. Maybe I love you too," he whispered.

They kissed, and the kisses were passionate.

Nobody ever disturbed the private sessions, the therapist thought as he locked the door. He lifted Cora's nightgown. She was not wearing panties, and he had his way with her for the first time. They both knew to be quiet. She later promised not to tell.

He visited her in her room late that afternoon, just before going home. There was no roommate to watch as she opened Rick's fly. He had not told her to. She just did it when he stepped close while she just sat there.

On Friday sex was easier, but Rick was happy for the weekend. It was an opportunity to consider his guilt. He had not made love to his wife in months, and now he was once again risking his career for ten to fifteen minutes with a mental patient. No way would he do it again.

On Monday, he got away with it when he volunteered to take Cora her lunch and things just got out of hand. Tuesday, the private session started with her sobbing declaration of undying love; and concluded by her proving it. Again, he had not told her to.

———

Tuesday night Rick could not sleep. His wife had long since quit doting and probably didn't notice. He could hear her breathing loudly, almost snoring. She wasn't the pretty girl he remembered marrying. Cora would have bathed before going to bed.

He had nobody to talk to, which struck Rick as funny since all he did was listen to those crazy people all day.

By dawn he had figured it out. He would talk to the psychiatrist—not about himself, but about Cora. She should be transferred. Not to the open unit. Out. He was going to recommend the psychiatric unit at Shand's Teaching Hospital at the University of Florida.

He would tell the psychiatrist that she was uncontrollable. Had to fight her off at all sessions. She would tell him about her dreams that they were in love. Now she was insisting that they were having an affair. How absurd! She was acting just like Heather during her second admission to the hospital, and the psychologist wasn't going to go through that again. He would suggest that they nip the problem in the bud.

By late in the evening, Rick had somehow managed not to have the talk with the psychiatrist. It seemed like something came up each time he gathered the nerve to have the little conversation that would cure his problem.

———

He had become bold over the last seven days. Any excuse was automatically accepted by the staff, so breaking little rules was not noticed.

Rick entered Cora's room. Felt powerful. Lustful. Just like every other time, he convinced himself that this would be the last. He closed her door, but there was light from the window.

Cora smelled good. She had just showered and her hair was still wet. She whispered, "I love you. Close the shades first."

He did as requested, but not without first checking all the windows in the open unit. A glance at somebody walking by half-dressed would be more than just a little exciting for Rick.

Cora was lying in the bed, naked but covered with a sheet. Since Mildred had died, she still had no roommate to watch them as he kissed her lips. His right hand went under the sheet, and he fondled her breasts before putting his fingers between her legs. He pulled his pants to his knees but did not remove them.

Two minutes had passed since he had adjusted the shades. Then, just as he was penetrating her, the door opened. Within seconds it closed.

Rick jumped to his feet; adjusted his clothes; and left the room. Entering the hall, he heard the phone ring. It was for him. Carol Robertson to inform him that Dr. Whitaker, the psychiatrist, needed him immediately.

"We have been looking for you for ten minutes," the head nurse said.

"I'll be right there. She couldn't sleep and needed to talk. She's still fragile, you know."

CHAPTER 2

CAROL ROBERTSON COULD NOT sleep, and she did not want to talk about it. At least she did not want to talk to her husband.

James Peter Robertson was a good man and easy to talk to. That was what had brought them together in the first place. It was a strong marriage—especially for the 2000s. It was Carol's second, and for nearly five years, she had somebody she could really talk to about anything.

"Why don't you tell me what's wrong? I know something is wrong."

"This is something I just have to work out for myself, Jim. Go to sleep."

"No, damn it! If you're mad at me, let it out."

"It's not you."

"Then tell me about it."

The conversation went in a circle for the umpteenth time.

Carol knew it was her fault. She hadn't molested Cora, but she could have stopped it. She should have reported the psychologist when she saw them through the window. She felt dirty and sick. She resolved to make a report in the morning, but that might just complicate things.

Sometime during the cool spring night, she remembered meeting Cora's sister, the one who had come back from the emergency room and acted so concerned. "Call me if we can do anything," the sister said just before leaving. Head nurse Robertson had made assurances that all was well now and nothing could go wrong in the closed wing.

She awoke before dawn, and at 6:45 a.m., Carol was looking at Cora's chart. Nobody noticed, even though it was several hours early for her to report to work. Maybe she was "making up" hours. The hospital was lenient on that. It was okay to take a little extra time at lunch here and have a hair appointment there. Just be sure to make it up. There was always paperwork to do.

Regina Smallwood Baker's name and address were in the chart. She got the phone number by asking Siri on her iPad. By seven o'clock, they were talking.

"Hello."

"Hello, is this Regina Baker, sister of Cora Smallwood?"

"Yes, why? What's wrong with Cora now?"

She sounded groggy at first, then awake, then exasperated, all within several seconds.

"No. Nothing. I—we—just think maybe Cora should talk to somebody. Maybe you could come see her."

"What's this about? Isn't that all she does? I mean, talk to you people all day? I know she talks to that psychiatrist, Rick something. She kept talking about him in the emergency room."

"It's just that sometimes they'll talk to family about things that happen…" The head nurse stopped to consider what she was saying. She didn't want to say too much. "We just…it's all right."

Regina interrupted, "What's happened?"

"Nothing."

"To whom am I talking?"

"Never mind." With that, Carol hung up feeling worse than ever.

She had helped nobody. Now this Mrs. Baker was obviously upset. And, she thought, *What a coward I was. How stupid. I just hung up in that poor woman's face. She'll call for sure. How am I going to explain all this now?*

The worst part was she felt like a traitor. She had almost broken the unwritten code. She had all but betrayed the whole hospital.

Fear had set in. It was the fear that had been instilled and taught in nursing school; and that had been repeated so often in every hospital in which she had ever worked. Nobody ever said it, but everybody who works in a hospital knows that if you see certain mistakes, you should turn your head. Try not to be a witness. Problems are handled in-house, without public scrutiny. Be silent. You can be forgiven for breaking almost any rule. You will not be forgiven for breaking the unwritten code of silence. After all, medical malpractice suits are out of control.

Carol left the hospital. She went to the Waffle House for coffee since she could not eat.

———

Predictably, Regina Baker called the hospital but nobody knew what she was talking about. The nurse who had the unfortunate luck to handle the call was courteous but firm.

When she finished the call and replaced the phone receiver, the nurse said to an orderly, who happened to be wasting time in the wrong place, "That woman is as crazy as her sister. Maybe they should be roommates."

The nurse had been up all night. She was tired, and it suddenly dawned on her that the orderly was not doing his job. She began raising hell. The orderly picked up a bedpan and disappeared down the hall.

Visiting hours began at 3:00 p.m. Regina would be in her sister's room. She knew they had to talk, but she had no idea what they were going to talk about.

———

Cora hated Regina.

Growing up, they went through the same things with their father, but somehow Regina had avoided him when the actual touching started. Regina was strong and would yell and threaten. Their father would cower.

Cora was timid when it came to her father. He made her feel guilty if she did not give in. She could not remember when he first began coming into her room during the middle of the night.

She tried to block it out of her mind. She couldn't. Unless sleeping under sedation, she knew that the nightmares that woke her included a child—barely more than a toddler—with Cora's face. She remembered her awful teen years, when he would come to her whenever he was sober enough to be aroused.

Why had her mother not helped, Cora often wondered? She had to have known what was going on. If she loved her, then why didn't she help her? Her mother was just as bad as her father, maybe worse.

Once Cora confronted her mother, who only sobbed.

"I don't believe you," her mother said. "If it would have happened, I would have known."

Mrs. Smallwood knew that Cora was only making it up. Otherwise, why did she wait so many years to ask the questions? To confront her?

Cora knew that her mother knew. Denying it made her feel dirty. Filthy.

At school, Cora was never popular. It was probably because she was not happy, even though she was smart and had no difficulty making good grades.

She had lost her virginity years before she reached puberty. That made it easy for her to be with the young boys who wanted to try it for the first time. Why were they never friends afterward? She knew that they were laughing at her in the halls of the junior high school. She hated explaining to her mother why she never had a steady boyfriend like the other girls her age.

Had she ever actually had intercourse with her brother, Richard? Cora could not remember. She remembers kissing him and him fondling her. But she had read an article in some family magazine that experimentation among siblings was "normal."

Richard was never mean to her like Regina was. He would even arrange dates for her as they got older, and their two years difference in age seemed less important. In fact, Cora had just weeks earlier broken up with Stanley Malloy, Richard's most recent "best" drinking buddy.

The sister was a different story. Regina was one of those courageous types who found strength in adversity. She was fourteen when Cora's baby boy was born. She always wondered whom he looked like. It was not until she was older that she understood why he had been placed with an adoption agency.

Regina had left home that same year and moved in with her grandmother on the Phillips side of the family. Grandpa Phillips had died the year before Regina's arrival. Her grandmother never asked her why she left. She was afraid to know. Talking was the last thing their family ever did.

High school wasn't so easy for Regina; but seemed easier when she changed schools after running away from home. After graduating, she made her own arrangements for scholarships at Santa Fe Junior College in Gainesville. That's where she met Kenneth Baker.

Ken was going to school on the GI Bill and other government subsidies that he earned during his three years in the Army. She did not know if his discipline was the result of his military training or the strong family values that seem innate in children who are raised on small rural farms.

When Regina and Ken were married, the only person from her family that she invited was Grandma Phillips, and she could not attend. With that, Regina felt that she had finally and totally divorced herself from her childhood. She felt clean. She did not care if she talked to the people who had tried to destroy her life and childhood ever again.

Regina was three years younger than Cora and was sixteen when Cora's daughter Renee was born. Cora had insisted on keeping Renee, even though her father had said that "the Smallwoods won't give a home to a bastard." Cora moved out. Got her own room in a weather-beaten boarding house near downtown Starke. She truly believed that she could support them both on minimum-wage earnings from her job at Jiffy Mart.

The younger sister was always fearful of the type of life Renee would have. Cora was an erratic mother, alternately showering Renee with love and then leaving her with any stranger when it suited. Renee lived on a diet of junk food and colas and learned to call any number of men "uncle."

Two years after marrying Ken, Regina called Cora and told her that she could no longer stand by and watch Renee face the sorry prospects of their own youth. She offered to take Renee and raise her as her own. Cora said that she would never give up her baby. That's when Ken made an appointment for him and his wife to meet with a lawyer.

William Forrester was twenty-eight when he graduated from the University of Florida College of Law. He had spent one year prosecuting criminals for the State Attorney's Office and then joined the largest insurance defense law firm in Jacksonville. After four years and a partnership, he and three others started their own firm, Moran, Smith, Forrester & Dees. Although business was not as good as they had hoped, it wasn't bad either. Three out of four of them were young and they were all hungry. They took any case that came through the door.

Bill liked trial work—criminal and personal injury trial work. However, in those early years, he had yet to make the reputation necessary to get enough work in those areas to keep him busy, let alone keep up with his share of the overhead.

There seemed to be plenty of domestic and family law work around, and he began to develop a reputation for that. At least half of his time was spent on divorces, child custody, and the enforcement of child support. It was bitter work, but it paid the bills.

When the young lawyer was told by Regina and Ken what they wanted to do, he let them know that such a suit was impractical. There was no way a judge could legally give them custody of Renee unless Cora consented. Regina was obstinate.

"Cora can't afford a lawyer. Can't you just draw up the papers and see what she'll do?"

"I can do that, but it won't be cheap. I charge two seventy-five per hour and keep accurate time sheets. The more she fights, the more expensive it will be, and I'll look to you for payment as we go along."

He didn't know how much it was going to cost, so Ken had borrowed $5,000 from his parents. He wrote out a retainer check for $3,500, knowing it would likely cost more. He did it for Regina. He knew what she had suffered in childhood. He knew why she wanted to protect Renee from the same thing.

Ken loved Regina and knew that he would love Renee.

It was nearly seven o'clock on a Wednesday night, two weeks later, when the papers were served by a Bradford County Sheriff's officer. In a small town like Starke, it was easy to figure out when Cora got off work. He refused to quit banging on her door until she answered. It took more than five minutes of pounding, but his persistence paid off, and he avoided a repeat trip later.

Cora yelled, "Coming!" And a half a minute later, she was answering the door, clad in a bathrobe and streaming wet hair. She had just finished her third shower of the day and had only just heard him.

The burly officer said, "You have to sign these papers, ma'am."

Startled, Cora looked at his face. "What are they for?"

"I don't know, but it looks like somebody wants custody of your kid. Now sign here and take these, ma'am."

Cora did as she was told. She began to weep. She closed the door and walked backward into the corner of the small room. She sobbed as she read the "COMPLAINT FOR CHILD CUSTODY." She wanted to give Renee a hug, but realized she had no idea where the child was playing. She could have been with any number of residents of the boarding house.

She didn't understand many of the legal words in the legal papers, but the sordid allegations of fact were clear. Her sister was saying that she was neglectful and abusive and unfit to be Renee's mother. She did as she always did when she felt dirty. She undid her robe in the living room and let it fall. She took a shower. Only afterward did she begin to look for Renee.

Regina called, but Cora would not talk to her. She pushed the off button and put her cell phone on silent. *I will not give her up. I'll die first*, she thought. *No judge is going to take my baby away.*

Two days later she did not hang up when her father called and said that the phone was on speaker and her mother was listening.

"We got subpoenas this morning from the Sheriff's Office. We went to see our lawyer, and he told us that we would have to go to court. We got copies of the Complaint that Regina made out. What are you trying to do, Cora?"

Mr. and Mrs. Smallwood were like Cora. They were scared. They knew that they would have to testify, and they didn't want a judge asking a lot of questions.

Her father called Cora a "slut" and a "whore" and told her that she didn't deserve to raise a baby, "even a bastard like Renee." Her mother stayed silent, as usual.

Arrangements were made for Cora to sign the papers giving Renee over to Regina and Ken. Although she was given liberal visitation privileges, Cora rarely made the forty-mile trip to see her brown-eyed baby in Jacksonville.

———

Cora hated Regina.

She hated seeing her in the emergency room when her wrist was being bandaged. She told her to stay away. Now Head Nurse Robertson was telling her that Regina was back again and waiting to see her at Greenview Psychiatric Hospital.

They had nothing to say to one another at first. Regina broke the ice.

"How's your wrist?"

"Fine."

"Everything okay?"

"Great."

It was like when a late-night television host tries to interview a ten-year-old. No real conversation, and everybody's glad when it's over.

After more silence Regina finally decided to take the direct approach. She told Cora about the phone call from somebody in the hospital. She told all of it, through the part where she called back and the nurse didn't know what she was talking about.

"I don't know what you're talking about either," Cora said. Those were the most words she had spoken at one time since Regina got there.

"Have you been injured? Has anyone hurt you?" Regina began to pry.

"No, everything is wonderful." Finally, Cora began to talk. "I really mean it. Wonderful! I'm in love. Really."

"Who is it?"

"I can't tell you his name, but he works here."

"You can't or you won't tell me?"

"I promised I wouldn't. He's going to teach me how to fly when I get out. I'll introduce you to him after we're married. We'll get Renee back."

"What are you talking about?" Regina demanded. "How do you know he loves you? You haven't been here long enough to know anybody, much less fall in love."

"You would be surprised how much you can get to know somebody when you talk a lot and let out all of your feelings." Cora was going on. Maybe, she thought, she would make her sister jealous.

"Who can you talk to that much?" Regina responded without thinking. Then she knew. "Are you talking about that psychiatrist you told me about after you slit your wrist?" She was practically yelling, and she knew she had gone too far.

Cora sat stiffly and crossed her arms. She said, "He's not a psychiatrist. I'll tell you that. But don't ask me any more questions. We aren't going to tell anybody until I get out. I promised I wouldn't tell, and you're the last person I'd tell. Why don't you leave?"

Cora wouldn't say another word. When Regina left, totally frustrated, Cora took a shower and remembered that she had not asked about how Renee was getting along.

CHAPTER 3

ALL CALLS IN THE psychiatric hospital went through a nurses' station. The landlines in the closed unit were for incoming calls only.

Nurses were only allowed to use their cells during breaks. Patients of the closed unit had no phone. Cora could not even get to the nurses' station. In the open unit, she could call out on a landline if she wanted.

There was no way for Cora to contact Rick unless he was in her wing. It was late when she saw him going into the conference room with another patient. He was avoiding her and she knew it.

Her medicine was brought on schedule. There was an extra capsule this time, and she was asleep in twenty minutes.

The next day Cora met her new roommate. Patients seldom got to know other patients' last names. The hospital tried to keep things confidential. Roommates, however, were an exception.

Alice had been admitted during the night. She was in her late forties and carried on like a magpie. She never stopped talking.

This was Alice's fourth admission to Greenview Psychiatric Hospital. She actually liked the place. It sure beat the alternative of being alone and at home.

She let it be known that she was rich. She lived in one of those colonial mansions with six columns supporting the portico in front. To get to it off the main road, US 27 where it is only two lanes, you had to travel through a good portion of her twelve-hundred-acre horse farm near Ocala. She had been born and raised in Michigan. "Grosse Point, Michigan," she told Cora as though she should be impressed.

Alice took little time before going into the details of her life. She had been happily married and had three daughters. Her oldest would have been in the Olympics, she was sure. At fifteen Christie was a great equestrian according to her mother. She rode thoroughbreds and always won. When they went to horse shows, if another child did well, they offered large sums of cash for that child's horse. Christie's horses were "made" horses. The finest that money could buy. The family moved to Ocala to train full-time.

Alice's grandfather and her husband's father were partners in the automobile industry. They had accumulated sufficient wealth so that their children and their children's children would never have to work. Alice had been happy as a child and as an adult. She was also happy as a wife and a parent until that ended four years ago.

Alice and her family were all going to watch Christie at a horse show near Orlando. Rather than sleep in a hotel, they decided to go early in the morning when there would be little traffic. John, her husband, was an early riser anyway.

They left their home at 4:30 a.m. and had made their way to Interstate 75 South. The kids were in the back seat sleeping on each other's shoulders.

It was so sudden. Alice and John were chitchatting away when they were hit head-on by a flatbed truck with its lights off, on the wrong side of the highway. The truck driver was killed. The autopsy blood test revealed a blood alcohol level of .21.

Her husband and the two younger girls were also dead at the scene. Christie seemed alert at first, but a hematoma inside her skull caused pressure on her brain. She had gone into a coma before the ambulance could get her to the hospital for the first of several surgeries.

Alice bruised her right knee—nothing else.

The first time she tried to kill herself with pills was the same day she agreed, under pressure, to allow Christie's life support system be removed. It wasn't that she believed the decision was wrong, she had explained; she just "wanted to get back with John and the girls in heaven."

Alice could afford a private room at Greenview Psychiatric Hospital, but she preferred to have somebody to talk to. She liked roommates.

Cora did not have to ask. Alice loved to talk about the previous "visits" to the psychiatric center. She had made friends. One friend was a psychologist, Richard Taggart. She told Cora about how they had become friends. The last time she went home, she had used her money to find Rick.

"It wasn't hard," she allowed, as though she, not a detective, had done the work. "Darling, was he ever surprised when I showed up at his house. I had presents for him, his wife and his girls. I really wanted to meet the girls and take them horseback riding where my girls used to like to ride."

Cora could not believe what she was hearing, though she did not say a word.

———

That afternoon she saw Rick. He could not avoid her for two days in a row. They were scheduled for a private session, and they were alone for the first time since the night somebody walked in while they were in bed.

Cora was not coy. She was hurt. She had to find out.

"Rick, you told me you were not married. You never told me you had children. Tell me the truth."

"I never lied and I never told you I wasn't married. I have children just like you. You know that." Rick looked Cora straight in the eye and talked as if he was disgusted with the conversation.

In his peripheral vision, he saw the razor in Cora's right hand. Razors were not allowed in the closed wing and he did not know how she had gotten one.

"I'm going to kill myself," she said with tears streaming down her face. "Why did you do this to me?"

Rick walked up to Cora and grasped her right wrist with his left hand. He held her arm to the side. He did not try to take the razor. He did not call for help.

He wrapped his free hand around the back of Cora's neck and pulled her to him. He kissed her with his mouth open and more passionately than ever before.

He let go of her as he stepped back. The staff psychologist opened the door and before leaving her alone in the room, he looked her in the eyes.

"Goodbye, Cora," he said as he closed the door.

She looked at the door. It should have been open at least twelve inches. Cora ran to her bathroom. Now she was sick and kneeling next to the toilet, crying. Her mind was made up. She would end it now. She was prepared to die. She would take a bath and cut her wrists. She would watch the red disappear down the drain while fading off to sleep. She remembered a similar scene from a porno flick she had watched with her brother, *The Devil in Mrs. Jones*.

The tub filled. Cora got in and submerged herself in the water. She felt dramatic as she deliberately raised the razor that the staff psychologist had left with her. She was no longer nauseous. When she had first come to the hospital, she had overdosed but was pretty certain she would be saved. When she cut her wrist last week, it was superficial. She did not want to die; she wanted to be with Richard in the closed unit. Now he had left her with the razor. If she used it, was there any chance that she would be saved? Was she ready to die?

No. He wasn't worth it. She was hurt, but most of her life she had been hurt. Cora—smart and pretty but not loved.

She finished bathing and went to bed.

———

Regina was frustrated. Why couldn't she free herself from the family? Maybe she was the crazy one. But she couldn't just forget it.

When he came home, she talked to Ken, who became thoroughly angry. Not at Regina, but at the hospital; the kook of a psychologist; whoever it was who felt the need to call but didn't have the gumption to do anything about what she knew. He was mostly mad with Cora, who continued to be a pain in the ass; who kept his home in an uproar. Everybody said she was smart, so why was she so crazy?

He suggested an appointment be made with Bill Forrester. It had been years since they needed a lawyer, and he was the only one they knew. When they got custody of Renee, the lawyer had returned some of the retainer. He explained that he had expected the matter to take more time, but since Cora didn't fight, they were entitled to a return of fee.

Whoever heard of such a thing? Obviously, they were lucky. They had an honest lawyer.

Over the years, when their friends needed a lawyer, Regina and Ken recommended Bill. Usually, however, their friends went to somebody with full-page ads and slick TV commercials. One of those mills that promised a "free consultation," but you were lucky to get past the efficient call screener.

It usually went like this:

MILL RECEPTIONIST:"Law firm."

CALLER: "Yes, I think I need to talk to an attorney."

MILL RECEPTIONIST: "One moment, please."

MILL PARALEGAL: "This is Jane Doe. I understand you need an attorney. How can we help you? What kind of case do you think you have?"

Caller starts to explain facts from the time she graduated from the sixth grade.

Mill paralegal cuts her off.

MILL PARALEGAL: "Were you injured? Have you been arrested? Do you need a divorce?"

Caller tries to get to the point but isn't used to this and skips through high school.

Mill paralegal cuts in again, not as nice as before.

MILL PARALEGAL: "Well, don't tell me all of that. Just tell me what you need."

CALLER: "I want a free consultation. You are the lawyer; I need to know if I need one."

MILL PARALEGAL: "No, I'm an assistant."

At which point the caller may hang up or spend fifteen minutes more only to learn that the "free consultation" must be in the office; and will only happen if the case is easy and doesn't involve taxes. The "free consultation" in the office usually turns out to be another screening—this time with another paralegal and some young, just-out-of-law-school professional who has never been in a courtroom, much less tried a case.

In fact, in those law firm mills, the senior partner may have never tried a case. But he knows how to plead you before some criminal judge after a plea bargain (and he knows how to twist your arm to plead guilty or nolo contendere—Latin for "no contest").

He can also settle your run-of-the-mill automobile accident case with the other drivers' insurance company (and he knows how to twist your arm to take the offer). He can also do an uncontested divorce in less than a month.

Easy money.

If it turns out that your case is not simple (say it's products liability, medical malpractice, or a wreck with big damages), he knows just how to shift you off to another firm for a referral fee of 25 percent for doing nothing but giving a "free consultation." The new firm is the one you should have gone to in the first place, but how were you to know? The ad for the new lawyers was not as flashy. They just started advertising and didn't think to put in "free consultation." After all, nobody who represents regular people charges for the initial consultation.

The law firm of Moran, Smith, Forrester & Dees had developed over the years since Regina took custody of Renee, Cora's love child. It was one of those firms to which the "mill" attorneys referred complicated cases. Bill Forrester had begun developing a reputation for good work before the U,S. Supreme Court decided that, after two hundred years, it was a violation of the Constitution to keep the law profession from advertising.

(Admittedly, now, after thirty years of heavy advertising, a few of the advertising firms had actually developed some really good trial lawyers. A rarity.)

Bill Forrester was a driven man. It was more the norm than not for him to work fourteen to sixteen hours per day. He believed in being prepared and often commented that most of the cases he won at trial was because he out worked his opposition. He had many friends but did not have much time to be with them. He enjoyed being with his girls but did not see them nearly enough.

Forrester was an imposing man of six-four who could dominate the courtroom. He also dominated his law firm, where he was the administrative lawyer (hiring and firing) in addition to all of his other work responsibilities.

No question, year after year, when firm profits were divided, Bill Forrester was responsible for at least 75 percent more income than any other partner. Notwithstanding, he was content with the relationship with his partners and they with him.

Forrester could seem gruff in the office because of his no-nonsense disposition. Ultimately, however, the staff knew that he was a fair man, and his secretary, Rosa, was content despite the long hours expected of her. It was kind of a badge of honor that she could keep up with his demands.

The lawyer was a dapper dresser. He liked to look sharp. However, his personal office was a different matter. His filing system was to have one stack of documents here and others there—on the floor, on chairs and any other surface available. The cleaning crew gave up on straightening his office. Emptying the wastebaskets was sufficient.

When Ken Baker called to make an appointment, Bill took the call directly from the receptionist. "Of course I remember you," he said. "How's...how's your little, uh, girl?" He forgot the name but wanted to make sure Ken knew he remembered the case.

Thirty seconds of chit chat, then Bill tactfully asked why he was being called. Unlike when he represented the Bakers before, Bill was now a busy lawyer, and he had learned to get to the point without being impolite. (He might be impolite with his staff but certainly not to clients.) He still took calls straight from the receptionist when he could, especially if the caller was a former client. Bill liked repeat business.

"My wife would like to come in to get some legal advice."

"Sure, what's the problem?"

"My sister-in-law. She may be having a problem at Greenview Psychiatric Hospital. She's a patient."

It took the former client five minutes to explain while the lawyer asked probing questions. Ken told the lawyer what Regina had told him that Cora had told her.

Ken Baker was thinking "advice." Bill Forrester was thinking "lawsuit." An appointment was made for a few days later when Forrester would be back from depositions in Boston.

CHAPTER 4

"WHILE WE'RE WAITING FOR an appointment with the lawyer, I'm going to do something. I'm going back to the hospital, and if Cora won't report it, I will." Regina was talking to herself as much as to her husband.

At exactly 3:00 p.m., she was waiting to see her sister. She was mad. Mad at the hospital and mad at Cora. Now she was told that something was wrong and the patient would not take visitors. "Then I want to talk to whoever's in charge," she insisted.

The receptionist informed her it would be a long wait. "Maybe you can make an appointment and come back tomorrow."

"No way! Then I'll talk straight to the psychiatrist—Dr. Richard something."

"You mean the *psychologist*, Mr. Taggart? He's the only 'Richard' treating patients in the closed unit. Isn't your sister in the closed unit? He's a *psychologist*," she concluded rudely.

"I'll see him."

"He's gone for the day, I'm afraid. Why don't you make an appointment with him too?"

Regina stormed out. She would have slammed the door, but it was automatic. "Damn it!" she muttered to herself.

Halfway to her car, she was startled when she was headed off by a woman she did not recognize. The stranger's words were rapid.

"Ms. Baker, I'm Carol Robertson. Aren't you Cora Smallwood's sister? I recognize you from when she was transferred out of the ER."

Regina froze to gain her composure. Several seconds would pass before she replied.

"Yes, I'm her sister." After another moment of hesitation, she spoke again. "Yes, I'm Regina Baker, and I recognize your voice. So, who are you? Why did you hang up on me? I'm going to get my sister out of here. I already have an appointment with my lawyer. You're in trouble."

Regina was spitting out the words too fast for a response, so the stranger interrupted.

"Please! Hold on! I'm sorry. I just wanted somebody to know. I may have been sticking my nose into other people's business. I should probably have kept my mouth shut."

"What's wrong with Cora? Tell me. What's going on? I want it clear. What's going on?"

"She didn't tell you?"

"No! Hell, no! So, you tell me! Are you going to tell me what's going on?"

"Ms. Baker, please calm down. Give me a minute. I've initiated an investigation because of your sister's possible affair with one of our staff. I didn't actually see anything, but when Cora was so withdrawn today, I requested an investigation. The hospital will get to the bottom of this."

For the first time in days, Head Nurse Carol Robertson felt better. It was like confession. She told Regina Smallwood Baker all she knew. She had caused the hospital to investigate, and she would be able to tell all again. Her only question was whether Mr. Taggart would be arrested or only fired.

———

When Cora was discharged one week later, she didn't know an investigation had occurred. She did realize that Rick was still there and would only glare when eye contact was unavailable. In fact, most everybody treated her differently, and she was uncomfortable.

Cora had not bathed in days, but her appetite had sure improved.

CHAPTER 5

RICK WAS RELIEVED AFTER Cora left. The staff had
been supportive of him. All except Carol Robertson. But she wasn't
pressing the issue.

During the investigation, things got hairy. A staff social worker,
Gladys Lake, had been ordered to help the incompetent boob from
HRS do whatever she was asked. She had some leads, but when
Marybeth Jones, the Health and Rehabilitative Service's snoop, quit
asking questions, so did Gladys. After all, she had been told to cooper-
ate, not volunteer.

Things got hairier when the cop asked questions. Lucky for the
psychologist, he never got around to Rick. The cop caught the flu.
Then Detective Officer Wright simply adopted the HRS report. He
didn't plagiarize. He just wrote, "See HRS report." It all ended there.
Well, practically.

Rick Taggart had been saved by the government.

It's true, he thought, *if the government is involved, you're home free.*
Government is bureaucracy. The police and HRS are government, and
you can count on government people to get bogged down. Rick counted on it, and he was cleared.

Now everybody avoided Cora like the plague. Staff would whisper
and point when they saw her in the hall. She was a psychiatric patient,
and she didn't have a chance. On the other hand, everybody but the
head nurse liked Rick, and she had been overruled.

Damn the head nurse.

After coming into the room that night without knocking, she made
a mistake. She should have reported what she saw, or thought she saw,

rather than waiting until days later. Now she was that "bitch" who, with absurd allegations, demanded the investigation.

It did not matter that Head Nurse Robertson felt "obligated," as she called it, to get involved. She admitted to Ms. Jones of HRS that if she had been sure of what she saw, she would have reported it immediately. Rick's story that he was counseling a depressed Cora Smallwood was explanation enough for HRS and the cop with the flu. After all, it was corroborated by an orderly who would have remembered.

Nobody seemed to remember, or Carol Robertson did not point out, that the lights had been out—even the night-light. On the other hand, Don, the orderly, reported his clear memory that the door was never completely shut. He would have noticed.

That same orderly and some of the nurses now dubbed the patient "Crazy Cora."

When Cora checked out, Rick Taggart was relieved. He repeatedly reminded himself that everybody knew he was a victim. The victim of a vindictive witch hunt. Thank God nobody could believe Crazy Cora.

Rick could concentrate again. He was good at what he did, and the proof was the many letters in his file from former patients and families of former patients. They praised him for all he had done for them and their loved ones.

Rick was patient with patients. He was kind. Could win their trust and be adored by people he helped. He was especially loved by the older women.

Alice was a wealthy patient who returned to the hospital every so often. Her letters praising Rick were typical.

Ladies and Gentlemen:

You should know that you have a gem in Richard Taggart. He saved my life and I am so thankful. I do not know how I could live but for him. I have been so depressed so many times since my family passed away. That is why I keep coming back.

With Rick and his gentle counseling, I can stand to live. He gives me something for which to look forward. Thank you for having such a wonderful person to help me and others.

Sincerely,
Alice Pierson

P.S. The rest of the people at the hospital (meaning the staff) are also wonderful.

Rick never tried to take advantage of people like Alice. He liked helping people and was really good at it. That's why he became a psychologist.

Nobody is perfect, and Rick would remind himself of that whenever situations would happen like with Cora. Each time when they would finally leave, he promised God and himself that it wouldn't happen again.

He knew he wasn't perfect, but he was a good psychologist who knew he could get control of his urges.

When he was younger, Rick had never been overwhelmed with urges. Through college, everything was okay. He married just like everybody else and didn't look at other women.

Now, life at home wasn't like it had been at first. He was a virgin when he met his
wife-to-be. Sandy wasn't.

She had been married before to a medical student. They had been living in Atlanta while the doctor-to-be attended med school at Emory. Hers was a promising life until her first husband died of a heart attack one afternoon. Just like that. He fell down on the side of the road and died while jogging in preparation for the River Run, a 15 K race held annually in Jacksonville.

Rick met Sandy while visiting Atlanta. At that time she was still working as a secretary at Emory Law School. He had dropped by for an application and to ask a few questions. Never actually applied, but he was thinking about it. She had helped from behind the desk, and by pure coincidence, they had mutual friends in Macon.

Sandy was eight years older, but they hit it off. They dated—taking turns on the weekend. He would drive to Atlanta one weekend and she to Macon the next. Rick was still a student working on his master's. Was young and good for her. Mostly he had a way of listening. He paid attention.

In turn Sandy taught him some things about life, and they fell in love.

Although "Mr. Taggart" wanted to become "Dr. Taggart, PhD," Sandy became impatient after they married and had moved to Macon. He was qualified to get a job as a psychologist now. He could go to school on the side and get his PhD. Could write his thesis at the same time he worked. She was, after all, tired of them living off her salary as a legal secretary. She would complain that his parents had not supported them one bit after they married.

Even though they moved to Gainesville to be close to a university, Rick never started on the PhD. He never started his thesis that he swore he would write on narcissistic personality disorder. He was going to start but never did.

If Sandy's first husband hadn't died, she would have been the wife of a wealthy man. He would have become a doctor years ago, and she could have quit working and would have never gone back again.

Sandy would dwell on the past, and over the years, she and Rick grew apart. Even the children didn't help things.

They stayed married, but for years they hadn't been in love. Rick didn't seem to listen anymore, and they didn't talk much. Maybe that was better. At least they didn't argue.

Rick Taggart couldn't remember when he first started feeling the urges. Maybe it was after they quit talking. Anyway, Cora was gone, and Cora would be the last person who would make him give into his urges.

The rec room was hardly ever empty because of Old George, who was almost always in there. He never noticed anything. He stared at the TV and never changed the channel. If anybody did, it didn't matter. George still stared at the TV.

When Rick would talk to Old George, it was always in the rec room. George didn't say much, but he could talk. Would talk to Rick but wouldn't take his eyes off the TV.

Old George was alone in the rec room when the new admittee, JoAnne Manchester, entered. She had been admitted against her will and had no idea what she'd do to pass the time. It was a Sunday, and she had been told there would be no group sessions. She could watch TV if she wanted.

Even dressed in the light cotton gown worn by most of the patients in the psychiatric hospital, it was obvious that Jo was a handsome woman. She held herself in that particular way that the upper crust is taught. Except for her garb, she was not typical of the other patients.

Jo was hooked on Valium and other prescriptions available to people living the good life. She had been nervous, and Valium had helped at first. Then she got hooked. She would wash the yellow pills down with vodka—Absolut Vodka. It made the Valium work faster and different. She also took pain pills—Percodan and Tylenol #3.

The pain pills came after being in a fender bender. The ER doctor had prescribed Tylenol #3, and then her orthopod's prescription was Percodan. The second doctor had not read the ER report on prescriptions, and neither of the doctors had inquired to learn that the family doctor had prescribed the Valium.

She wanted to stop, but Jo was hooked on legal drugs. Kind of like Elvis. The difference being when the doctors cut her off, nobody was around to help her fill prescriptions. She started going from one doctor to another. Eventually, each would declare that enough was enough, then cut her off.

Jo became an embarrassment to her old money Vilano Beach family. At gatherings, she would raid the bathroom medicine cabinets of the hosts. At one party in a cousin's mansion on San Marco Club Road, Jo excused herself no fewer than fourteen times in order to thoroughly check every bathroom for narcotic medicine.

San Marco Club Road of Vilano is located between the St. Augustine and Ponte Vedra Beach and is believed by the local inhabitants to be the most elite road on the First Coast. Indeed, if one were to read some of the original deed restrictions—since declared unconstitutional—one would think that the addresses on that road were used for inbreeding. Until recently not a single black resident of North Florida had become a member of the ocean front San Marco Yacht Club. Certain white people were also restricted from the club. The San Marco Yacht Club of Vilano Beach was for the old money passed down from one generation to the other. It was not for the new rich who had earned it themselves.

JoAnne Manchester was finally arrested for writing her own prescriptions on a pad she had stolen from her fifth-generation doctor uncle. It was a scandal, and the family would tolerate her no longer.

In lieu of criminal prosecution, she was admitted into the Greenview Psychiatric Hospital the following Sunday.

———

Normally, S. Richard Taggart, psychologist, would not have been at the psychiatric hospital that Sunday. He was making up time he missed during the Cora Smallwood investigation.

As he walked by the room reserved for pool, TV, checkers and cards (if you could find a full deck), he saw the striking, tall, dark-haired woman he had not seen before. Rick entered and practically ignored her as if Old George was the only one on his mind.

"George, is anything good on TV?"

George nodded. He always nodded when asked that question.

"We need to spend some time together this week. I've got some tests arranged for you to take on Tuesday. After that, maybe we can get together with some of the other people. Maybe we can go over to the university track and watch the Florida Gators run in circles."

After a pregnant pause of ten seconds, Old George replied, "I'll just watch TV."

Enough time had been spent with Old George. He had served his purpose. Now he could act like he noticed the stately woman for the first time.

"Hello, I'm Rick," he said with extended hand. "We'll probably get to know each other while you are here."

"I doubt it," she said with an affected air to her voice--not uncommon to women raised and trained in her old-money neighborhood.

Rick stepped closer. Only slightly closer, but close enough to break the comfort barrier. The invisible barrier—when somebody breaks it, that somebody is too close. Maybe the person is being a bully. Maybe the person is flirting. You're uncomfortable either way.

Rick looked Jo straight in the eyes. She stood her ground. When he put his hand on her shoulder, she stepped away, closer to Old George, who continued to watch TV.

Nothing else happened, and they both felt relieved. Jo didn't feel like being hit on. Rick used the opportunity to take control of himself.

He knew he could control himself and his urges.

CHAPTER 6

BILL FORRESTER, ESQUIRE, RETURNED from Boston. Rosa, his ever-patient assistant, met him at the airport.

"How did it go?" she asked.

"The depositions went well" was his reply. "Actually, they went better than well. I think we got enough information to nail them, but I'm glad I didn't send an associate. An associate would have been befuddled by the insurance lawyers. I hate it when I have to litigate with Fred Boseman."

Rosa said, "His secretary isn't too nice either."

"Then they're a match. I'm gonna have to go back to Boston to finish this thing. Every time we got solid information, he told the witness not to answer the follow-up questions. Now we'll have to have another hearing to get an order to make them answer. The judge will wonder why the case isn't moving along."

"But you did get what you needed?"

"I got enough, but there's more. You know we have a bunch of these same type of cases and it will help to have them nailed down on their positions early."

"Well, everybody at the office missed you." Rosa lied.

"I'm sure," he said sarcastically. "I wish I had somebody I could send to take these depositions who would be tenacious and not get sidetracked by that SOB." The lawyer paused, then mused, "Well, maybe the new one could have handled the deposition and Boseman."

Actually, Forrester had a lot of respect for Fred Boseman as a lawyer. It wasn't the fact that his adversary was an insurance defense lawyer. Heck, Forrester had represented insurance companies after he was an assistant state attorney and before he started limiting his work to representing plaintiffs. Most of Bill's friends were trial lawyers. civil and criminal; prosecutors and defenders. How many times had he said, "Good trial lawyers should be able to represent any side of any case?"

Boseman was smart and knew how to represent his clients. He wins his share of cases. But that didn't mean that Forrester had to like him as a person. And he didn't. The feeling was probably mutual.

Bill also had a lot of respect for the new associate, Elizabeth Kelley. She had handled herself well at other depositions as his adversary. After that his firm stole her from the insurance defense firm at which she was on a fast track to partnership. She had not solicited the new job, but joined the plaintiff's firm when offered a 50 percent raise.

Maybe she would be somebody he could rely on to handle tough discovery matters. He would try her out in time. Let her cover some of the easier stuff first.

———

Forrester had been to Boston to take depositions in the Zimmerman case. It was a products liability file that was typical of many he had handled in the past.

Products liability cases were often referred to him by other lawyers because they are more complicated than the average fender benders. You sue the designer, manufacturer and seller for sending out defective products that hurt people who are using them. Using them like the product is expected to be used. The victim doesn't know he's in danger, but the defendants do. Or at least that is what Forester tried to prove.

Remember those Ford Pinto cases with the exploding gas tanks? Some poor guy is sitting at a stoplight when he is rear-ended. Instead of getting a whiplash as you would expect, the car goes up like a bomb, and the driver is fried.

Ford knew it had a problem but didn't change the design. The people driving the Pintos had no idea that a minor accident might burn them to a crisp. The inter-office memos said Ford would rather pay a few claims than recall the cars. So, Ford refused to do anything about the problem until a jury got mad and awarded a victim over $100 million, after he was made to look like a monster and hurt twenty-four hours a day. After this victim got Ford's attention with the help of a lawyer and an Alabama jury, Ford fixed the Pinto. Most of the verdict was punitive damages, and Ford actually paid a whole lot less, but they changed the product to make it safe.

Not all cases are so famous, but changes have been made countless times when juries have forced the manufacturer to be responsible. For example, look at the asbestos cases where manufacturers hid letters for decades. Letters they had written that said they would rather pay off the widows than slow down the profits. How about the three-wheeler all-terrain vehicle cases? Lawsuits made the manufacturer stop making them; now we have four-wheeler ATVs.

Bill Forrester felt good about handling product liability cases. The Zimmerman case was no exception.

Roger Zimmerman broke his back on the job. He was a car carrier driver. He drove those trucks that carry ten to twelve cars from the import docks to the dealerships. He was also required to drive the cars on and off the truck and to tie them down securely with chains.

A chain broke while he was tightening down a car to secure it to a truck. It was like when somebody suddenly lets go of the rope when you have a tug-of-war. You fly backward. Only, when the chain broke, Zimmerman fell down against a steel tread and then to the ground. A paraplegic, he would never be on his feet again.

While in Boston, Forrester had learned that the manufacturer could have predicted Zimmerman, or some other driver, was going to end up like he did. In one year alone, more than 1,700 out of 5,000 drivers were hurt while loading or unloading those kind of trucks. They lost more than 20,000-man days from work that year alone. Thirty years ago, another system had been designed to stop those injuries. The manufacturer had not adopted the new design, and Zimmerman was the victim.

Forrester hoped that he could force them to change the design with the help of a Florida jury.

When Bill got to the office, Elizabeth Kelley met him at the car. She caught him checking her out as she walked to the car. She acted like she didn't notice. That does not mean that she didn't feel harassed.

Liz Kelley was about five-four or five-five. Pretty face with full lips. Nice figure. Really nice.

"How did it go?" she asked.

"Okay, I guess."

"A new client is coming in at four thirty. Do you mind if I sit in?"

"Who is it? What's it about?" He snapped the questions.

"Somebody named Smallwood. She's coming in with a family named Baker."

"Is that today? I planned to leave early. I've been fighting for three days to get what Wilson Vans, with the help of their lawyer, has been trying to hide from us. Wilson Van

Carriers, Inc. builds those trucks Zimmerman fell on. Are you familiar with the case?"

He had not answered her question, but Liz listened. Forrester was just shifting gears. He continued to complain about having to travel to Boston with Fred Boseman being the only human he knew there. Boseman was no company at all. The trip, like most for business, was lonely.

After verbally punching it out all day like a prize fighter does with his fists, he would return to his hotel room. He would go to a fine restaurant. Alone. Not wanting to go to bed early, he would spend time in the hotel bar until some other person on a trip for another reason would strike up a conversation. Invariably, the lonely traveler, or the bartender one, would start asking for legal advice. One or two martinis on the rocks later, he would return to his room; watch the late news; and go to sleep.

The next day was more of the same. Fight for twelve hours. Go to the hotel. Eat a lonely dinner. Hit the hotel bar. Then go to sleep.

When Bill had finished commiserating, Liz reminded him of her original question. "Do you mind if I sit in with the Bakers and Ms. Smallwood?"

"Sure. Maybe you'll work with me on the case. Tell me what you think."

———

Regina and Kenneth Baker showed up at the office with Cora Smallwood at twenty minutes after four. Forrester was on the telephone but cut the conversation short to keep the clients from waiting. He didn't like to act like a doctor. He wanted to be punctual. No reason to fill up a reception room with waiting bodies.

The Bakers looked neat. Spiffy. Not so, Cora.

Her hair wasn't really brushed. It hung down oily, and you could tell she hadn't bathed lately. When she spoke, she was quiet. She mostly mumbled her words as she avoided eye contact with the lawyers.

It took about forty-five minutes, between Regina and Cora's narration, for the story to be told while Bill listened, and Liz took notes. Regina had convinced Cora to come to the lawyer's office because there had been no satisfactory result after the investigation by the state HRS and the local police.

Forrester summed up his evaluation of the case.

"The problem is, it will be your word against his. It doesn't matter if I believe you. You will have the burden of proving what happened. Not only will it be hard on you, it will be hard for you to convince a jury that a psychologist is lying and that his mental patient is telling the truth."

Liz blushed when she heard the callous words reminding the potential client of the purpose of her hospital stay. She had the good sense to keep her mouth shut and listen to her more experienced, if abrupt, counterpart.

For the first time since the handshake and the preliminary chit-chat which was directed by Forrester at each new meeting, Kenneth Baker spoke.

"What do you suggest? Do you think we should just forget it?" He sounded like he hoped Forrester would answer in the affirmative and this thing would be finished.

Before Bill could answer, Liz, who had kept silent since the original introduction, chimed in. Forrester gave her a quizzical look. Amazed that she was butting in and not leaving him in control.

"No," she said, "it won't cost too much for us to at least order the medical records. It would be helpful if we could look at the investigation report from the police and HRS. Since we have a hospital involved here, we can probably take an unsworn statement from Taggart and maybe some other people too."

Forrester hated it when somebody else was suggesting ways for him to spend money. Getting the medical records was not free. Taking unsworn statements would cost several thousand dollars—not to mention the value of his time. Still, not wanting to appear out of harmony with his new associate, he turned the conversation to practical matters.

"Yes, we can do what Ms. Kelley is talking about. But until we know what we are looking at here; until we can evaluate the case; we would be unwilling to front the costs. I expect it'll cost about five to six thousand dollars to gather the records and pay a court reporter when we take the statements. If we decide to handle the case from there, we will front the rest of the costs. That is, if you want to hire us on a contingency fee basis."

Regina looked at her husband. She knew he would front the costs, and he signaled his agreement with a nod. At the same time, Forrester explained contingency fee contracts.

"I'm willing to handle the case on an hourly basis the same way the insurance company lawyers will be paid. Most people can't afford that and would rather hire us with our fee being paid only if we win. Some people call it 'the average man's ticket to the courthouse.'"

He pointed out that his automobile mechanic at the Chevrolet dealership charged $125 an hour for labor. Parts were separate. On an hourly basis, win, lose or draw, his firm would be paid like the automobile mechanic—but at a higher rate, $350 per hour for associate time and $600 per hour for his.

"You can expect us to spend one to two thousand hours on a case like this if we go all the way through trial. This kind of case is complicated from a legal standpoint, and the hospital won't simply roll over. They'll fight with excellent lawyers. The hospital's insurance company will also hire Taggart a lawyer who will fight us hard."

"You mean they will have two law firms against one?"

"That's right, Mrs. Baker. Sometimes there are more than two against one, but we will get by."

The other option was a contingency fee contract. The kind of contract that big business and doctors are constantly attacking. They want to cap the contingency fee at an amount so small as to make it not worthwhile for the lawyer to take their case. Then regular folks won't be able to hire a lawyer. When they can't afford to pay an hourly wage, regular folks would be no match for the trained lawyers that would be against them.

It was agreed that if Bill was successful in handling Cora's claim, his fee would be 40 percent of whatever was collected. Although Taggart's lawyer would get paid win, lose or draw, Forrester was taking a chance. If he lost, his fee would be zero. In addition, he would have to eat the costs, which would probably run over $100,000.

The new clients left just before six o'clock.

Forrester had wanted to go home early. Probably about four rather than the usual eight or later. After the trip to Boston, he wanted some rest.

By the time he finished reviewing the correspondence, pleadings, junk mail and other papers that had come in while he was gone, it was after nine o'clock. It would take him the rest of the week to catch up on the cases he had ignored while he was working on the Zimmerman file. He left the office for the night at just before ten.

Forrester was at least slightly frustrated each night when he left the office. There were nine attorneys in the firm of Moran, Smith, Forrester & Dees. Hardly ever was anybody around when he left.

The partners pulled their own weight. They were the original partners who formed the firm on February 1, 1999. Each had a different specialty. A tax/probate lawyer, a lobbyist/rainmaker, a commercial and real property litigator and Bill Forrester.

The partners were loyal to one another. Forrester, the complex tort litigator, did not mind that they got home to their families at a reasonable hour. The associates were a different story.

There was plenty of work to be done, and there was no chance that anybody could ever be totally caught up. Maybe Forrester wasn't hard enough on the associates; or he demanded too little. Maybe he just wasn't a good role model; a good leader.

He remembered when he was an associate with the defense firm. It was the same insurance defense firm that Fred Boseman was still with.

In fact, Forrester and Boseman had tried cases together, on the same team, when they were younger.

However, when Forrester was a defense lawyer, he put in lots of hours and would try to work until the last partner had left. He billed by the hour back then and was the highest biller without padding his time sheets.

Why were his associates not similarly motivated? Why was his usually the last car remaining in the firm's parking lot when he would leave for home?

If not for home, his favorite watering hole.

———

As he was leaving this p.m., the light was on in the library. The janitor must have left it on, he thought as he changed his route from the front door to turn it off.

"We can sue for battery and negligence. Do you have any other theory?"

Bill was startled to hear the feminine voice. "What are you doing here?" he asked Elizabeth Kelley.

"I'm intrigued by the Smallwood case. I was just researching the med mal statutes to see if we should put them on notice first," she answered.

"Oh." He was still surprised to find somebody else at the office—especially an associate.

"Thanks for letting me sit in today."

"Sure. No problem."

"I still want to do a little research before I leave."

"Don't stay here too late. I need you to cover a deposition tomorrow early."

"I know," she replied. "Rosa told me. I've prepared."

"Good. Well...good night. Don't forget to set the burglar alarm before you leave."

"No problem."

The lawyer was intrigued as he walked to his car. "Maybe she is different," he said to himself as he pulled out of the parking lot.

CHAPTER 7

DOCTORS HAVE A STRONG lobby that coordinates its efforts with the lobbies of big business and the insurance industries. They are the three wealthiest lobbies, and they know where to spend their money. In Florida it's spent in Tallahassee, the capital.

It's interesting what money can buy. Special laws have been passed to protect doctors when they cut off the wrong leg. Legal traps have been laid to protect the medical community from its victims. As a result, most lawyers are unwilling to handle medical malpractice cases. Those who are willing require that two criteria be met before taking the case.

Bill Forrester knew that cases against doctors and hospitals are expensive and complicated. Local doctors are not going to testify against each other—much less testify against the hospital where they have privileges. Before he would handle a medical malpractice case and risk the time and money it takes to win, he would make sure that the victim's damages were great. Secondly, liability must be obvious. It simply didn't make sense for him to take on the medical community unless the proof was solid.

———

Bill asked Liz to lunch the next day, which was unusual for a person who normally only spent about twenty minutes scarfing down leftovers that he stored in the office refrigerator. He agreed to spring for the tab at the nearby sandwich shop located four doors down and across the street from the office.

The Desert Sandwich Shop was takeout and fast lunches. There were no tables, but they found two spots next to each other at the counter. They could choose between a "rider salad" or one of the twenty different kinds of sandwiches. They could choose which bread but most people ordered the "rider," which is pita with a pocket.

It didn't take more than a minute for an older man to ask, "Have you decided what you would like?" Forrester liked the rapid service, which would keep him out of the office for the minimum length of time. The food was good too.

"I'll take a turkey on rider bread all the way and a large unsweetened ice tea."

"And you, ma'am?"

"Sweet tea and a rider salad, thank you."

The shop was operated by the Salem family, the first of whom came to America from Palestine in 1949. Three generations worked in the shop, with the oldest having a Middle Eastern accent and the youngest talking with a slight Southern drawl.

The place was busy, as usual. As they waited the few minutes it would take before their lunches were delivered, Bill introduced Liz to a man who had gone to law school with him.

"Judge, I'd like for you to meet Elizabeth Kelley, who has recently started with our office."

Liz stood from her stool and extended her hand as she said, "I sat second chair in a trial before Judge Whitman just a few months ago. It's nice to see you again, sir."

"It's nice to see you, Ms. Kelley. You'll enjoy working with Bill, if you like those ridiculously long hours and if you have no social life."

The judge was smiling as he described the reputation of Liz's new task-master. Bill was relieved when the conversation was interrupted by the delivery of a meal that included at least a third of a pound of meat. It gave the judge an opportunity to leave the two lawyers as he hunted an empty seat.

Sounding disinterested while putting mayonnaise and mustard on the pita, Bill said, "I like your work, Liz."

He waited for her response. Time passed. Finally, she asked, "*But* what?"

"What do you mean?"

"I can tell you've got something on your mind. So you like my work. *But* what?"

"But I have my own way of doing some things."

"Did I do something wrong?"

"No. Not really."

"So why did you ask me to lunch? People at the office say when you ask somebody to lunch, they can expect the worst."

"Is that what they say? Really?"

"You know it is. Have I done something wrong?" she repeated.

"You know when we met with Cora Smallwood and the Bakers yesterday?" Bill was ready to get to the point.

"Yes."

"I was going to turn down the case."

"So why didn't you?"

"Because you started talking. I would have preferred that you had sat in and just listened. Once you started talking, I felt like I needed to back you up."

"I see."

"If we're going to work together, you're going to have to follow my lead."

Liz's feelings were hurt. Bill Forrester had the reputation for being, and was, in fact, a hard-ass. Nevertheless, he was an *experienced* hard-ass lawyer; more successful than most; and most importantly, he was a partner.

"I understand, boss," the associate said. "I'm sorry, boss. It won't happen again." Before he had asked her to lunch, he knew she would be hurt, and she was hurt.

"Listen. We're going to work together. There's no problem, but I've got to tell you when I've got a problem. I'm the one who will spend the money on this case, and I pay the bills. That's why I want to do the picking and choosing."

"I understand, boss. I won't say anything in the future in front of clients."

"That's not what I mean. Just don't obligate the firm. I'll do that. I would not have taken the Smallwood case, but you obligated us. I backed you up. Now, you work it up. If it goes to trial, you can sit second chair. If it doesn't develop, we'll eat our losses early. It's just harder to withdraw than to turn down the case in the first place."

Everything that needed to be said had been said. Bill finished his lunch within five minutes. Liz didn't have much of an appetite. She took what was left of her salad back to the office. She'd eat it for lunch in the kitchen tomorrow if the lettuce wasn't too wilted.

There was one thing more nagging at Bill's craw as they entered the front door of Moran, Smith, Forrester & Dees. He decided to get it out of the way now.

"By the way, I don't like to be called 'boss.' We work together, so don't call me 'boss' anymore. Okay?"

"I understand," she said quietly, as she wondered why she had decided to take this job.

———

Bill had his children half the time. It was something he and his ex had worked out in the divorce so he could see his children more than just on the weekends. For two weeks at a stretch, Jane and Deborah stayed at his house, followed by the next two weeks at the home of his former wife.

He hired a live-in housekeeper shortly after the divorce. Because he worked and he worked long hours, she saw the children more than he did. He knew he would always regret the time he wasn't with them but justified it by the money he made. How else could he pay for his house, his support and the house of his former wife? And the private schools? And the riding, piano and dance lessons? And....

By 9:30 p.m. Bill was ready to go home. His children were at their mother's for her half the time so he decided to go by the River House, his favorite watering hole, for at least one martini. He could put off going home. It would be lonely when he got there.

There was the light on in the library again. This time he wasn't surprised to see Liz at the books.

"When are you going home?"

"As soon as I finish some research."

"How long? I don't like you walking to your car alone, and I'm leaving."

Bill Forrester knew that his attitude about her staying late was a contradiction. He was usually annoyed that he was the last one to leave.

"Go on. I'll leave in twenty minutes," Liz insisted.

"Are you at a good stopping point?"

"Maybe, but I'm not finished."

"That's okay. How about let's go…join me for a drink, and we can talk about Smallwood."

It was almost a command, but it wasn't rough and she agreed to meet him when she was finished. The River House was out of her way, but they agreed that would be the place.

Liz showed up thirty minutes after Bill had drunk his first martini and had ordered his second. He was slightly agitated that she had made him wait, but the vodka with a lemon peel twist had relaxed the courtroom warrior who intimidated people even if he didn't want to.

He was sitting on the outside deck overlooking the St. Johns River which, at that location, is more than three miles wide. It wasn't a full moon, but there was enough light to see all the way across. The wind was faint but created a little chop that was mesmerizing, like a fire on a cold night. When Liz showed, the spell of the water was broken, and Forrester came to his feet.

"I began to think you had stood me up."

"I'm sorry. It's not like this is a date."

Bill just smiled and made a gesture with his hand for her to sit down.

Liz continued, "I would have left later since I didn't finish the research. I guess I'll finish it tomorrow."

"What's so important? What are you drinking?" Bill made both inquiries in rapid succession.

"I'll just have a beer. Any light beer is okay." She paused and then Liz said, "The Smallwood case. I'm working on the Smallwood case. I think we can file suit without going through the med mal crap. I wanted to make sure."

"I think we can too, but we won't. I see no reason to give the hospital a built-in appeal."

Just that fast, hours of work had been invalidated for Elizabeth Kelley. She had to control her frustration. No, she wanted to lash out. She didn't. Maybe she should have asked him first. She was determined she would learn.

"On second thought, cancel that beer. I'll have a Johnny Walker Black with water."

She drank it fast; excused herself and went home—leaving Bill with the tab.

CHAPTER 8

JOANNE MANCHESTER WAS SICK. She was in the hospital because they knew she would be sick. Her family had the money and could afford the detox program. It was a lot better than jail.

She was addicted to legal narcotics, and the best course was to admit her. The family had once considered having her committed to a mental facility. They assured her they were only looking out for her, not their reputation. She was not a willing patient but had finally agreed in order to avoid being forced. First, she would have withdrawal, and that's what made Jo sick. Physically sick. Next, they would deal with the mental so she could stay clean.

Maybe it wouldn't be so bad after all, she convinced herself. If she was off the pills, she could still buy alcohol.

Rick had not expected to see her one way or the other. She might be his patient, along with that of a psychiatrist. Or she might work with another psychologist altogether. He saw her only because she called to him as he walked by her private room.

Jo wasn't calling Rick because he was Mr. Taggart, the psychologist. She called him because he was walking by.

He went to her door and looked in.

"You're the guy from the TV room, aren't you?" Jo asked.

"Yes. I'm Rick Taggart. I see you aren't feeling too well."

"I'm sick as hell. I want to leave."

"You'll be all right," he said nicely. "Just give us a few days."

"I'll be dead in a few days."

"You want me to get a nurse?" Again, he was nice.

"I want you to get me some pills. I'm sick."

"I'm sorry, but the nurse handles that. I'm only a psychologist."

Then Jo did the unexpected. She did what Rick wished she hadn't done. She raised her arms with the gown in her hands. She was naked except for the panties. Rick stared and didn't remove his eyes. He couldn't remove his eyes.

"I've got a good body, and I will do anything for some help. Please just help," Jo pleaded.

"I'll tell the nurse you aren't feeling well," Rick said as he turned from the door, the image of her naked body firmly imprinted in his mind's eye.

As he walked away, he could feel the erection. He put his right hand in his pocket to hide the arousal. He was embarrassed and felt like everybody would notice. He didn't say anything as he walked past the nurse's station.

⎯⎯

The next morning at home was like every other. He was supposed to be at work by 8:00 a.m. His wife had to be to work by nine. He woke up before six.

Sandy feigned sleep until he had left. There was no conversation. Things were as usual. He may have been bitter, but he had his work. He helped people.

Rick began to back out of the driveway but then deliberately stopped before making it to the street. He didn't bother to pull forward again. He took the keys from the ignition and fumbled around the ring until he found the one that fit the house lock. He opened the door at the side of the house, which opened into the kitchen. Sandy looked at him startled and pale as she hung up the phone.

The psychologist didn't stop to talk. He walked to the bathroom—to the medicine cabinet. The pills were on the cabinet shelves. He took the little yellow ones. His wife's pills. Valium. Took the whole bottle and put them in his pocket.

Leaving the bathroom to retrace his steps through their bedroom, he was met by Sandy. She didn't say anything, so he did.

"Why are you following me?"

"It's my house! This is my bedroom."

"What are you doing up? I thought you were asleep." He knew better, but he continued. "I wasn't even out of the driveway. You just couldn't wait for me to leave. Of course, you never can wait for me to leave."

Sandy stayed calm, though Rick obviously wasn't. She said, "Did you forget something in the bathroom? Do you need my help?"

"Forget it."

"Of course. You never need my help."

"I've got to go. I'll be late."

Rick looked at his wife. They hadn't spoken so many words to each other at one time in months. He was no longer the man who would listen to her. They never talked. They never argued. They simply shared the same house and the same bed. They slept in the bed, but that was all. There was no love, and they didn't make love. They existed under the same roof. That was all.

Rick was ready to leave the house for work. When he got home, they could exist together again. The man walked past his wife through the loveless bedroom and into the hallway.

She spoke. "Rick, stay home today. Let's go back to bed."

"Are you serious?" he responded sarcastically. "Sandy, I've got to go."

"Okay, Rick. Whatever you say. But I think...."

"What do you think?" He cut her off.

"I think we...we should get divorced."

Rick hadn't expected that. One second she wanted him in bed. Now, she was talking divorce.

"Really, Rick. It's over between us. I've already seen a lawyer. We can be divorced in less than a month. That's who I was calling in the kitchen."

"Why?"

"Come on Rick. There's no marriage. You have your affairs...."

"What are you talking about... *affairs?*"

"Please, Rick. I know."

"You mean you think you know."

"You talk in your sleep. I don't know what you're saying. I do know when I hear a woman's name like..."

Rick was flushed. He wasn't sure what she knew. He felt sick, like he was going to vomit. He interrupted. "Damn you, Sandy."

That was all he could think to say. He knew the words didn't make sense in context with what was happening. He had never cussed his wife before. He was afraid of what she was going to say.

"Who is JoAnne, Rick? Who's Cora? Somebody at work?"

"I don't know what you're talking about."

"Those are the latest ones. It doesn't matter, though. There's nothing for us to stay together for. Our children are gone now. Anne works. Lilly's in college. They know. They'll understand."

"Whatever you say, Sandy. It's always whatever you say."

"Say? We never talk. We never 'say' anything."

Sandy was late to work, but she had done it, and she hadn't buckled under. They would be divorced in a month. He could see his girlfriends, and she didn't care. She would have her own life now.

She never really loved him, not even when they were first married. But she had liked him. When did she fall out of like? She couldn't remember—just as she couldn't remember when they stopped making love. Stopped arguing. Stopped talking.

Although she had planned the divorce, things were not planned for that morning. It had been easier than she had expected. She hadn't even needed to relax beforehand. She hadn't needed her little yellow pills.

He was supposed to be at the hospital at eight o'clock. It was after eight before he left the house. Had he not gone back into the house, he would've been at work early. Of course, he would not have had the pills in his pocket.

"My wife's leaving me."

That's all the explanation Rick gave, and the response was predictable. He was forgiven for being late because it was her fault. Everybody understood how Rick felt. He had been let down by an unappreciative wife.

He couldn't help thinking about it, but as the day settled down, Rick accepted his fate with Sandy. He was, in fact, relieved, though he had never really thought about divorce before. For several years, he hadn't thought much about his wife--much less divorce.

Now, as the reality of it set in, Rick began to fantasize. He would get a girlfriend. He could meet somebody away from work. That would be nice. Somebody younger. Prettier than Sandy.

Then he thought about the children. Sure, they were grown, but that didn't matter. Telling them that their parents were divorcing was an awful thought and an awful job. Since Sandy was the one who wanted to split, Rick decided that she could tell them.

———

Rick could not help thinking about JoAnne Manchester --the handsome lady who had exposed herself. Unfortunately, she had not been assigned to any of his groups. She was still detoxing. That didn't matter. He knew that she wanted him as much as she needed him. And what a body. He remembered that body, but he could barely remember her face.

Between groups he found reasons to go by her private room. She was sleeping the first time. The next time she wasn't there. He saw her with a visitor in the rec room, the place where they had first met.

He heard Jo say that she "needed to get out of this place." She was pleading. Whoever she was pleading with just shook her head.

An hour later Rick made his third trip by Jo's room, where she was lying on her bed crying. The psychologist entered uninvited. He would comfort her.

"Hey lady. Why so glum?" He sounded cheerful. "You should be feeling better. If you aren't, you will be soon." Now you could hear the excitement in his voice.

Jo looked up contemptuously. She had developed that look over a lifetime of being raised as one of the chosen few. She knew how to communicate disgust without saying a word. She knew how to ridicule people with words that if written in black and white would not sound like ridicule. She knew how to make people feel uncomfortable.

Jo also knew how to use people who usually sought her approval because of her high status in life. She had, after all, been born and raised in Vilano Beach, the old family/old money neighborhood.

She stopped crying and didn't look so pitiful when she said, "You may leave."

Rick didn't leave. He was a psychologist, and he knew how to handle people. Especially patients.

"I am not so sure you mean that. You really shouldn't want me to leave. I can help you. I can help you feel better."

"I don't need *your* help. Do you intend to leave?" she asked dryly.

"I have something that will help you, but maybe I made a mistake. I thought you really did want my help when you asked me yesterday."

By this time Jo was sitting up erect and stately. Rick had his hand in his pocket and had moved closer—through the edge of the comfort barrier. He withdrew his hand and the bottle of pills, which were instantly recognized for what they were by Jo.

Jo's mannerisms changed. He hadn't actually offered the pills, but she knew they were there for her taking. She struggled with herself only briefly. She wasn't really ready to get off the drugs. She had admitted herself as a patient only upon the coaxing and insistence and threats of her family and the criminal authorities. She knew she could handle the drugs. In her heart of hearts, she did not believe she was an addict. She also knew that what he had in his hand would stop the pain and nausea. She only wanted to relax.

Jo said, "I'm sorry if I've acted poorly. I know you only want to help." In the most demure voice, she said, "I'm sorry for my behavior toward you. It's not your fault. You know, for the life of me, I don't remember your name."

"Rick. I'm Rick Taggart. I run groups here. Maybe you'll be in one of the groups when you feel better."

"I would like that," she responded.

Jo was focused, and he knew that she was. He opened the cap to the bottle and poured two Valium into his hand. Then he closed the bottle and returned it to his pocket.

Palm up, yellow pills in the center, he stepped within reach of the patient. She reached out to take the pills, and when her hand met his, he clasped it. She gave no resistance when he brought her hand between his legs, then released her hand and the pills.

Jo knew what he wanted, and she stroked him. As she did so, his now empty hand found her breasts as he stepped even closer. Jo stood up to make it easier for him to touch between her legs with his free hand.

Rick couldn't stay any longer but knew he could come back. He left her with the Valium, which she swallowed without water and without the usual vodka chaser.

Rick Taggart was going to be a single man again. He knew JoAnne Manchester was of fine breeding. Cora had fantasized about seeing him after she was released. He was now fantasizing about being with JoAnne when she got out of the hospital.

CHAPTER 9

IT TOOK SEVERAL MONTHS for Moran, Smith, Forrester & Dees to gather the medical records from the Greenview Psychiatric Hospital. Upon request, they were supposed to be provided within thirty days. The hospital delayed the production of the records, and there wasn't much that could be done about it. By the time the records were collected, it was nearly autumn and the statute of limitations to file a lawsuit was running.

The firm also collected Cora Smallwood's hospital and medical records going back to when she was a teenager. The records were extensive and varied. However, they had one thing in common. Since she was a teenager, her consistent psychological diagnosis was histrionic personality disorder. Although that diagnosis was never abandoned, more recent diagnoses included post-traumatic stress disorder associated with the sexual trauma. While her records reported that she had bouts of depression, consistently she was also diagnosed as being manipulative.

Liz next made arrangements for Cora to see a psychiatrist, Dr. Rudolph Lewis. For purposes of the lawsuit, it was important to have one person who would painstakingly go through the records as well as meet with the client. This was preliminary stuff, used to sum up the problems and quantify the damages created by the most recent treatment. The doctor, who charged $5,000 to review the records, would not agree to the mention of his name in the event of litigation

In the conclusion of his report, he wrote, "I agree with the diagnoses of post-traumatic stress disorder, which is associated with premature sexuality coupled with histrionic personality disorder and depression. Such diagnoses may be, indeed, probably are, interrelated to her home environment during her formative years. Further, I would expect that a person with such diagnoses may cope by being manipulative. Her records are replete with history of Ms. Smallwood's tendency to be manipulative. Of course, the patient with those diagnoses should be treated, as that was the purpose of her being admitted to Greenview Psychiatric Hospital. The treatment reported by the patient, which included sexual modalities, falls below acceptable standards of care...."

Liz handed the report to Bill.

"What do you think?" she asked after he had a chance to review same.

"Well, if it was a sworn affidavit, it would be enough to place the psychologist and the hospital on notice of our intention to file a medical malpractice case."

"You don't look pleased."

"The problem is the diagnosis. It says she is manipulative, and the defense is going to jump on that."

"You mean there's no reason to believe her over the psychologist with a good reputation."

"I mean that even though she was a patient, they're going to try to twist it around and make it look like she manipulated him. He'll be the victim."

Forrester wanted more reliable data before he would be willing to spend more time and much more money. Maybe he would have been right to turn down the case in the first place. Already, the Baker's $6,000 cost deposit had been exhausted and the firm had spent twice that again.

In addition, more than sixty-five attorney hours had been invested, and they had hardly started. Now Liz understood what Bill had been irritated about. After four months the case still boiled down to the client's word against the defendant's. There were damages, but the damages might not be obvious to the trier of fact. Especially since the client was manipulative consistent with a histrionic personality disorder. The diagnosis was not caused by the hospital. It was caused by a family life that no one should endure.

Thank God the new associate had a lot of other cases to work on that would almost for sure be money makers. On top of that, she was going to be sitting second chair to Forrester when they picked a jury in the Zimmerman case the following Monday.

When suit is filed, you must assume that it will actually go to trial. Most cases don't, but you have to assume that they will. Otherwise, you will be sitting in the courtroom unprepared.

When settlement negotiations break down and trial is looming, the focus on that case increases exponentially. The last couple of weeks before trial, you have to concentrate on details. Pictures must be blown up to the size of posters; PowerPoint slides are created; arguments are practiced; and jury instructions are prepared. You meet with the witnesses; write out questions; summarize depositions; and research, research, research. The lawyers and the staff work overtime and through the weekends.

At the same time, the costs skyrocket. If the case is being handled on a contingency fee basis, and if you lose, not only will it all have been for naught, but the firm will also have to eat those costs—not to mention salaries for secretaries and paralegals and the other overhead expenses.

———

Over the last several months, Liz and Bill had learned to work together. He gave her great leeway and relied on her discretion on how to handle things. However, she learned early that if he gave advice, it should be taken as an order.

She had her own case load, which she handled with only loose supervision from Forrester. The supervision and control were considerably more apparent when she worked with him on big cases.

"You're the first associate that he's ever trusted," Rosa had confided.

"What do you mean?" Liz asked.

"Usually, he's accused of micromanaging the cases. It looks like he pretty much lets you do what you want."

"What do you think that means?"

"It means you're a better lawyer than the others. Or maybe he's just mellowing."

Liz actually appreciated the help that Forrester gave her. Bill had tried cases and had survived the battles of litigation. Each battle brought its own scars, but each was also a learning experience. He obviously wanted to pass on to Liz those experiences that can't be fully appreciated until a lawyer risks ego, time and money.

In time Liz realized that she was being molded by Bill Forrester. She took him as a mentor and worked his long hours. She tried to learn to think like he thought.

She figured out that Bill was not only a workaholic but also liked being a workaholic. He also liked being referred to as a workaholic and being able to expect more effort from people than they would otherwise be inclined to give.

Not long after she had been with the firm, Liz started declining lunches with other associates and friends outside the office. A long, leisurely forty-five-minute or one-hour lunch was simply out of the question for her. She ate because it gave her strength, but, like her mentor, she brought her lunch. She would eat in the firm's kitchen and time it so she could spend the fifteen or twenty minutes with him.

They would talk about their cases as they wolfed down the food. Usually, a sandwich or leftovers brought in by Forrester when his housekeeper had prepared too much for his children—when he had his children. While they were preparing for the Zimmerman trial, lunch was a good time to discuss the other files. Her time sheets would reflect the conversation while they ate.

Yes, this work was being done on a contingency fee basis. However, Bill Forrester learned to keep timesheets while working for an insurance defense firm for several years after leaving the State Attorney's office. He insisted that the lawyers and paralegals keep timesheets now. From time to time, in certain cases, he would be able to tax attorneys' fees against the other side. However, the real reason for keeping time sheets was so that when a case was finished, it could be determined how much the firm made per hour.

"Do you have time to talk to me about the Smallwood case?"

"What do you need? Are you having problems deciding if there was malpractice?" he inquired.

"I just haven't worked on many malpractice cases in the past. The statute is totally unfair to the victims," she reported as though the other lawyer did not know it already.

"So, what's new?"

"Do you think we should file the report we got from Dr. Lewis as a basis for our notice?"

"Not unless you want to be sued. We agreed to leave him out of the litigation. Besides, we need more than a report. The law requires a sworn affidavit."

"Okay, so how do we find somebody who is willing to swear to the malpractice? Obviously, the hospital records don't report that Cora was molested by one of the psychologists. Her psychiatrist at the hospital while she was a patient refused to believe her over Taggart. Any suggestions?"

Forrester didn't answer immediately. He was thinking as he removed the leftover pilau (Southernese for chicken and rice) from the microwave.

"If we sued them, we could take depositions to see if anybody knows anything. Of course, we can't sue them yet because of the special legal protection provided by the statutes."

"So you don't have a suggestion?"

"I have a suggestion." He thought some more while stuffing a large fork full of the rice into his mouth. "Here's what I suggest. Take a sworn statement from Ms. Smallwood. Actually, you can prepare a written statement and have her swear to it. Describe in brief words what she claimed happened."

"Okay."

The instructor went on. "There's a psychiatrist in Atlanta that we have used before to review medicals. He probably won't get involved in the actual case either. But that won't matter if he'll just sign an affidavit. Ask Rosa what his name is. I used him in the Freeman case. I don't remember his name right off. Rosa can tell you."

"The Freeman case?"

"Yeah. Send him the records, along with Ms. Smallwood's affidavit. Ask him to assume that the statement is true. I think that you can get an affidavit from him saying that in light of her records, it would be medical malpractice by the hospital if she is telling the truth. Is there anything in the records?"

"The investigation is referred to in her records. Just briefly. If there are anymore records about the investigation, they will be in the hospital files, which the law doesn't let us have and we'll never get."

"I know. The statutes exempt discovery of anything that would help the victim patient." He was being sarcastic.

"So you think we should file suit if I get the affidavit? You're willing for the firm to go whole hog?" Liz asked.

"It's your call," Forrester replied, looking her in the eyes.

The conversation turned to the Zimmerman case, and ten minutes later the lawyers went back to work.

———

The sworn affidavit by Dr. Phillip E. Townsend, MD, Psychiatrist, Atlanta, Georgia, was received six weeks later. He had only charged $5,000 and was willing to testify.

In the meantime, Forrester and Kelley tried Zimmerman before six jurors and an alternate in the super modern Duval County Courthouse.

———

After waiting for a verdict for hours on end, the lawyers returned to the office triumphant. Forrester stuck his head into his partner's office.

Peter Dees asked, "Did you get a verdict?"

"The jury gave us eight million for the driver and one hundred seventy-five thousand for his wife's consortium claim. I don't know if that's enough for the loss of her ability to have sex with her man for the rest of their lives. They've been married for twelve years."

"It sounds like a good verdict to me. I would have never thought that they would let you take it to trial. I thought they would settle that case."

Forrester said, "I thought they would've settled it, too. That's why you have to assume you'll go to trial when you file suit."

"What are the costs?" Dees asked.

"I'm not sure. It was ninety-two thousand before the trial started, and I think it'll be at least another fifty thousand."

"So, if you had lost, we would have had to eat over one hundred forty thousand?"

"That's right. It takes a lot of money to blow up pictures the size of posters. The real money was spent on the doctors and engineers for their time before trial and testifying at trial."

"Do you have any idea how many hours were spent on the case?"

"The lawyers' and paralegals' time sheets show nearly a thousand hours before the trial. Who knows how much time the secretaries have in it?"

Dees chuckled. "Who says the only motivation for a trial lawyer is to avoid a fractured ego? Thank God we don't lose many of those cases. If we did, it wouldn't take long to go bankrupt." The conversation had already taken longer than Forrester had expected when he stuck his head in the door. Now it seemed like Dees' office had become a gathering place for a partners' meeting as the news of the verdict spread through the firm. Of course, Forrester did most of the talking and he wanted to talk about Liz. He couldn't quit singing her praises.

"She really is a good lawyer. We work well together, and she's a heck of a lot more organized than I am," Forrester reported several times.

In another part of the office, Liz was being pigeonholed by secretaries and the other associates.

"He's a genius," she reported. "He laid out the case like a professor would to his class. Before it was over, the jury understood kinetics, human factors and complicated engineering principles. They could speak the right lingo."

"What was their defense?" another associate asked the rising star.

"They wanted the jury to say that Zimmerman was responsible since he knew that the car carrier trucks were dangerous in the first place. They didn't buy that when Bill showed them that alternative systems were being used in Europe and had been suggested twenty years earlier here in the United States. If Mr. Zimmerman lived in Europe, he wouldn't be a paraplegic. He wouldn't even be hurt. In Europe they don't use chains for the job. They use straps and hydraulics to tie down the cars. The drivers don't have to act like acrobats in order to try to do their job."

"Was there any comparative negligence?"

"The jury said no. Zimmerman was doing everything that the other drivers do when he got hurt. Bill proved that most all the drivers will eventually get hurt doing the same job unless the company makes some design changes."

A gleeful Rosa added, "A few more verdicts like that, and they'll make the changes."

Liz said, "Yeah, but the sad thing is that Zimmerman will be in a wheelchair for the rest of his life because Wilson Van Carriers won't pay thirty-five hundred dollars per unit to make it safe. Our economist testified that, over his lifetime, when you take into consideration everything from his medical bills to his lost wages to replacement of wheelchair parts, the economic impact will be more than three million."

Another associate couldn't contain himself. He said, "Yeah, and the big business lobbies are now working with Congress to limit the amount of damages people like Zimmerman can collect. They want to cap damages at about two hundred and fifty thousand and, at the same time, cap contingency fees so that they're so low nobody can afford to handle complicated cases."

The lawyers were exhausted. Within a couple of hours, the adrenalin high was wearing off. Forrester called for his co-counsel. They might go celebrate with a drink, but she was nowhere to be found. He was equally unsuccessful when he tried to locate his children, who were with their mother somewhere or other but not at home.

He decided to do a little paperwork before returning home alone. When he left the building, it was ten forty-five.

CHAPTER 10

DR. PHILLIP TOWNSEND'S AFFIDAVIT, based on the medical records along with the statement from Cora Smallwood, said that both the psychologist and the hospital had provided treatment "below acceptable standards of care." After more than a year of work on the case, the lawyers were ready to file suit. However, under Florida law the eventual defendants in medical malpractice cases have to be put on notice before suit can be filed.

So the day following receipt of the doctor expert's opinion affidavit, one copy was sent certified mail to Richard Taggart and another to Greenview. Taggart's was returned unclaimed. It took another thirty days to track him down.

In the meantime, Raymond Jones, CEO and hospital administrator, went haywire. Within twenty-four hours, he had contacted the insurance company; met the attorney chosen by the insurance company; and arranged a meeting of all nurses and staff who had ever met Cora.

The meeting was called for a particular purpose. Damage control was important, and it was important to start damage control immediately. After a short briefing by Jones, the defense lawyer was introduced. He took over.

"Thank you, Mr. Jones." Nodding to his audience like a politician, he said, "I'm Fred Boseman." Many laughed when he told them that he had already learned the so-called "victim" was always known as "Crazy Cora." Head Nurse Carol Robertson did not crack a smile.

Boseman told them what to expect. Somebody else would represent the psychologist individually. There would be attempts by Forrester to divide them. "He will try to divide you at the depositions to come."

The defense lawyer wanted to spend some time on this subject. "Depositions are sworn statements," he told them. "Many if not all of you will be subpoenaed to a court reporter's office to give a deposition. We will arrange for you to meet with us in advance. Then you will be sworn and asked to tell the truth, and we know that you will."

"You will be giving testimony, just like you were in a courtroom. All of the lawyers will have a chance to ask you questions. In fact, your answers to those questions asked at your deposition may be presented directly to a jury. That is done by reading your deposition, which will be transcribed; or, if it is taken before a videographer, it will be edited and shown to a jury."

"In other words, depositions are sworn testimony before trial which may be substituted for live testimony at trial. In any event, in the end, the hospital will be found not guilty, if there is a trial…, I say, 'if there is a trial' because we're going to try to have the case thrown out of court."

Boseman knew that the plaintiff's lawyers would want to nail the hospital. He expected that Taggart probably didn't have any money and Taggart's lawyers would be paid by the hospital's insurance company. They would coordinate their work.

"Just stick together. We will win," he assured his audience again.

Boseman did not give the assembled a chance to speak or ask questions. He was instructing them. He did not want them to volunteer information that would hurt their chances. Without telling them to lie, he told them what to say.

"We all know…." (How would he know? He hadn't worked in the hospital. Nevertheless, nobody questioned him.)

"We all know that Cora Smallwood's diagnoses consistently emphasize her ability to manipulate. Nobody questions that she is smart. Like a fox. She has been in this hospital several times—not to mention all of those other places. She is a manipulator (Now he was planting a seed.) who does not know truth from fiction. There is only one thing this case is about. She and her attorneys want to manipulate the system and want to get rich off of us."

Boseman went on acting and declaring and unifying the nurses and staff. He was the cheerleader and quarterback rolled up in one. He expected to be interrupted by applause as he explained how they would go about getting out of this mess.

"You know," he went on, "her claims were investigated by the HRS and the police. We were cleared before because we did what we were supposed to do. Let's stick together and we'll be okay."

Boseman was now one of them. They could call on him at any time. After twenty minutes of instructing, he was finished. He would have liked to have stayed and answered questions, but he had another appointment. The defense attorney, the best that money could buy, left.

Head Nurse Carol Robertson, whose hand had been raised nearly the entire time, never got to open her mouth nor enlighten the attorney about what she had seen. Boseman knew better. Before the meeting ever started, Jones had warned him about "Nurse Robertson, the troublemaker."

It took more than six months more before suit could legally be filed. Cora was the victim/plaintiff of medical malpractice. If her lawyer made a procedural mistake before filing suit, the case would be dismissed. It doesn't matter how legitimate the case is; it can be thrown out of court on one of many technicalities.

During the procedural delays, the defense can circle the wagons to thwart the victim's efforts to recover damages. Unsworn statements can be taken, but they aren't binding. If the person later changes her story, the statement cannot be used to prove she is lying.

One other thing. During the legally mandated delay, medical records may be amended, changed or lost.

Up until she started working with the plaintiff's firm, Liz Kelley never thought about the complications associated with representing victims. Now she felt something was wrong with a system that was purposely skewed in favor of the medical community.

"Will you read this Complaint?" Liz asked Forrester as she handed him the document which would finally put the court process in gear.

After reading the complicated pleading, Forrester was impressed. "Very good," he told her while handing the papers back. "I see you have it styled to file in Jacksonville. What made you think to file it here rather than in Gainesville?"

"I know they can change the venue, but why should they? We know the defense lawyers live in Jacksonville and this is where our offices are."

"So you figure that since it's more convenient to handle the case here in Jacksonville, they won't move to change venue to Alachua County?"

"Convenient? Yes. In addition, the insurance companies won't have to pay their lawyers for extra travel time every time there's a hearing. Insurance companies always like to save money."

"Good thinking." Forrester praised,

Suit was filed after more than eighteen months from when the lawyers had met their client. Less than six months remained before the running of the statute of limitations.

Liz was like a race-horse chomping at the bit. She sent deposition subpoenas to every person whose name was found in the hospital's records. The results were not good.

One after another, nurses, social workers, orderlies and psychologists swore that they knew nothing about the allegations. The only thing they did know was that you could not trust Cora. Crazy Cora. Manipulative Cora.

Each admitted having met with the defense lawyers before the depo. They had each been reminded that Cora's diagnoses were PTSD coupled with a histrionic personality disorder. Each had been reminded that Cora was manipulative. In other words, she could neither be trusted nor believed. It was Cora's word against the psychologist's, and each witness believed the word of the latter.

How about Head Nurse Robertson? She was no longer "head nurse." She was now a staff nurse who had transferred to another psychiatric hospital near Orlando, that was owned and operated by the same conglomerate that owned and operated the Greenview facility. That information came from others since, due to the transfer, Nurse Robertson's subpoena had not been served. Without it, there was no reason for her to show up.

When Liz reported the dismal results of the depositions to the man who did not like to be called "boss," he wasn't surprised. "What did you expect?" Forrester asked.

"I thought somebody would have seen something," she replied.

"You thought? Actually, you hoped. Do you really think anybody would admit it if they really did see something?"

Liz said, "I'm learning just how tight the medical community is. There's definitely a conspiracy of silence. If it's not a conspiracy, it's a powerful unwritten code."

"You're learning, Liz."

"What if we go to trial, and it's still her word against his?" Forrester did not mince words. "We will lose. It's just that simple. Are you still glad you took the case?" He was smiling, but he was serious.

"I believe she's telling the truth."

"I believe it, too, but that doesn't necessarily mean that we can win," Forrester reminded her.

"So, what are you saying?"

"So, I'm saying that unless we find something pretty soon, I want to cut my losses. I don't intend, if I can help it, to fund this case through a trial unless you can find a witness who will help. Can you think of any place you'll find somebody?"

"I've taken a lot of depositions, but we didn't get everybody served with their subpoena."

"Why not?"

"Some have quit, and some have transferred," she told him naively.

Forrester almost hoped those depositions would never be taken. The case was already getting expensive, and it looked like it would probably be a loser. Associates didn't think of the cost end of it, but he had to. Short depositions end up costing at least $1,000 each by the time they are transcribed. He was financing the case, and it could be like pouring money into a pit.

Forrester asked, "When is Taggart's deposition being taken?"

"We're trying to set a mutually convenient date, but it hasn't been noticed yet."

"If we haven't already dismissed the case by that time, I want to take that deposition. I want to do the questioning." Forrester was emphatic.

The associate agreed.

———

A couple of months later, Rosa, at Forrester's direction, arranged an appointment for the Bakers and Cora. Unbelievable. Cora had gained lots of weight over the last year. She had been chubby. Now she was fat. She came in wearing a muumuu type sack dress, and it was obvious she hadn't taken a bath in a while. She smelled rank.

He had called the meeting because he wanted to cut his losses. He figured that after he explained how bad things were going, they would take his advice and allow him to dismiss the case. Forrester did the talking.

"I started Richard Taggart's deposition, but we didn't get a chance to complete it. We've got two lawyers against us, and they're playing games. One's representing the hospital and the other Taggart. There's no question they're in cahoots, and we can handle that. It's just that it slows things down and gets more expensive."

Kenneth Baker asked the next question as though the answer would make a difference. "Who's representing them?"

"Lou Barrymore represents the psychologist. He's got a good reputation, and he's tough. Fred Boseman's hired for the hospital. He's the same lawyer that was against us not too long ago when we were representing some folks named Zimmerman. He'll be thorough, and he's smart."

"They both have reputations for winning. They will give no quarter, but if they tell you something, you can trust it to be true."

The follow-up question was, "When are you going to finish the deposition?"

"I don't know for sure. It should've only taken about three or four hours in the first place. We've already been asking questions for six, and we've got a long way to go. Every time we start getting any real information, Boseman or Barrymore, one, interrupts. There's no way to agree on the time of day."

"Have you scheduled to finish it?" Ken was asking the same question again but in a different way.

"Not yet. That's what I wanted to talk to you about. The transcript for what we've already done will be about twenty-five hundred. Before I keep spending money, I want to hear your thoughts."

It was still Ken. "What you're wondering is if Cora should dismiss the case. Right?"

Forrester was being the diplomat. He got his point across, but he didn't want it to sound like he was forcing the issue. He did, however, let them know that not one positive thing had come out of months of discovery.

"I tend to agree that the case should be dismissed. Of course, it's not up to me," Ken said.

"I don't care," Cora whispered without making eye contact.

Regina was the last one to talk. She said, "We'll follow your advice. That's what you're being paid for."

Forrester felt relieved. Of course, he was not being paid. He had to win to get paid. He had not yet won the case, but the clients had agreed that he could cut his losses—both dollar-wise and manpower-wise. He would work out a deal with the defense lawyers that would allow him to drop the suit if they would waive trying to collect the costs that the defense had incurred.

He was sure that the deal would be no problem. After all, Boseman and Barrymore would impress their clients with their obvious skill in bringing the plaintiff and her attorneys to their knees. They would be heroes.

They were on their feet and leaving when Regina said, "I can't believe that nurse lied."

"They all swore the same thing," Forrester assured her as he ushered the trio to the door. "None of them admits to knowing anything that's helpful."

"Yeah, but why did she call me in the first place?" Regina was questioning in passing.

"Who?" asked Forrester.

"The head nurse, Carol something," Regina answered. "You know, Roberts, Carol Roberts. Something like that."

Now it was Liz's turn. She had not butted in before now. She knew better. The words came out automatically. "Hold it. Just give me a minute."

Forrester's look was one of annoyance as Liz reviewed notes from the file. Nobody talked. All, except Cora, stared at Liz and waited for her to speak. Cora stared at the floor.

Finally, the associate said, "There is no Nurse *Roberts*. There is a Nurse *Robertson*. Her depo hasn't been taken. Remember, I told you she had transferred. We haven't reset it."

"That's it," Regina said. "Her name is Robertson. Carol Robertson."

Forrester gritted his teeth while suggesting they sit back down.

Regina explained that she probably would not have known anything if that nurse hadn't called her. Then she told about the conversation in the hospital parking lot. She apologized that she had forgotten to tell the lawyers about Robertson the first time they had met. She was sorry. She had delivered the information but not the source of it.

It was agreed before the clients left that Nurse Robertson's deposition would be taken. If she wasn't helpful, the case would be dismissed.

———

Before her deposition, Carol Robertson met with the defense lawyers as she had been instructed.

"Hello, Ms. Robertson. I'm Fred Boseman. I've been retained to represent the Greenview Psychiatric Hospital.

"It's a pleasure to meet you."

Boseman went on. "This is Lou Barrymore. He's representing Richard Taggart. Do you remember Mr. Taggart? He was a psychologist at the hospital."

"I remember him," she said without explanation.

"Well, since we'll be representing you at this deposition...."

The nurse cut him off. "I thought you said you were representing the hospital? I don't believe I need to be represented."

"Oh, no. Of course not. It's just that the law says that if we represent the hospital, we also represent its employees. That's the reason I'm here."

"If you say so." Carol Robertson wasn't acting as friendly as they had hoped. Then she asked, "Why do we need to meet anyway? I only plan to tell the truth."

Boseman said, "That's all we want you to do. It's just that we want to make sure that you know what to expect at the deposition."

"Besides, we know Bill Forrester," Lou Barrymore added. "We don't want you to get blindsided."

She said, "As long as I tell the truth, I don't see how I can get blindsided."

"You probably won't. It's just that sometimes the truth can be twisted to make it seem like you're lying, and we want to make certain that we can prepare you so that that doesn't happen," Boseman said.

The lawyers were frustrated. The witness had made it known that she did not want to meet in the first place. When they ignored that, she had not asked them what to say, and they were concerned when she refused to tell them exactly what she intended to say.

To bring her into the fold, they did most of the talking. They told her what everyone else had sworn to, but she did not seem to listen. She did not respond. The only thing she would agree to was not to volunteer any information unless asked.

The lawyers for the defense had reason to be concerned, and they knew it. Cora's complaint had been investigated by the hospital, HRS and the local police. They had kept from the plaintiff's attorneys, through legal manipulations, the investigation reports from the hospital and HRS. The police report contained few details and no names, except that of Cora Smallwood.

On the other hand, the defense lawyers had the reports. Had read them within thirty minutes of first being retained by the insurance company and had hoped Nurse Robertson's deposition would never get taken. Now they had to prepare for the worst.

Neither Boseman nor Barrymore told Carol Robertson to lie. They would never do that. That could get them disbarred. Still, if her story was the same as the other hospital personnel who testified, nobody would ever be the wiser. The hired guns for the defense knew that and had hoped they could, without saying so directly, influence this nurse to be a team player. All they needed her to say was that the patient was not believable. After all, Cora was crazy.

When the pre-depo interview was finished, Barrymore and Boseman were uptight. Up until now, the case had been going well. They had tried to stall the deposition of this nurse, but Forrester had persisted. They knew he must know something, and they were concerned.

———

It was the day before Robertson's deposition. Liz rapped once on his office door before picking a path through the piles of paperwork placed methodically across his floor. Without uttering a word, she stood in front of his mess of a desk until he acknowledged her presence. He just looked up from his computer monitor and keyboard with a weary, agitated look.

"I should have waited," Liz said." Would you like me to come back?"

"No. What's the use? I've already lost my train of thought."

"I'm sorry. I just wanted to talk to you about that deposition in Ms. Smallwood's case for tomorrow."

Forrester asked, "Is it on my calendar?"

"It's on both of our calendars, but I would prefer if you took it."

"Why? I have total faith in your ability and your instincts."

"Thanks, Bill. I mean it. It's just that if what Regina Baker said is accurate, the good defense lawyers will be pulling no punches."

Sarcastically Forrester inquired, "Do you think there's a chance that the witness will lie?"

"I just think you would be better at exposing it if she does. Besides, you have more experience fighting lawyers in this situation."

Forrester knew what she was talking about. If the deposition went badly for the defense, the lawyers would be objecting at every turn. The objections would be worded to tell the friendly witness what to say. If the witness got too wordy and was giving too much information, they would interrupt her in mid-sentence.

"I'll take the deposition. You come along and take notes."

"You mean you're going to allow two lawyers out of the office at the same time for one deposition?" She was teasing the man who would have never allowed it if she had made the suggestion.

CHAPTER 11

BILL FORRESTER WAS A skilled lawyer who was not easily sidetracked. Hadn't been intimidated in years. He would ask the questions while Liz took notes.

"What is your name?" Forrester asked.

"Carol Robertson."

"Where do you work?"

"Wekiva Springs Psychiatric Center."

"Did you ever work for Greenview Psychiatric Hospital?"

"Yes," she answered. But did not leave it at that. In direct violation of the instructions from the defense lawyers not to volunteer information, she continued, "I was transferred from GPH to Wekiva. Both hospitals are owned by the same company, Good Health Hospital Associates, Inc."

Barrymore boomed, "Objection! Move to strike as unresponsive."

"Same objection, same motion," parroted Boseman.

Forrester was unphased. "When were you transferred?"

"Objection, not relevant," said Barrymore.

"Same objection," said the other attorney.

"About nine months ago," said the witness.

"Why were you transferred?"

"Objection! She can't know why she was transferred." That was Barrymore's method of telling the witness to say that she didn't know.

The other lawyer said, "Objection, not relevant."

The witness said, "I think it was because of this case."

"Why do you think that?" Forrester prodded. Knowing now he had an ally.

"Objection, not relevant," said Barrymore.

Boseman was more forceful. He said, "As the attorney for your employer, the hospital… and you . . . I instruct you not to answer that question."

Robertson answered anyway. "After I told the higher-ups what I had seen; and after the investigation; I got a lot of pressure. I think they were trying to force me to quit. I wouldn't quit, and I doubted they would fire me. I got the silent treatment. Then I was told that they needed me at Wekiva. It's near Orlando. When I was transferred from GPH to Wekiva, I was no longer head nurse."

Boseman interrupted. "Ms. Robertson, you are speculating. I instruct you not to speculate."

"Go on," said Forrester.

"I told her not to answer," Boseman said emphatically.

"So?" said the plaintiff's lawyer.

"So ask a different question," demanded Boseman.

"After she finishes answering the last question."

"She has finished!" Boseman emphasized the word "has."

"Have you finished, Ms. Robertson? If not, please continue," Forrester instructed his ally.

Over defense lawyer protestations, the witness continued. "Orlando isn't close to my home, and my husband works in Gainesville, so I said I couldn't go. I was told to quit or be transferred. I felt it was because I had told what I saw."

"Why didn't you quit?" was Cora's attorney's next question.

"You know you can't ask that," shouted Boseman.

"Is that an objection?" Bill asked the hospital's lawyer. Then he looked at the witness and repeated, "Why didn't you quit?"

"First, I have almost enough years to retire from this company. Besides, I broke the 'code of silence,' and getting another job around here will not be easy."

You can guess the next question. "What is the code of silence?"

Bill Forrester knew the answer but wanted it on the record. The defense lawyers adamantly objected.

The witness answered. "It's not written, but everybody knows if you say something that will cause a doctor or hospital malpractice problems…well, you just don't do it."

"If you do, are you ostracized by your fellow employees?"

"Objection."

"Objection."

"You can say that," the witness responded.

As the deposition went on, former Head Nurse Robertson spilled her guts. Like she was talking to a psychiatrist, not a bunch of lawyers.

She told about seeing the kiss while Cora was still in the open unit. Before Cora had tried to kill herself with a razor. She wasn't sure it was Cora at first. Later, after the HRS investigation, she had checked the records to make sure. She didn't know why the investigator had not checked it out. Maybe it was because she had said she could not be sure it was Cora. Had only "thought" it was Cora.

The deponent admitted, even now, she was still not 100 percent sure it was Richard Taggart that she had seen kiss Cora in front of the window. Thought it was Taggart and still does. He had the same build. And, of course, she had an unobstructed view into Cora's room from the other corridor that day more than a year ago.

The defense lawyers were going berserk. Objected to every question. Moved to strike every answer. Forrester kept asking questions, undaunted. The nurse kept responding with volunteered information if she thought the lawyer had missed something.

She talked about going into the room and "catching" the couple, Cora and Rick, together. No, she could not swear they were having sex. "They looked like they were caught. Caught having sex," she volunteered. It did not matter anyway. He was breaking the rules to be in there in the first place, alone and in the dark. "Why had he been so insistent with his excuses when she had not asked any questions?" she asked rhetorically.

"Objection!"

"Move to strike!"

She continued, "HRS didn't want to know what I *thought*, just what I *knew*. The police never talked to me. It just makes me wonder…"

Boseman couldn't take it any longer. Once again he interrupted the witness. This time he boldly declared, "This deposition is over."

"You're kidding," said the plaintiff's lawyer, who had been caught off guard. Then sarcastically he added, "Are you just tired of hearing the truth?"

"I'm not kidding. I haven't got any problem with the truth either. You said this deposition was going to take two hours at the most, and we've now been going over three and a half." Boseman's voice boomed as he stated his position.

Now Barrymore wanted to say something. "Listen, Bill, I have another deposition in Jacksonville that starts at five o'clock. From here in Gainesville, it'll take at least two hours to get back to the office. We can come back and finish this some other day."

"If the judge lets him," insisted Boseman. "If he had stuck with the relevant questions, we would have been finished way before now."

Forrester was now composed. He met the unpleasant sound of his adversaries with the most pleasant of voices. "I don't think so, gentlemen. Lou, you can call your office and cancel the other depo or get somebody to cover it. We aren't stopping this one until I'm finished."

Sounding almost embarrassed, Barrymore said, "Okay, let me call the office."

"Bullshit!" Boseman exclaimed. "This deposition is over. Let's go Ms. Robertson."

She did not move. "I'm okay. I want to get this over with."

Boseman's face was crimson. Barrymore was exhausted. Forrester took off his coat and resumed questioning for forty-five minutes more.

Finally, he turned to Liz and whispered, "I don't think I have anything else. Have I missed anything?"

She whispered back, "Ask her why Taggart's no longer with the hospital."

Following orders, Forrester asked, "Ms. Robertson, do you know that Mr. Taggart is no longer with the hospital?"

"Yes."

"Do you know why?"

Boseman got a second wind and practically yelled, "She can't possibly know. Ask Mr. Taggart!"

"Objection," chimed Barrymore.

"I think I know why," said the willing witness.

"Please tell us." Forrester loved it. He and the witness both ignored the objections.

"He was forced to leave. There was another investigation, in-house. A patient claimed he was giving her pills. I don't know the details."

Forrester could not believe what he had just heard. He opened his mouth. The words came out, "For sex?"

Barrymore and Boseman went wild. Ballistic. The court reporter did her best to get it all down as lawyer talked over lawyer.

Finally, Robertson answered, "I don't know for sure. There was speculation…"

After more of the same from the defense, Bill asked his last question. "What is the name of the patient?"

Carol Robertson hesitated. As she opened her mouth to answer, she was interrupted for the umpteenth time by the lawyer. Her lawyer. The lawyer representing the hospital. Fred Boseman.

"Ms. Robertson, don't answer that. You can't answer that. You know it. That information is privileged." He took a breath. "If you answer that, you will be reported to the Department of Professional Regulation. You could lose your license. You know that."

"It's true," agreed Barrymore.

"Did anybody turn Mr. Taggart into the DPR? He still has a license." She was angry as she queried the defense lawyers.

Boseman did not hesitate to respond. "That's not the point."

Forrester said nothing.

The witness declined to answer.

Returning to Jacksonville took more time than normal since Bill was driving. Liz would've driven straight back. Instead, he turned into Johnnie's Hideaway, a honky-tonk-type bar on US 301 near the little speed trap town of Waldo. In his customary way, he didn't ask his riding companion what she thought. He just turned into the parking lot.

"It's going to be too late to get anything done if we go back to the office now. Let's have a martini."

It was only a little after 5:00 p.m., so Johnnie's wasn't crowded yet. As they took their seats, Liz told the waitress, "I'd like a Johnny Walker Red and water."

"Make mine a vodka on the rocks with a lemon peel twist," Bill ordered.

It was happy hour, and the bartender gave them each two glasses of their favorite liquid. She also put out a snack basket of party mix. Bill picked out the peanuts and ate those first.

"You ever had a drink here before?"

Liz's answer surprised him a little. "I've been here a couple of times on the weekend for line dancing."

"You like country music?"

"Sometimes. It's fun."

"I've never been here at night. Does it get rough?"

"It's more redneck than rough. It gets crowded with people mostly from Cora's hometown, Starke."

The two lawyers enjoyed the chitchat conversation. Nothing important being talked about. He told her about supporting Waldo's local government when he got a ticket for going thirty-two in a thirty-mile-per-hour zone. Liz had gotten one there for failing to come to a complete stop at a stop sign. She still protested her innocence.

As the duo continued to unwind, the conversation switched to Cora's case.

"Can you believe that deposition?" Liz's question was rhetorical. "When did you know she was going to help us?"

"As soon as she volunteered that she had been transferred, I knew we would not be dropping this case. I'm not sure if it's a curse or a blessing, but we'll be going all the way now."

Liz stroked his ego. She told him how brilliant his questioning was and how she admired his composure. She could not say the same for Barrymore and Boseman—especially Boseman. She called them the "B and B twins." They would be using that term for months while the case progressed.

Noting the obvious, she said, "The B and B twins are shook."

"They have reason to be."

"Do you think they'll want to settle now?"

"Not yet. Right now, we can only nail Taggart. Unless we can nail the hospital, they'll only offer peanuts, if anything."

"I know the hospital will deny they knew anything he was doing, but what about the insurance? Taggart's covered under the hospital's policy."

"Sure, but there's no coverage for intentional acts. What he did to Cora was no accident."

"What do you think about Ms. Robertson saying that there was another victim after Cora?"

"We ought to be able to track that down one way or another. If they made a police report or something like that, we can find out. But again, although that will help us against Taggart, we still need to show that the hospital knew of Taggart's propensities before Cora complained." Forrester smiled before adding, "It's too bad we don't represent the pill victim."

Liz was serious, "Do you think Cora was the first?"

"Probably not, but who knows? I do know that unless we nail the hospital, we won't get paid."

Liz sipped her Scotch. Then she said, "It's hard explaining to our client that we could get a big verdict against Taggart but collect nothing. We could collect from the hospital because it has money and assets. That's why the hospital bought the insurance. How much of a verdict could Taggart pay?" Then she answered her own question. "Probably little or nothing."

Bill took another mouthful of party mix. Swallowed. Then went back to the subject. "Our job is to prove the hospital vicariously liable. If Greenview knew what Taggart was doing before he got to Cora, we could prove negligence. Then, whatever Taggart did, the hospital would be legally responsible."

"There must be more victims," Liz concluded as she concluded her second Scotch.

"Then find one who was before Cora," Bill responded while standing to leave.

The party mix basket was empty.

———

Back in his fairly new Suburban Silverado, Forrester invited his associate to join him for dinner. It was more of a command. She took it as a compliment and agreed to be company. It would be like a celebration.

His girls were, once again, staying with their mother, and he need not get home early. They could take their time. Forrester chose the Hilltop Club, a restaurant located between Jacksonville and Orange Park where you count on a good meal. He chose a reasonably priced, but good white wine, Mandavi sauvignon blanc, from the special list. She ordered blackened grouper. He a medium-rare sirloin strip.

The wine was finished before they finished supper. Another bottle replaced the empty one.

After almost two years of working under his tutelage, Liz had grown to really admire Bill Forrester. He worked hard and was smart. However, she had never seen him like he was this night.

By the time they had finished supper and most of the second bottle of fermented grape, Bill was relaxed. Completely relaxed. Charming and witty.

They sat and talked until their glasses were empty. He was complimentary and told her how he appreciated her work. They did not mention any specific cases after he had admonished "no shop talk."

When Liz informed him that she "must wash [her] hands," he stood as she left the table. Although seemingly a gentleman, he peered intently and admired her figure as she walked to the powder room. He thought back to when they had first met on opposite sides at a deposition. Now, as then, she was slim, close to five-six, with perfectly shaped legs. Her auburn hair had grown to shoulder length, but the way she pulled it back exposed her elegant neck.

When she returned to the table, he stood again and stared at the sharp features of her face. Nice lips. Brown eyes. Found her nearly irresistible, though he knew he would resist since she worked for him. After all, inner-office liaisons were strictly verboten at Moran, Smith, Forrester & Dees. Maybe that was why he had been so aggravated the day she was hired by his partners without his acquiescence. Maybe in the back of his mind he thought someday they could get together.

The first time they met, he had fantasized about her being with him. Now that she was an employee, they would never be together in the biblical sense.

"Would you care to go the River House for a nightcap and dancing?" This time his voice was not that of a commander but was instead genuinely pleasant.

"I would love to, but I really don't think we should. It's getting late and it's a school night."

Bill did not protest. Rather, he jested. "You're probably right. Don't be late tomorrow morning."

"I won't," she said. "It might make my superiors angry."

———

At seven thirty that morning, they had met at Bill's house to drive to the deposition in Gainesville. It was fourteen hours later when they got back to her car, which had been left in his driveway.

He opened her door and closed it when she stepped into her Subaru Outback. Liz lowered the window to thank him.

Forrester leaned forward but said nothing. She said nothing too. They looked at each other until a voice from the garage broke the silence. It was the live-in housekeeper and nanny for his girls.

"Is that you, Bill?" Dorothy's voice was tentative. "I heard the garage door open. I just wanted to check."

Liz Kelley was in her own bed before midnight wondering what would have happened if the voice had not called out. In her mind's eye, she could see him turning and walking toward Dorothy. He waved as the automatic garage door closed.

———

The next day at the office, neither the man nor the woman seemed different. Neither acted like they had almost kissed the night before. It was back to work as usual, with long hours and a short lunch break in the kitchen. Both Bill and Liz were behind in paperwork, having spent the full day out of town.

Bill offered Liz some leftover meat loaf that he had stored in the firm's refrigerator for more than a week. She declined as he cut slices and laid them on wheat bread covered with ketchup. Instead, she microwaved a frozen hot dog fresh from the freezer.

"Let's put off finishing Taggart's depo," Bill said between mouthfuls. "If we ever ID his victims, I want to ask him about them. After his deposition is finished, we can't go back."

"Whom should I set?"

"Set everybody whose name came up at the deposition. Set the policeman and the HRS investigator first."

Yes, things were back to normal.

CHAPTER 12

"THIS IS LOU BARRYMORE," he said as he answered the phone.

"Lou, this is Fred Boseman."

"How do you think Bill and his associate celebrated last night? I know how I'd like to celebrate with that woman."

"If you said that about somebody in your own firm, it might be considered sexual harassment. In that case, you might get sued just like your client, the psychologist." Boseman chuckled.

Barrymore knew why Boseman had called. He wanted to get back to the real subject. "What more could that nurse have said to hurt us? Do you think she has it in for the hospital, or what?"

"I don't think they helped us much by moving her out of town. Anyway, we can't make the facts. We just have to do the best we can with what we got.

Neither of the lawyers mentioned to the other that "they" had failed in their quest to hide the facts.

Boseman went on. "I still don't think they have anything on the hospital. Forrester understands that. He won't get paid unless he can nail my client."

"How did I get to represent the easy target?" Barrymore really wasn't complaining; it just kept the conversation going.

Now Boseman got to the point. "I was thinking of calling the insurance adjusters. It may be better to settle this case now before something else comes up when it's too late."

"Fred, I really don't believe they'll be able to hold the hospital responsible. If my upstanding client is guilty of being with the Honorable

Miss Smallwood, I would bet that she was the first. There's no way they would have kept him on."

"We're lucky he doesn't represent that Manchester woman," Boseman said. "If we can settle this case early, he may never learn who she is. I suspect he's looking for her now."

It was Barrymore who called Elizabeth Kelley after the short meeting with the insurance adjuster. A business decision had been made to offer up to $100,000. Taggart's lawyer specifically and purposely asked for the younger of Cora's lawyers rather than her mentor. It was agreed that he and Boseman would come over to talk. Barrymore started with, "We may have been hurt by Nurse Robertson, even though I find it hard to believe her."

"I don't believe her either," agreed Boseman.

"So what are you here for?" asked Liz.

"Litigation like this is expensive," Barrymore responded. "We got a call from the insurance company. They wanted to know how much more we were going to have to spend to defend this case."

Now it was Boseman's turn to lie. "You know the company is paying both of us. It gets expensive. There are a lot of depositions to take. So, we have calculated how much it'll take to defend this case to the end."

Liz asked, "Do you have an offer? If so, tell me. I'll ask Bill to come over, and we can talk together."

"You can ask Bill to come if you want to," said Barrymore. "There's no reason to talk to both of you, and I thought that you were lead counsel on this case." He was trying to flatter her.

Liz may have been a little flattered. In any event, she asked matter-of-factly, "What is the offer?

Boseman looked at Barrymore. Barrymore said, "They gave us permission to offer fifty thousand dollars. They want to stop the bleeding now."

"I think we might be able to get another ten thousand." Boseman chimed in.

They were negotiating. There was no reason to offer the full amount of authority at once. If they saved anything off of the $100,000, there would be pats on the back and congratulations.

"I think the case is worth a lot more than that," was the young lawyer's response.

"Maybe. Maybe not. Frankly, I don't know why the insurance company wants to settle in the first place. I think they're offering this in good faith. You can't get to the hospital and you know it. Even if the jury believes Miss Smallwood…."

"Believes her and Nurse Robertson," Liz blurted out before Barrymore could finish the sentence.

"She didn't really see anything," Boseman said. Anyway, if the jury believes her, we will get a directed verdict for the hospital. He wasn't doing it for the hospital, even if he did those things you claim. The hospital is not at fault."

Lawyers puff that way. They try to put their best foot forward. They act like they aren't scared of anything. Contrary to appearances, all three at the negotiation table were concerned about their respective client's position in this case.

———

Ethically, all offers must be conveyed to the plaintiff client. It would be necessary for Liz to explain the offer to Cora and the Bakers. Forrester suggested that she make an appointment and meet with them. He would be going out of town and the clients ought to know about the offer as soon as possible. "Tell them face-to-face," he directed.

If the offer was rejected, the firm would continue to fund the litigation. Liz didn't have to worry about the expenses. After all, she was an associate. She had mixed feelings for other reasons.

On the one hand, Attorney Kelley had a feeling that they could win. Taggart was a dirtbag. That could be proven. They only needed to find victims before Cora. If they could do that, they could prove that the hospital "knew or should have known" that Taggart was a dirt bag.

On the other hand, she was concerned that if the offer was rejected, the client might get nothing for the humiliation.

Liz explained it all at the meeting with Regina and Cora. It was not Kenneth Baker's case, and he did not show up. Were it not for his wife wanting him to, he would not have come to any of the meetings at the lawyers' office. He didn't care much about Cora, but he did care about his wife.

Regina hadn't really wanted to come to the meeting either. She had grown tired of the lawsuit. She had escaped her family years ago and now this was keeping them together. At least it kept her and Cora together; she had been able to keep Renee out of the fray.

Liz said, "Cora can take the offer or leave it. As it stands, if she takes it, she ends up with about ten thousand dollars after attorney's fees and costs and after paying you back for the original retainer. If you wait, they may increase the offer, or they may withdraw it."

Regina asked, "What about Taggart? If she takes the offer, what happens to him?"

"The insurance company will pay and that'll be it. Nothing will happen to him unless somebody else comes along and sues later," the lawyer explained.

"So at this stage, Cora gets about ten thousand dollars. On the other hand, the worst that can happen is she gets nothing."

"That pretty much sums it up for right now. We really do need to know the answer as soon as possible."

It wasn't Regina's case, but she was doing all the work. Questions called "interrogatories" had been sent and had to be answered. Cora couldn't or wouldn't help, and it made Regina bitter.

She knew things were not going to get easier. She had tried to avoid Cora for years, and now it was like they were in this together, but Regina had to do the work and answer questions like:

"List the names and addresses of each and every doctor who has treated you for each of the last ten years. As to each, provide the date or dates of treatment and the nature of the treatment."

It took her hours to research and respond. She still was not sure she had listed everything.

Another interrogatory only took moments to answer: "Describe in detail how the events you allege to have occurred affected or changed you."

Responding for Cora, Regina wrote: "Do not bathe."

She was tempted to add the obvious—"Cora smells bad."

When Liz pressed for an answer, Regina wanted to say, "Cora, take the offer." Instead, she said, "Cora, I think you should turn it down. If we don't take this to trial, that bastard will keep on hurting people."

Without looking up, Cora said in her quiet voice, "I don't care. Whatever you think."

———

After the B & B twins were told the offer was rejected, they conferred before calling back to offer $75,000. Like the one before, this offer was rejected. They were humiliated when they made the last offer for $100,000. It was rejected, too.

CHAPTER 13

RICHARD SMALLWOOD WAS PISSED off when he got the subpoena. Why was this thing still going on? Almost three years had passed since Cora was in that hospital. How long do these things take?

"What the hell is this for?" he asked the deputy serving the subpoena.

"I don't know nothing about it," the deputy answered. "Somebody wants to take your deposition."

Richard Smallwood was pissed off because he did not trust lawyers. He had been in a deposition before and didn't like it. You get there, and they can ask you anything. He wondered why nobody had told him the subpoena was coming.

The deputy had also asked for his father, but he wasn't home. It was the same home where Cora's brother was still living.

Richard was two years younger than Cora. She was thirty-three. He was thirty-one. They had grown up in the house together with their aging parents and Regina. Regina had been the strong one, the one who left as a teenager.

When he was younger, he knew what was happening to Cora. He could hear the old man come into her room through the uninsulated sheetrock walls. The house was a modest house, but not a run-down shanty. It was in a neighborhood that had been developed in the 1950's. There were three bedrooms and a den, which had been converted into Regina's sleeping quarters. Cora's room and Richard's were side by side and separated by the width of a two-by-four stud. Richard could hear what was happening to Cora, but for years he didn't know it was sex.

The parents were older when they married. Florence Smallwood, a timid housewife and mother, was in her late thirties and pregnant with Cora when the marriage ceremony was performed in Folkston, Georgia.

In those days, if you wanted to get married in Florida, blood tests were required, and waiting for the results could take a week. There was no waiting period if you got married in Georgia, and Folkston was right on the Florida-Georgia line. It was a small town about as big as Waldo. But in a way, it was like Las Vegas to North Floridians. No glitz, of course, but an easy place to get married with no questions asked.

Rosco Smallwood was forty when he married his pregnant bride. He had a good job with the Seaboard Coastline Railroad, and Florence was anxious to marry. She had never been married before and was tired of being called "old maid" or "spinster." Rosco had been married twice before.

His first wife and childhood sweetheart, Linda Hazel, had died along with their baby during childbirth. They were both seventeen at the time. War time. Vietnam. She died soon after he had enlisted in the Army and while he was a recruit doing basic training at Fort Benning.

He followed the war from Vietnam into Cambodia and back again. Was a cook but also saw combat. Although he did not receive the Silver Star nor Bronze Star, he was awarded the Purple Heart after a shrapnel wound took him temporarily out of action. Rosco seldom talked about his experiences overseas.

He met his second wife before being shipped back to the States. Binh was from South Vietnam and had a hard time adjusting to American ways. The language was not the only barrier. Rosco's clannish Florida cracker family. That was the biggest barrier.

The family had seen Rosco only off and on for almost four years when his enlistment was up. He had lost Linda Hazel and his baby just before being shipped out, and they expected that he would still be mourning their deaths. For the family, the "oriental" woman was unexpected and her ways unacceptable.

Binh left without notice and pregnant less than two years after the marriage. She never wrote and neither did he. Heck, he wasn't even sure where she could be found. Although papers were never filed, he told people they were divorced. Rosco never followed up and never knew if their baby was born. He never wondered if it was a boy or a girl.

Railroad jobs were hard to come by. They were good jobs if you could get one and he stayed with the railroad for more than thirty years. He was a foreman with a good pension when he retired.

In his prime, Rosco was a little over six feet. Was strong, tough and capable in the railroad yard. At home, he was caustic, short-tempered and constantly ridiculed his third wife. Though he seldom beat her, he would admit that he would occasionally "have to slap her to keep her in line."

Florence was timid. Rosco felt strong. She kept the house and cooked their meals. He doled out the money and frequently reminded her about how lucky she was to have him.

Florence Smallwood stuck with Rosco Smallwood and never considered divorce.

When Richard first started hearing his father go into Cora's room, he did not understand what was going on. When the old man would leave, he could hear Cora sob, but for years did not know why. When he was eleven, he saw his father lying naked next to Cora in her bed. Her door was open. The only reason he saw it was because he was not supposed to be at home. Florence was grocery shopping and Cora had stayed home from school sick. Richard had played hooky from school, which was less than one-half mile from their house. It was an easy walk.

Through the open door, he saw Cora with their father. Watched for less than a minute and, even though he had not been detected, got scared. Not because he saw what he saw, but because he knew his father would beat him for not being in school. He slipped out of the house, leaving no one the wiser.

Richard Smallwood never forgot that day. That was the first time he knew what was actually going on in the next room when Cora would cry—quietly.

It was not unusual for Richard to get beaten by his father. He was not a good student and repeated the first and second grades. To help his self-esteem, he was thereafter socially promoted in succeeding years. When Richard would bring home his report card, Rosco would beat him. Would also beat him for other things like letting the screen door slam; playing the TV too loud; or crying "for no good reason."

Richard was only beaten by his mother once. That was when he told her about seeing Cora and his father in bed together without any clothes on. He was only asking her what it meant, but she slapped him and beat him until he admitted it was a lie. After all, his father was a good man.

While in the ninth grade, at the age of sixteen, Richard Smallwood dropped out of school. That year, before dropping out, was the only time in his life he was popular. He was the only kid in his ninth-grade class who had a driver's license, and his mother would let him drive her six-year-old sedan that he called "the tank." He had wheels.

Most of the kids in the class were fourteen. They liked the older boy. It was exciting to ride around in a car, and even the girls would go driving with him.

All that ended seven months after his sixteenth birthday. The day he loaded three boys, himself, and three girls into "the tank." It was a Wednesday afternoon and they were skipping school. Had planned it on Tuesday.

The plan was to drive to Kingsley Lake and go swimming. It was one of those eighty-degree days in March, which is not atypical for North Florida. Kingsley Lake is only about fifteen miles from Starke. Half of it is owned by and fronts a military facility, Camp Blanding. The other half is dotted by houses on one-hundred-foot lots. Most of the houses are owned by people in Jacksonville and Gainesville as "summer places" for water-skiing and fishing. Although the lake is crowded in the summer, it is practically empty in March.

The teenagers pulled into the driveway of a house that would not be occupied for a few months. Unfortunately for them, the house next door was owned by a permanent resident. She got suspicious upon see-ing seven teenagers swimming in front of an empty house that should have been empty until June. Besides, the neighbor wondered why they were there on a school day. They were obviously children.

The woman stepped out to her screened porch, from which she would normally view the lake unmolested by flies, gnats and mosquitos. "What are you kids doing out there?" she called out.

Richard yelled back, "None of your business, bitch!"

Another boy gave her the finger.

"You better get off that property! I'm calling the police," she yelled.

Richard was content to ignore her, but the other teenagers scrambled and coerced him back to his mother's car. With four in the back seat and three in the front, he turned the key and gunned the accelerator. The old car wheeled into reverse out of the driveway.

Now he would be cool. Instead of turning back toward the main road, which would have taken them back to Starke, he went the other way. He bumped over the curb in front of the house where the lady lived; then drove in circles making doughnuts in the yard. In seconds, a good portion of her lawn, as well as a newly planted spring garden, was destroyed.

Next, the kid, who was for the first time popular, swung the car back on the road while yelling obscenities at the woman he knew would never forget him. Yelled obscenities to the woman who had dared to take on Richard Smallwood.

Before the end of the block, the car was going almost seventy miles per hour. Richard slammed on the brakes and tried to turn left at the same time—the way he had seen cops do it on TV. His passengers were screaming when the right-hand back door popped open.

Melissa Rowe was thrown from the car to the asphalt and killed instantly. Nobody else was hurt.

Richard Smallwood did not attend Melissa's funeral. He was no longer popular.

———

A wrongful death lawsuit was filed against the minor and "his parents, guardians and next friends, Rosco Smallwood and Florence Smallwood." When they got the suit papers, Richard was beaten. Just as he had been beaten the afternoon of the day Melissa Rowe was killed.

The case was settled short of trial for the Smallwood's insurance policy limit, $100,000.00.

Richard was a juvenile, and he lost his driver's license for one year.

Cora still lived at home when Richard had the accident. Regina had long since left. He was lonely, and Cora befriended him. She was an ally, and he needed her affection.

He understood sex by now. He had seen it in the movies and on TV and on the internet and in magazines. He did not read much but looked at the magazines Rosco Smallwood kept stacked in a corner of his clothes closet. The boy had found them when he was thirteen and in the sixth grade.

He had never actually had sex but did for the first time on the day the suit papers were served because of Melissa Rowe's death. It was after he had been beaten by his father.

The parents had left to get away from the house and their offspring. Richard was ordered to stay in his room. Cora joined him just to listen to what he had to say. She would hear his side of the story. Would comfort him because she hated their father, too.

The sixteen-year-old boy attacked her almost immediately. She was shocked when he told her to undress like she did for Rosco. Cora began to cry, so he threw her to the bed and did what he had seen in a movie on cable TV.

He never forcibly raped her again. They had sex again several times, but that stopped by the time he was twenty and she was twenty-two. After that, he arranged for her to have dates with his friends. Like the date she had just before the last time she was admitted to Greenview Psychiatric Hospital.

Over the years, Cora had been treated for psychiatric problems in several psychiatric centers by several psychiatrists and psychologists. Her medical records were voluminous. They contained volumes of notes and reports by the doctors. Those reports were the basis for her obtaining social security benefits soon after Regina had taken custody of Cora's daughter, Renee.

Now the records would be reviewed for other purposes. Litigation purposes.

The records were like juicy gossip. They spoke often to the facts surrounding her abuse at the hands of her father, brother and brother's friends. Because of her lawsuit, all the records were available to the defense lawyers, who had them reviewed and summarized by a nurse working full-time for Boseman's firm. The defense knew everything about Cora and her family.

There are two parts to every lawsuit. The liability portion determines if the defendants are at fault. The damages portion gives the jury a basis for setting an award.

If the jury ever found the hospital responsible for Taggart's behavior, the defense lawyers wanted to show that it did not matter anyway. After all, Cora was damaged goods in the first place. What did it hurt if Taggart had an affair with her while she was a patient? What were the damages?

Barrymore and Boseman decided to test the waters. They would take the depositions of Cora's earliest predators. Her father and her brother. They would decide later how to use the evidence at trial.

Richard Smallwood had been deposed before. He had been grilled by the lawyer representing the estate of Melissa Rowe, deceased. Her parents attended the deposition to see the boy who had killed their oldest daughter.

Richard had tried to act unconcerned. Nonchalant. Wanted to act tough like his father. It was not his fault. Melissa had wanted to go swimming.

He testified, "I didn't make her skip school. It was not my idea."

Caroline and Wade Rowe wept openly at the deposition. They wondered what their daughter had seen in Richard Smallwood. He was thin and lanky. Wore jeans, a Harley-Davidson T-shirt, and work boots to the deposition. It looked like he was trying to grow a beard, but he had patchy places on his cheeks. The beard on his chin was black and uneven.

Why had their daughter been with him? He was not her boyfriend. He was a dropout who did not have the decency to send flowers to the funeral.

Of course, money would not buy their daughter back. They would have preferred the law of the jungle and the law of the Old Testament. The law that said, "An eye for an eye and a tooth for a tooth."

Before the Rowes ever went to a lawyer for help, the Smallwoods' insurance representative called on them. The evening that he knocked on their door was less than a week after the funeral. The visit was unexpected, but Mr. Rowe let the insurance adjuster in.

"Mr. Rowe?"

"Yes."

"I'm Hal Crawford with Worldwide Insurance."

"Who?"

"Hal Crawford. I'm with the insurance company that insures the Smallwoods."

"Did you make an appointment with my wife?" the father asked incredulously.

"Oh, no. I just wanted to come by to tell you that we couldn't be more sorry for Melissa."

Mr. Rowe wanted to end the conversation there. He said, "Thank you. Now, if you don't mind, we would like to be left alone."

The adjuster had been trained not to leave them alone. He said, "Have you hired an attorney?"

"We haven't even thought about it. Why do you ask?"

"Sir, I don't want to bother you. We'd just like to get this behind us, just like you would. We know that money will not buy Melissa back, but…."

With tears coming from his eyes, the father pushed the adjuster out of the house and slammed the door in his face. He chose not to tell his wife what he had witnessed.

Two days later they received a letter on stationery from Worldwide Insurance Company.

Dear Mr. and Mrs. Rowe:

This is in follow-up to my meeting at your house on March 28. I realize that at this time you may not be thinking about settling your case for the death of your daughter, Melissa.

Believe me, we at Worldwide have nothing but condolences for the tragedy you suffered. With that in mind, we are prepared to settle your case on behalf of the Smallwoods for $25,000.00.

Please call me at your earliest convenience so that we may prepare the appropriate paperwork to put this unfortunate matter behind us.

Very truly yours,
Hal Crawford

The Rowes were horrified. They had heard of ambulance-chasing lawyers but for some reason were unaware of the tactics of the insurance companies. They had never considered hiring a lawyer, but with letter in hand sought legal advice from Scott Watson, P.A. Watson was a one-man firm in Starke with a good reputation.

At first, the Rowes were determined to take the case to trial and bankrupt the Smallwoods if possible. After Richard's deposition, they realized it was not his parents, but him, they were after. They were after a minor without a job who did not have a pot to pee in nor a window to throw it out of.

As they wept at his deposition, they changed. Now, they hoped they would not have to go through the ordeal of trial. When the $100,000 insurance policy limits were offered, they accepted.

The fight was out of them, and the fight was over. The money would help to send their other four children to the University of Florida in Gainesville.

He never wanted to be deposed again. Now, because of Cora, Richard Smallwood had received a subpoena signed by somebody named Lou Barrymore.

He wondered how this lawyer would try to embarrass him. He did not know much about Cora's case except that if she won, he thought he would borrow some money. Giving his deposition was not worth it.

Richard Smallwood was definitely pissed off when he was handed the subpoena.

When the deputy served the other subpoena on Rosco Smallwood, he was expecting it. His son had told him that it would be coming. Still, Cora's father had hoped maybe they would leave him alone. He was older now and looked older than his age. Things that would not have bothered him when he was younger, scared him now—especially when it came to legal matters.

Before the subpoena, when he first learned about Cora's case, he tried to talk her out of it. Somehow, he knew that sooner or later somebody would bring him into the fracas. Cora didn't care if the suit was dismissed or not.

"It's up to Regina," she said. "Why don't you call her? They're Regina's lawyers."

"They're your lawyers, not Regina's," he explained to his oldest daughter. "Call and tell them to drop it."

At that point Cora would have done it. She would have dropped the case. She usually did what her father told her. Long ago, she had quit fighting him. Unfortunately for Rosco, Richard was present for that conversation.

"What the hell are you telling her to drop the case for? It's her case, not yours. Not Regina's. What can it hurt for her to get some money?"

Just as Cora had quit fighting the old man, the old man had long since quit fighting Richard. The argument ended with the case at status quo.

Later, the old man thought about calling Regina. Ask her to make sure the case was dropped. He didn't, though. There would be no use to it. They had parted ways years ago when she left home to live with Rosco's in-laws.

Besides, Regina was strong. If she wanted something, she could get it. After all, she got Renee, Cora's little girl, who he had not been allowed to see since.

For the same reason he was scared when Regina went after custody of the child, he was scared now. He was scared that there would be testimony or a trial. He was scared that the past that he wanted to forget might come out. He was scared that he would go to jail.

What was the statute of limitations for crimes relating to sleeping with a daughter child, Rosco wondered.

When Rosco got the subpoena, he blasted Richard. "See! I told you that damn case should have been dropped. No! You had to talk her out of it."

"Shut the hell up. And while you're at it, go to hell, you old bastard!" Richard was yelling at the old man.

The boy had not been afraid of his father for years. The last time he was beaten by the old man was after they had been sued because of the death of Melissa Rowe.

It was not like the old man had not tried. He went to beat Richard about a month after the case had been settled. The boy had taken his mother's car to a honky-tonk place on a Friday night. He showed a fake ID and proceeded to get drunk on beer. Coming home, he was stopped and put in jail for DWI and driving without a license.

The judge insisted that the parents attend the court hearing and was furious with Rosco for not controlling the boy. It was the same judge who had sentenced the juvenile delinquent after the accident that killed the girl. He threatened to charge the father with some crime, probably child neglect, if he did not get control.

When they returned home, Richard knew what was coming. He knew Rosco would beat him, so he countered with a baseball bat. He ruptured his father's spleen and broke three of his ribs.

At the hospital, it was reported that the patient had fallen off a ladder while cleaning the gutters on the house.

Richard never moved from his boyhood house. He would come and go as he wanted, and nobody asked questions. The Smallwoods were not exactly a close family, and they didn't talk much. After both men received a Subpoena for Deposition, however, they needed to talk.

It was the old man who explained why they did not want the deposition to happen.

"They'll want to know everything. That's the way lawyers are."

Richard knew what that meant, though he had never confronted his father with what he knew about him and Cora. Likewise, he suspected his father knew about his relationship with his sister.

"So, what do we do? I just won't show up," he said boldly.

"And they'll probably put you in jail for contempt."

In truth and in fact, while the court can hold somebody in contempt for ignoring a deposition subpoena, it hardly ever happens. It's too much work for the lawyers and the judge. The Smallwood men didn't know that. They became convinced that they would go to jail if they ignored the subpoenas. They were also concerned that they would go to jail if they didn't.

While Rosco and Richard were sweating it, the B & B Twins were yucking it up in Boseman's office. They worked hand in hand and planned the strategy for the Southeastern Fire & Casualty Company, which employed them both. They worked together to keep Crazy Cora from getting too many dollars.

It was Boseman's idea to take the deposition of Cora's father and brother, although Barrymore actually signed the necessary papers. It was Barrymore's name that was burned into the memory of Richard Smallwood.

Initially, Barrymore had asked, "Do you really think their testimony is necessary?"

"Of course not," Boseman responded.

"Then why spend the time taking the depositions?"

"Think about it, Lou. We know from her medical records that she was abused in the beds of both of the men in her family. Don't you think if we subpoena them, they'll pressure her to settle for what we've offered?"

Barrymore thought about it for less than a New York minute before forming a wry smile. He said, "Don't you know they'll be squirming when we quote directly from her records?"

Boseman chuckled on cue. "They're the ones she ought to be suing."

They were into it now. Barrymore said, "Maybe the Smallwood men are better hung than Taggart."

Between giggles, Boseman added, "That would explain it. You think Forrester will object if I ask to see the evidence?"

The B&B Twins howled.

Then they stopped laughing when Boseman's partner, Gary Mahon, came through the open door. He closed it.

"We are going to be defending our own lawsuit. Everybody can hear you yucking it up about that poor girl's awful situation. Nobody but you guys think it's funny."

"I'm sorry," Barrymore immediately and sincerely responded. He knew the implications. He might not get sued, but he would be a witness.

Sexual harassment is a legitimate cause of action. Any woman hearing the banter had every right to be offended. Any woman working for the law firm had every right to file a complaint. A hostile workplace complaint.

As he prepared to leave, Mahon said, "I'm serious. You need to cut it out. I will make the apologies for now. I hope you figure out how to make your own apologies later."

CHAPTER 14

EXCEPT WHEN HE HAD to travel, Bill Forrester liked his work. When working, time passed quickly. Sometimes he would take on one last twenty-minute task before leaving the office, yet hours would pass before he looked up again. When in the office, he could get engrossed in his work.

On the other hand, time dragged when his work caused him to travel. There was too much time to think about his own life. He was a successful lawyer, but things had not worked out as he had planned. Especially when it came to his family. When it came to the things that really mattered.

Forrester had planned to have a big family with lots of children. He wanted girls mostly, but boys would be okay. He longed to come home to a wife who was really glad to see him. Whatever it took, he would give her, if she would be happy when he drove into the garage.

It would be a piece of cake, he figured. Like his own father, he would work hard; be successful; and be adored. When he was young, he could not fathom divorce. By the time he was forty-two, he had been divorced twice.

The first marriage began and ended while he was still in college. He was heartbroken when he found his young wife in bed with another man. The other man had been his friend in college and they both graduated with degrees in business administration. However, after Forrester went to law school, his wife's bedfellow took a job in Gainesville. Then, during the time he spent studying in the law library, his old buddy and his bride spent time together. Fortunately, there had been no children, though she had promised them as soon as he got a full-time job.

Five years later he was a young lawyer, a rising star, and once again a married man. His second wife was as beautiful as the first and promised him all the children he wanted on the day she proposed to him. She was a perfect woman, he thought. She was young, vivacious, and possessed a wicked sense of humor. She already had a degree from Florida State, but she wanted to be a housewife.

Within four years, they had two girls. His income rose steadily as he became known as one of the most successful young lawyers in the state. Within six years, she was spending more after-tax dollars per month than his before-tax annual salary the first year out of law school. Within ten years, it was divorce number two.

The second wife had left him because "he simply wasn't around enough." Besides, she "needed her space." Naturally, the "space" could not be maintained if she got a job. She got the house, most of their assets, alimony and child support. The monthly checks were written with bitterness at first. You get used to it, though, and he wasn't so bitter anymore.

Forrester swore never to marry again. Heartbroken twice, he vowed not to be vulnerable again. Now he was lonely—especially when he traveled.

Forrester landed in Newark on Monday night at nine thirty. Checked into the Hilton located across from Penn Station. By then it was a quarter til eleven.

One of his clients had had his hand nearly chewed off by a paper shredder designed and manufactured in New Jersey. The plastic shield had broken the second week after it had been set up and the blades were exposed. It was another products liability case.

When he checked in, there was a message waiting from the most reliable associate he had ever employed, Elizabeth Kelley. It read, "Please call whatever the hour. Very important. Liz."

Instead of going to the hotel bar for the martini he had planned before turning in, he went directly to his room to place the call. Put his briefcase on the king-size bed and hung his clothes bag in the closet.

Sitting on the bed, he fumbled for his cell while he read the message again. It did not have her phone number on it.

"Damn," he muttered to himself.

There was seldom reason to call Liz, and he sure as hell didn't have her numbers memorized. Neither her cell nor her home number. (He would fix both problems as soon as he got back to Jacksonville. He would add her numbers to his contacts.) The lawyer asked Siri to get the landline number, but that was unsuccessful. Then he punched the number for long distance information in North Florida.

"What city, please?" It was a computer voice.

"Jacksonville Beach."

The computer came back again. "What name, please?"

"Elizabeth Kelley."

"At the request of the customer, the number you seek is not published," the computer reported.

He knew Rosa's number and thought about calling her. Since it was nearly midnight, though, he decided against it. Instead, he left the room; entered the elevator; and went back to the first floor to the lounge for the martini he had planned in the first place. Whatever it was could wait until tomorrow.

Bill sat down at the bar. There were two empty seats between him and the next person and only three lonely people altogether. He broke the silence when he ordered.

"I would like a Stoli martini with a lemon peel twist, straight-up."

The bartender, Debbie, smiled. She said, "Dry?"

"Enough Vermouth so that I can taste it." He smiled back.

When she served him, the lawyer engaged the attractive woman with small talk. "Can you think of any reason why anybody would have an unlisted number?" Then he answered his own question. "Maybe if there is a bill collector chasing her. Otherwise, can you think of a reason?"

The bartender agreed that she could think of no reason. She did not embarrass him with the information that her phone number, too, was unlisted.

By 1:00 a.m., he had brushed his teeth and turned in. A wake-up call was ordered for 6:30 a.m., and he was asleep in less than thirty minutes.

The slumber was broken just as he reached R.E.M. Bill stopped the obnoxious sound of the phone when he picked it up on the fourth ring. It was his associate and it was two thirty in the morning.

"Hello," a sleepy voice said.

"Bill, hello, Bill? This is Liz."

"Yes, this is Bill Forrester." He still wasn't awake. "Who is this?"

"It's Liz, Bill."

"I thought it was the hotel."

"Didn't you get my message?"

"Oh, yeah, but no number." He was waking up. "Why don't you get your number listed?"

"Bill…Barrymore's been shot."

"What?" Now he was really awake.

"The guy I've been seeing told me that Barrymore was shot."

"Barrymore's dead?" he asked.

"According to my friend."

"How?"

"At first, they thought it was a car wreck. It turns out he was shot."

"Shot?"

"They're speculating he was shot from an overpass on I-295. The police aren't sure. Probably some kid thinking it's cute to shoot at passing cars."

"Who is this guy who told you?"

"Wayne Milton. He's in the State Attorney's Office. He knew I had a deposition with Barrymore in the morning."

"I know Wayne. You've been seeing that guy?" Forrester asked incredulously. "He's practically my age."

"Not really." She was flippant. "Anyway, what should I do?"

Bill had lost, then regained his composure. He said, "What did they say on the news?"

"I don't think it was on the news. I kept flipping channels to see."

There was silence, and then Bill spoke. "I liked Barrymore and his theatrics. He would fight you, but he wouldn't lie to you." He thought for a moment. Liz didn't interrupt the silence. "Tell Rosa to have LaMee Florist send flowers to the funeral."

"Okay."

"And also send one hundred dollars to his favorite charity."

"Okay."

"And I'll be back tomorrow night or the next morning. It depends on how long things take up here. Mark off my calendar for the funeral."

"What about the depositions?" Liz asked.

"I don't know how long they'll take. It depends on what they try to hide."

"Not your depositions!" Liz was obviously frustrated with the lack of communication. "What about the depositions in the Smallwood case? The depositions I'm supposed to take?"

"Oh." He thought for a second. "I guess that's why you called me."

"Well, yeah. That's why I called. I'm sorry if I woke you."

"I'm sure they're canceled," Bill said. He was feeling tired again.

"I couldn't get in touch with his office. Depositions start early and they're going to be held in Starke. It's at least an hour and a half to get there from where I live."

"Liz, if you can't get in touch with somebody that says different, you better go. Otherwise, Boseman will probably take the depos without us."

"Okay." The conversation was winding down. Forrester didn't want to hang up without saying one more thing.

"Liz, didn't you know that at Moran, Smith, Forrester and Dees, every lawyer's phone should be listed? Otherwise, we may miss a new case call."

"Thank you, Mr. Forrester."

Mr. Forrester could not go to sleep again until nearly 4:00 a.m. His mind was reeling. At first, he thought about Barrymore, with whom he had litigated dozens of times. After he had relived those memories, he thought about Liz, his associate who was dating a lawyer in the State Attorney's Office.

———

Liz didn't get much sleep either. She was up before six and left her high-rise condominium on Jacksonville Beach at a quarter to seven. The first of the Smallwood depositions was scheduled to begin at eight thirty.

Since Rosa was usually the first one at the office and was there by seven thirty, Liz used her cell phone. Rosa told her there were no messages. She also agreed to handle the florist, then arrange for the charitable donation.

When Liz entered the conference room at the Bradford County Courthouse, the court reporter had already arrived. Five minutes later Boseman showed up. Nobody came from Barrymore's office.

The two lawyers waited until 9:45 a.m. before asking the court reporter to prepare a Certificate of Non-Appearance. Neither witness had showed.

When Liz got back to the office, Rosa gave her a message. "Lou Barrymore's office called. They were sorry nobody could go to the depositions. They will reschedule everything in the Smallwood case. His secretary told me things are chaotic."

———

"Trust me, Daddy, we don't have to go to the courthouse. There won't be no depositions," Richard Smallwood told his father on the day before the scheduled day.

"I wish you was right. I don't want somebody coming out here and arresting me for not showing up."

"Nobody's going to arrest you, Daddy. That Mr. Barrymore is just not going to be taking our depositions. I was told to tell you that so you wouldn't show up for no reason."

———

Two weeks later to the day, the old man got another subpoena. Same deputy.

"How many times can they set these things?" The old man was hoping against hope that the man with the papers in hand could— would—help somehow.

"They can harass you as long as they want. Lawyers have a license to harass."

"They ain't going to harass me forever."

"That's why people hate lawyers. Lawyers can get to anybody. Doctors. Businesses. Anybody. Sign here," the deputy said handing over the papers.

As the old man followed orders, he was asked, "Is Richard Smallwood here?"

"Nope."

"Tell him I'll be back. I'm getting used to this place."

The man in uniform was being clever. The old man didn't think it was funny.

When the deputy left, the old man went back in the house and sat for a while. He drank a glass of sweet tea from the refrigerator and stared at the specks of grease that stained the wall above the stove. Finally, he got up and walked into where his wife was in the living room.

"I'm leaving, Florence."

She looked up from the TV and nodded. She didn't say anything, though it was unusual that he had told her his plans. He usually came and went as he wanted. Then she was distracted again by the talk-show host who was interviewing a former congressman who had lost his job and now served as a talking head for the network.

Rosco stared at his wife a minute longer before turning to the door and walking out. He got in his ten-year-old Ford F-150 pickup and backed out of the driveway as Richard drove up in his mother's recently purchased, used Toyota Camry. Neither son nor father waved or acknowledged the other, who was no more than fifteen feet away.

As Rosco drove off, he saw the same car that held the deputy with the papers pull in behind his "chip off the old block."

The old man drove north. He didn't drive fast or recklessly. He paid little attention to the scenery until an hour later when he crossed the Florida/Georgia line.

He continued to travel north on U.S. 301 toward Folkston. It had been years since he had been there. To him, it didn't look all that different than when he and Florence made the trip to get married.

He drove around a bit. Just looking. After a while, he took back roads and made his way over to I-95. As he turned into the parking lot marked with a sign, "Welcome to Georgia Visitor Center," tears were pouring. This was the first time he had cried in more than sixty years. He had not even cried in the war as had his comrades in arms.

He took the perpendicular parking place farthest from the building that housed the State of Georgia Visitor Center. The cement block building was about one hundred yards away. There were at least ten spaces between him and the next vehicle.

It was almost 4:00 p.m. when he took the .38 caliber Smith & Wesson from the glove box. He cocked the hammer and pressed the muzzle of the gun at his temple. The explosion that forced the bullet out of the barrel went unnoticed outside. The noise had been muffled to little more than a "pop" beyond the closed windows of the pickup.

The old man had flinched just as he pulled the trigger. He was still alive and partially lucid when discovered at ten minutes after seven by a tourist from Maryland. Rosco was pronounced dead before the ambulance delivered him to the Brunswick General Hospital.

Florence Smallwood insisted that Cora bathe and put on a clean dress before the two of them went to the funeral.

Regina did not go.

CHAPTER 15

NEW LAWYERS SHOULD SIT second chair to more experienced lawyers during trials. That's the way they do it in England, and that's the way they train new lawyers at most good law firms. The new lawyer gets experience without making mistakes at the cost of the clients.

When she was with the insurance defense firm, Liz sat second chair at three trials. Two settled before the case was finished. The third went to the jury. The plaintiffs got a verdict on that one—but only about half of what had been offered before trial.

At Moran, Smith, Forrester & Dees, she was assigned solely to Forrester. He liked to try cases alone, but had acquiesced to pressure from Liz and his partners so that she could get training. She sat second chair to him eight times during the first eighteen months they were together. Forrester would let her put on two or three witnesses during each trial, but all of the arguments were left to him. Overall, the results had been good.

They had settled three of the cases during various stages after a jury had been picked. Four of the other five trials had resulted in verdicts considerably higher than the pre-trial offers. They had lost the one other trial outright to one of Lou Barrymore's partners, Laura Griffin.

After Barrymore was murdered, Ms. Griffin was assigned to take over the defense of Rick Taggart, psychologist. Unlike her predecessor, she was one of those attorneys who others don't quite trust.

Although they had fought tooth and nail, Boseman, Barrymore and Forrester had been cooperative. Accordingly, they avoided a lot of wasted time and unnecessary hearings. They could rely on each other's verbal agreements, which were designed to make the case run smoother.

It is important that lawyers trust each other if the pre-trial work is going to go smoothly. In South Florida nobody trusts anybody. Each lawyer tries to set traps to screw the other. That isn't the way it normally works in North Florida, but Ms. Griffin was originally trained in Miami.

If you had an agreement with Ms. Griffin, you better confirm it in writing. Otherwise, when it suited her, she wouldn't remember the details. When she took over the Smallwood case, Forrester thought it advisable to write a multi-page letter confirming agreements. He copied Boseman to establish the status of things. Ms. Griffin would never have agreed had Boseman not pressed. She thought Boseman's interference was all but treasonous, but she went along under duress.

From the time she took over for Barrymore, things ceased to run smoothly. It took judges' orders to get the parties to agree on mundane matters. Ms. Griffin billed her client for preparation and attendance at hearings that would have been unnecessary with her predecessor.

Things calmed down a little when Judge Howard Coker threatened sanctions after Ms. Griffin couldn't explain why she had set depositions of Cora's psychiatrist without coordinating calendars with opposing counsel. She had set the deposition during a week when Forrester had three trials scheduled. "This is a waste of judicial time and your client's money," the judge admonished. "How do you expect them to be in trial and attend depositions at the same time?"

———

Long ago, Forrester had learned that it is the plaintiff's lawyer's job to get the cases set for trial as soon as possible. Most cases will settle before trial but not before pressure is applied by a pending day certain. The job of the defense is to get cases put off. The longer it can be put off, the better it is for the defense. Sometimes it takes so long to get a case to trial that the victim dies. At that point the case is worth less—or nothing at all.

As it turned out, a week before the trials, Forrester's paper shredder case settled. The two car wrecks didn't.

"We'll have to ask the judge to continue one of the trials. I can't be in two courtrooms at the same time." Forrester was discussing strategy with his associate.

"Why don't you let me try one of them and you try the other?" Liz didn't want to sound like she was begging, but she was.

Like most trial lawyers, Forrester was egotistical. That would explain the next words out of his mouth.

"I wouldn't mind, but I think our clients would."

"Let me ask them. I know more about the Rodriguez case than you since I've worked it up. Mrs. Rodriguez will probably prefer me."

His associate had developed her ego nicely, Forrester thought. Remembering his desire to sit first chair back when he was a criminal prosecutor, he said, "Fine, you try Rodriguez."

She was surprised. She had hoped, but she was still surprised. "I'll ask the client," she said confidently.

"You do that."

In the same courthouse in different courtrooms, Mr. Forrester and Ms. Kelley each picked a jury that following Monday.

———

Liz felt confident throughout jury selection; during presentation of evidence; and through the final argument of her first solo trial. She had prepared for this and was well trained.

With her in the courtroom was the feeling of practicing law on the moral high ground. She was a plaintiff's lawyer representing plaintiffs. Victims. Victims of somebody's poor behavior—whether deliberate or careless.

That gave her the advantage at trial. Not a legal advantage, but a moral advantage.

At this trial she was representing Mr. and Mrs. Rodriguez, who had been in a wreck on a six-lane road on their way home. An eighty-one-year-old gentleman going to visit his children and grandchildren was about to miss his turn. He crossed from the far left to the far right lane just in time to cause his right rear bumper to smack the couple's left front bumper. The damage to the cars was minimal.

Unfortunately, when Roberto Rodriguez slammed on his brakes trying to avoid the accident, Janie's right knee slammed into the dashboard. At first her knee was sore. Six months later, a degenerative process called "chondromalacia" was diagnosed by the doctors. Arthroscopic surgery was performed, but the damage was permanent though not disastrous.

The defense claimed the accident was Roberto's fault or he at least contributed to it. Besides, it was argued, the condition was probably pre-existing since Janie had twisted the same knee ten years earlier during cheerleading practice in high school. If that wasn't enough, the jury might buy the theory that with so little damage to the cars, there could be little damage to the passenger. Kelley counted on the jury doing the right thing when she turned down the last settlement offer for $20,000. She ignored the innuendo from the defense lawyer that a Southern jury could not award a fair verdict to someone named "Rodriguez." Especially since Roberto was a dark-skinned Hispanic while Janie was fair. The counteroffer was $55,000.

The three-man, three-woman, two-black, four-white jury came through with a verdict for the victim. $210,000. No comparative.

Trial work is hard. Trials are harder. The lawyer is always exhausted from the fight. Exhausted from being on the edge and being alert for hours on end.

It doesn't matter what the case is worth; or if it's your first, tenth or hundredth trial. When a lawyer gets a verdict, it's ecstasy.

She did not try to hide the fact that she was ecstatic when the verdict was read. It seemed that almost everybody in the courtroom was happy with the result. A black woman juror darted over to give Janie a hug. With a twinkle in his eye, one of the men jurors whispered to Liz, "We would've given you more if you had asked for it."

The elderly defendant wasn't upset. He had insurance and had wondered all along why the insurance company had not settled before trial. The insurance adjuster chalked it up as a business decision. He had won some cases he thought he would lose, and this one just went the wrong way. On other days, there will be other courtrooms. One person in the courtroom was devastated, however. The defense lawyer. James Stevens's ego was shattered. Not because he had been beaten by a woman. Not because it was Liz's first solo. Lawyers, like athletes, don't like to lose. He was devastated because he had lost.

Another person in the courtroom, Wayne Milton, was all smiles. "Where do you want me to take you for your celebration dinner?" the handsome lawyer from the State Attorney's Office inquired.

"I feel like having fun. How about a Japanese restaurant where they chop and cook your meal in front of you?" You could hear the excitement in her voice.

"Do you want me to pick you up at your condo?"

"No. It's already after seven. How about we meet there in about an hour? I want to run by the office first."

Not a soul was there when she dropped off her briefcases. Dinner wasn't exactly what she had hoped for, either. Something was missing. It wasn't that Wayne didn't massage her ego. He did. It was just that she wanted somebody else to listen to her recount the trial; blow by blow.

It was about a quarter of eleven when Wayne asked, "One more Sake?"

"No, thank you. I have a long drive back to the beach."

It would take her fifteen to twenty minutes to get to where she lived. She wanted to go home alone and declined when Wayne offered to join her later.

As she entered her condo, she checked her voicemail. There were three messages.

The first was from Rosa. She said, "We're all proud of you. When can we pop some corks?"

The next message was the one she wanted to hear. Bill Forrester said, "I heard about the trial. Good job. Congratulations."

The person who called with the final message did not identify herself. "Ms. Kelley, this is ... never mind. I'm calling about Rick Taggart. The person you need to find in Jacksonville is Manchester. Jo Manchester. Also Heather. I don't know the last name. I think it starts with an *M*. Heather M. In Gainesville."

She played the message again and again before putting the voice with a face.

Nobody was surprised when Liz did not show up at the office until mid-morning. She was carrying herself with that victor's confidence. Kind of a strut.

She stopped at nearly every office so that each colleague could congratulate her and ask questions about the brilliant way she had conducted the trial. She was beaming and full of energy, though nonchalant when responding with details.

Lee Forrester met the victor coming down the hall. In Southern fashion, he strode up to Liz with his arms out and gave her an enthusiastic hug. Lee was not only a retired policeman and her mentor's uncle; he was the investigator at Moran, Smith, Forrester & Dees.

"Good job!" he said. "I don't believe Bill would have done as well."

"Thanks," she replied. "Do you know when he'll be finished?"

"Rosa said closing arguments will probably be this afternoon, if it's not too late to let the case go to the jury. Otherwise, it'll be tomorrow morning."

"I want to watch the close."

"Maybe you can give him some tips." Lee was smiling.

She quit smiling and changed the subject. "Lee, somebody called last night about the Smallwood case and left a message."

"Yeah."

"We need to find a couple of witnesses. One is in Jacksonville and the other is in Gainesville."

"Who are they?"

"Apparently more people who were in the hospital at the same time as Cora Smallwood."

"Do you have names? Addresses?"

"Names only. Joe Manchester in Jacksonville. The other one's from Gainesville. No last name. It's Heather something. Her last name starts with an *M*."

"Great." He was being sarcastic. "You're going to have to get some more on that last one."

"I'll let you know when I do."

There was no closing argument. Forrester returned from the courthouse at lunchtime. He had settled the case for $225,000.

"When they offered a hundred grand, I told them it would take at least two twenty-five. They knew I was serious. I couldn't go back to the office with less than you," he joked with Liz.

"And they believed it?"

"Must have. Before trial they only offered thirty-six thousand."

"You got their attention." Liz smiled when she said it.

"No, you did! Everybody in the lawyer's lounge was talking about how well you did." The mentor was beaming. He was truly happy for her and was glad to have this chance to talk about it.

"Will you have time to celebrate tonight?" Forrester was asking her out.

Taken aback, she hesitated. "I'm sorry. I can't. I already have a date."

Forrester looked embarrassed, but as Lee walked up, he was able to keep his composure. It gave him an opportunity to tell about the case he had just settled and removed him from the awkward conversation with Liz.

When the lawyer ran out of steam, the investigator switched the subject.

"It seems to me that I remember that you used to go out with a 'Manchester' girl."

"That was years ago," Bill answered. "I'm amazed at your memory. That was before I was married."

Lee said, "I thought so. I thought I remembered her. A good lookin' woman with black hair. Wasn't her family rich?"

"They were well-off. So what do you need her for?"

"We don't need her. I was just thinking maybe you would know some of her relatives. Liz said there may be a witness named Joe Manchester here in town. Did your old flame have a brother named Joe?"

"Her sister's name was 'Jo.' No *e*. At least they called her that. Her real name was JoAnne."

"A sister?"

"JoAnne. JoAnne Manchester. She's a flake. I've seen her from time to time. She's almost always drunk."

"Liz says she's a witness in the Smallwood case," Lee reported.

Liz chimed in. "When you've got a minute, I've got a message you need to hear."

Forrester said, "After lunch. I'm tired right now."

"Can I take you to lunch?" Liz questioned.

"Sure."

"Out of the office?"

"If you insist," Forrester answered, "but in the refrigerator, I have some leftover spaghetti that Dorothy fixed." His pride had been saved. The two of them ate at the Desert Sandwich Shop. They didn't get there until nearly one thirty, but stayed and talked about their victories until well after three o'clock.

Back at the office, Liz played her voicemail for Bill. He recognized the voice immediately. It was Carol Robertson, their ally.

It only took Lee a couple of days to find JoAnne Manchester. She was now living with friends in Tampa. Yes, she remembered a psychologist named Richard Taggart. No, she had never heard of Heather. Cora either. Would she talk about her relationship with Taggart? Absolutely not!

She was only mildly interested to know that other women were claiming to be victims. Nevertheless, the witness asked several questions about the Smallwood case.

She refused to give a recorded statement.

By this time the case had been filed for well over a year and a half, and it had been more than three years since Cora had left the hospital. Of course, it had taken most of two years before suit was allowed to be filed pursuant to the medical malpractice laws.

As she had done about every thirty to forty-five days, Liz wrote her client an update letter with a copy to the sister. Communication with clients is important, and letters can be quicker than phone calls or meetings.

She told them that the case was not moving along very fast. The death of Lou Barrymore had slowed it down even more. Depositions and hearings were being rescheduled, etcetera.

She also wrote about the anonymous phone call. "We have found Jo Manchester. We have no clue who Heather M. is."

A week after mailing the last letter, Liz got her first phone call ever from Cora Smallwood.

"Hello, this is Cora Smallwood." Her voice was quiet; depressed; sad-sounding. Liz could imagine Cora staring at the floor with the telephone in hand.

"Hello Cora. Things are moving along. Did you get my letter?"

"That's why I'm calling."

"Okay. Good. How can I help you?"

"Heather was there at the hospital when I was there."

"You know Heather?"

"I don't know her, but I remember her."

"What's her last name?" she asked with anticipation.

"I don't know. I just remember her."

Let down.

"We need to find her. We know she lives in Gainesville. Do you remember what she looks like?"

"She's young. You would probably say she's cute. She hated being there."

"Where?"

"In the hospital."

"What color is her hair? Her eyes?"

"I don't remember. She had a good body. She was big, you know."

"Fat?"

"No. Big."

"You mean large breasts?"

"For her size."

"Oh." Liz paused, thinking. "Can you remember anything that could help us find her?"

"All I know is that she had a visitor one time. He was in a uniform."

"Military?"

"No. Police."

It was like pulling teeth to get information from Cora.

Liz asked, "Gainesville Police?"

"No. Alachua."

"Alachua? She was visited by a policeman for the Town of Alachua?"

"Yes. They looked a lot alike. He was probably her father."

"How do you remember this?"

"They always told me I have a good memory."

"Can you remember anything else?"

"No. I never really talked to her. Bye."

Just like that, Cora hung up.

When Liz reported the conversation to Lee, he said, "I thought she was crazy."

"She has her problems."

"How could she remember the cop from Alachua?"

"Her sister says Cora is smart in spite of the family history." Then Liz asked, "You think you can find Heather M. with that information?"

"I'll drive down there and talk to every policeman in the town. They can't have many. There are only a couple of red lights in Alachua. I'll let you know something in a week or two."

CHAPTER 16

THE SMALLWOOD MEN FAILED again to show for their depositions. Liz Kelley, Fred Boseman and Laura Griffin waited for thirty minutes at the Bradford County Courthouse before calling it quits. Cora's team of lawyers did not care if the depositions ever got taken. Boseman would have given up.

Not so for Ms. Griffin, the lawyer who took over for Barrymore. She filed a Motion for Contempt.

Judge Coker could not be persuaded to have the witnesses locked up even though they had also failed to appear at the hearing. The judge did agree to sign an order promising jail in the event of another "no show." An "ORDER TO SHOW CAUSE."

A copy of the order was sent to Smallwood house. Cora's brother was pissed off when he read it.

———

She was easy to intimidate. Always had been. So when Richard Smallwood got to his sister's house, he did not try to coax. He went right at her.

"Cora, you need to drop that lawsuit."

"What do you mean?"

"I got a order from a judge saying they'll put me in jail if I don't give some testimony."

Cora asked, "Why do they want you?"

"Who the hell knows?" Richard sounded angry. "It don't make no difference. You need to drop the lawsuit before somebody else gets hurt."

"Hurt? What do you mean?"

"You already killed Daddy with it. You need to call them lawyers and tell them to settle. If they ain't paying, drop it."

"How did I kill Daddy?"

"Why do you think he shot himself? Because of you and that damn lawsuit. It's your fault."

Cora had not thought of her father's death as "her" fault. She had been numb to it. She felt nothing when he died. No love. No hate. Nothing. It amused her that the brother thought she had caused the old man to die, but it did not bother her. It did not matter one way or the other. No victory and no defeat.

"They said they would settle. Regina says that it's not enough. You need to call Regina."

"To hell with Regina. Call the damn lawyers yourself and tell them you'll take it." He paused, "How much they offer anyway?"

"I don't know. They're Regina's lawyers. You'll have to talk to Regina."

Richard slapped Cora. Slapped her hard.

"I ain't talked to Regina in years. I ain't going to now. And ... I ain't going to give no deposition. They just want to ask questions about the family."

Cora didn't say anything. She didn't react to the slap on her face. She was not crying in spite of the hand mark across her left cheek. She did nothing.

"This place smells. You smell. I'm not going to jail for a stinking bitch like you." As he said it, he swung and hit her, this time with his fist.

She fell to the floor and just looked at him. There was no resistance. There was no emotion.

Richard yelled, "I thought you hated Regina like the rest of us! What has she ever done for us? Call and tell her the case is over, or I'll be back."

Cora's sibling left. Blood was dripping from her nose. Onto her clothes. She just sat on the floor.

———

Uninvited, Florence Smallwood came to her daughter's house that same night and found Cora a bloody mess. It was unusual for Florence to visit even though they lived in the same town.

The blood had coagulated hours ago. It had dried on Cora's face and on her dress. You could see where she had wiped her face with her hand and she had not washed it. She was eating a Domino's pizza that she had bought with part of the Social Security money she got every month.

"Honey, you used to be so clean. What's the matter?" The old lady didn't ask how the blood got there. She just took a dishrag and wet it. Then started cleaning Cora's face while Cora just sat there.

"Richard tells me that you're planning to settle your lawsuit. Is that right?"

"Maybe," Cora responded.

"I don't know why everybody is so upset about all this. Your brother's real upset. There's some judge's order that says he's going to go to jail. I guess that's it."

"Why is he going to go to jail? Is it because he hit me?"

"I'm sorry he hurt you, honey. You know he didn't mean it." The old lady sounded tired as if she had said the same words many times.

Florence continued, "He's going to jail unless this suit of yours is dropped or unless he goes to something at the courthouse where they ask a bunch of questions about the family. Your daddy was supposed to go too. I guess he won't be going, though."

The old lady was there on Richard's behalf. She was an ambassador trying to save her son, but Cora didn't care. It became obvious that it was going to be up to Regina if the case was going to be settled. The old lady was not about to call Regina.

Before she left, Florence cleaned the place, where Cora lived alone. There weren't many dishes, just litter from the wrappers of fast-food burgers, french fries and pizzas.

Florence Smallwood had lived a tough life too. Had been her abusive husband's third wife. Had never left him and patted herself on the back for that. She felt like a martyr.

During the marriage, she had refused to let herself believe what she knew was happening with her offspring. She didn't exactly know why things had gone wrong when it came to her children. Regina had left home early. Richard was wild and mean. Cora was the smart one when she was a baby, and the old woman didn't know what had caused her to change.

Cora was able to care for herself. She could do things. She just wouldn't do things. Somebody had helped her file for Social Security when Renee was born. When the money started coming in, Florence helped Cora find the HUD housing.

For a long time, it seemed like Cora was doing just fine. She was always clean. Her house was tidy. She had plenty of dates.

There was no way anybody could blame Cora's recent condition on her deceased husband, Florence thought. Cora had been out of the family house for years and never visited except when Florence picked her up and insisted that she come over.

Now that her husband had died, it seemed like things were worse than ever. As far as the old lady was concerned, it just didn't make sense.

It didn't make sense that all of a sudden Richard was upset about his sister's lawsuit. She couldn't control Richard, and Rosco hadn't been able to, either. She didn't like seeing her daughter beat up, but she knew that it would not be the last time. She was scared of her son, although he had never struck his mother.

———

Over the years, the Smallwoods had learned a way to deal with Cora when things went wrong. If she got caught shoplifting, taking drugs, or doing some other foolish thing, she could easily be admitted into a hospital. Social Security would pay for her stays. She would usually come out better than when she had gone in.

If Cora did not want to go, a court procedure could be used. An involuntary hospitalization order could force her to go.

The next morning, the mother filled out the papers at the courthouse. Cora was picked up and went passively with a representative from the Sheriff's Office to Macclenny Psychiatric Facility. It seemed an easy method to keep Cora away until after Richard had given his deposition.

Nobody had told Cora's lawyers that their client's father was no longer with the living. Must not have been important. It was learned when Liz, for the third time, went to depositions at the Bradford County Courthouse.

Richard Smallwood had finally come to give testimony. He believed the judge's order that said that he would be held in contempt.

Between Laura Griffin and Fred Boseman, any questions that would have been relevant to the case were asked. Of course, he denied that he had ever had sexual relations with his sister. He testified that he did not know of any relations she had had with her father.

He said, "If Cora told them things about me to anybody, she was lying. She has a problem with lying."

Ms. Griffin jumped on that remark. "Are you saying that Cora Smallwood may say some things happened to her even if they really did not?"

"I never did anything to her, that's for sure."

"And you don't know if she's telling the truth when she alleges that Mr. Taggart had inappropriate relationships with her. Isn't that true?"

"How would I know?"

"But you do know that just because she says something doesn't mean it's true, don't you?"

"If she said some of them things about me, then that wasn't true. That's all I know."

After Griffin and Boseman had finished, Liz was about to report that she had no questions. For some reason, she changed her mind. Maybe it was because she didn't like him and just wanted to make him feel uncomfortable. In any event, she did ask questions, but only a few.

"Mr. Smallwood, this is the third time your deposition has been set. Are you aware of that?"

"Yes."

"Why didn't you come to your depositions when they were set before?"

"I don't know what you mean."

"Well, you know that your deposition had been set about six weeks ago and you didn't show up."

"I forgot about it. My father had died. I just forgot about it after that."

"Were you at a funeral at the time?"

"I don't know if that was the day of the funeral or not."

"Okay. Why didn't you come the first time it was set?"

"I thought it was canceled." He was lying, but his lies were fluid. There was no hesitation.

"Why did you think they were canceled?" Liz was pressing on a subject that she knew didn't make any difference. Maybe she was just curious.

Richard Smallwood looked Liz right in the eye and responded as though she must be the stupidest person in the world to even ask such a question. "The lawyer who subpoenaed me was shot and was dead. Wouldn't you think it was canceled if you was me?"

Liz thought for a moment. "No further questions," she announced.

CHAPTER 17

LIZ FELT UNCOMFORTABLE ON her ride back to Jacksonville. The deposition had not hurt the case. The psychological records were replete with descriptions of Cora's liaisons with her father and brother, though Richard had denied the incest. As far as the case was concerned, it really didn't matter one way or the other. The facts were a given, and the records confirmed that Cora was from a dysfunctional family.

Regina had survived it. Cora had not.

She was in and out. In and out of various psychiatric institutions. Had she not been so vulnerable, Rick Taggart would never have had a chance. The issue, as Liz saw it, was not what caused her to be in the hospital in the first place. The issue was that she was in the hospital because she needed help. Her psychologist did not help. He took advantage of her hospitalization and her mental problems. Then he took advantage of her.

Liz was sure that the defense would never call the brother as a witness. They could not call her father. The testimony was irrelevant.

But the testimony made Liz sick, and she got sicker as she drove home. Alone in the car, she said out loud, "I killed Lou Barrymore."

———

When Liz arrived at the office, she tried to find Bill. He would not be back for hours, so she tried to call Wayne Milton, the prosecutor she respected and knew intimately. He wasn't in either, so she left a message.

She really didn't want to talk to anybody else about it. She had plenty of other work to do, and she set about busying herself while she waited for a return call. She wanted advice from her mentor; or, to ask questions of the man who worked daily with the local police. The latter called before the former returned to the office.

"Hellooooooooo, baby," Wayne Milton said in a way so as to mimic the Big Bopper when he sang "Chantilly Lace." He was obviously in a good mood which had been brought on by the message from his significant other.

"Hey, Wayne."

He could immediately tell from her voice that her mind did not match his. She was down.

"I got a message you called. Don't tell me you're canceling tonight."

"I'm not canceling. But, can it be just the two of us?"

Wayne had been looking forward to a dinner party at his brother's house. Six people altogether.

"We can't. It would be unfair to cancel at the last minute." He was taking charge, albeit with tact.

She really did not want to go out at all, and now being with others was the last thing she wanted to do. She wanted to talk with Wayne or Bill. She was not in the mood for small talk with people she hardly knew.

"All right, but I don't want to be out late," she said begrudgingly.

"What's the problem?"

"Nothing. I'll talk to you later."

"Liz…."

"It's really nothing."

"What?"

"Forget it. I'll see you later."

"Okay. I'll call and cancel," he volunteered.

The timing was perfect. Wayne got just the response he thought he would. Just the response he wanted.

"No, no, no. Forget it. You're right. We should go." She tried to sound cheerful. "Pick me up here at the office around six thirty."

Liz hung up, frustrated. She had wanted to talk about something, but the conversation never got off the ground.

Five minutes later Liz got another call. It was Wayne again.

"What's the problem, Liz?" He no longer sounded like the Big Bopper. He sounded humble.

"I just want to talk."

"Tell me. What's the problem?"

"Lou Barrymore."

"The lawyer who got killed?"

"Yes."

"What about him?"

"Do you know anything about the investigation?"

"Only what I told you and what I read in the papers. They think some kid shot him from an overpass when he was on I-295."

"Can you find out what the police know?"

She was finally talking about what had bothered her all day. It turned out the man in her life who should know something didn't. The man said, "I'll see what anybody knows, and we can talk about it tonight."

"Before we go to your brother's?"

"How about I call you when I know something?"

"Thanks, Wayne."

Wayne called back for a third time just fifteen minutes after they had hung up. "Liz, what's going on?"

"Have you already found out something?"

"No. I haven't even tried yet. What am I supposed to do? Just say my girlfriend needs some information?"

"Forget it," Liz snapped.

"Seriously. What's going on?"

"We'll talk about it tonight. Don't keep calling." She hung up.

Her voice sounded troubled. Irritated. Three calls and her boyfriend knew diddly.

Now she would wait for Bill. She had only worked on civil cases since getting out of law school. She had sued people and had defended people being sued. She was ill-equipped with the little criminal law she had learned in school.

Bill Forrester, on the other hand, had been an Assistant State Attorney and had established his reputation while a trial lawyer doing criminal prosecutions. He had defended plenty of criminals after that. Knowing she could talk to him and rely on his judgment, she had no intention of telling anybody else what she thought.

It was after five o'clock when Forrester called the office. He asked for Rosa.

"Ms. Kelley wants to talk to you," was the first thing Rosa told her boss.

"It'll have to wait. I'm just calling from the car to tell you that I am not coming back to the office today."

"Okay, but how about talking to Ms. Kelley? She's asked at least five times when you would be in."

"Okay, but first go over my messages and what's on the calendar tomorrow."

It took twenty minutes for the lawyer to finish his business with Rosa. It was mundane stuff, but he didn't want to face it the next day.

When they finished, he said, "Thanks, Rosa. Now transfer me to Ms. Kelley."

"Wouldn't you know it?" Liz could not be found. When the secretary reported this to Forrester, he instructed her to let Liz know she could get him on his cell for the next ten minutes. Five minutes later, Liz got the message and immediately returned the call.

"Forrester," he answered.

"Thank goodness, Bill...."

He cut her off.

"Liz, I'm not coming back to the office. I've got my girls, and we're going to see a baseball game. I'm running late to get home. Rosa says you wanted something."

"You're not coming back to the office?" She was exasperated.

"No. What do you need?"

"I need to talk to you. I've waited all day."

"Liz. I can't come by the office. I promised my children." He waited. She said nothing so he said, "What do you need? Is it a problem?"

"I need to talk to you right away."

"Go ahead and talk."

"Not on the phone."

"Hey. Why don't you come to the game with us? We can talk." He sounded upbeat.

She wasn't upbeat when she said, "I can't. Wayne and I are going to his brother's for a dinner party." She hesitated. "Can we get together to talk later tonight?"

The two agreed to meet at his house. Ten o'clock.

———

On the way to the dinner party, Wayne Milton let her know that he had not been able to find out anything about Lou Barrymore's death. He promised that he had tried. He had been told by somebody, who had been told by somebody else, that there were no real leads.

Jacksonville had made the national news years earlier because cars along I-295 were being stoned and shot by teenagers. When Barrymore was shot, the city was back in the undesirable limelight. However, this time there had been no leads at all.

Liz was less satisfied. Unlike her usual self, she was quiet through cocktails and dinner. At nine o'clock, she told Wayne that she needed to leave. She did not care that the dinner party was ruined since Wayne had to drive her back to the car she had left at the office.

The drive was quiet. The lack of conversation frustrated Wayne more than leaving early.

His voice was not gentle when he finally said, "Liz... damn it. Liz... will you quit acting like a woman and talk to me? What have I done? What's the problem?"

"What does that mean?" she quipped.

"What does what mean?" He responded while pulling into the parking lot.

"I am a woman. So how does a woman act?" she snapped as she left his car; got into hers, and drove off.

Liz lived at the beach, and Wayne could not help but notice that she drove in the opposite direction. He thought about following her but decided against it.

Liz drove directly to Bill's house, which took about thirty minutes. When she got there on time, he wasn't. The live-in housekeeper had a pot of coffee ready and served Liz in the living room, where she had nothing to do but read hunting books and magazines for the next thirty minutes.

Bill finally got home, but she still didn't have his immediate attention. It was after eleven before the children were to bed. The teenager had been no trouble, but the ten-year-old was wired from Coca-Colas, cotton candy, and other junk food.

Finally, Bill asked, "What's wrong? Did the case get blown out of the water somehow?"

She wanted to tell him that she thought he was rude to the nth degree. She had been wanting to talk to him all day, and now it was getting close to midnight. She held her tongue.

Liz said, "I really need to talk to you. You know criminal law, and I don't...."

He interrupted. "I haven't done much criminal law in years."

"It doesn't really matter. I need your advice. I think Cora's brother killed Lou Barrymore." She blurted it out.

Bill was deliberate before answering. His mind was turned onto work again. He thought about the potential for a conflict of interest. He could not really think of one, but he wanted to think it through.

After the pregnant pause, he asked, "What makes you think so?"

"He didn't confess or anything. It's just that we took his deposition. I had no intention of asking him any questions. I don't know why I did. I guess I was curious. All I asked him was why he hadn't shown up for the previously scheduled depositions."

"Okay. Then what?" Bill probed.

Liz reminded Bill that Barrymore had been shot and killed while Bill was out of town. Her friend with the State Attorney had told her. She had immediately called Bill and left a message. It was late, and he had not returned her call because he didn't know her number. That didn't matter. She stayed up late waiting for a return call. While she waited, she listened to the radio and watched the news on TV. She wanted to find out as much as she could about Barrymore's death. Apparently, the shooting had occurred too late in the day to make the news. Nobody carried it. She remembered that well. The next day, nothing was in the newspaper either. It simply had not been an item until the day after Barrymore had been shot.

"During the deposition, I asked him why he didn't show up the first time. He said he didn't think there was any need to. He said the reason he didn't show up was because Barrymore had been shot and Barrymore was the one who had subpoenaed him."

When Liz finished, Forrester was not quick to respond. Finally he asked, "Are you sure there was no way for him to know Barrymore had been shot?"

Liz thought about it but didn't say anything at first.

"I'm sure of it."

"When did you figure all this out?"

"On the drive back from Starke. It was like turning on a light bulb. I've been wanting to talk to you about it all day to get your advice. I feel like I killed Lou Barrymore. If I hadn't filed the lawsuit... I know that may not make sense."

"You're right" he said abruptly. "To blame yourself for doing your job does not make sense!"

Bill kept thinking about what she had told him, but didn't say anything more for a while. He walked to the kitchen and returned with a cup of coffee before talking.

"No big deal, Liz. Just tell the police. I mean, it's a big deal that Barrymore was shot, but it's not a problem as far as the case is concerned. Did you tell your boyfriend? What's his name?"

"Wayne Milton. No, I didn't want to tell him until I could talk to you. I asked him what the police knew about it, but he couldn't find out anything. I didn't tell him why I wanted to know."

———

Liz started her drive back to the beach after midnight. It was 1:00 a.m. before she got home.

She and Bill had decided to wait until the next day to file a report about what she knew. They thought about all of the explanations Richard Smallwood could give. The evidence was conclusive, they decided.

Bill considered it clever that she was the only one who picked up on the implication of Cora's brother's testimony. That's what made her a good lawyer, Bill thought. She picks up on the details. She punches holes in people's excuses.

———

Liz drove into the parking lot of the condo. She went to her designated spot; got out of the car; and walked toward her building.

"You're finally home."

She wasn't expecting it. She was startled and she practically turned and ran. Then she realized that she recognized the voice. It was Wayne.

"God, you scared me. What are you doing here?"

"Where have you been?"

Neither his question nor his voice was pleasant. It had gnawed in Wayne's gut since he let her off and watched her turn the wrong direction. When he first saw her, he was relieved that she had not spent the night out. The relief turned to anger. The anger raised Liz's ire.

"What's it to you?" That quick. She was irritated and her voice showed it.

"I just want to know where you've been. You insisted on leaving dinner early. Obviously, you didn't come back to the beach. You have been acting strange all day."

Liz wasn't ready for this and didn't want it. She turned back toward the building and started toward her condo.

The prosecutor grabbed her by the arm. That was a mistake. The moment it happened, she knew they were finished as a couple.

It was one thing for him to be concerned about her. Instead, he was jealous. That might have been nice under other circumstances. Tonight Liz was stressed and was not going to tolerate his behavior.

She yanked herself away, unlocked the door, and went into her condo. She said nothing.

Sure, Liz would have enjoyed his company, and would have liked to talk to him about her discovery. She was not about to put up with a bully. Wayne was left standing there with a gnawing in his stomach. He had fouled up.

———————

Jacksonville is the largest city in the United States—area-wise. In the 1960's, through a process known as "consolidation," the city limits were expanded to meet the boundaries of Duval County. Through the process of consolidation, the Sheriff of Duval County became the top law enforcement officer. The Jacksonville Police Department became known as the Jacksonville Sheriff's Office.

The day following Liz's revelation that she knew who had killed Lou Barrymore, Forrester called the Sheriff of Duval County. The Sheriff had been a detective when Forrester was a prosecutor. On more than one occasion, they had worked together to convict some slime-ball. The two had become solid friends, and Forrester could call him direct.

After initial pleasantries Forrester said, "One of my associates believes she has information about Lou Barrymore's death."

"Who?"

"Lou Barrymore. You remember. It was during your election, he was killed by a sniper on I-295."

"Oh, you mean the lawyer. I haven't heard anything about it in a while."

"The only reason I am calling you is because I want to avoid the runaround. Would it be possible for you to direct us to the detective in charge of the case?"

From there, Bill explained to the Sheriff what Liz thought she knew. The Sheriff assured him that somebody would be in touch before noon.

Forrester knew from his days doing criminal law that there was almost always an element of luck to solving a murder case. Usually, the police would take down whatever information they could find offhand. If the murderer was working alone, he seldom got caught.

Most cases were solved when the perpetrator made the mistake of confiding in somebody. A lot of times, an angered girlfriend who had been dumped would call the police with what she had learned during pillow talk. There was seldom any real investigation where one part of the puzzle led to another like you read about in mystery novels.

Forrester would say, "In real life, there are no Sherlock Holmeses."

With luck, coupled with the brilliant mind of his associate, Lou Barrymore's murder might get solved.

Within thirty minutes after the call to the Sheriff, a Detective Wilson Prescott called. Arrangements were made for the detective to meet with Bill and Liz in the lawyers' office. By that afternoon, there was an all-points bulletin placed in all North Florida counties for "Richard Smallwood—suspected of murder."

CHAPTER 18

RICHARD SMALLWOOD WENT TO the Miss Q Lounge & Liquor Store. It was a dimly lit place on US 301 just south of Starke. He got there by the early afternoon after his deposition. He had planned to just buy a pint of Ancient Age bourbon. Instead, he decided to spend some time flirting with the bartender.

The Miss Q was equipped with two pool tables that you put quarters in. Most people played eight ball. Richard was typical of its clientele.

He was wiry and tough—tattoos that showed on the back of his hands; smoked cigarettes; became boisterous with liquor, which was served at happy-hour prices, day and night. Like most of the other patrons who frequented the Miss Q, Richard seldom had a full-time job. He could get day-labor work and would sponge extra money off his mother.

Like the bartender, Gloria, Richard was on track to age prematurely. He would go from being tough, to looking tough, to withering. He would stay lean, but after a while the sockets of his eyes would grow to look hollow. He had already lost two molars from his left upper jaw, which was only obvious when he smiled or you watched him from the side. Eventually, his permanent teeth would be replaced by dentures.

You could tell that at one time Gloria had been attractive. Had she been raised in Vilano Beach in a home like JoAnne Manchester's, she would still look good. As it was, she looked mid-forties even though she was only thirty-four. If you looked her right in the face, you could see that her left eyelid drooped a little. Scarred by the backhand of a former boyfriend.

Her three children were being raised by their grandparents. As though she were a good mother, she would talk about them often with customers at the bar. In reality, she would only see them from time to time at her parents' house. Her visits would end with her children staying and her being lent the money she needed for one thing or another.

Richard started the conversation with a trite comment that he knew would get the desired response.

"Them lawyers are all sons of bitches," he said. "I just spent most of the day answering questions about a bunch of bullshit."

Gloria followed her cues as she poured the customer a drink. "I know what you mean about them lawyers. You can't satisfy them. They're just after the money."

As Richard acted tough like one football player bumping chests with another, Gloria listened. When he flirted, she acted just a little embarrassed. She would agree with his conclusions; sympathize with his misfortune; and provide anecdotes to supplement his in order to keep the conversation rolling. At the same time, she kept the patron ordering drinks. She would expect at least a 25 percent tip when he got ready to leave.

By nine thirty Richard had reached that point where the liquor had caused him to act obnoxious when Gloria's attention was focused on other customers. By ten o'clock, he was belligerent and picking fights. To the extent they could, most customers ignored him, but the skilled bartender knew his behavior was bad for business.

When Cora's brother spilled a half-filled bourbon and Coke, the liquid ran down the bar and onto the lap of a man who was sitting two places over. He was a big man in his late forties who had been quiet and kept to himself for more than an hour. He had ignored Richard for all that time. Now he turned to the young punk and glared.

Gloria had seen the same scenario too many times and wanted to defuse it. She grabbed a towel to soak up the liquid.

"I'll have another one of the same," Richard demanded.

"Hey, honey, I think you've had enough for tonight. Why don't you just pay up, and I'll see you tomorrow?" She was no longer sure of her tip.

"I'm okay. Just pour me another bourbon and Coke."

Gloria said, "Sure honey, if you'll clear your tab now. This drink's on me."

It seemed like the situation had been handled. She mechanically scooped the ice into the glass; poured the brown stuff into the shot glass; and poured that container over the ice while pushing the right button to fill the glass with Coca-Cola. She placed it on the bar in front of him as he withdrew the wallet he kept in his back pocket hooked to a chain.

Richard laid a fifty-dollar bill on the counter, which was more than enough to cover his several hours of drinking. The big man continued to glare, almost daring the young man to make some sort of move.

Gloria picked up the fifty. She laid it on the cash register without opening the drawer. The money would stay there until he left unless he asked for change. This way, she would be assured of her tip.

Things were still tense.

The big man continued to stare at Cora's brother; who in turn, even drunk, began to feel intimidated.

Gloria slinked down the bar as if nothing was going on. She would make small talk with other customers. Two minutes passed. Just two minutes. But they passed slowly for Gloria, Cora's brother and the big man.

The tension was broken by Richard. When he stood up from his stool, his first step landed on a piece of ice on the floor that had gotten there when he spilled his drink. It was like stepping on a banana peel.

Whatever balance he had left after all of the drinks was gone. He really couldn't help it when what was left of the drink in his hand went flying into the lap of the big man.

"Oh, Jesus!" Gloria yelled as the big man caught the falling younger one.

"Oh, Jesus!" Gloria yelled again when the big man punched Richard in the stomach; making him react as would the recipient of the Heimlich maneuver.

"Oh, Jesus!" Gloria yelled a final time as Richard vomited all over the startled big man.

What could he do? He was taken completely by surprise when the vomit spewed on his chest. In turn, the big man wanted to vomit as he threw Richard to the floor; kicked him once hard in the thigh; tore his own shirt off and flung it down.

The big man, disgusted, stomped out the door; got in his pickup and drove north.

None of the redneck patrons wanted to help Richard to his feet. He was a mess, and the place smelled like puke. The ruckus was not unusual for the Miss Q, but the aftermath was. The customers looked for Gloria to take charge.

"Oh hell!" Gloria said while coming around the bar.

She brought with her the cloth she used to wipe the bar. She placed the damp rag on Richard's face and cleaned him like a nurse would a patient.

"Won't one of you creeps help me get him up?" Gloria was angry with this disruption in her regular duties.

With that, a woman in tight jeans, about forty, came forward and helped the barmaid pick the soiled customer off the floor. Warren, a regular, also came forward to help the honky-tonk Florence Nightingales. With help from the woman in tight jeans, Warren volunteered to put Richard in his truck so he could "sleep it off." As Gloria mopped the already permanently stained floor, the situation would return to normalcy. Some of the patrons went back to shooting pool, while others returned to their regular spot at the bar—facing the bar well and peering through empty eyes.

At least Gloria could be pleased that her tip from Richard was several times more than usual.

CHAPTER 19

"ROSA! HAVE YOU SEEN Ms. Kelley?"

You could hear it in his voice. Bill Forrester was excited about leaving town. At the same time, he was anguished about leaving the office and his work. It seemed like ten minutes didn't go by when orders weren't barked at somebody. It was days like this the office staff dreaded most.

Rosa got the worst of it. He couldn't get along without her--especially on the last day before he left town.

"Ms. Kelley is in court arguing a motion to dismiss. She should be back in about half an hour." Rosa was saying this as she entered his office carrying several folders stuffed with papers that he planned to read on the trip.

"How'd I ever go off on these trips before we hired her?"

"It's nice that you have somebody you feel confident can handle emergencies while you are gone," Rosa agreed.

"I really don't know how I managed before," he repeated earnestly as Rosa stepped around a stack of files on the floor between his desk and the door.

———

This time the trip would be longer than usual. He was not going for business. He was packed and ready for a safari in Zimbabwe, the African country formerly known as Rhodesia. It was summertime here. Winter where he was going below the equator. He knew he was ready to go, but he wasn't sure the office was ready to be without him.

It wasn't his first safari, and he knew what to expect. He would be hunting in the Dandy area on the Zambezi River where three countries border one another. He would stay in a safari tent camp and be able to look from the banks of the great river and wave to citizens of Mozambique as well as Zambia.

His memories of Africa were bitter sweet. Bitter because the woman who had accompanied him before had since broken his heart when she announced that she no longer wanted to be married. Sweet, because together in Africa, they had experienced adventure and constant romance.

His companion for this trip was his best friend and hunting buddy, Kevin Malone. Bill and Kevin had literally hunted the world together. They had hunted Canada and the great western states—Texas, Wyoming, Oregon, Idaho and Alaska. They had also been together in Africa, Australia, and Europe. Each time had been an adventure—each different from the others.

Kevin was a lawyer too. He and Bill met while they were in law school, and each learned that the other enjoyed the outdoor life of hunting and fishing. On weekends in their younger days, if they weren't hunting rabbits, quail, doves and waterfowl, they were fishing for the large-mouth black bass, abundant throughout the Florida freshwater lakes.

As the two grew older and more successful, they began planning trips out of the state. The more successful they became, the more frequent the trips. Then Bill's divorce. Now, after several years, Kevin had lured Bill into going again.

This time the lawyer went to Rosa's office. Not because she was his secretary, but because she was his confidante.

He confessed, "I really wish I wasn't going. There's just too much work to be done for me to be leaving town."

"Mr. Forrester, everything is going to be handled. You should just relax and forget the office for a while."

"Thank God I didn't leave three weeks ago when all that mess about the Smallwood case was coming down."

"Ms. Kelley handled that well. She still kept the client in spite of her family."

"That's what I mean. Liz does things right. She has good instincts. But that doesn't matter, I've got to tell you that I worry to death trying to get out of here."

"It's always hectic getting away, but you'll enjoy the trip," Rosa was still reassuring.

"It will be a relief to get on the plane. Then there's nothing I can do about anything. I'll try to call from Johannesburg."

"You already told me that." Rosa was speaking with authority now.

She had been through the same process maybe a dozen times over the years. He would work day and night making certain that everything was finished and would leave enough work to keep her and the rest of the office busy for a month. He would call at some midpoint of his journey to learn that nothing had gone wrong, and then nobody would hear from him again until he walked into the office. He never called on his return trip, and that kept everybody a little off balance.

The only real difference this time was that he had somebody he respected to take up the slack. Elizabeth Kelley and Bill Forrester were the proverbial Fred and Ginger. They worked hand in glove.

Forrester rambled back to his office and went over his checklist one final time. This list included everything from the articles he was taking on the trip to the details of the work that should have already been completed.

"Do you mind if I drive you to the airport?" It was Liz who was standing in his doorway now.

Forrester looked up. With the usual aire, the one that made him such a pain in the ass, he said, "It's not really necessary but if you want to…."

An hour later, the two were in his Suburban for the twenty-minute drive.

"Yesterday, Judge Coker set the trial date for the Smallwood case," Liz told the driver.

"When's it set?" Forrester asked.

"Second week in December."

"You couldn't get it set sooner?"

"He set it for two weeks. I told him it wouldn't take but a week at most. Fred and Laura insisted that we would need two weeks."

Forrester pondered the thought for a moment before responding emphatically. "They just want to delay the trial Why not? They can keep billing their files. A lot of people think that it's the insurance companies who want delays so they can make interest on the money instead of paying people like our client."

"You think that's wrong?"

"Yeah. I don't think it's the insurance companies, Too much regulation in Florida. They have to set reserves and hold the money until the case is over."

Bill continued. "Delay is also a defense tactic. When I did defense work, I used the same tactic. Delay puts pressure on the plaintiff to settle for less than the case is worth. Besides, who knows? Witnesses may move or disappear. Hell, the plaintiff may die."

"I know that's what you think, and you're probably right. You know, I'm kind of glad it's not sooner. Joanne Manchester says that she will refuse to testify. She doesn't want her private life in the courtroom."

"Subpoena her anyway. We won't force her to testify, but we won't tell her we won't. Maybe she'll come around."

"If she doesn't testify, it's going to be Cora's word against Taggart's. The jury will probably believe Taggart. Any suggestions?"

Bill snapped back. "If we don't find another victim, we'll have to rely totally on Nurse Robertson." Then he asked as if he didn't know the answer, "Has Lee found our other witness yet?"

"You mean Heather?"

"Yeah. That's who I mean. Has he found her?"

"He knows who she is. He's even talked to her father. He claims he doesn't know where she's gone but promises to get back to us if he finds out."

"Tell Lee that won't do." There was irritation in the lawyer's voice since several weeks had passed and the witness still had not been located.

The couple was nearing the airport entrance. They talked about other cases, and Liz reassured her superior that she could handle whatever came along. He knew that she'd put in the hours, but it was not in him not to worry.

As they made the loop into the airport, almost as an aside, Bill queried, "Have you heard anything else on Cora's brother and the Lou Barrymore murder?"

"I really haven't. It worries me too. He must know by now he's wanted. I'm kind of frightened that somehow he's going to get Cora even more mixed up in his problems."

"Don't worry about that. Nothing we can do about it anyway."

"I'm sure you're right, but I thought it was stupid that they put on TV that he was wanted. He couldn't have been that hard to find."

Bill shrugged. "So be it."

In front of the airport, with the help of a skycap, William Forrester, big-game hunter, unloaded his bags from the Suburban. He checked his duffle and rifle case. Destination Miami. From there, non-stop first-class to Johannesburg; then to Harare, Zimbabwe. A bush plane would take him and Kevin to a small airstrip near the border of Mozambique.

Liz had moved into the driver's seat. She would arrange for Bill's luxury four-wheel drive to be taken to his home. Before driving off, however, she decided to watch him disappear into the airport.

Just as the automatic doors opened, Bill turned around; returned to the driver's side; and motioned for Liz to lower the window. At the same time, he leaned forward toward her and, for an awkward moment, stared at her attractive face.

Liz did not resist the eye contact. The body language seemed obvious. She was not going to withdraw if he made his move.

Bill's eyes watered as his mind raced with thoughts of his former love, his marriage and family. The extended pause was ended when he said, with composure regained, "Liz, please call Dorothy every so often to make certain that my girls are okay. I'll miss them."

As he turned, he said inaudibly, "I'll miss you too."

Liz only nodded.

The anxiety of leaving had been replaced by the thrill of anticipation. Forrester ordered and received a vodka and grapefruit juice after being seated comfortably in first class. By chance, seated next to him was T.W. Boyer—another lawyer and best-selling author of *This Book*, a legal thriller. Boyer's books were almost always about somebody seeking revenge in the courtroom. He spent most of the flight to Miami working on a new manuscript.

Comfortable now and with drink in hand, Forrester contemplated the recent events. He had come within an ace of violating a fundamental rule in his office. Had come within a gnat's ass of ruining a perfectly good working relationship with his star associate.

In Miami, he would call the office and learn that all was fine without him. He did not ask to speak to Liz.

CHAPTER 20

ALL IN ALL, THE flight from Miami to Johannesburg was uneventful. One American co-passenger made the mistake of attempting debate on the ethics of hunting. She withdrew when eavesdroppers chimed in.

"Tourist hunting is a major portion of our economy. Without it, there would be little conservation on the entire continent." Such were the words of a Zulu businessman sitting on an aisle seat in row two.

He and his companion were returning home after having spent two weeks in Washington, DC, headquartered at the South African Embassy. They were with that country's Department of Tourism and wanted to set some people straight.

The companion started spewing facts and figures. "It amazes me," he concluded, "that so many Americans are so ignorant, yet feel they must express idiotic opinions. It is empirically obvious. Where there is hunting in Africa, the animals are abundant and increasing. Where there is no hunting, the poachers see to it that the herds are depleted. Take the elephant, for example. In South Africa and Zimbabwe, our elephant population is controlled and growing in numbers. On the other hand, there is no hunting in Kenya and their numbers are falling."

The tall, thin black man had it out of his system now. He looked at the fellow passengers in nearby first-class seats as though to challenge any disagreement. Nobody wanted to be "ignorant" nor "idiotic." Nobody rose to the bait. Except for occasional air turbulence, the rest of the flight was smooth.

Things did not remain as calm in Jacksonville. One of those television programs that help police capture bad guys did a feature on Richard Smallwood. It was aired the same night that Bill left the country.

Until he called the office after flying all night and landing in Johannesburg, he didn't get the news that Liz had been on television. He wished he had not called in. There was no other news. Nobody needed his advice. And, being a half a world away, there was nothing he could do anyway.

He turned off his cell. He would not be using it again until he was back in the states. Maybe all the way back to Florida. It was time to relax.

It seems that Richard Smallwood had been injured that night he was in the Miss Q. At some point before being placed in his deceased father's pickup, either Gloria or one of her helpers unchained and pinched the biker's wallet. (Kind of like what the lady known as Lou did in Robert Service's "The Shooting of Dan McGrew.")

The fist in the gut that he received from the big man had ruptured his spleen. Either that or the wreck that happened less than a mile north, when he hit a telephone pole.

Having not buckled up, the back of his head broke the back window. He took another good blow when his head continued backward and struck the toolbox that was mounted on the bed of the pickup, just inches behind the back window.

This definitely was not a good day for Cora's brother:

1. He had gone to a deposition and was hammered by the lawyer.
2. He had let Liz (although he did not yet know) discover he had something to do with the murder of Lou Barrymore.
3. He had gotten drunk.
4. He had spilled a bourbon and Coke across the bar and pissed off a guy twice his size.

5. He had stumbled when he was getting ready to leave and gotten a fist in his gut.
6. He had forgotten to pick up the change from the fifty-dollar bill he had given the waitress, Gloria.
7. He had had his wallet stolen.
8. He had ruptured his spleen.
9. He had wrecked his truck and busted his head wide open.

That wasn't the end of the bad news.

Life Flight was dispatched to the accident scene. Richard was unconscious when loaded up and flown to Shands Teaching Hospital in Gainesville—a trauma center and part of the University of Florida campus.

The paramedics explained to the ER nurse that Richard was a John Doe. Had no ID when they found him at the accident scene. Of course, his truck could have been traced, but such paperwork would become confusing, crisscrossed, and unlikely to ever match up with the John Doe anyway.

The paramedics also reported that they were concerned that the patient had head injuries and neck problems, and his collarbone was definitely broken.

In spite of all of his problems, one good thing happened to Richard Smallwood. The cops investigating the accident scene did not give him a ticket for DWI. Maybe they would have if they had found his wallet. Without it, the paperwork was just too much to make it worthwhile. Besides, if the John Doe died, what would be the use?

The trauma team at Shands did a remarkable job. A CT scan revealed that he had a hematoma inside the front part of his head. A contrecoup injury from when the lick on the back part of his head caused his brain to smash forward on the skull. The residents working with the seasoned surgeons had an opportunity to view the brain close-up when part of his skull was removed. As it would turn out, the small sliver of brain that was cut out would be reason enough for Richard to have the flat affect to go along with his already environmentally damaged personality.

The patient was in and out of his comatose condition for six days. More than ten days passed before he would talk and his chart was changed from "John Doe" to "R. Smallwood." There was no reason for anybody to put two plus two together and remember that an all-points bulletin issued the day following Richard's mishaps at the Miss Q was directed at this patient.

Weeks passed and he was still a guest at Shands for the purpose of re-habilitation. He grew stronger with physical and mental therapy. Was due to be released the same day Bill Forrester boarded South African Airways.

Richard did not go through the regular release procedures and was not in his room when police detectives came with a warrant. He had watched the same TV program as that watched by whoever it was that recognized him as the Shands patient with massive injuries.

The program announced his name and showed pictures from when Richard Smallwood was in junior high. There was an explanation that he was older now and dangerous. Although it wasn't relevant to the kill-ing of Lou Barrymore, the host of the TV program described Richard's youth and his causing the death of the young girl, Melissa Rowe.

A picture of Liz Kelley was displayed to the audience. She had not consented to it, but it made good TV.

The reporter said, "Undisclosed sources revealed that Elizabeth Kelley, a well-respected lawyer from Jacksonville, Florida, broke the case when she noticed certain discrepancies at a deposition of Mr. Smallwood in another yet unrelated case."

Liz was not watching TV when she was so aptly described by the serious-faced reporter. She learned about it when Rosa called and found her at the office. It was after nine, and she was just calling it a day.

Rosa said, "You won't believe this. They had a program about Richard Smallwood. It showed his picture and Lou Barrymore's…and yours."

"Mine? You're kidding."

"No. They said you—'a respected lawyer'—broke the case, and they showed your picture."

"Oh, great. Who knows? Maybe it's good for business," she replied sarcastically after a pause.

She got a few more details, and the conversation ended.

That night it took Liz a long time to go to sleep. Her mind was not on work. She had become frightened knowing the nut, Cora's brother, probably knew about her. He might want some sort of revenge.

Why wasn't Forrester around for advice?

In fact, Richard's first thoughts were not of revenge. In fact, revenge had not crossed his mind. Revenge required emotion, and he had little.

He just wanted to get away from Shands.

Stealing a car was a lot less problem for him than stealing clothes. The nightgown with his fanny hanging out would not do. He finally hit pay dirt when he found somebody's penny loafers, jeans and blue button-down collar, long-sleeve shirt (one of those shirts with a pony emblem on it instead of a pocket) hanging on the back of a door. The clothes, which probably belonged to some yuppy doctor, were a little big on him, but fit good enough for nobody to notice as he walked out.

Walking down the hallways, it seemed like he was in a maze. "Imagine trying to find somebody here," Richard mumbled to himself.

There were long halls with no doors on either side. Other halls were dotted with doors. The offices of doctors of various and sundry specialties. Before his stay at Shands, he did not know one specialty from another. Now he had been treated by about a dozen different ones.

Something caught Richard Smallwood's eye as he went by one door that was open. It led to an office, and a woman's handbag was sitting on a chair beside a desk. Nobody was sitting there. He could hear voices, but nobody was around. It was so easy.

He just stepped inside; picked up the purse; stepped out; and continued his journey through the seemingly never-ending corridors.

As if somebody were shepherding him from there, he came to a sign for the restroom. It was a picture of a stick man and stick woman with a line in between. There was another sign with an arrow showing how to get to the emergency room. He went into the restroom first, where he rifled through the purse.

With nearly three hundred dollars in "his" pocket, a Visa card, two Mastercards (one gold), and a Discover Card, he headed out the ER door. Then he was lucky again. Somebody had pulled up and had parked her late model white Ford Mustang behind one of the ambulances near the ER entrance. The engine was running. Somebody must have followed somebody into the hospital.

Richard just got in and drove away.

One of those large department stores that end with "mart" was still open when the hospital escapee pulled into the parking lot. He wanted to use the credit cards quickly before they were reported stolen.

He loaded the cart with clothes and shoes his size. He grabbed thises and thats and a big duffle bag. His shopping only stopped when they announced that the store would close in ten minutes.

The gold card chip was pushed into the machine. In a bit there was a "ding" and the machine said "approved." In a few seconds there was a line for a scribbled signature, then a paper ticket, which he scrunched up and placed in his pocket.

Richard drove north toward Starke.

Not once had he gotten excited or scared. It had to do with that part of the brain that got hurt in the wreck. Of course, he could hardly care less. And, of course, notwithstanding the flat affect he would live with for the rest of his life, he knew and understood the troubles he had with the police chasing him and all. He understood survival.

Richard understood a lot of things. Mentally, emotion was the only thing he was lacking.

The Miss Q closed at 2:00 a.m. Last call had been a half hour earlier. Gloria was locking up at 2:30 a.m., and she was alone.

"Do I get any change?"

Richard's voice startled her.

Gloria did not recognize him at first. He needed to shave. Although his beard was not thick, he had stubble on his chin and over his lips. Thin hairs covered the rest of his face. What really threw her off was the crew cut. His head had been shaved for the operation. Scars could be seen on the head underneath about a quarter inch of hair.

Finally realizing who he was, Gloria said, "Hey, baby. I've been worried about you. Where you been?"

She acted cheerful, but she was scared.

"Let's go back inside. I need some money. You took my wallet."

"I don't know what you mean," she said. Then she tried to brush him off. "Come back tomorrow. I'll give you drinks on me."

Richard responded quietly. He was not upset. "I said open the door or I'll kick your ass right here." His eyes were staring right at hers.

"Hey, honey. You know I've got children. I've got to get home." It was an easy excuse.

The former customer raised his hand to hit her. He would have too. He had had enough, but she opened the door, and they walked in.

"Where's my change from my drinks?"

Gloria said, "Honey, I don't know what you mean. Besides, there's no money here. The owner puts it in the safe every night."

She was behind the bar. He went behind it too. The cash register drawer was open and empty. He opened the other cabinets and drawers one at a time.

Gloria was scared. Petrified. She had been beaten by men before, and she did not want to be beaten again.

While he was looking in the cabinet where the owner kept a pistol, she reached under the bar and grabbed a black tube. Just as Richard turned around with pistol in hand, she raised the tube toward him and pushed the release. He inhaled some of the tear gas, and more sprayed right in his eyes. As he fell to the floor, she ran out.

The engine to her 2004 pickup started with the first turn of the key. It was only then that Gloria knew she was free from the man who was about to hurt her. She had not wasted time closing the door to the building. Nor did she call the cops until she got to an all-night convenience store several miles away.

Richard Smallwood, fugitive, had plenty of time to recover enough to grab the pistol and leave. He drove to Lake City and purchased a ticket for the first bus available. It took three days before anybody started wondering about the car that was left in the Greyhound parking lot.

CHAPTER 21

BILL FORRESTER WAS ON the other side of the world.

He and Kevin were met by a bush pilot when they arrived in Harare. Twenty minutes later they had cleared Customs. Unlike during trips to Ethiopia or the Sudan, no bribes had been requested and none paid.

With their gear in hand, they loaded the one-engine bush plane and flew another hour and a half before landing on a grassy area that supported two air socks. They were met at that "airport" by Trevor Smythe and Tomi Makubu, their professional hunters, who drove them in a Land Rover for another two hours to their final destination.

The vehicle had been modified for safari. The doors had been removed as had the roof. The windshield was up but could be laid over the "bonnet." There was a special seat erected in the back of the vehicle so hunters could sit a few feet higher than the driver and more easily observe the game.

By the time the four had arrived in camp, solid friendships had been established.

The safari had been booked several months earlier at the largest hunting convention in the world. It is put on annually by Safari Club International (SCI), which plays host to twenty thousand or more hunters from throughout the world. A thousand or more booths and exhibitors are set up for the purpose of selling everything from ancient first edition books, to the adventures that are recorded in same. Tomi was sharing a booth with a booking agent when Kevin met him and arranged the African safari for the purpose of hunting Cape Buffalo and various plains animals. It took little convincing for Bill to agree to set aside a couple of weeks from the office.

———

The safari camp was what Bill and Kevin had expected. From past experience, both knew that the professional hunters and staff went all out to provide first-class accommodations. Sure, they would be sleeping in tents under mosquito netting over their beds. But the nights would be cool, and the air was unpolluted.

"God, this is beautiful." Bill's voice was full of enthusiasm, and his mind was at ease following the long journey.

"Would you care for something to drink?" Tomi asked as he opened a beer in a dark brown bottle for himself.

"I'll take orange juice," Kevin ordered.

Bill wanted the traditional pot of hot tea.

As they rested, their bags and rifles were efficiently delivered to the tents that had been assigned. Each tent provided a window view of the major river of Africa and was erected beneath thatch to maintain constant shade. Within each was a bed, bed stand, mirror, basin and pan for washing. There was also a pitcher of previously boiled drinking water.

The camp dining area was large and contained the comforts of a grand hotel. The walls were made of clay with wide-open areas to allow an unrestricted view of the fast-running Zambezi. The thatch roof provided the desired shade. Within the dining area were two tables capable of seating ten each. To the side was a sitting area with large rattan-type chairs fitted with overstuffed, down-filled cushions. They were arranged around an ironwood coffee table upon which were multiple photo albums and assorted books written by turn-of-the-nineteenth-century hunters.

Between the dining area and the river was an array of chairs positioned around logs that would be burned every evening before supper. The weather in Zimbabwe is similar to that of Georgia or North Florida and can be fairly chilly at night and early morning during the hunting season. The warm fire in the evening would always be a welcome addition to the camp when the hunters returned from search of game.

On this day there would be no hunting unless Bill or Kevin really wanted to go out for the afternoon. That was unlikely, if for no other reason than both were suffering. The adrenaline rush, associated with arriving at their destination and learning the lay of the land, had worn off. The men were not really nauseated, but they did not feel good. They felt clammy, tired, and sleepy.

"Tomi, if you don't mind, I'll have a shower and then a nap," Bill said.

The PH said, "I expected you would. Most everybody from your country wants the same thing. I don't know a better cure for jet lag."

Hot water had already been delivered to the showering place. It was designed for privacy—basically thatched walls with bamboo mats. There was no roof, but overhead hung a gravity-operated contraption that allowed the user to mix hot and cold water to the desired temperature. Camp staff boiled water and replenished the tap throughout the day.

"We'll wake you in a few hours if you are not already up," Tomi informed the two Americans as they parted company. "If we don't wake you, you'll probably come about and be hungry at one or two in the morning. Jet lag cannot be cured that way."

Regardless of the time differential and the jet lag that went with it, Bill was relaxed. He was relaxed in a way he only experienced when thousands of miles from the office, in the middle of nowhere. If there was an emergency, it would take at least six days to do something about it.

His mind was at ease as Bill drifted to sleep.

Kevin woke on his own and was with Davidad, the head of the camp staff, when, in a most proper way, the latter woke Bill as the sun was setting.

"Sleep well?"

"Unbelievably. What time is it?"

"Time for cocktails," Kevin replied.

"I'll be there in ten minutes."

"We won't wait for you." Kevin was lighthearted. "By the way, do you know that you talk in your sleep?"

"I've been told that before. Why, did I say anything bad?"

"Not that I know of. But who is Liz?"

Dressed in khaki and a down vest, the American walked from his tent to the fire less than seventy-five yards from the Zambezi. Comfortable chairs were being used by several people taking in the warmth. Bill did not recognize all of them.

The view of the setting sun on the river was like something out of a movie. The chatter of baboons in the faint distance mingled with the grunts of the hippos leaving the water to graze on the high grass along the riverbanks. This was an absolute perfect place for cocktails each evening before dinner.

Kevin remained seated as Bill approached. Not so Trevor. The perfect host inquired earnestly, "Feeling better?"

"Yes, thanks," Bill said as his eyes scoped the people around the fire.

As Jon-Jon, the cook's helper, stepped forward, Trevor asked, "Would you care for something to drink?"

"Scotch and ice, thank you."

Jon-Jon faded away to fetch same, while Bill admired his red sash and fez. His attention was broken when Trevor, in his good-natured voice and impeccable manner, said, "Bill, you must meet the other hunters who will be here with you. They were out when you came in."

The two stepped toward the fire as an older gentleman in his late 60's sixties stood with right hand extended. Bill grasped the hand as Trevor made the introduction.

"I would like for you to meet Felix Bauer."

As the two men shook, Forrester asked, "German?"

"No. Austrian. This is my daughter, Ingrid."

The lady did not stand as she extended her slender right hand, which the American grasped firmly, but in a different way than he would a man's hand. He grasped it differently than he had her father's a moment earlier. His thumb extended to the back knuckles; his fingers crossed her palm.

"Ingrid?" Forrester paused after repeating the name. "I'm Bill Forrester. It's a pleasure to meet you."

His eyes practically glued onto hers for several seconds before he turned to find his seat in front of the fire where he would wait for his Scotch. She noticed his not-so-inconspicuous glance to her left, un-ringed hand.

Before Bill could say anything else, Trevor said, "Ingrid and Fritz arrived yesterday. They are hunting with Johnny."

"Johnny?"

"Johnny Finley. I think you and Kevin met him in Las Vegas. He and Tomi will be back shortly."

"Sure. Johnny Finley," Bill replied, although he had absolutely no recollection of who Johnny was. In fact, he must have met a hundred professional hunters at the Safari Club convention. and couldn't remember most of them. It really didn't matter. He knew things would be sorted out shortly, and he was content to watch and learn.

Kevin was pretty much in charge of the conversation and was telling tried and true "war stories" about past hunting adventures. No doubt he had a knack for telling stories and jokes. What endeared Kevin to the others was that he always made himself the brunt of the jokes.

When it was Fritz's turn to talk, Bill learned that he was an engineer and industrialist. Ingrid, his only offspring, had hunted with him since she a child. His wife, who did not like the outdoors so much, would be eagerly awaiting their return.

It was hard to get Trevor to talk much about himself. He was a typical professional hunter, someone who, in Africa, serves many and various roles.

Not only must a PH be an outstanding woodsman, capable to spot and judge animals and their spoor, but he is also the host with a quick laugh, impeccable manners and who speaks the King's English. Trevor's and Johnny's ancestors probably came from England or Germany several generations earlier, about the same time other Europeans were conquering the American Indians. Tomi, a black African, trained as a PH shortly after the Rhodesian War.

A good professional hunter should be able to drink heartily without getting drunk and without losing composure. He should be a man's man and a woman's man clad in khaki shirt and shorts that accentuate his muscular body. His footwear is a short chukka boot that just covers the ankles and rounds out the healthy, outdoorsy look.

Bill wondered if he would be competing with the PHs for Ingrid's attention.

Ingrid's attention. That's what the lawyer from Florida wanted. He knew it almost immediately. And, as a Southerner, he felt almost obligated to flirt with this most handsome woman.

He did it at first by just looking at her whenever the conversation allowed it to be proper. He would not stare like some mesmerized child. He would look at her until she would catch him looking, and then he would act a little shy.

He knew he had plenty of time unless she was swept off her feet by a PH. If that happened, so be it. After all, he was in Africa for hunting—not romance.

Cocktails lasted almost exactly one hour. It would be like that every evening. Then Jon-Jon would quietly announce that dinner was prepared and served.

As with any fine dining experience, multiple waiters would serve the meals on freshly ironed tablecloths. The multiple courses and the multiple wines from which to choose would be offered to the ladies first, then the other guests. The professional hunters would be served last—but just as formally.

The wines of South Africa are some of the best in the world. Kevin's favorite was the the Cape Pinotage. He often joked, "it's not the vintage of the wine; it's the size of the jug that counts.

As much as anything else, the reason Bill returned to Africa again and again was to sample luxurious five-star cuisine and formality in an otherwise informal, rugged environment.

Tomi and Johnny Finley arrived just as the others were being seated. They apologized for having been detained in a meeting with the local tribal hierarchy. An accounting of the animals taken by a just-finished safari served to keep the conservation efforts on track since it was the locals who would share in the proceeds realized.

Tomi brought other news. "The Chief had just reported jailing a poacher. Apparently the man was setting snares and creating painful traps for the game animals."

"The locals aren't allowed to take animals?" Ingrid asked.

"As in your country, not without permits," Tomi answered. "It is against the law for a band of poachers to indiscriminately maim or kill animals, then sell the meat and keep all the profits. The safari outfitters, unlike the poachers, simply do not allow indiscriminate killing and the torture brought on by snares."

Johnny added, "There is an organization known as Campfire that has become quite successful here. It distributes the money from the sale of the permits to the locals. They also use the money for conservation programs and the maintenance of parks and equipment."

Almost as though it had been rehearsed, Tomi spoke again. "It actually works quite well. We have a lot of cooperation with the local tribes, who do not hesitate to protect the natural game resources and in return receive a bounty for turning the poachers over to the game rangers for proper punishment."

"It's a shame, but true, that in those places where Campfire does not have a strong influence, the game animals have been poached out of existence," Trevor waded in. "It's just not like Europe, or the States, for that matter. In Africa, game must have value or there is no game."

The propaganda having been explained and concluded, Tomi asked, "Trevor, what has the cook prepared for us tonight?"

"It's a roast from the Bushbuck that Ingrid took yesterday afternoon."

"Splendid," he replied as he took a seat.

Through all of the conversation about poachers, the other man had yet to introduce himself. Before he had another chance, Bill extended his hand and said, "Aren't you Johnny Finley? I think we met in Las Vegas."

Johnny smiled and said, "You, sir, have a very good memory."

CHAPTER 22

INGRID. INGRID KLINE. NOW, she is a hell of a woman. Nobody would call her a girl. Physically, she is the type of woman that men notice. The type of woman that most men would feel inadequate to approach.

She is a large woman. Not the least bit fat, but big-boned with broad shoulders and a firm body. Her legs are shapely but not skinny. The way she looks, a man can tell she is not flat-chested, but he cannot tell the size of her breasts; even though she always holds herself erect, shoulders back.

How about her face? Green eyes—kind of hazel. Her lips are between thick and thin—like Loretta Young's in the 1940s. She wears little makeup and pulls her hair, dark blond and thick, straight back into a ponytail not longer than her shoulders.

Ingrid Kline is a big, handsome woman whose presence is noticed—imposing and intimidating. You can tell she is wealthy and used to wealth, although she never speaks of it.

Her clothes on safari had not been bought willy-nilly in some discount department store. Instead, she looked like she had walked out of a catalog from Holland & Holland or Dunns.

Unlike what you would expect of an Austrian, her English vocabulary, which she speaks with only a tinge of an accent, is that of a scholar. She also speaks Italian and French well enough to order from any menu. Her training was in Europe—from country to country.

Other than one trip to Alaska, she had spent no time in the United States.

The day after arriving in the Zambezi camp, Bill Forrester was full of questions. Having finished a breakfast that included fried tenderloin of Bushbuck, eggs, cheese and English muffins, he left camp with Trevor in the Land Rover, which was sans roof and sans door.

Likewise, Kevin had left with Tomi. Fritz and Ingrid were hunting together with Johnny Finley.

Trevor asked in good humor, "Do all barristers ask so many questions?"

Bill smiled and replied, "How could any man not ask questions about that woman?"

"I only just met her myself. Johnny has hunted with her before but never before with her father. She and her husband hunted here three years ago."

"Her husband? Is she divorced?"

"No. She is a widow. Her husband was a doctor of some sort. He died in a plane crash somewhere in Alaska."

"Hunting?"

"I think so. Bear or moose."

As if comparing venues, Bill said, "Alaska! Now that's tough hunting."

The PH answered back in a voice that showed that he was not amused, "So I've been told. You hunt for weeks for a single animal, and you still may not be successful. I think I'll stick with Africa."

"It's just different," Bill said with the authority of having experienced both. "Here you see hundreds of animals a day and live in first-class accommodations. There, you may not see anything but birds for days; you eat what you can out of a can; you sleep in a tent erected over freezing tundra; and you don't bathe for two weeks at a time."

Reverting to his favorite subject of the day, Bill asked, "Do you know how long it was before she found out about her husband?"

"Johnny says immediately. She was with him and the pilot in a bush plane. She was the only one who survived."

"She, a woman like her, was going hunting in Alaska?"

"I suppose—unless she was just there to take pictures."

"When did all this happen?" Bill was still asking questions, and he was interested in the answers.

"A year or two ago. She's back here with her father to sort of gather her wits, if you know what I mean."

"I think I do."

The conversation ended when Trevor, uncharacteristically and inappropriately allowed, "I suppose she'll never have to work—being the widow of a doctor. Did you ever know a doctor who didn't have megabucks?"

Bill did not reply, but the silence did not last long. Fresh spoor from a herd of Cape buffalo was spotted and the PH, his hunter, and a skilled tracker, Hundz, followed from there on foot.

———

Three days passed. Bill had yet to take a buffalo. He had seen hundreds of the huge, fierce wild oxen, but not the one he wanted. He wanted a buffalo bigger than the one he had taken several years earlier when he had made the trip with Karen, his former wife, who would eventually break his heart.

Of course, he had dated since then but had not fallen in love. He did not want to fall in love—at least not until his children were on their own.

He still had the Southern gentlemanly charms that he used to flirt and play sweet games with the opposite sex. He had used those charms on Elizabeth Kelley when they first met at deposition; and when he next saw her at her interview with the firm of Moran, Smith, Forrester & Dees. He wasn't certain how well his charms had worked with her, and he did not think that they would work so well with Ingrid.

Of course, he only saw her at supper and just before, when they would have drinks together, along with the other hunters, PHs, and occasional guests. Ingrid and her father were usually long gone by the time Bill ate breakfast. Lunch was generally handled in the field.

They had all gotten to know one another. A must for staying in the same camp. They were becoming friends, sharing stories, and reporting the luck of the day; each day.

"You are trying too hard, you know." It was Trevor breaking the mid-morning silence as they and Hundz were strolling back to the

Land Rover. Bill had again declined the opportunity to take a buffalo of less quality than that for which he had come to Africa.

"I'm not worried. If I don't find the right buff, I'm still having a great time."

"I don't mean buffalo. We will get your trophy. I mean Ingrid. You are simply trying too hard."

Pause. "It shows, huh?" Pause. "Actually, I may give up. I think Johnny Finley has caught her for this trip."

Bill knew that it was not unusual for women on safari to become infatuated with the PH. Chapters in many of Bill's collection of old first edition books report stories about affairs on safari. It is easy to understand. The mood is set to give the professional hunter the advantage over matters of the heart. He is in his own element, giving directions and making decisions that may mean the difference between life and death. The PH is the leader. He is clever. On safari he is the hero to man and woman alike.

Add that to the romance of Africa, and the PH can have his way with many women.

Trevor said, "Johnny will not get in your way. First, he is married, and he loves his wife. He just loves to flirt, that's all. Besides, the policy in our camp is to avoid short romances on safari. It simply complicates things."

"I can imagine. I have a similar rule in my office." As he said that, for the first time in several days, Bill thought consciously of his associate, Elizabeth Kelley.

"Don't change the subject," Trevor said as he again flashed his easy smile. "I don't think that the Austrian beauty has a thing for Johnny anyway."

"No?"

"No. She is not here for romance."

"Then why?"

"She just loves Africa. Like you. The two of you have a lot in common. Just don't try so hard."

Back at the Land Rover, Trevor suggested they break the ritual of packed lunch. "It's early," he said. "Do you mind if we go to the camp for our mid-day meal?"

The expected reply was forthcoming. "Why not?"

An eland roast had been served the night before and was being served for lunch as sandwich making. Naturally, it was served on a tray with cheeses, lettuce, tomato and various other garnishes. Few delis offer more. Indeed, few offer as much.

"Hello gentlemen," a familiar voice said. "Do you mind if I join you?"

Always polite, Trevor stood, forcing Bill to do likewise.

"Not at all," he said as Ingrid took her place.

Bill started the conversation. "I thought you'd be hunting."

"I took a nice Kudu this morning and decided to take the afternoon off. My father, on the other hand, went back out.

"Do you mind if I take the afternoon off with you?" Not timid.

"Of course not," she replied

Trevor had not said a word. But, having listened, he gathered his sandwich and said, "Then I'm off to do some paperwork, unless you need me."

———

Before that afternoon, Bill and Ingrid had become acquaintances. By sundown, the two were fast friends. They talked about everything, and the talk came easy. It was the kind of talk that brings people together.

Ingrid liked that Bill was a self-made man. She enjoyed hearing about his Army days. He was not the kind of Middle East veteran you see in the movies who cannot get the war out of his system. He was like the vast majority of the veterans of the longest war who had had the same experience. He, like they, was only bitter because his country refused to wage the war to win; train the locals and come home.

Bill told her about his days at the University of Florida. He tried to explain American football and his love for the Gators.

Ingrid seemed fascinated with tales of courtroom battles—his successes and his failures with the juries. She was relieved to learn that the O.J. Simpson trials were not typical, except maybe for California. Bill did not opine his thoughts of the guilt or innocence of O.J. He did opine that the judge in the criminal trial had let the system down and that trial was more of a circus than the normal courtroom scenario.

They did not dwell on his unsuccessful marriages, though they did dwell on his daughters. Bill had brought out an album of pictures of his girls. In good spirit, Ingrid seemed to take delight in stories about each.

Likewise, Bill was fascinated by the life history of his new-found friend. Typical of a trial lawyer, he had dozens of questions about her experiences in so many countries of Europe. In turn, she taught him how to say, "May I have a vodka on the rocks?" in four different languages.

Her father had established their family fortune before she was born, but she took none of it for granted. She admitted that she was her father's extravagance. He doted on her and always had. Theirs was the relationship that Bill hoped for with his daughters. She explained that it worked because of their mutual attraction for the great outdoors.

That had also been her attraction to her husband, a surgeon, who had met success early in life. Hans Kline was only thirty-nine when the bush pilot had taken the wrong course through some mountains. The passage had narrowed. Too tight to turn around. They had crashed, and her husband died instantly. The pilot died within the hour after having become conscious only once. She had waited at the plane for two days before being found and rescued by hikers.

What about children? She had one; also a girl. She was yet uncertain as to whether little Helena would also take to hunting and fishing.

"She is being kept by my mother while Daddy and I hunt Africa."

By evening Bill Forrester and Ingrid Kline were infatuated. Mutually infatuated. He was convinced that they would be lovers before the end of safari. She did not betray her thoughts.

———

After three more days, Bill had still not taken a Cape buffalo. He had taken a fine warthog as well as several other plains game trophies. However, he had come to Africa primarily to hunt "buff."

The conversations with his PH would daily turn to the excitement of the hunt.

"The Cape buffalo is one of the most dangerous animals in the world," Trevor had repeated. "He is the type of breed that will hunt the hunter."

"I guess that's what makes it so exhilarating. There's always the element of danger."

"Bill, you know we've stalked dangerously close to several bulls that most any hunter would find to be exceptional trophies."

"Yes, but we've found none larger than I've taken before. I hope I haven't become too tiresome"

"Actually, I appreciate clients like you. It makes the hunt more difficult but the results more satisfying."

"Let's keep trying until we find one with all the best qualities. Thick, hard bosses, a deep curl, and plenty of width." So far, he had found many bulls that met all but one of the called-for criteria he had set as a goal. His most difficult task on this trip had been to find a bull with massive horn width of forty-five inches, plus.

"We'll keep at it and as long as you do," Trevor reassured

———

Just prior to this trip, Rosa had reported seeing a television program obviously prepared by an anti-hunting group. Parroting the commentator, she had asked why he was so set on taking "trophies."

"When a trophy is taken, doesn't that deplete the best of the herd?" Rosa had asked. "What are you doing to the gene pool?"

It was like Forrester was addressing a jury. "The trophy animal is usually the oldest of the bunch. More often than not, he is no longer a breeder, but he still competes with the other animals for food—a scarcity when the herds are in the thousands." He ended his argument by reporting, "A goodly number of the animals I've taken over the years would not have made it through the next winter."

In the end he was not sure that Rosa had been impressed. However, she did allow, "Until I become a vegetarian and quit wearing leather shoes and belts, I won't complain. You always seem to have the right answers, anyway."

———

On the seventh evening of the safari, Bill approached Ingrid in the presence of her father.

"Any chance you would consider hunting with me tomorrow?"

She turned to Fritz. "Father?"

"Of course. Why not? Bill seems to need some luck. Maybe you'll bring it to him." The response demonstrated that the father was fond of the American he had only recently met.

The next morning, as had become the custom, Hundz led the way on foot after striking spoor. Trevor followed next, with Bill and Ingrid alternately taking the third position. The tracking was accomplished in single file.

When Bill was in the fourth position, he admired the stature of the woman in front of him. Her waist was small for her frame and was accentuated by the way the olive drab short-sleeve shirt was tucked into her pleated khaki pants. Her belt was dark leather and carried a matching cartridge pouch along with a small case in which she inserted her German-made, high-quality binoculars. As time passed, her shirt became wet with perspiration which, under the circumstances, Bill thought was kind of sexy.

Hundz carried water, lunches and other essentials. The PH and both of the "hunters" carried high-powered rifles. Nobody ever gave thought to asking Ingrid if she would like assistance. She did not, and to have asked would have been insulting.

Though they were traveling through rough terrain, the hunters were careful to be quiet. They made a conscious effort not to step where they would make noise. Twigs and leaves that would break and crunch were avoided as they made their way, following the spoor.

The acute awareness of the possibility of danger kept them all keenly conscious of their surroundings. They were constantly aware of their senses being tested to the limits while traveling through thick places with limited visibility.

The four would follow the rambling herd by relying on Hundz, who could detect the most minuscule sign. Down one hill and up another. Through dried creek bottoms of warm sand where each step would sink several inches deep. Around and between thickets of bushes—each with thorns that would grab and tear clothing as well as rip the skin of the person who did not pay attention. The terrain was always changing, and the change was delightful for those who loved the outdoors and could experience it in this unique way.

When Hundz stopped, they all stopped. Like when he pointed to a klipspringer, a small antelope that seems content to live in rocky areas at the base of worn-out mountains untold millions of years old. It was in that same area that they witnessed a female leopard spring on a rock hyrax, reducing it to a mid-morning meal before disappearing out of sight.

Twice that morning, Hundz had stopped and then guided the others around two different snakes—a puff adder and a green mamba. Both are extremely poisonous but serve the useful purpose of rodent control. Snakes were left unharmed as the hunters continued their search.

Each time Hundz made the discoveries and pointed them out to the hunters, all of the communication was in silence. He would point, but nobody spoke.

That procedure was broken after having moved along this way for just more than two hours. This time Hundz froze and yelled, "Bwana! Bwana!" He was pointing in the direction of thick bush directly to the right of the quartet.

In a split second, everybody saw what the trained tracker had already seen. At first, there was movement in the grass. Then the long grass parted maybe thirty yards away. The black animal looked like what a matador must see—only it was bigger; the horns were wider and thicker; and the hunters had not had the benefit of the picadors.

Bill was shouldering his .375 H&H magnum.

Ka-boom! Ingrid had not hesitated, and the first blast was from Ingrid's rifle. The two-thousand-pound beast was hit but still closing.

Now Bill's rifle was to his shoulder. The giant animal had lowered his head and was swinging it wildly. *My God*, Bill thought, *how does something so huge move so quickly?* All he could see was blackness in his scope. He had to remain calm. He had to squeeze the trigger. But before—

Ka-boom! a ton of powerful muscle stumbled not fifteen yards away with Trevor's shot; but kept coming as bolts were maneuvered to jack another bullet into place.

How can it keep coming? Bill's mind was racing. He had to stay calm. There was no time to think. This was not like the slow motion in the movies. The charge was here! The beast was here! The shot had to be placed right and now!

Ka-boom! With Bill's bullet, the Buffalo fell within fifteen feet; but was struggling to recover.

Ka-boom! Ka-boom! More shots fired in rapid succession by the PH and then Ingrid.

Then there was silence. For several minutes, just silence.

Hundz was the first to speak. Hand extended toward Bill, all smiles, he said, "Bwana!"

Instead of shaking hands, Bill hugged the little man like he was his brother. Then he hugged Trevor with body language that said, "Thank you" without words. It was Ingrid's turn next, but this time he did not just hug.

As if they were the only people in the world, Bill bent her backward and kissed her like that sailor kissed the woman in Times Square after World War II. They released. Then he pulled her close and kissed her softly while she kissed back over and over and over again.

Trevor and Hundz talked to each other in some African language that neither Bill nor Ingrid understood.

The Cape buffalo was mature but smaller than several that Bill had previously turned down. So what? He knew this would be the hunt he could never forget. He knew that this would be the trophy that he would remember and think about most often.

The four were in camp soon after lunch. There were no other PHs or tourist hunters around. Graciously, Hundz left with the skinners while Trevor found some sort of work to do that would not require him to interfere with his clients.

Ingrid and Bill spent the rest of the daylight hours getting to know each other in one of the most perfectly romantic places on earth.

———

"God, man, it was thrilling and terrifying at the same time," Trevor told everybody during cocktails.

The chairs were empty as everyone stood around to enjoy the excitement. The fire with its low flame provided sufficient lighting for the reenactment gestures as the story was repeated multiple times. Nobody noticed the grunts of the hippos that sent sound waves down the Zambezi, whose shores were maybe fifty yards away.

Ingrid gave the credit to the brave tracker. "We would have all been killed had Hundz not given us that extra moment before the charge."

"When it was over, I was exhausted," Bill allowed. "I felt like I had run a marathon, but I hadn't moved two feet. I know it was the adrenaline, but I could hardly catch my breath when the buffalo fell right there in front of us. I mean, he fell within touching distance!"

To put the danger in proper prospective, Tomi recounted a story about a professional hunter and his client being killed only months earlier. It seems that a Cape buffalo had been wounded as dusk came, and it had been determined that it was too dangerous to track at night. The PH, tracker, and the client returned along with the client's wife and son the next morning, early. The wife and child were left with the Land Rover and from there had witnessed the horror of an unexpected buffalo charge. Both her husband and the professional hunter were hooked and gored repeatedly by the horns; and both died from the inflicted wounds. The tracker survived only because he was able to avoid the charge by climbing a nearby tree.

"Trevor, why do you think the animal charged you today? Why didn't he try to avoid you?" Kevin had asked the obvious question.

"It was poachers," Trevor said with disgust. "Damn those poachers. If only they had been charged. I wish the beast had killed them. If we can catch them, I want them put in prison."

"Poachers? This was the work of poachers?"

"Those coward bastards! The buffalo had been snared. There was a cable wrapped around its right hind leg. It had obviously been set for an elephant, and this poor creature had unfortunately wandered over the trap. I can't imagine how long he was held to the tree before the snare came loose. Maybe days. His leg was a bloody mess and infected."

Tomi continued the thought. "Of course, he was enraged. It is no wonder he hated the next human being that came along."

It was obvious that every hunter and every professional hunter around the fire had great respect for the animal that had almost taken some of their lives. They loved the animals but condemned the cowards who set the snares. Any injured animal is dangerous. People included. But a creature that is more than a ton of muscle and horns can really create havoc.

"Poachers are not hunters. They are random killers that have little respect for the wild animals that roam free," Fritz concluded.

"Where is Hundz?" Bill changed the subject. "I want to propose a toast and make a presentation."

The small black man had to be summoned from another campfire where he was telling the tale to his friends. You could tell he was tipsy from the home brew he had been drinking before being invited to join the foreigners. At first he declined but then accepted a glass of South African Merlot.

"I'd like to propose a toast to Hundz," Bill said as he lifted his glass high. He wanted to be sure that everybody knew that he was serious, so he paused. With stern face, Bill continued, "To Hundz, who saved our lives and showed absolute courage when he stood firm in the face of the charging buffalo. To Hundz, who was the only one without a weapon yet stood his ground with the rest of us."

"To Hundz!" the others repeated.

Hundz said nothing, but you could tell he was embarrassed. The brave man had only done what he knew was expected of him.

Then Bill did something that was totally unexpected. He said, "Hundz, I have a gift for you."

With that, he handed the tracker his .375 H&H magnum rifle that had been used to stop the charge. Bill was still serious. "I would like for you to have this rifle as a token of my appreciation for saving my life and that of my companions." He was talking like he was making a speech at the Rotary Club. "Hopefully, if there is ever again such an attack, you will have the opportunity to defend yourself."

Bill's presentation had taken everyone by surprise. The rifle was expensive by American standards. In Africa it was a magnificent gift, the cost of which would represent the value of more than a year of the courageous man's salary.

Almost inaudibly, Hundz said, "Thank you, Bwana. Thank you." His eyes watered but no tears fell on the cheeks that had been purposely scarred when he had been elevated from youth to manhood.

———

By suppertime, the events of the day had been thoroughly discussed. That is, they had discussed all of the events that had occurred in the field. Nobody mentioned what had happened when they returned to camp. Nobody reported that Ingrid and Bill had fallen in love.

———

On one more occasion, Ingrid hunted with Bill. Mostly, though, she spent the days with her father as originally planned. The evenings, on the other hand, were dedicated to the American.

The two now stood next to one another whenever the group would have cocktails. Sat next to each other during meals. You could see the way they paid attention and thoroughly enjoyed each other's company.

It became obvious to Felix as well as the others that Bill and Ingrid had formed a special relationship. Of course, they were totally discreet.

CHAPTER 23

KEVIN TOOK THE DIRECT flight back from Johannesburg to Miami, while Bill rearranged his to accommodate a few days in London.

As they were departing company, Kevin teased. "Leave it to you, Bill. Who else would go across the world to fall in love?"

"Who says I'm in love?"

"How about everybody from her father to the cook? On our way out here, I thought you really had a thing for that woman lawyer in your office."

A smile was Bill's reply.

"Don't get married before you get back to Florida." Now Kevin was smiling. "But if you can't wait, I'll fly to London to be in your wedding."

The two friends shook hands and departed company.

For the first time since leaving Jacksonville, Bill was alone. Alone in the sense that there was no companion on the non-stop British Airways flight to Heathrow. Ingrid had flown Air Zimbabwe with her father to Frankfurt. She would connect from there to London.

For once he was enjoying being alone. It gave him time to think. Not about work, but about his African experience. About falling in love and the giddiness of it all. It had been a long time since he had felt giddy.

The seven-hour flight gave him plenty of time to reflect about Liz, too. He did not have the giddy feeling with her. Did that mean he did not love her? If he did, he would never admit it.

Liz and Ingrid. Ingrid and Liz. Physically, both were striking, and both were smart. He had grown to admire one for her skills in the courtroom. The other for her passion for the outdoors.

During the time he spent on the airplane journey, he was missing both of the women in his life. By the time he arrived in Heathrow, he was thinking only of the one who would join him later that day.

———

Bill checked into the hotel across from Windsor Castle.

Reservations had been made before they left Harare in spite of the problems associated with the African country's antiquated telephone system. A satellite phone was fetched by his PH. He did not even try to call the office.

Why should he call the office? He would be home in a few days anyway. There was no reason to learn whatever problems may have cropped up while he had been gone. Let others in the firm solve any problems. Let Liz solve them.

———

They had planned to tour the castle on day one; Stonehenge on day two; and finally, the Crown Jewels in the Tower of London before flying out to their respective homes. As it actually happened, they seldom left the room. And then, only because room service failed to offer a full menu.

"We fit, Ingrid," he whispered.

"What do you mean?"

"I've never been so excited about a woman. We fit mentally and physically. I want to hold all of you at one time."

"Yes. We fit" she whispered back.

For two days they had not wanted for conversation. It flowed, and the two were happy.

To Bill Forrester, this woman was as exciting as the experiences they had shared. Willingly, she was his companion, friend and lover.

They were together because she wanted to be with him, and she wanted to do the things that he wanted to do.

She wasn't like his first wife who usually bitched when he wanted to go off for a long weekend of hunting and fishing. Bill knew Ingrid would not bitch. She would go with him and love it.

———

It was their final night together before either mentioned it. It was Ingrid who started.

"Bill, when we first met, before that day with the buffalo, you told me you would never marry again."

"I know I said that."

"I feel the same way."

What had she just said? Had he heard her right?

"Don't say anything," she whispered. Holding her index finger perpendicular to her lips as if to say, "Shhhhhhh." Then she continued to whisper, "I know we can never be married in spite of our affection… in spite of our love."

He continued to say nothing.

"I love you, and I know you love me. We could be perfect for each other, but we are not."

Still no response.

"You will forever be the other love in my life. Hans was the first."

Now Bill spoke. "I know what I said. I've never planned to marry again. Maybe I was wrong."

"You probably are wrong, my darling. You probably should get married again. Maybe you will."

"And you?"

"You know it cannot be 'us.'"

Of course, she was right. Before she said it, he had already thought it through. She had the guts to say it first, and it had caught him off guard.

Bill Forrester had found the most exciting woman he could imagine. She seemed perfect. She was smart, statuesque and beautiful. More importantly, she loved to do the things he loved to do. They were lovers, and they were in love.

On the other hand, he could not just pack up and leave for Europe. He couldn't just leave his children and his roots. Besides, he had too many financial obligations for it to make any sense.

It was pretty much the same for Ingrid. She was Austrian. She could move to America, but she would not be happy there. She was sure that Helena could adapt. She was equally sure that she could not. They agreed to keep in touch. Perhaps they would go on hunts together; or she could be a tour guide for him and his children on trips to Europe. Likewise, she promised to visit America. Perhaps often. Time would tell.

They spent the rest of the day in the room together, loving and making memories until it was time to go.

CHAPTER 24

WHEN HE LANDED IN Miami, it was just after dawn. By the time Customs said it was okay to bring his hunting rifles back into the US, it was almost noon.

"This is ridiculous," he told the agent. "These are hunting arms, not machine guns, for crying out loud. I thought I would avoid all this harassment since I had the paperwork prepared in advance."

The Rambo agent didn't smile as he took the hours necessary to make sure the American citizen was not a terrorist.

For more than two weeks, he had been relaxed. Thoroughly relaxed. Africa had that effect on him. Now, just within moments of stepping onto American soil, he was changed from Bill Forrester, relaxed international hunter, to William Forrester, hard-driving litigator.

Now it was time to get back into work mode. Workaholic mode. When he returned to the office, he knew he'd face crushing paperwork that had piled up. Everybody on his staff would be firing questions at him. His was the advice they sought, and his was the advice they trusted.

Had it not been for the hassles in Customs, he would have been back in Jacksonville in the early afternoon. Because of the hassles, he had missed his connecting flight and it would be evening before he returned.

He pondered the idea of calling the office and getting started on this particular Tuesday afternoon. His habit after such trips was to simply show up at the office and nonchalantly return to his hectic pace. He declined to change his habits, and he declined to call the office.

Instead, he opened his smartphone for the first time since he had called the office from London on his way to Africa. Hundreds of missed calls. He ignored them. At least a thousand unopened emails.

He ignored them. He scanned Drudge for news information. He also bought a two-day-old *New York Times* and a current *Miami Herald*. Nothing disastrous had happened, he learned.

The federal government was still spending billions on pork barrel projects. As usual, the Congress and the President were not getting along; and essential and "non-essential" jobs were being handled by the bureaucrats in their bureaucratic way. He mused at the little piece on Hillary Clinton and wondered if she would ever be consoled.

Reviewing the international news, he confirmed that the same wars and civil wars were being fought. Some fairly close to where he had been hunting. He also learned, at least according to the internet, he should have felt in perilous danger when in Johannesburg. Apparently a crime spree had been waged despite the best efforts of the African National Congress.

There was no reason to expect anybody to meet him at the Jacksonville Airport after the last leg of his trip. It was late afternoon. Besides, nobody knew when to expect him. Still, there was a slight, totally illogical, emotional letdown when he got off the plane and recognized no friendly faces. The first positive of the day was when he found that all of his bags had arrived in Jacksonville together. "Wonder of wonders," he mumbled to himself.

It cost sixty bucks for the trip to Orange Park, where he would find his car in his garage. The only real problem was, he had to listen to the Uber driver make idle conversation for forty-five minutes.

"Been on a long trip?" The driver had probably asked the same question a thousand times to a thousand different travelers.

"Yeah, I went to Africa and then to England."

"Africa? You been huntin'? What'd you get?"

Bill's smile could not be seen from the back seat. He only replied, "I had an adventure."

"Been gone long?"

"A couple weeks. I guess I'm glad to be home. I see that Jacksonville is still in one piece. Is there anything I should know about?"

Bill had changed the subject, and the driver picked up from there.

"No. The weather's been good today, but we've had a lot of rain while you were gone. I guess that's good for the aquifer."

Bill thought to himself, *I wonder if this man really knows anything about the aquifer.*

Then he replied, "Well, I guess that's good for people who don't have a sprinkler system." Both men chuckled, even though the comment didn't really mean much.

The conversation lulled, and Bill was happy with that. But the driver must have felt uncomfortable and thought he needed to spice up the ride with more talk.

"I guess you haven't heard about that nut they're looking for."

"Nut. What nut?"

"Some dude's been on a rampage. Most recently, he killed his mama down in Starke. Before that, he killed some lawyer up here, and then he shot a shrink down in Gainesville. They think the shrink's gonna live, though."

"Somebody shot a lawyer? That's what I do for a living. When did all this happen?"

The driver had stumbled into a subject that Bill was interested in. "You're a lawyer? What kind of cases do you do?"

"I sue people. Do you know the name of the lawyer? The lawyer who got killed."

"I don't remember his name. He shot him a while back—months ago. Then he escaped from a hospital and started going after these other people. At least that's what the paper says."

"Are you talking about Barrymore? Lou Barrymore?"

"I'm not sure what the man's name was. All I know is his mama lived in Starke, and that's where he used to live, too. It's been all over the news and on television almost every day lately."

"Today's news?"

"Maybe."

The lawyer's mind was at work. It had to be Richard Smallwood. Now he wished he had called the office while he had had all that time in Miami. He had seen nothing about this when he scanned Drudge, the *Miami Herald* and the *Times.* Why should there have been? This would be a North Florida problem, and Miami was like another world.

Jacksonville was like South Georgia. Miami was like South New York City and North Cuba mixed together.

The driver kept blabbering, but Forrester was thinking, not listening. Finally he interrupted. "How about pulling into the next convenience store so I can buy a paper?"

Within several minutes the driver complied.

Jacksonville's paper, *The Florida Times Union*, had nothing about Richard Smallwood in Section A. At the bottom right-hand corner of the first page, Section B, "Metro," was the article.

Other than identifying the victims and the chief suspect, the article didn't say anything that the driver hadn't. Another article on the third page quoted Richard Smallwood's physician from Shands Hospital.

Dr. Ernest James, head of neurosurgery at Shands Hospital, treated the suspect after a car wreck. Dr. James revealed that a portion of the suspect's brain was damaged in the accident.

As a result, it is entirely possible that my patient has a personality change rather than a change in intellect. The unfortunate result of injuries such as he has sustained is that he may be without what we commonly refer to as a conscience....

It was dark when Bill finally got home. He paid for the Uber and used two keys to get in the house. His housekeeper was watching TV in the kitchen.

"Bill?" Her voice was shock and fright. "Good God, you nearly scared me to death. I didn't know you were coming home today."

She had gathered her wits and was on her feet. They hugged in traditional Southern style.

"It sure is good to see ya," she said.

"You too, Dorothy. Are the girls at their mother's?"

"Yeah. If I'd known you were going to be here, they would've been here too. I know they've been missing you. I talked to Rosa this morning, and she didn't know you were coming home either."

"I should've called." He meant it.

"I guess you heard about that man whose family you're representing."

"Not until just a few minutes ago," he answered. "How did you know our firm was representing his family?"

"Miss Kelley, that woman who brought you home that time, is almost always mentioned when they bring it up on the news. She always says that she has no comment."

"I guess I ought to give her a call after I've had a chance to talk to the girls." Bill was saying that while he punched in the "girls" listing in the "favorite contacts" directory on his cell. The phone rang at his former house, where his former wife still lived.

A pleasant robotic voice directed him to leave a message, and he complied.

The world traveler took a shower, then garbed himself in khakis, cowboy boots and a short-sleeve shirt he had purchased from Ducks Unlimited. It was not office attire, but it was after dark, and there would be no clients. As he passed Dorothy in the hallway, he told her that he did not know what time he would be back. He would continue to call the girls from his car.

After driving just a block, he remembered something. He had forgotten to bring a pistol. It was back to the house, where he opened a small portable safe and retrieved a .22 magnum, manufactured by North American Arms. It was a miniature five-shot revolver, about the size of a Derringer, that fit easily into his trouser pocket without making much of a bulge. It was loaded with four rounds with the hammer seated over the empty chamber.

The fact that Richard Smallwood was on the loose was not the reason he took the gun along. In the early 1990s, laws had been passed letting Florida citizens carry concealed firearms if they could qualify for a permit. They first had to complete a safety course and have a background check. Since then, Forrester usually carried a pistol—especially after one of his law partners had been mugged on the way to the firm's parking lot. After a while, carrying the small pistol was a habit that made him feel at least a bit more secure.

Back in the Suburban, he tried to call his children. Still no answer. He thought about calling Elizabeth Kelley. Found her in his "contacts," then decided not to.

"It doesn't matter," he muttered to himself. "She wouldn't be home anyway. She never gets home this early."

He asked Siri to call his office. The phone rang four times, and then he heard his own voice. "You have reached the law firm of Moran, Smith, Forrester, and Dees. Your call is important to us. Please leave your name and number at the sound of the tone and someone will be in touch shortly. Please speak slowly."

When he arrived, the building was empty except for the cleaning lady. He sat at his desk and then punched in the number of his former wife's home again. Again, neither she nor the children answered. So, he settled into his leather chair and began the task of sorting out business. He forgot about trying to make contact with his children or Liz. His incoming box was stacked with papers.

Forrester could tell that while he had been having adventures in Africa, mundane work at the office had gone along fairly routinely. There had been no business disaster, and Elizabeth Kelley had taken care of all minor emergencies.

It was after midnight when he walked into the parking lot and then drove away for home. Still didn't know anything more about Richard Smallwood and decided he would get his answers the next day.

CHAPTER 25

RICHARD SMALLWOOD KNEW HE had troubles. He was not scared, but he knew it was not like when Melissa Rowe had died. He was a juvenile when that happened, and it really had been an accident. A reckless accident.

Lou Barrymore's death was no accident.

In Richard's mind, Lou Barrymore needed to die. After all, Barrymore was the one who sent the subpoenas that literally drove his father to suicide. Richard had rationalized that it had scared his father to death. The fact that he hated his father did not matter. It was a family thing.

The killer reasoned further: Lou Barrymore was one of the lawyers trying to keep his sister from getting the money she deserved from the hospital. If she ever got any money, he figured she would loan him some. Barrymore was between him and the loan.

He thought the subpoenas would stop with the death of Barrymore. It had been planned well, and it should've worked. Barrymore should have died, and that should have been the end of it.

Every day for a week, the youngest man in the Smallwood family had followed the lawyer when he left his office at the end of the day. He always took the same route to his home, located on several acres in northwest Jacksonville.

Richard did not follow him down the drive to the large English Tudor house with the circular driveway in front. Behind the house were horse barns in a special area where his daughter and wife trained their jumpers. From the road he was unable to see Barrymore and his family act like a family completely different from the Smallwoods.

By the end of that week, Richard had a plan. It was an ideal set-up. Jacksonville had been in the news off and on for years because of punk vandals who would throw rocks and shoot guns at the cars of travelers on I-295. They had caught one kid shooting a .22 from the pedestrian overpass. It was an easy set up.

On the particular day of his death, Lou Barrymore made it even easier. He worked late enough so that the five o'clock rush-hour traffic was over, but it was still daylight. Richard Smallwood had his father's pickup truck. He followed the lawyer west on I-10 and then passed him at the intersection with I-295.

As his plan took shape, he was actually amused. When he passed Barrymore, he honked his horn, although it was not necessary. Then he waved at his would-be victim before flooring the pickup to get way ahead.

Several miles later, near the pedestrian overpass, he practically slammed on the brakes and pulled to the shoulder of the road. He turned off the ignition to stop the vibration of the idling truck. Without hesitation, he slid open the back of the truck cab window, which had been an "extra" when the pickup had come off the assembly line.

In another fluid motion, he grasped the 7 mm magnum bolt action deer rifle equipped with a cheap but adequate scope. It was a high-powered rifle that Richard had stolen out of another pickup when somebody had stupidly left the cab open while running into a Quick Mart convenience store for a pack of cigarettes. The rifle had been in plain view, ready for the taking, in a gun rack in front of the back window.

Now Richard had the rifle, which he pushed through the back window as soon as he had squirmed around 180 degrees. Almost as soon as the rifle was shouldered, the killer could see Barrymore's car in the scope. As the distance closed, he could see Barrymore in the cross-hairs and heard the expected explosion.

Almost simultaneously, Barrymore's car swerved to the left at sixty-five miles per hour; crossed the median and the southbound traffic lanes; then rammed a substantial pine tree thirty yards beyond the shoulder.

Before that moment Richard had never been sure that his plan would work. As he turned the ignition key, he knew for sure it had worked. He put the pickup in gear and drove north.

From the rear-view mirror, he witnessed the forming of a traffic jam as would-be helpers pulled to the shoulders of I-295.

———

As it turned out, the deposition that he had feared so much was not so bad. When it was over, he figured it had really been his father who scared him. After his wreck on the day of his deposition, being scared would never again be a problem for Richard.

That did not mean that he wanted to die. On the contrary, he wanted to live. That's why he fled the hospital. And that's why he decided to meet Rick Taggart personally.

———

Rick Taggart was miserable. It was the lawyers who made him miserable, and there were a bunch of lawyers paying attention to him.

Lawyers can make anybody miserable, and that's why lawyers are constantly under fire. They do work for little people against those who are otherwise insulated from attack. Good lawyers can even up the playing field between tough businessmen and the regular folks.

It's not only mobsters who lawyers persecute. Doctors, politicians and big corporations don't like it when they're sued by lawyers. Held accountable by lawyers.

Rick Taggart did not like it either.

Before the lawyers, things had always worked out in the past. He had worked it out himself whenever his urges had become indiscretions. But not now. Not since the lawyers had been involved in his life.

First, it was Bill Forrester and Elizabeth Kelley. Then his own lawyers turned on him.

His own lawyers, supplied by the hospital, started out on his side. They said they believed him, a well-respected psychologist, not Crazy Cora. Now they were acting like he was infected with the plague. Now they only talked settlement and damage control.

Because of those damn lawyers, the Department of Professional Regulation and its investigators were getting involved. He was afraid that the prosecuting lawyers from the State Attorney's Office would turn on him next. That would be the worst. He could go to jail because Cora Smallwood and the lawyers would not leave things alone.

When he learned that Forrester and Kelley had turned down the settlement offer, Rick Taggart knew that he was being persecuted because the lawyers were greedy sons of bitches.

As if all that were not enough, his wife had hired her lawyers for a divorce. They would not leave him alone either. Laura Griffin did not do family law, so Taggart had to hire another lawyer who would drain his assets at two to four hundred dollars per hour.

To make matters worse, he was paying $1,000 a month for an apartment because his wife had been given the house by the divorce judge—another lawyer.

It was no wonder Rick Taggart was bitter when he opened the apartment door to a stranger. Without being asked to, the stranger walked in. Extended his right hand and said, "You're Cora's doctor. I'm her brother, Richard Smallwood."

Rick grasped Richard's extended hand out of habit. It did not dawn on him that both he and the stranger shared the same name and both had shared Cora.

Almost immediately, Rick was frightened. He remembered the news reports and knew that the stranger was wanted for the killing of one of the lawyers in the case in which he was the main character.

He had still not opened his mouth when Richard sat down and said, "We have the same problem."

Rick said, "What do you mean?"

"Lawyers. We both got a problem with lawyers. The same lawyers."

"Is that why you killed Lou Barrymore?"

"I only meant to scare him," was Richard's excuse.

"Just tried to scare him," the psychologist repeated as though conducting a therapeutic conversation with a patient.

"Yeah, and now I want to scare that woman lawyer who's after us both."

"You want to scare Elizabeth Kelley," he repeated in his own words.

"Yeah. It could do us both some good."

This time the psychologist did not repeat. He mused for a moment before speaking. He thought what a pain in the ass lawyers are. His wife's lawyers. Cora's lawyers. Elizabeth Kelley, in particular.

"How?" he finally asked.

"How what?"

"How would it do us any good?"

"Are you kidding? It's her who's pushing this whole thing. Her with Cora's help."

"So Cora would be next?"

"Not necessarily. Usually Cora will do what I tell her. She's probably told you that. She could settle this case, and everybody'd be off your ass and off my ass."

Rick knew he had more problems than all the lawyers put together. He was conversing with a sociopath who needed more therapy than Cora ever did. There was nothing to do but keep talking while he planned a way to get rid of the uninvited guest. Unfortunately, unlike Bill Forrester, he was not an "armed citizen," and the criminal probably had a gun.

"What do you have in mind?" Rick asked.

Richard did not answer. Instead, he asked questions. "When's Cora's and your trial? A month away?"

"More than two months."

"She going to have some more depositions?"

"Probably. Not mine. It's been taken."

"Mine too. How about court hearings?"

"Probably."

"Your lawyers tell you when they're going to be?"

"Sometimes. Not always."

"But you got a right to know. Right?"

"I guess."

Now, the high school dropout was ready to share his plan with Cora's psychologist.

"That bitch is unpredictable," Richard said. "I've tried to follow her. Never can figure out where she's going to go. If I knew where she was going to go at a certain time, I could do something about her."

"Which bitch?"

"Cora's lawyer."

"I thought you said you only wanted to scare her."

Ignoring what Taggart had said, Richard gave instructions. "Call your lawyers and find out what's scheduled. You tell me, and I'll follow up from there."

The psychologist knew that there was no need to argue. His visitor was psychotic. Putting him off was the best he was going to be able to do. Sure, he wanted Elizabeth Kelley out of his life, but there was no urge to see her dead. Being involved in a killing would only add to his problems when the nut in his apartment eventually got caught.

"What happens if I don't like your plan?" Taggart asked.

"You got a better plan?"

"I haven't given it any thought one way or the other. I just don't like your plan."

"If you ain't got a plan, you gotta go along with my plan." Taggart didn't say anything, so Richard kept talking. "I ain't believing you don't want to go along with this. Is that what you're telling me?"

Richard was calm, but Taggart wasn't. There was no way to reason with the psychotic. He decided to take a control approach.

"Mr. Smallwood, you have to leave now!"

"I ain't leaving."

With that, Richard confirmed Rick's worst fears as he drew the .38 caliber pistol that had been recently stolen from the Miss Q Lounge. He didn't point it at Rick. He was simply, calmly making his point. He didn't raise his voice.

Richard said, "You gotta be part of my plan. Otherwise, there ain't nothing to keep you on my side. I planned both sides of this before I came here. Either you have to be on my side, or not."

It was obvious what "not" meant, and Rick should've played along. The smart thing would've been to go along or act like he was going along. But he was scared, and scared people do dumb things.

Taggart said, "I don't want to help—" He did not have a chance to finish the sentence. He did not have a chance to say, "But I'll call the lawyers and find out what the schedule of things are."

Calmly, Richard Smallwood raised the pistol without saying anything. He did not take aim. Just pulled the trigger and watched the man who had caused all his problems get lifted off his feet and then crumple to the floor.

As at the hospital, he did not run from the apartment. He just walked out and casually got into the car he had purchased two days after leaving Shands. Ninety-nine dollars down: instant financing: and monthly payments.

Not one of Taggart's neighbors opened an apartment door to investigate the source of the explosion when the .38 caliber bullet exited the barrel of the pistol.

In less than an hour, Richard was in familiar territory. First, he drove by Cora's. Then he was at the house he had called home for most of his boyhood. Most of his life. It was the first time in a while. He had avoided Starke since leaving the hospital because he expected that the police would expect him there.

In fact, the Jacksonville Police had visited his mother on the morning following the report from the bartender that he had stolen money and a pistol. The Starke Police had agreed to keep an eye on the place in case Richard showed up. Their patrols were less frequent as the days passed.

Richard did not bother to knock, but the door was locked. With little effort, he entered through the window to his old bedroom. He walked directly from there to the place where his mother had spent so many evenings and nights. As anticipated, the television in the little living room was blaring.

Mrs. Smallwood didn't seem surprised to see her son. She was weary but not surprised.

Over the years she was often weary. Weary of an abusive husband, an abused daughter, and an uncontrollable son. Regina would have been a bright spot in her weary life, but she left young and had little contact with the Smallwood family.

Florence Smallwood did not put out her arms to hug her son, whom she had not seen for weeks. Her son made no effort to hug her either.

"The police have been here," she said as she snuffed out a cigarette.

"I'd have imagined that."

She turned her attention back to the TV.

"This is all Cora's fault," Richard said. "I tried to help her. If she wouldn't have brought that lawsuit, everything would be okay. Daddy'd be alive."

His mother did not answer.

"I tried to work something out with the psychologist too," he said.

Mrs. Smallwood said, "I know. It was on TV earlier."

"What was on TV?" Richard asked the question with no real emotion, but he was curious.

"They said you shot him like you did the lawyer. They're looking for you. You're driving a white car, aren't you?"

"They said I was driving a white car? If I shot him like you said I did, how'd anybody know I talked to the dead bastard?"

The mother did not answer the question while she lit a fresh cigarette. After blowing out the smoke, she said, "You better leave. I expect they'll be checking over here directly."

"I went by Cora's. Where's she gone?"

"She's moved. Regina's helping her out until her case is over."

"She move in with Regina?" he asked.

"No."

Richard left the living room and went into his bedroom. He took a few clothes and stuffed them in a pillowcase. Before coming out, he looked in the back of his closet, and it wasn't there. The rifle he had used against Barrymore was missing.

He walked into the living room and stood in front of the TV. Ms. Smallwood said nothing. He pushed the button to make the TV go off.

"Would you mind putting that back on?" she asked.

"Where's the gun? Where's the rifle?"

"The police came by here the same day you were on TV the first time. I told them I had never seen it before. They took it with them."

She used both hands to push herself up from the couch. Walked slowly into the kitchen, opened the refrigerator, and poured some sweet iced tea into a glass. Walked the few steps back to the living room and toward the television. She was going to turn it on.

The lanky man had stood in one place all the while his mother had gone to the kitchen and returned. As she went around him, he said calmly, "You better give me your keys. You said they're looking for my car."

"I won't have nothing to drive if I do that," she replied. "Besides, I suspect that car is stolen or something."

She bent down to turn the TV back on. Then the son did what he had seen his father do so many times over the years. He hauled off and slapped her across her left cheek with his right hand.

That got her attention, all right, and knocked her back off balance. The tea sloshed out of the glass and onto the floor as she raised her hands to her face.

Crying, she whimpered, "Richard...."

"I said, give me your keys."

At the same time, he slammed his right fist into her stomach. The old lady doubled over and the remaining part of the tea, glass and all, crashed to the floor. She grabbed her stomach as she was falling and crumpled up into a heap. Then she vomited uncontrollably.

"Where's the keys?" His voice was loud, but it was not emotional.

Florence Smallwood couldn't hear her son. She couldn't talk. When she tried to catch her breath, she could taste the vomit. Her mind was whirling, and she wanted to sob as she passed out.

Richard leaned down and turned his unconscious mother over on her back. She vomited again.

The next morning, a Starke policeman patrolling the area noticed the white car in the driveway. It was just past seven when he entered the house and found Florence Smallwood still on her back, the way Richard had left her.

Rescue declared her dead, and the autopsy confirmed that she had drowned by the inhaled aspirant.

Richard was nowhere to be found. Nor was his mother's car. Nor her purse.

CHAPTER 26

WHEN YOU RETURN FROM a trip, an adventure, like Africa, you want to talk to people. You want to tell people about what you've seen and experienced. Forrester had been thwarted in his efforts to do just that.

Customs had fouled him up; his children were not home; and nobody was at the office when he finally got there. Maybe, he thought, he should have called and told them he was coming.

When Rosa got to the office the next morning, there was no problem figuring out that he had been there. Piles of incoming mail and pleadings and other legal documents had been read and shifted to her. There was enough dictation to keep her busy for days. She knew more would be coming while she tried to catch up.

Rosa was undaunted. She had been through it before. It was always like this after his adventures—or after a two week trial.

"May I get you a cup of coffee?"

Rosa looked up and saw her smiling boss, who didn't like to be called "boss," standing in the doorway to her small office. She smiled back.

"No, thank you. But if you want some, I've already made a pot."

"Any disasters while I was gone?" he asked, hoping for the right answer.

"None that Ms. Kelley couldn't handle. Actually, everything's been pretty calm around here, except the Smallwood thing. Maybe you haven't heard about Cora Smallwood's brother."

"I could hardly sleep last night thinking about it. I've read what's in the papers and Dorothy told me a little."

"I know Ms. Kelley hopes they find him. Everybody's pretty concerned."

Forrester changed the subject. "Have you heard from my children? Is everything okay with them? I tried to call them at least a dozen times last night but only got the voicemail."

"Nobody knew when you were going to be home. I got a call from Karen yesterday afternoon. She was asking about when to expect you. I told her I didn't know. She told me that she was taking the girls to her parents' house in North Carolina for a week. Do you want me to try to get them on the phone?"

"If they left in the afternoon, I'm sure they would have stayed at a hotel somewhere on I-95 or I-26. How about trying off and on during the day to reach them?" he instructed.

"Sure."

Forrester disappeared from the door; poured a cup of coffee; and made his way through the maze of paper in his office and into his chair. Almost immediately Rosa appeared.

She said, "I forgot to ask you how you're doing. We missed you around here. According to Mr. Malone, you had quite an eventful trip."

Finally, someone was interested. "He told you about the charge by the Cape buffalo?"

"He told me about Ingrid," Rosa answered, partially smiling.

He hardly finished reciting the details when other employees of Moran, Smith, Forrester & Dees started drifting in. Practically everybody, lawyers, secretaries and paralegals found an excuse to make it to his office. They would listen briefly while he told about the buffalo charge, but they were more interested in new-found love. Lee confessed that he had a bet with several people that Forrester would be married by the time he got home. Of course, he had gotten odds.

When things calmed down, he called Rosa on the intercom. "Where's Ms. Kelley?"

"Maybe she didn't want to talk to you about the European woman," Rosa responded lightheartedly.

"Really, where is she?"

"I really don't know. Maybe you should ask the Judge."

"Is she sick?"

"No, I don't think so. I think the Judge asked her to do something for him."

Everybody referred to Brett Moran as the "Judge" because he had served one term on the circuit bench. He decided not to run for reelection even though he probably would have been unopposed. Instead, he wanted to form a law firm with younger lawyers who had appeared before him and showed talent. At first the judge was considered the senior partner, but when it became obvious that the recruits could pull their own weight, the status of each was equal.

Forrester knocked on the door and waited the few seconds before being invited in.

"Good morning, Judge," Forrester started.

"Welcome back, Bill. I talked to Kevin Malone, and he told me you had an especially good time on this trip."

"It was different. You know I love Africa, and I will be going back again."

Like everybody else, the judge had a twinkle in his eye. He said, "I understand there was more to Africa than hunting this time. When will we get to meet the European bombshell?"

"So, Kevin told you, and you're the one who told everybody else in the firm about Ingrid."

The judge avoided the question. He said, "So her name's Ingrid."

"Don't plan to meet her any time soon." With that, Forrester changed the subject. "Judge, they tell me Elizabeth Kelley isn't coming in today."

"True."

"Something wrong?"

"Probably not. I guess you heard about the media putting our Ms. Kelley's face all over the television and the newspapers. It has something to do with your client's brother."

"I read about it yesterday."

"Well, the police suggested to Wayne Milton, who in turn suggested to me, that she ought not to be in an obvious place until they catch the Smallwood boy."

"So, you sent her on vacation?"

"You know better than that," the Judge replied in a less than pleasant voice. "She's staying with a friend and taking all of the out-of-town depositions for a while. She comes in from time to time, but nothing regular."

Though he didn't have the right, Bill felt a tinge of jealousy. Could the "friend" be the young Assistant State Attorney?

"How about the Smallwood trial? Is she preparing for it?" Forrester asked.

"I'm sure she is. I attended a hearing the other day in her stead and your absence. They were talking about a continuance based on the circumstances."

"Was it continued?"

"Not yet. The judge wants to have another hearing. You know, Bill, the trial will be a surefire sideshow for the media."

Forrester said, "I've thought about that since yesterday. None of this has helped us any. It's going to be harder to expose Taggart as the creep that he is. Now that he's a wounded man, they'll play it for all the sympathy they can get."

"That's going to be a problem, I agree," the Judge said.

"I guess that's as good as any excuse for them to try to delay the trial."

"It's more than an excuse, Bill. That Smallwood kid is dangerous and a menace."

By evening, Forrester felt that he was back into his routine. He was fairly content. He had had a chance to talk to his children who at least acted like they missed him.

It was around eight o'clock, and everybody had left the office except him. He had no thoughts of leaving for several hours more. That's when he had that funny feeling you get when somebody's looking at you. He lifted his head over a pile of papers that Rosa would be filing the next day.

"Good evening, Mr. Forrester."

His heart leaped as he heard the familiar voice from the familiar face. There she was standing in the doorway. Neat, prim, appropriately and professionally dressed. The wonderfully attractive woman.

He wanted to rush over and put his arms around her. Instead, he awkwardly stood up behind his desk.

"Liz, how are you? I really wasn't expecting you tonight."

She smiled.

"The Judge tells me you are staying with Wayne Milton, and that I shouldn't expect to see you around here for a while."

"He told you I'm staying with Wayne Milton?"

"Well…no, he said you were staying with friends. I just thought…"

"I thought I told you that Wayne and I are no longer an item." Her mind reeled back to the night that Wayne Milton grabbed her by the arm and demanded to know why she had not come directly home from the dinner party.

"I guess you did say that. I'm sorry to have assumed."

"No problem," Liz said. "I thought I would pop in and do a little paperwork. Besides, I heard you had shown up at the office."

For thirty minutes, at least, they were like old friends. He told her about Africa, and she told him about Smallwood. Neither mentioned Ingrid.

Blaming it on jet lag, Forrester decided to call it a night. "Liz, have you eaten?"

"No, and I would love to if you promise we can have drinks at the River House afterward."

She had never acted so familiar, and it excited him. "Agreed," he said.

"Why don't we meet at Sarnelli's, if you're in the mood for Italian? It's only a few blocks from the River House."

———

Liz left the building first while Forrester made dinner reservations. Bill grabbed a briefcase full of papers before turning out the lights and setting the alarm. As was his habit, he exited; locked the door; and proceeded around the corner of the building with his hand gripping the small .22 mag nestled in his pocket.

Just as he rounded the building, the automatic arm of the parking lot gate raised, and Liz drove through the opening. He got into his Suburban and watched her turn left, then right onto the road that would eventually lead to the interstate; then the exit for Sarnelli's. Forrester would be driving the same route.

He was excited that she had been so receptive. More excited that she had suggested drinks at his favorite watering hole. Maybe that was the reason he paid no particular attention to the older model Toyota Prius that pulled from the curbside parking space.

By the time Forrester left the parking lot and took the appropriate turns, he was less than a block behind the Prius. Could see Liz's taillights further ahead. As he thought about her, his pulse was beating more rapidly than before.

Liz's taillights were more clearly visible when the Prius switched from her lane to the right-hand lane. Forrester didn't have to drive any faster. He was closing the gap between the cars as her brake lights signaled that she would be caught by the traffic light that changed from green to amber to red.

Now Liz came to a complete stop in the left-hand lane. Forrester still had paid no particular attention to the Prius that was pulling up in the right lane beside her.

"What the hell is that?" Bill exclaimed out loud. He could see a hand extended from the driver's side of the Prius. Was somebody asking for directions? No.

The gap between Bill's car and those stopped in front of him continued to close. Now he could see more clearly. The extended hand held a pistol that was pointed toward Liz.

No hesitation. Forrester slammed the accelerator to the floor of the Suburban.

Wham!

There was a jolt, and he could feel the seat belt tighten against his chest as he rammed the Prius through the intersection. At the same time, he heard a "pop" and saw a flash.

The Prius crashed into a telephone pole with the Suburban still attached.

Bill threw open the door to make his move to get out but was yanked back by the seat belt. He felt tangled in the airbag. He fumbled with the seatbelt button and was finally able to free himself at the same moment he saw the door of the Toyota open. A figure was scurrying to get out.

Without thinking, Forrester's hand went back into his pocket, where he retrieved the small .22 magnum that he had hoped he would never have to use. The younger man, holding his left arm with his right hand, turned to run as Forrester reached him while extending the pistol against the body—the body of Richard Smallwood.

"You move an inch, and I'll blow your guts out! Do it!"

"What the hell are you doing?" the thin, lanky driver of the Prius asked in a voice that was serious.

"Where's the gun?" Forrester demanded.

"I don't know what you're talking about. My arm's broke."

Without protestation, Richard Smallwood laid down on the pavement. He was on his right side with his right hand continuing to cradle the left arm.

"Liz!" Forrester yelled as he continued to point the small pistol at his client's brother.

Liz stood beside the open door of her Volvo. "I called 911 on my cell."

"Are you all right?" he asked in an excited voice that could have been heard a block away.

"I heard him shoot. He missed me. What about you?"

Now Forrester started shaking as the adrenaline rush was taking its effect. "I'm okay." He was almost inaudible. "Where's his gun?"

"I think he dropped it when you hit him with your car. I'll try to find it," she volunteered.

"Why don't you just stay where you are," Forrester directed with a harsher tone than was necessary.

As a mob began to gather, Forrester was aware of the siren and blue lights. Within minutes North Florida's most infamous criminal was in custody. An hour later the detective told the lawyers they could leave. The police would continue to try to find whoever it was that had picked up the missing pistol.

"He must have lost the pistol when his arm slammed against the metal frame of the door when I rear-ended him," Forrester theorized. "He took a pretty good blow. His arm's broken. You may want to take a picture of the bruises to confirm that it was out the window when I hit him."

"It's not that we don't believe you, but the pistol would be a good piece of evidence," the detective assured him. "Without the weapon, it might be hard to convince a jury that he not only missed the lady, but also her car. That's a pretty big target."

Forrester spit out the words. "Then convict him of killing his mother. Convict him of shooting Richard Taggart. Convict him of killing Lou Barrymore."

"It'll be up to the State Attorneys from here. You've done your job."

―――――――

"Are you still hungry?"

Liz didn't reply. She took his face in both of her hands and gently pulled him toward her. There they were in the middle of Bay Street, but he did not resist. The kisses that the reporters caught on film were for more than just mere appreciation.

CHAPTER 27

THE ARREST OF RICHARD Smallwood made headlines on all local channels as well as the *Florida Times-Union*. There were multiple articles. On a separate page was a picture of Bill Forrester and Elizabeth Kelley. She was kissing him like he was a hero soldier returning from the wars. All the articles made Kelley seem greater than life. After all, she was the one who had cracked the case of the murder of Lou Barrymore.

The paper let the readers know that Richard would also be charged with the death of his mother and the shooting of Rick Taggart, psychologist. It was obvious to the writer that the stalking of Elizabeth Kelley was in retaliation.

The articles only alluded to the lawsuit against the hospital and Rick Taggart. The reporters hadn't had time to thumb through all of the court files open to the public. Because Cora was a victim, her name was not mentioned.

The lawyers figured that there would be multiple follow-up articles. The coverage would last for days. Articles written about the civil lawsuit would always refer back to the crimes that resulted. Articles about the criminal prosecution of Richard Smallwood would refer back to Cora's case against the hospital and Rick Taggart.

———

Bill's former wife showed the newspaper articles to the children. When Deborah called her father the day after the heroics with Richard Smallwood, she was genuinely concerned. She mostly wanted to make certain that he was safe and unharmed. If she was curious about Liz, she didn't let on.

The ten-year-old, Jane, was another story.

"Daddy, are you in love?" Jane asked.

"Probably, but don't tell your mother." He was teasing.

"Mommy already knows." Jane was serious. "She wants to know when you're going to get married."

"Tell her she'll be the third to know, but I wouldn't hold my breath."

"Will you tell me?"

"Jane, honey, your daddy has no intentions of getting married. If I ever do, before I ask the question, I'll talk to you first. Is that okay?"

Jane seemed relieved.

The people in his professional life saw it differently. Some were excited that a perfect couple had emerged from among them. Others were jealous because Ms. Kelley would be getting special attention. Both Liz and Bill knew the rules. Office liaisons lead to trouble and special problems. The Judge waited a couple of days before asking his partner.

"I have no intentions one way or the other right now," Forrester said.

"I understand, Bill, but you know that this sort of thing can disrupt the office."

"I know."

The Judge continued. "We may believe that nepotism is okay; but workplace romances create a different problem altogether."

Was he concerned? Yes. But the Judge was not pressing. Was actually easygoing. Bill knew the score. He had been attracted to Elizabeth Kelley before the firm ever hired her. He had grown solidly fond of her and had resisted romantic overtures for the better part of three years. The circumstances of that one particular night were different.

He mused that in less than one month, he had experienced two life-threatening situations. Each had created the ideal setting for romance. The romance with Ingrid could go nowhere. On the other hand, things could happen with Liz, if she wanted it and if he was so inclined.

Bill told the Judge, "She and I haven't really talked about it yet. I'll have my girls for the next couple of weeks. Let's just see what happens."

"I'm not going to tell you what to do, Bill," the judge said. "If you want to talk about it, just let me know."

"No matter what, Liz is helping me with some important cases. I don't know what I'd do if I lost her right now."

The judge responded with a pleasant smile. "Then do what you can not to lose her."

———

Two weeks after Richard Smallwood had been arrested, Liz came to the kitchen where Bill was eating lunch. It was just past two o'clock.

"Cora Smallwood is in the conference room."

"I didn't know she had an appointment," Bill responded.

"She didn't. She just came in and asked for me. She's not with her sister. She said she caught the bus up here and walked from the bus station."

"I really don't have time to talk to her right now. You handle whatever it is."

"She wants to know what the last settlement offer is."

"Why?"

"She says she wants to settle her case."

"You serious? All we have to do is hold off, and the settlement offer will get a lot higher. If we find a couple of witnesses, a jury will give us more than they'll ever offer."

Liz had Bill's attention.

She continued, "You won't believe why she wants to settle."

"She wants us out of her life because of her brother?"

"No. She actually likes us. As weird as things have gotten, it doesn't seem to bother her. She and I have had that conversation."

"So, tell me. Why does she want to settle?"

"She says she wants to have some money to hire her brother a good lawyer. She talked to him, and he's convinced that the Public Defender will do a lousy job."

"That's bull. With all the charges he has against him, a Public Defender will do as good or better than anybody he could hire off the street. In fact, Assistant PD Don Register is the lawyer I would want to hire if I were charged with murder. He's truly dedicated and a heck of a good lawyer."

"Maybe you should talk to her."

Bill stashed what was left of his leftovers into the refrigerator. He put on his coat and straightened his tie before entering the conference room. Cora was sitting there quietly.

She had gained a lot of weight since the first time he saw her. Her hair was oily and stringy. She was dressed in one of those pull-over muumuus that needed to be washed. It would never be attractive on her, but it could be clean. She smelled as though she hadn't bathed in a long while.

Cora looked at him and didn't say anything. Then she looked down at the tips of her fingers, where her fingernails had been chewed beyond the quick.

Forrester spoke first. "Hello, Ms. Smallwood. Ms. Kelley tells me that you've been talking to your brother."

She did not look up. She nodded.

"I guess he's pretty mad at us for getting him arrested."

"No. He doesn't seem mad at anybody."

"But he thinks you ought to settle your case."

"Yes. So do I," she said almost inaudibly.

"Have you talked about this with your sister, Ms. Baker?"

In a soft voice, Cora said, "I hate Regina. I've always hated Regina."

"Don't you think you ought to at least talk to her before you make a decision to settle?"

She shook her head.

Cora Smallwood was the client, not her sister. Forrester knew his bounds and knew his responsibilities. The client employs the lawyer, not vice versa. It was Cora who had the right to take the case to trial. She could also settle at any stage and could require her lawyer to demand settlement.

However, the lawyer has a right, if not a responsibility, to let the client know his thoughts; and let her know if he thinks she's making a mistake. He knew Cora was making a mistake if the purpose of the lawsuit was to get the most money possible. Settlement would also be a mistake if the purpose was to punish the hospital and to punish Rick Taggart.

Cora stood her ground for the most part. She did finally agree to give them two days to do their best to negotiate a better deal. She also agreed that they could talk to the sister that she hated.

———

Richard Smallwood had called his sister from the telephone that he had access to once a day in the Duval County Jail. He didn't reach her the first time he tried on the night he was arrested. He had no desire for her to fire the lawyer that had assisted in his arrest. That would take hate—an emotion he didn't possess.

By the time brother talked to sister, he had already appeared at his bond hearing. No bail had been set. There would be no bail for a person accused of multiple murders.

At the same hearing, the Public Defender's Office had been appointed to represent the young man charged.

It was a shot in the dark. Every day Richard had dialed his home phone, collect. He knew his mother wouldn't answer, but Cora finally did.

"Hello, Cora. This is Richard. I'm in jail."

In a soft voice, Cora responded, "I know."

"I have been arrested."

Still soft, "I know."

"I need your help. You're the only one who can help me. You know Regina hates me just like she hates you."

Cora did not respond, and there was a pause.

Then Richard said, "Cora, you know I always loved you. Regina left us, and she never loved you. Now they tell me Mamma's dead, and I've been charged with killing her. You know I wouldn't never hurt Mamma."

Cora responded softly, "I know."

"I've got to have your help. I need a real lawyer. A Public Defender won't do me no good, and that's who has been appointed to me. He ain't even come to see me at the jail."

Another pause. He continued. "You can hire me a lawyer. I need for you to hire me a lawyer. You know lawyers are expensive, and I don't have no money."

Cora responded softly, "I know."

"I know that you've been offered money to settle your case. Think about it, Cora—if it wasn't for your case, I wouldn't be in here."

"I know."

"Daddy's dead because of you. He couldn't take it, and that's why he shot his self."

"I know."

"That must be why Mamma's dead, too. I didn't kill her. Somebody with your case probably did."

He waited for Cora to respond. She finally did. She said softly, "I know."

"Cora, I love you. We are the only people left in our family. Regina's not part of the family. You gotta help me get out of here. You gotta get me a good lawyer."

"How can I help?" Cora was still quiet and soft-spoken.

"Make the lawyers settle your case. You're gonna get plenty of money from the case. I know they've offered money. If you settle the case, you can help me hire a lawyer and have money left over."

The conversation went on from there, even though Cora already felt guilty. She was guilty for the deaths of all involved. It was her fault, not her brother's.

It was her fault that she had let her father touch her; and she only let her brother touch her because he loved her. She knew it was all her fault.

It was also her lawsuit. She understood her rights, and she could tell the lawyers to settle the case. They would have to do what she told them.

She agreed to help. That's why she showed up at the office alone and without an appointment.

Calling Regina didn't help a bit. She insisted that there was nothing she could do. Richard always had the ability to control Cora, and Regina was tired of beating her head against the proverbial wall.

"They should pay," Regina concluded. "I hope you can convince Cora to change her mind. I doubt you'll have any luck."

"Cora deserves more," Liz said. "She was abused as a child at the hands of your family."

"Don't remind me."

"It's just so frustrating. Because of the abuse at an early age, your sister was in the hospital, where she was abused by the people who were supposed to help her."

"They should pay, I know. There's just nothing that I can do to help you, Ms. Kelley."

"So be it. We'll get the best settlement we can under the circumstances. They've offered fifty thousand dollars. Mr. Forrester will be in touch with the other lawyers."

———

Forrester called the hospital's lawyer first. Fred Boseman had been with the case all along and had the ear of the insurance company. Both lawyers knew the routine. They would beat around the bush before getting to the point.

"Do you think you have a conflict of interest, Bill?" Boseman asked.

"Where is the conflict?"

"I don't know. It just seems that you may be a crucial witness of some sort. After all, your client's brother shot my client, and you in turn were instrumental in his arrest."

"So what?" Forrester was getting a little perturbed and was off track as far as taking the conversation where he wanted it. "I've researched the issue. I don't think you're going to be calling me as a witness, and I don't think there's any conflict. You already took his deposition, so you can read it at trial if you want. I don't believe that he'll be given the chance to appear live, anyway."

Boseman let it drop. "So, what are you calling me about, Bill? If it's scheduling matters, why don't you just let your secretary call mine?"

Forrester said, "We're concerned that the judge is going to continue the Smallwood case. My client really doesn't want a continuance. She wants to get this over with in spite of her brother's worst effort."

Boseman said, "I can't imagine that we won't have a continuance. My client can't come to trial wounded."

"Save that for the judge. Maybe he'll believe you. It doesn't really matter what I think. Anyway, if you want to settle this case, now is the time to get it settled."

"We've offered you fifty thousand dollars."

"You know that's not nearly enough. Punitive damages will be several times that."

"How much are you thinking about?"

"I think we should get at least the policy limits. I'm doing this off the top of my head, but I think there's two million in limits. The umbrella policy provides another ten million. We're talking the underline policy."

"I don't remember the policy limits either," Boseman lied. "It doesn't really matter, you know they aren't about to offer that kind of money."

"They should. But she's not looking for that much if we can settle without a continuance. Anyway, tell your client we'll take five hundred thousand."

Without hesitation, Boseman said almost sarcastically, "Get serious."

"I am serious. What do you think the case is worth?"

"I haven't really thought about it lately. I know they aren't going to offer you that kind of money, and I'm not going to recommend it," Boseman replied.

"Find out what they'll offer. We aren't going to give the case away, but if it's going to settle, it should settle now."

"I'll see if I can talk to the adjuster. It'll probably take a few days before I can get back."

Forrester didn't have a few days. "If we're going to settle this thing, I want to settle it without spending a lot more money. We're spending money by buckets getting prepared for a trial that may continue." Forrester was trying to sound convincing and sure of himself.

Boseman recognized what was going on. Forrester had lost control of his client. Maybe not complete control, but he had definitely lost some control. If there was a time to settle, it would be now.

Boseman said, "I'll try to contact him today. If not, I'll be in touch in the morning."

It was now time for the conversation to take a 180-degree turn. The lawyers finished it by talking football and their predictions about the Florida Gators and the Florida State Seminoles.

Three prosecutors were assigned to put Richard Smallwood behind bars. The crimes had been committed in three different counties. Lou Barrymore had been shot and Elizabeth Kelley shot at in Duval County. The crime against Richard Taggart was in Alachua County, as was at least one grand theft auto from near Shands Hospital emergency room entrance. Bradford County was where he would be charged for robbing the Miss Q Lounge and bringing about the death of Florence Smallwood.

Since the arrest for the most recent crime was in Jacksonville, that's where the prisoner would stay for now. The prosecution would be conducted by Assistant State Attorney Lance Nichols.

He had some high-profile cases on his hands and he knew it. He also knew that none of the Smallwood cases would be a slam dunk. He concluded early on there were problems with all of the cases in all of the counties.

There were no witnesses to the death of Lou Barrymore, and Richard Smallwood was not about to confess. The ballistics report from the high-powered rifle had been inconclusive due to splintering when the bullet went through Barrymore's windshield.

The problem with attempted murder against Elizabeth Kelley was that the shot intended for her had not even hit her car. The pistol had been jarred from Richard's hand at the same time his arm was broken. To compound the problems, the gun had been stolen at the scene by one of the onlookers and had never been recovered.

Down in Bradford County, Florence Smallwood had been beaten up while nobody was around. The case against Richard for that crime was based on purely circumstantial evidence. As for the robbery at the Miss Q, Gloria was the only witness, and she wasn't all that willing to be tangled up in legal matters.

Of course, they had a good case against Richard for the shooting of Taggart. However, that case had sympathy. A brother was defending the honor of his sister. Taggart, as a victim, would not invoke sympathy from a jury. Besides, attempted murder and aggravated battery did not bring the sentence that Richard Smallwood deserved.

If all of the cases could be tried together, things might be easier. That would never occur.

Finally, there was one more obstacle, and that was the biggest problem. A part of Richard's brain had been removed. Maybe it had not been removed at the time he killed Barrymore, but that didn't necessarily matter. There was no question but that the defense would claim the client could not assist because of irrefutable brain damage.

The prosecutor knew that the defense would rely on insanity as well as other defenses consistent with the mental status of Cora's brother.

CHAPTER 28

FRED BOSEMAN DID NOT call Cora's lawyers the following day as promised. It wasn't really his fault. The insurance company's adjuster had been informed of the conversation but had not made an immediate decision. In turn, the adjuster had promised to get back with Boseman.

Forrester knew time was running out, but he didn't want to sound desperate. He didn't want to call Boseman and say, "I'll take the last offer." It irritated him that, no matter what, he would be settling the case for less than it was worth. He didn't have time to negotiate, but that was his client's fault.

The adjuster had asked Boseman's thoughts about settlement. He told the insurance person that the case could be disastrous. The demand was $500,000. Although that was not unreasonable, Boseman told the adjuster, "I believe they'll take a whole lot less."

When the adjuster finally got back with Boseman, he told him that he could offer up to $350,000. "Let's see what happens with that," the adjuster directed.

———

Cora had not called back, and Forrester had his marching orders to settle the case. No wonder he was relieved when Rosa told him that Fred Boseman was on the phone.

"I'm sorry I didn't get back with you yesterday. I had a tough time getting the company to offer anything more than they've already offered." That was Boseman's way of letting Forrester know that there was room to negotiate.

Boldly, Forrester told him, "You know we haven't demanded enough. I really don't have much wiggle room for negotiation beyond what I told you the other day. Did they offer the half million?"

"Not hardly. The company doesn't think the case is worth anything. They're more interested in the embarrassment to the hospital than anything else."

Forrester was aggressive. "So, you're telling me you don't have anything more to offer?"

"No. That's not what I'm saying."

"What are you saying?"

"They told me to offer you one hundred thousand to get rid of the case. Frankly, that's more authority than I thought they would give me."

Forrester had no room to negotiate. He had to take what he could get. It was frustrating to be put in such a predicament since the case had started developing so well.

"Get serious! My costs are almost that. She won't settle for free." Forrester's voice was controlled, and there was not a trace of satisfaction with the offer.

"Bill, they are serious. I told them you wouldn't take one hundred thousand, but what can I do?"

Here Boseman had authority to offer $350,000 but would earn major kudos if he could settle the case for less. He was as skillful at negotiations as anybody.

"Tell them to forget it." Forrester was bluffing again.

"Don't hang up on me, Bill. The only reason my client is interested in settling is because they want to stop the bleeding. They want to stop spending money on this case. Tell me what your client will really take."

"I already told you what she would take. A half-million." There was a pause before he continued the bluff. "Maybe if we could get the money within a couple of days, she would be willing to take three-fifty."

Forrester had said the magic number. With that, Boseman knew that there was plenty of playing room. It was his turn. "If I get authority for two hundred fifty thousand dollars, will you take it?"

"I bet you have authority for more than that already," Forrester said.

"I don't have authority for it." He continued to lie. "I think I may be able to get two-fifty, but I can't keep going to the well. If she's not going to take it, tell me. I don't want to go and ask them for two hundred fifty thousand dollars if that's not going to settle the case. I don't want to lose my credibility with the company."

"When you have the authority to offer two hundred and fifty, let me know. I'll take it to the client. I won't recommend it one way or the other. The case is worth more than that."

Boseman felt great. He had authority to settle the case for $350,000, and he believed it was worth a half a million up. Something was going on, and it really didn't matter to him what it was. He was confident he could settle the case for $250,000 but did not want to seem too eager. Show his hand. Maybe he could get it for a little less.

"I'll call you back this afternoon, after I've talked to the insurance people," the defense lawyer said.

———

"You weren't talking to somebody about the Smallwood case, were you?" Elizabeth Kelley had overheard the last part of the conversation from her mentor's doorway.

"Yeah, I was talking to Fred Boseman. He's playing cat and mouse, and it's frustrating because my hands are tied by the client."

"Maybe you're lucky he was being so coy. I've got good news. You should hold off taking any offers."

"Have you talked to Cora Smallwood? I've got to know. They're about to offer a quarter of a million dollars, and she told me to settle for fifty thousand dollars."

"I didn't talk to Cora, but I just got a call from the State Attorney's Office."

"And?"

"They are plea-bargaining big time, with Richard Smallwood's lawyer."

"So soon?"

"Maybe getting it over with quick will be good PR."

"Maybe."

"Before they offer a deal, they want to run it by the victims. They consider me one of his victims." By this time Liz had removed several files from a chair and was sitting in front of Forrester's desk.

She had mixed feelings. She was scared of Richard Smallwood. Since the very beginning, however, she wanted to take Cora's case to trial. Wanted a jury to determine how much it was worth.

She had a good chance to block any plea bargain negotiations if she wanted to. If she did, she knew that the civil case would be settled. On the other hand, she could take a lot of pressure off the State Attorney by cooperating and helping with the plea negotiations.

With her support, the prosecutor would get his headlines, and they would not be negative. He could tell the press that one of the victims would rather a deal be made than show up in court. Elizabeth Kelley would back him up even if Barrymore's family did not.

"What's the deal?" Forrester asked.

"Lance Nichols is afraid of an insanity defense. He may be right. Cora's brother is wicked. That's for sure. He may also be insane."

Forrester asked, "Do you know who's representing him?"

"The Public Defender's Office in Jacksonville. Lance said the Assistant PD is somebody named Dale Black."

"Dale Black. He's been a PD for years, and Dal's a good lawyer."

"That's what Lance said."

"Have they made an offer?"

"Not yet. Lance Nichols wanted to run it by me and the other people before he made the offer."

"And?"

"He's going to offer to waive the death penalty if Richard Smallwood will plead guilty straight up to one charge of first-degree murder and one charge of attempted murder. The other charges will be dropped. First, though, he wants to see what they're willing to take."

"What did you tell them?"

"I told him I would support him as long as he pleads guilty on at least one murder charge, first degree; and if his sentence will make certain that he stays in prison for at least twenty-five years."

"When are we going to know something?"

"They want the deal before his next appearance in Circuit Court. Lance wants to wrap it up immediately. Otherwise, he's going to go all the way."

Forrester thought for a minute. "This is awfully quick for a deal. He must have a lot more holes in the case than we thought."

"The big hole is the insanity defense. The papers make it all sound so simple. Apparently, it's not so open-and-shut."

"Are you for it, Liz, or do you just want to try our case?"

Liz's eyes watered. "We're lucky Cora didn't fire us immediately. I want to press this case. There are a lot of bad people. Richard Smallwood's not the only one who ruins lives."

"How about the case down in Starke? Our client's mother's death? And Taggart's shooting in Gainesville?"

"That's part of the whole package. One plea bargain for all the cases. The other State Attorneys have agreed."

———

When Boseman called, Forrester felt more secure. He had not been able to get in touch with Cora, but the only reason she had wanted to settle was to get money for her brother's lawyer. If the plea could be worked out with the Public Defender, that would not be necessary.

Boseman was upbeat, but Forrester was no longer so eager to conclude matters.

Of course, the defense lawyer had not been in touch with his client. Why should he have contacted them? He already had authority to settle the case for $350,000. When they hung up, he was confident that a deal could be struck for $100,000 less.

"I think I can get two hundred fifty thousand dollars if you will take it. It's more than I think the case is worth, but they want to get it over with."

Without hesitation, Forrester said, "I already asked her. She said whatever I recommend. I told her two hundred fifty thousand dollars is not enough."

Boseman's voice betrayed his frustration. Now he was going to have to offer more. The more he offered, the less impressed his client would be. His client would be even less impressed if he failed to offer all of his authority when the case could be settled for that amount.

"How much?"

"Maybe three hundred fifty thousand dollars."

Forrester was leaving his options open. With the way he phrased his words, he could see where Boseman was going. If the money was offered, he could say his client rejected it. He would always have the option of going back now for the $250,000. Mostly, he wanted time.

"I'll call you right back," Boseman said. "I'm going to call my client."

Forrester knew what that meant. The hospital would be offering the $350,000. He was even more resolved to thwart the settlement.

He told Rosa he was going to leave for the afternoon. He didn't want to talk to Boseman. He invited Elizabeth Kelley to drive with him to Starke to find Cora. With the help of Liz, he may be able to get more time to negotiate.

They hadn't got out of downtown when Forrester's cell rang. It was Rosa.

"Mr. Forrester, you have a phone call that you might find important."

Hands free, Forrester said, "I told you I didn't want to talk to Boseman. What else could be important?"

"Ms. Smallwood's on the phone."

"Oh."

"Would you like me to patch her through?"

"Please."

Within seconds a quiet voice was heard through the speaker phone. "Hello?"

"Hello. This is Bill Forrester. I have you on hands-free. Ms. Kelley is with me, and I'd like for her to hear whatever you have to say. Is that okay?"

"Yes."

"We were just heading your way. I'm glad you called. That will save us a trip to Starke."

"I'm not in Starke. I'm in Jacksonville," the quiet voice replied.

"Why are you in Jacksonville?"

"I was visiting my brother."

"I see."

There was no response on the other end. Finally, Forrester said, "Are you still there?"

"Yes."

"Is there something you needed to talk to me about?"

"Have you settled my case?"

"That's what we wanted to talk to you about. They've offered a lot more than they did before. I haven't accepted yet since you gave me extra time to negotiate."

"I don't think we should settle."

"You just said, 'Don't settle'?"

Her voice was so soft he was not sure if he had heard her right. He repeated, "You said, 'Don't settle'?"

"Unless you want to," Cora answered so softly, they could barely hear.

"No! No! Really, I think your case is worth more."

Forrester could hardly care less what had motivated his client to change her mind. He would not ask and take a chance of her flipping again.

Liz followed up. "Cora, this is Liz Kelley. As he said, I am here with Mr. Forrester. What made you change your mind?"

Forrester had not asked, but she feared not the consequences.

"Do you still think I should not settle?" Cora was vacillating.

"Oh, no! I mean yes. I think you should not settle. I was just curious." Liz realized she had asked a dumb question.

Forrester broke in. He wanted to stop the conversation. "I'll tell Mr. Boseman to forget it," he said.

"Okay," said the soft voice. Then she said, "I don't think he's guilty. He only tried to hurt Rick because Rick hurt me."

"Did your brother tell you that?"

Liz was asking the questions again. Forrester gave her a dirty look.

"No. Mr. Black, his lawyer, told me. He was visiting Richard at the jail. He said he was working for free. They wouldn't let me see Richard, but I got to see his lawyer. Then I called Regina."

"You called your sister?"

"Yes, before I called you. She wouldn't tell me what to do because she hates me and Richard. I just decided to do whatever you want me to do with my case. Is Mr. Black a good lawyer?"

Forrester jumped to answer. "One of the best. Your brother's got one of the best lawyers in the State. You can trust him to do a good job."

When the conversation with the client ended, the lawyers were flabbergasted. An amazing turn of events.

The phone rang again. Rosa said it was somebody from the newspaper to ask Liz questions about the plea bargain. Another call was patched through to the car phone.

The reporter asked, "Is it true that you don't care if the prosecutor drops the charges against Richard Smallwood?"

Of course, the question was out of context. But at least the lawyers knew that a deal had been made. With the deal, there would be no more reason for Cora to change her mind a second time.

It was four o'clock. No need to keep driving toward Starke, and there was a ton of work to do at the offices of Moran, Smith, Forrester & Dees.

Bill turned east onto Butler Boulevard. He said, "I want to make another call. After that, why don't we go to the beach?"

"What about work?" Liz was asking the question from the perspective of an associate. From the perspective of a woman, she knew the answer without asking.

"What about work?" he asked back as he kept on driving east.

This would be the first time he would spend the night at Liz's home in Ponte Vedra. He had that tingly feeling as he drove along the boulevard that would exit at the beach. Still, he was distracted because he couldn't stop thinking about the case.

The last thing Bill Forrester wanted in the case of *Cora Smallwood, Plaintiff, versus Richard Taggart, et al.,* was a continuance. Client control was a problem. He wanted to try the case, but the client could force him to settle whenever she wanted. He knew if the case was put off, it might never be tried.

Liz had a flair for numbers. She punched the right ones in for the opposing counsel. The receptionist answered.

"Jones, Knight, Boseman, Montgomery and Connors." It was a pleasant voice.

"I would like to speak with Fred Boseman," Forrester said. "Please tell him that Bill Forrester is calling."

The call was screened again by Boseman's secretary. After a brief wait, the defense lawyer answered. He was using his speaker phone, and it sounded like he was in a tunnel.

The first words out of Boseman's mouth were "I think I can get three hundred thousand dollars."

Boseman felt nauseous because he knew he had blown it when Forrester responded, "Forget it."

"What are you talking about? Are you trying to tell me it's really going to take three hundred fifty thousand dollars?"

Forrester tried to contain the glee in his voice. "That was earlier. All offers are rejected, and all demands are withdrawn. It looks like we're going to have to try this case, Fred."

Boseman didn't want to sound desperate. Still, he realized that he was about to lose the opportunity to settle the case within the authority given him by his insurance client. He chose his words carefully.

"Bill, I know I can get the three hundred fifty thousand dollars you've demanded. You've done a helluva job for a case that nobody would have ever taken. We'll settle and go on to another case where you can beat me up again."

"Don't try to stroke my ego. I note that you didn't say that you could offer the three hundred fifty thousand dollars. You said you could go back to the well and get it."

"You can count on it."

Forrester could tell what had happened. He knew the defense lawyer was in a bind like he had been in a bind earlier. Boseman had not offered the money he had the authority to offer. Of course, that had put Forrester in a bind since he had had directions to settle for whatever he could get. What would Boseman's insurance client do if it found out that the case could have been settled for $350,000 except their lawyer had played games and had lost that chance?

"It's too late, Fred. We might've accepted an offer this morning, but not now. We'll just settle it the old-fashioned way."

"You mean let the jury do the settling?"

"You got it."

Boseman was not amused. Now he would try another approach. Be a bully.

"You told me you would take three hundred fifty thousand dollars. I stepped out on a limb with my client to get it for you. Now you're saying no. This is bullshit, and you know it." Boseman was practically yelling.

Forrester was at his best. He was in charge and calm with a hint of glee in his voice as he rubbed salt in the wounds of his adversary.

"Fred, remember. Your client still hasn't offered the three hundred fifty thousand dollars. You can tell them we won't take it."

The crucial part of the conversation was the next part. The judge had already implied that he would continue the case because of the publicity. Since that hearing, one of the defendants had been shot and was recovering from a pretty bad gunshot wound. The wound coming from none other than the plaintiff's brother, who would be using the family relationship as a defense to the criminal charges.

Forrester did not want the trial continued. Unless there is some sort of special advantage to be obtained, the defense always wants to put off the case. A continuance is good for the defense if for no other reason than witnesses may die. Of course, another good reason to continue is to give the plaintiff one more chance to die before trial. Then there are no damages.

Forrester said, "I'll be filing a motion for continuance in the next day or two."

This took Boseman off guard. A lawyer's knee-jerk reaction is to always oppose the opponent. Although he had every intention to file his own motion to put off the trial, if Forrester was filing the same thing, maybe he should give it some more thought.

"What are your grounds for a continuance?"

"Frankly, Fred, I don't want y'all to bring Taggart into the court-room looking like the victim."

"He is a victim. This case shouldn't have been filed in the first place. Now you want to drag him and the hospital through the mud and a trial for the headlines. You ask for three hundred fifty thousand dollars and now you say no when I say I can get it for you. Obviously, you want a continuance to drag out the publicity. If Taggart's not a victim, the hospital sure as hell is."

The plaintiff's lawyer stayed the course. He said, "I want the jury to see Taggart for what he is. I want them to see him as a sleaze."

The phone conversation ended without pleasantries.

Liz had to ask. "You don't really want a continuance, do you?"

"Hell, no. But you need to file the motion tomorrow."

"Should I title it 'Plaintiff's Motion for Continuance' or plaintiff's motion titled 'Please Don't Throw Me in the Briar Patch'?"

———

Nobody ever really knows if a trial will be tried as scheduled. You cannot take a chance. Good lawyers will tell you that you can never be totally prepared. You just have to be as prepared as you can be.

When Boseman received the Plaintiff's Motion for Continuance, he called the defense lawyer for Rick Taggart.

Laura Griffin answered the phone talking. "Did you get Bill Forrester's Motion for Continuance?"

"Good morning to you too, Laura. Yes, I got it. That's the reason I'm calling."

She ignored the slight. "What do you make of it?" she asked.

"I've been giving it some thought. I've decided to keep the options open. I don't think I'll be filing a motion."

"I agree," she answered as though she had already given it a lot of thought.

"He says that he doesn't want your client, Taggart, to look like a victim in the courtroom. I'm not sure he's being straight."

"That seems like a pretty good reason from the plaintiff's standpoint."

"Yeah, but I know Forrester too well. It must be something else. You know his case is not bulletproof."

"I think he has a pretty good case against my client, if you want to know the truth," Taggart's lawyer said.

"But what good does that do him? He can nail your client but not get paid a dime. He has to prove that the hospital knew or should've known what our Mr. Taggart was doing. Otherwise, there's no insurance to pay the verdict."

"You think there's a good chance that the hospital will be found 'not guilty' if the jury finds my client 'guilty'?"

"I think there is a chance, and I think Forrester thinks that there's a chance. I don't think that the Smallwood case is a slam dunk for the plaintiff."

"So, what do you think the problem is? Why did he file the Motion for Continuance?"

"Laura, I don't think he's prepared. Forrester likes to be really prepared before he goes to trial. I think he doesn't have his witnesses in line, and he wants more time."

———

Judge Howard Coker was typical of many, if not most, of the judges these days. He had been a prosecutor right out of law school for ten years before being appointed to the County Court bench. Five years later, he was elevated by another appointment to the Circuit bench. Now he enjoyed the security of a public job. Benefits paid for; no overhead; and no worries about making payroll.

Judge Coker knew criminal law about as well as anybody. However, typical of much of the judiciary, he had no real personal experience in civil trial work. Had had never represented a client other than "the State."

After law school and until he became a judge, he had never taken the time to master the Civil Rules of Procedure. No reason to. He knew the Rules of Evidence and the Criminal Procedure Rules backwards and forwards. Evidence rules are mostly the same for both civil and criminal cases.

This judge was a dedicated and smart public servant. After taking the bench, he went out of his way to study civil law and procedure so that he was competent and comfortable as both a criminal and civil trial judge. In fact, he was the type of judge before whom both the plaintiff and defendant lawyers enjoyed practicing.

His experience trying jury trials as a lawyer facilitated his ability to control the courtroom and would assure a fair trial. If either side crossed him, there would be hell to pay.

Although Judge Coker didn't smile a lot, he was not brash. He was always prepared and was generally courteous to the lawyers.

In chambers the judge was first to speak. "I read the Motion for Continuance and am inclined to grant it. I suppose, Mr. Boseman, Ms. Griffin, the only reason neither of you filed the same motion was that it was unnecessary in light of Mr. Forrester's."

Boseman spoke for the defense. "Your Honor, we didn't file a Motion for Continuance because we don't believe that there should be a continuance. This case has long been set for trial and my clients would like to get it over with."

Griffin couldn't contain herself. "They are tired of the publicity."

The judge was oblivious to the tactics of the defense. Forrester knew that his adversaries had risen to the bait.

Forrester said, "We filed the motion, Your Honor, because my partner said you had suggested it at the last hearing and we wanted to get the matter over with one way or the other. We are surprised at Mr. Boseman's opposition to the motion since he apparently seemed to be in favor of it at the last hearing when no motion was pending."

Forrester was not making a legal argument. He didn't want to totally tip his hand to Boseman, but he wanted to give the judge every reason to deny the motion. Judge Coker did just that. The trial would be tried as previously scheduled. It would commence in forty-eight days.

CHAPTER 29

THE COURT'S ORDER, IN addition to setting the case for trial, also required witness disclosure. The expert witnesses, who would be allowed to state their opinions at trial, had long since been disclosed. The experts included doctors to testify about damages and standards of care; and hospital administrators to opine that GPH could not possibly be culpable for Taggart's behavior.

The "non-expert" witnesses would be limited to testimony about what they actually saw, touched, or heard. The judge ordered the parties to exchange lists of non-expert witnesses exactly twenty-one days before trial.

In an abundance of caution, each lawyer provided the name of every conceivable person who might testify. That would keep the other side working and keep their own options open. It didn't mean that everybody who was listed would testify, but if the person's name didn't appear on the list, there was no chance.

Boseman phoned Laura Griffin. He had just received the final list of witnesses. He recognized the names of most of them. It was the ones he didn't recognize who concerned him.

"Laura, have you received the witness list from Forrester in the Smallwood case?"

"I received it a couple of hours ago. I was going to call you later."

"Do you have any idea who Heather Maxwell and JoAnne Manchester are?"

"That's what I've been doing for the last couple of hours. I've been trying to find out who they are without calling Bill Forrester."

"Same here. I didn't call him yet either. I wanted to talk to you first. Do you know who they are?"

"I've never heard of them before today." Her voice sounded angry. "That son of a bitch Forrester, probably had their names all along."

"Who are they?" You could hear the irritation in Boseman's voice as he tired of his

co-counsel not answering the question simply.

With unmistakable sarcasm, she said, "My prince of a client tells me that he 'thinks' that they were former patients of the hospital. He says he 'might' have been involved in their treatment."

"Don't tell me...."

"He swears he's never touched them." After a pause, she added, "Of course, he says the same thing about Cora Smallwood."

"Great. This is swell." It was Boseman's turn to sound sarcastic.

Before the day was over, an investigator had been dispatched to contact the newly disclosed witnesses. Within twenty-four hours, he reported that JoAnne Manchester had exploded and said that she had no intention of testifying for anybody at trial. She told the investigator that she had told Forrester the same thing. Her good family name was at stake, and she did not appreciate becoming part of a "side show."

Boseman asked the investigator, "Do you think she means it? Do you think she will testify?"

"I think she does mean it. It's up to you whether or not you take her deposition. She says that if you do, she'll tell all and that her testimony will 'blow you out of court.' On the other hand, she said that if she is called to testify by the plaintiff, she would 'blow them out of the water' and swear that nothing ever happened."

The defense lawyers decided it would not be worth the risk. They would not take her deposition. If she testified at trial, they would use her hospital records against her and "her good name."

"Tell us about Heather. Heather...what's her name?" Laura Griffin was questioning the investigator now.

"I don't think you have to worry about her. The address they gave us was wrong."

"You couldn't find her?" She continued the inquiry.

"I found her. She's a temporary resident of the psychiatric wing of a hospital in Miami. According to what I found out, she should be there for at least another month. Won't the trial be over by then?"

———

The plaintiff's team of lawyers was having its own problems when they got the final list of witnesses. It only took Liz about a half hour to find out from Cora who R. David Gobel was. Before the day was over, Lee had driven to Starke and back and was reporting to the lawyers.

"He says he's in love with her, and she's in love with him," Lee reported. "They only met about two weeks ago, and they're talking about getting married."

"Before the trial?" Forrester had to ask.

"He says that's up to Cora."

"Doesn't he know that this could destroy the case?" Liz asked rhetorically.

"I didn't ask him that. I suspect it's the case that's the main attraction here," Lee answered.

"How did the other side find him?" Liz was full of questions.

Lee didn't know the answer to that question either. His good news was that it was reported that he had refused to give a statement to the defense investigator. The bad news was that he was not able to refuse the subpoena for trial.

After fielding dozens of questions, Lee started to leave. Liz called him back.

"I've got to know. What does he look like?"

Smiling in his own special way while at the same time shaking his head, Lee said, "He's probably five foot eight or nine. Maybe two hundred and thirty or two hundred and forty pounds. It looked like he hadn't shaved in a couple of days, and he smelled at least as bad as our client."

"They must make a beautiful couple," Forrester remarked.

Lee started to leave again, but Liz stopped him again.

"Anything more on Heather Maxwell? We put her on our witness list just in case. We gave the father's address."

"I still haven't found her," Lee informed.

"No leads?" Forrester snapped.

"As I told y'all before, I found her father in Alachua. Other than learning her last name from him, he was no help."

"That was before I went to Africa." Forrester sounded weary. "What have you done since then?"

"A lot. What do you want me to do? Report every dead end? I'm still trying." Lee was reacting to Forrester's unpleasant tone.

"So?"

"Some people in her home-town told me she's in Miami. That's a big city, but I am still trying to find her."

"With the trial starting in a few weeks." Forrester confirmed the obvious.

"I'll do my best, boss," Lee said while turning to leave for the third time.

"Thanks," Forrester mumbled. "But don't call me 'boss.'"

CHAPTER 30

THE PROSPECTIVE JURORS WERE sitting on pews in the rear of Courtroom 612 of the Duval County Courthouse. There were thirty-two of them along with a dozen other people, mostly reporters, sitting behind the little railing known as "the bar." Judge Coker entered through the door strategically placed behind the chair on his bench.

He looked larger than life in his robe. He looked even more imposing because the bench was situated on a platform at least a couple of feet higher than the rest of the floor.

The bailiff ordered, "Everyone rise!"

Everybody followed the instructions.

After becoming comfortable in his leather chair, His Honor said, "You may be seated."

Again, everybody followed suit—with the exception of the defense lawyers.

Then Forrester noticed. Neither of the defendants was present in the courtroom. Their lawyers were present, but they were conspicuously separated by several feet. Both were standing.

Judge Coker asked the perfunctory question, "Are the parties ready to proceed?"

Boseman stepped forward. "Your Honor!" He was using his trial voice. His words were deliberate and enunciated with preciseness. His delivery was loud enough for everybody in the courtroom to hear. He especially wanted those thirty-two special people in the back to hear.

The judge said, "Yes, Mr. Boseman."

"Your Honor, we wish to request that another desk or table be brought into the courtroom. The plaintiff has brought charges against my client as well as Ms. Griffin's. We had no choice in this matter, but we do not want to sit at the same table and thereby give the jury the impression that we are working together on this case. Ms. Griffin's client and mine are as different and unrelated as are our defenses. We should be treated separately and appear separately in the courtroom."

Forrester was on his feet. Unlike television law, nobody in Jacksonville would address a judge from a seated position. Forrester's face was flushed. Before the judge could respond to Boseman's speech, Forrester was making his presence known.

"Your Honor, this is outrageous. If Mr. Boseman had wanted to make this speech, he should have done it at the sidebar. He is deliberately trying to create prejudice favorable to the defense, and the plaintiff moves for a mistrial."

Now Judge Coker was crimson. In a brash, hard voice, he ordered the lawyers, "Come to the sidebar!"

The lawyers obeyed by traipsing up to the edge of the judge's bench.

As they stood out of earshot from all but the court reporter, Judge Coker continued, obviously angered. "What is the meaning of this? You know I won't tolerate speaking objections in my courtroom. These kind of matters will be taken up at the sidebar! Do I make myself clear?"

Boseman was quick to respond. "We were not making an objection in the true sense, Your Honor."

"I will not tolerate speeches in front of the jury, Mr. Boseman. The same is true for you, Mr. Forrester. If you have a motion for a mistrial, you will make it at the side-bar. Do you understand?"

"Yes, Your Honor, but—" Forrester was cut off by the judge.

"No buts, Mr. Forrester. This is my courtroom, and I'm not going to have a trial out of control conducted in my courtroom. Do you understand?"

"Yes, sir," Forrester said.

"How about you, Mr. Boseman?"

"Yes, Your Honor."

Laura Griffin merely nodded with approval. She had not been the subject of the judge's wrath.

Elizabeth Kelley got things back on course. "Your Honor," she whispered at the side-bar, "may I suggest that rather than a mistrial that you ask the clerk to replace the prospective jurors who have already been tainted?"

"The trial has not begun. There can be no mistrial at this stage. However, I will accept Ms. Kelley's suggestion and ask the clerk to arrange for another thirty-two bodies to be brought in. When we come back in, we will have no further antics. I will also instruct the bailiff to arrange for another table to be placed in the courtroom so that the defense counsel can 'appear' to be separate."

———

It took the rest of the day to complete jury selection. In fact, it wasn't complete until nearly 7:00 p.m.

For the duration of the trial, a hotel room had been arranged for Cora. At the suggestion of Liz, she had been taken there after lunch. The jury had had the chance to see what she looked like, and there was no reason to make it appear as though she were helping in the selection process. Besides, her lawyers hoped that the lack of her presence might convince at least one juror that she was scared of Richard Taggart, who did stay in the courtroom throughout the process.

A representative from the hospital who nobody had ever seen before also stayed throughout. She was a handsome, but not too pretty, woman who served the defense's purpose of providing the hospital and the corporation that owned it with a human face.

At the conclusion of the long day, the jury consisted of two men and four women, along with two alternates, both men. Unlike those famous trials on TV, in Florida, civil jury trials usually consist of only six peers; and you need a unanimous verdict. Forrester felt relieved when it all was over. If the case could be tried with the six who were in the box, the jury would be fair. One of the alternates posed another problem.

The first six jurors were regular folks. Three white and three black. The alternates were also evenly divided along racial lines. He was pleased that none were bankers, who make a living by telling people "no" every day; and none owned their own business since mom-and-pop operators are always afraid that insurance rates will go up if they award a fair verdict.

His main concern was the alternate who swore he could be fair. The judge would not strike him "for cause," and Forrester had been forced to use his last peremptory challenge to remove a woman who said that punitive damages were unfair but swore, "I'll follow the law as instructed by the judge." Sure.

That left the plaintiff with the second alternate, whose occupation was the most dreaded by any plaintiff's lawyer. A juror who knew the ropes and knew how to answer the attorney's probing questions during jury selection. Answer them so that the judge would have no basis for disqualifying him. Alternate juror number two was an insurance adjuster.

Cora's lawyers could only hope that not more than one of the jurors would become ill during the course of the trial. Be replaced by the man who made his living trying to keep victims from collecting more than minimum settlements.

When jury selection was over, Judge Coker reminded the jurors that they were to talk to no one, not even among themselves, about the trial and the proceedings they would begin to hear the following morning.

———

At the end of a trial day, the judge can go home along with everybody else in the courtroom. He can come back fresh the next day and be ready to hear the evidence. Not so the lawyers.

Back at the office, Forrester worked on his Opening Statement. Liz reviewed the depositions of the witnesses who would be called the next day. She called them on the phone and reviewed their testimony.

Lee had agreed to meet Cora's lawyers at 9:00 p.m. He was going to help coordinate the witnesses. He would make sure they showed up on time and would admonish them not to talk to each other about the case. He would also give his final report on Rick Taggart.

"He hasn't gone back to work yet. I guess that's understandable since our client's brother nearly killed him." It was Lee reporting on his surveillance and on what the neighbors had told him about the defendant.

"I watched him. He spent most of the day in his house. I did see him walk to the car and followed him to a convenience store. He poured his own gas and actually looked fine."

Forrester asked, "When did you watch him?"

"It was Saturday. Two days ago."

Forrester said, "You should have seen him in the courtroom today. He moved around like an old lady."

Now it was Kelley. "He's been rehearsed to get the sympathy of the jury. Maybe we should've really tried to get a continuance."

"Yeah, and if we had, we probably wouldn't have had a client to take to trial. Who knows? She may have been married to that slob of a boyfriend." Forrester then looked at Lee. "What have you found out about his personal life over the last several months?"

"They fired him from the hospital. Or, he quit. I couldn't find out for sure."

Kelley said, "Maybe they're afraid of more lawsuits."

"Maybe. Anyway, he doesn't work there anymore."

"So, he doesn't have a job?" Forrester asked.

"No. He has a job."

"So, where does he work?"

"You won't believe it. He works for Levy County Middle School. It's in one of those rural towns south of Gainesville."

"You've got to be kidding. What's he do?"

"He was hired about nine weeks ago as a counselor. Of course, he hasn't shown up for work since he was shot." After waiting for everything to sink in, Lee went on. "I found out some more things too."

"Go on."

"First of all, his wife left him even before this lawsuit was filed. Apparently she was having an affair of her own while he was having his in the hospital."

"We knew they got a divorce from when we took his deposition."

"Well, the former Mrs. Taggart is now Mrs. Phillips. This time she's married to a Dr. Simon Phillips who's a foot doctor."

"A foot doctor? You mean an orthopedic surgeon?" Liz asked.

"No. He's a podiatrist. He's younger than she is, but maybe it'll work out."

"Maybe."

"Have you talked to her?"

"You know I have. Former wives usually make the best witnesses. That's not going to be the case this time. She hates him, but she's afraid to get involved. She told me he was weird, but she wouldn't give me any particulars. She said if we get a chance we should ask him about his "urges.""

Forrester squinted his eyes like he did sometimes when he was thinking. "What do you mean 'urges'?"

"That's the word she used. She said that it was a term he used a lot when he was talking in his sleep. She thinks it meant when he was going to do something weird to one of his patients...or when he felt proud of himself for not doing something weird. I don't know. That's just what she told me."

"Urges. I'll try to remember that if he takes the witness stand live," Forrester said. "Anything else?"

"Not really. He doesn't really date. There's a middle-aged lady he visits quite a bit. Name's Alice. Alice Pierson. I talked to her, and she thinks the world of him. She doesn't believe anything that I had to say about the case. She told me that if it hadn't been for him, she would've committed suicide a long time ago."

Liz lit up. "Her name's on Taggart's witness list. She will probably testify about his treatment of women in the hospital."

"Yeah. That's where I got her name. From the witness list. Maybe he treats middle-aged ladies different than he does the younger ones."

"I doubt they'll call her. I imagine she was listed for the purpose of giving us the runaround."

That said, Forrester scratched a little note on the side of his opening statement that had been typed in rough and semi-final form by Rosa. "Urges."

———

The next time Forrester looked at his watch, he was irritated with himself. Although his girls were staying with him at the time, most of the time it seemed like he worked too late to enjoy them. If he left the office right now, he wouldn't be home before midnight. He had to be in court by a quarter of nine the next morning. He would get to spend thirty minutes, at most, with his girls over a liquid breakfast and while driving them to school. He would be back in the office by seven forty-five.

He walked Liz to her car and kissed her in the parking lot. It wasn't a passionate kiss—just a peck on the lips. He still felt uncomfortable about having a relationship with a woman from the office.

CHAPTER 31

"LADIES AND GENTLEMEN, I want to first thank you for agreeing to serve as a jury in this case."

It was Bill Forrester beginning his Opening Statement. He had rehearsed it multiple times and would have little use for his notes. The Opening Statement was like the index to a magazine. He would use it to let the jury know what to expect the evidence to show during a trial. Similar to the way an index lets you know what to expect to see if you buy the periodical.

He used the next forty minutes to explain what the witnesses would say. The two defense lawyers would have a half hour each to tell their side of the story before the evidence was put on.

After Forrester told the jury about how Taggart had taken advantage of his position at the hospital, the defendants would have two chances through two lawyers to explain that it was really Cora's word against that of a psychologist. The defense would have a chance to point out that psychologists are in peculiar positions when they work with people who have been sexually active all of their lives. Patients like that fantasize about having relationships with somebody who is nice to them as Richard Taggart was nice to Cora.

Forrester had one chance to explain the testimony he expected them to hear from former Head Nurse Robertson. The two defense lawyers each had their chance to explain that the evidence would show that she did not actually "see" Taggart having intercourse with his patient. If anything, he was counseling her, and Cora manipulated him into what "appeared" to be a compromising position.

Neither side mentioned Heather Maxwell or JoAnne Manchester. Forrester wasn't sure he would get testimony from either of them. The defendants' lawyers were confident that the testimony would never be heard.

Both sides talked about the damages. Forrester had emphasized that the jury would have to rely on the testimony of experts. Psychologists and psychiatrists would both testify about the effect of having a person in trust take advantage of that relationship. It would last a lifetime. Her injuries were permanent. He challenged the defense to put on one professional witness who would testify to the contrary. He knew that there were none to be called.

The defense lawyers each took their turn down-playing the damages, "if any." The woman lawyer, Laura Griffin, was bold enough to point out the obvious. "Cora Smallwood was not a virgin. Nobody will testify that she was harmed physically in any way." Of course, that kind of talk was interspersed with challenges to Forrester to prove the allegations were true in the first place. The only witness was a psychiatric patient in a psychiatric hospital for psychiatric reasons—Cora Smallwood. "Consider the source. You will be asked at the conclusion of the case to judge who is telling the truth."

Boseman agreed that the evidence would show that the allegations were probably not true. "However, if they are true," he went on, "there will be no proof that such behavior was within the scope and course of his employment at the hospital. There will be no proof that the hospital knew or could have known."

It was obvious to Bill Forrester and Liz Kelley, but not to the jury, that the defense had coordinated their Opening Statements. They were sitting at separate tables for the purpose of appearances. The plaintiff's job was to demonstrate the separate tables were for appearances only.

When the Opening Statement was over, Forrester looked to the back of the courtroom where Rosa and Lee were sitting. The judge announced a ten-minute break, which gave them an opportunity to talk.

"I thought you did an excellent job," Lee said.

"You really did," Rosa agreed.

"What about them? I thought they got some good licks in early." Forrester was asking for Rosa's honest opinion.

"They did a good job," she said. "I guess it will be Tweedledee, Tweedledum the whole trial."

"I'm certain of that. Can you believe the judge let them have separate tables?" Forrester's question was rhetorical, and it got no answer. He looked at Lee. "Did you watch Taggart during the Opening
Statements?"

"I watched him. He was the perfect client most of the time. He sat
upright but held his stomach with his left hand and wrote notes with
his right."

"Did I ever shake him?"

"I think you got to him one time. It was what you planned."

"What'd he do?"

"He jerked up and stared for several seconds and then went back
to doodling."

"What are y'all talking about?" Rosa was asking both the lawyer
and the investigator.

Lee was the one to answer. "Didn't you see him? Didn't you see the
way Mr. Taggart, the psychologist, lost it?"

"When?"

"When Bill said he was going to ask for punitive damages. It was
when he said, 'And then you'll consider how much to award as damages. Damages to punish Rick Taggart so that he won't do it again.
Damages to punish the hospital so that it won't let it happen again.
Damages that will send a message home that people working in positions of trust will not be allowed to give in to their 'urges.'"

———

Putting Cora Smallwood on the stand as the first witness had been Liz's
idea. "She's our greatest asset and our greatest liability."

Forrester had the ultimate authority to make decisions. Liz wouldn't
buck him. But he respected his associate as a lawyer—a trial lawyer. A
trial was no place for him to get bogged down about his mixed feelings
for her as a woman and a lover; and the problems that were created by
her being a member of the firm.

Forrester said, "You know, if she's the first witness, she can blow the
case at the beginning."

"Maybe, but she can also put things in perspective. If she's awful, maybe the jury will forget it before we're finished."

After mulling it over, Forrester agreed. "It'll be hard to get her to communicate, but we can use her to get in all the evidence that we need to avoid a directed verdict."

A directed verdict was something that concerned both of them. There was no chance for a directed verdict for Taggart. The hospital was the concern. If Taggart got nailed without the hospital, there would be no insurance to pay the verdict. They had to prove that when Taggart acted, he acted as the hospital personified.

Things had looked up when they found JoAnne Manchester. Now she wouldn't testify. It would be useless to try to call her. Besides, she had promised to slam them if they did. In addition to this risk, JoAnne Manchester had been mistreated after Cora, not before. She could show a "modus operandi," but even with her testimony, they might not survive a directed verdict.

Heather Maxwell could do it since she had been one of his early victims before Cora. Too bad she was back in another hospital, and there was no way they were going to let her out to come to the Duval County Courthouse to testify.

It was decided that the best way to get past a directed verdict was to coordinate Cora's testimony with that of Head Nurse Carol Robertson, who had seen Cora and Taggart kissing. As head nurse, she was Greenview management. It was after she saw the kissing that the love affair had begun. They would argue that the nurse should've done something immediately rather than wait until the damage was done.

Forrester said, "You convinced me. I want you to call Ms. Smallwood as our first witness."

"You want me to take the first witness?" Liz confirmed.

"That's right. I want the jury to know that you're as much a part of this trial as anybody. Also, it doesn't hurt that you're a woman. Cora feels more comfortable with you."

"I hope she doesn't feel too comfortable with Laura Griffin."

Liz stood in the courtroom following the break after the Opening Statements. She had been outside working with Cora while Bill told the jury what the case was about.

Cora was smart, but easily led. She was depressed and sad.

"Your Honor, the plaintiff would call Cora Smallwood as our first witness." Liz Kelley's voice was clear and steady.

Boseman looked at Griffin. Griffin looked at Boseman. There was one disadvantage to them being at separate tables—they couldn't help each other with their notes. The reaction showed that they were caught a little off-guard. They had not expected Cora to be first since the plaintiff is usually put on at the end of a trial.

Cora stood up from the plaintiff's table with the urging of Bill Forrester. She walked slowly toward the witness stand. Before she got there, the clerk ordered, "Step forward. Raise your right hand and place your left hand on the Bible."

Cora had not been expecting that. It confused her briefly. The clerk demanded again, "Step forward."

Cora looked back at Bill Forrester and then looked to Liz Kelley. She didn't know exactly what to do. Forrester stood up as though he owned the courtroom and walked toward her. He took her by the left arm and brought her to the clerk, where she swore to tell the truth.

She looked disheveled. Less than thirty minutes ago, Liz had told her to brush her hair. When she had no brush, Liz gave her one. She may have made three swipes, but that was it. She took a rubberband and gathered it in the back like a ponytail. She had been persuaded to bathe the day before, but her hair still looked oily.

She was wearing a straight dress that went over her shoulders and down to the lower part of her calf. It had a fruit design on it—pears, plums and apples. The hem had come loose on the right side, and a red thread trailed behind her as she maneuvered her way to the witness stand.

KELLEY: Please tell the jury your name and address.

SMALLWOOD: Cora Smallwood, 4721 Granite Street, Starke.

KELLEY: How old are you, and what is your date of birth?

SMALLWOOD: I am 34 years old, and I was born on February 27, 1988.

KELLEY: Do you know Richard Taggart?

SMALLWOOD, *responding quietly*: I know Rick.

KELLEY: How long have you known him?

SMALLWOOD: About two or three years.

KELLEY: Where did you meet him?

SMALLWOOD: When I was a patient at the hospital.

KELLEY: Greenview Psychiatric Hospital in Gainesville, Florida?

SMALLWOOD: Yes.

KELLEY: How'd you meet him?

SMALLWOOD: He treated me. He was my psychologist.

As competently as any experienced trial lawyer, Liz Kelley took her client, the witness, through the testimony. She did not leave anything out. She wanted the jury to hear it all on the plaintiff's side of the case.

Cora talked about the first time they kissed in her room in the open wing of the psychiatric hospital. It had been her idea, but she didn't think that he had resisted.

She explained her attempted suicide and told the jury that she was not really trying to kill herself. She just wanted to be with "Rick." She had to fake the suicide attempt in order to get into the closed unit and in order to be close to the man she thought she loved.

She talked about their affairs in the secure area of the hospital. They made love as often as he wanted. Birth control was not a problem, according to him. She thought she remembered the night that Head Nurse Robertson caught them in bed together. However, she wasn't sure if she remembered.

KELLEY: Who did you tell about the affair?

SMALLWOOD: Nobody.

KELLEY: Why not?

SMALLWOOD: Rick didn't want me to.

KELLEY: Why did what Rick wanted matter?

Cora started to answer but she couldn't. She looked down at her fingers and just fumbled. Liz asked the question again. "Why did you care what Rick wanted?"

Cora looked up at Liz. Her eyes were red. Tears welled up and then dripped off. She didn't bother wiping them away. They ran down her cheek, and her nose began to run. She started to sniff, and then she started to cry. Really cry. She was sobbing.

Judge Coker looked down at the witness stand from his perch at the bench. He said, "Would you like a minute to get your composure?"

Cora didn't respond. She started crying louder. She had her face in her hands like a small child whose feelings had been hurt after being reprimanded by the parent she loved. She was crying like she was heartbroken.

"We'll take a ten-minute recess," Judge Coker ordered. With that, he left the courtroom, and the bailiff showed the jury to the little room behind the jury box.

It wasn't ten but rather fifteen minutes before the judge returned. Cora was composed, and the jury was brought back into the courtroom.

Judge Coker looked over the bench and said, "Madam Court Reporter, would you kindly read back the last question? Ms. Smallwood, would you please answer the question?" It was obvious the judge was going to keep the decorum of the courtroom. He was in charge and his questions were not so much asking as telling.

The court reporter read the last question from her stenograph machine, "Why did you care what Rick wanted?"

Cora didn't respond.

Judge Coker looked down at her again. "Did you hear the question?"

Cora nodded.

"Do you understand the question?"

Cora nodded.

"Please answer the question."

"I...I..."

She was losing her voice. She was looking at her hands again. The tears were welling up once more. She took a deep breath that could be heard throughout the courtroom. In fact, the courtroom was utterly quiet in anticipation of an important answer to what seemed not too important a question.

SMALLWOOD: I...I loved Richard and I would do anything for him, and he didn't want me to tell anybody.

KELLEY: Did you think he loved you?

SMALLWOOD: He told me he loved me. Richard always told me he loved me.

KELLEY: Do you mean Rick Taggart?

SMALLWOOD: His real name is Richard, but I call him Rick.

Cora was crying again. Not as hard as before, but she was still crying enough to make everybody feel awkward. Awkward staring at her on the witness stand; vulnerable and crying.

It took Liz less than an hour, including the recess, to ask the questions and get the responses that she had expected. She had not expected the tears.

Any trial lawyer will tell you that whether it's a criminal or civil case, the most damaging evidence will come from your own client. If you can survive the cross-examination of your own client, you can feel like you have a chance. Most often when a case is lost, it's lost when your own client takes the witness stand.

The direct examination is not so hard. The questions and answers are rehearsed. The client knows what's going to be asked, and the lawyer knows the response to expect. Direct examination questions usually begin with the words "who," "what," "where," "when," "how" and "why."

Cross-examination is different. The other side gets to lead. The asker literally puts the words into the witness's mouth. Leading questions often include the words "Isn't it true...."

It had been decided in advance. Laura Griffin would ask most of the questions of Cora Smallwood. Boseman agreed that she would come across more softly, as had Elizabeth Kelley.

GRIFFIN: Ms. Smallwood, do you need a break or are you okay to answer questions at this time? *(Her voice was nice; almost sweet. She sounded most concerned for the well-being of Cora Smallwood.)*

SMALLWOOD: I'm okay.

GRIFFIN: I have a few questions to ask you in follow-up of those that were asked by "your" lawyer.

(Cora did not respond.) Ms. Smallwood, do you know what "IQ" means?

SMALLWOOD: Yes.

GRIFFIN: Isn't it true that your IQ is over one fifty?

SMALLWOOD: I don't know for sure.

GRIFFIN: You don't know your IQ?

SMALLWOOD: I don't know my IQ exactly. They tell me I'm smart.

GRIFFIN: You've always been smart, haven't you?

SMALLWOOD: People have told me that I'm smart.

The questioner had made her point. Now it was time to shift to a different subject.

GRIFFIN: Isn't it true that you met Mr. Taggart while you were a patient?

SMALLWOOD: Yes. That's what I said.

GRIFFIN: And isn't it true that when you met him, you were in the open unit; the unit that was not secure?

SMALLWOOD: Yes.

GRIFFIN: And while you were in the open unit, you did not have to depend on him or anybody else for most things. True?

SMALLWOOD: Not in the open unit.

GRIFFIN: You went out of your way to meet Mr. Taggart. Get to know him. True?

SMALLWOOD: Yes.

GRIFFIN: You manipulated things to meet him. Isn't that true?

SMALLWOOD: I manipulated him? I don't know.

GRIFFIN: Well, by your own testimony, isn't it true that the first time you allegedly kissed him, it was in your room in the open unit?

SMALLWOOD: Yes.

GRIFFIN: In fact, it's true, isn't it, that you kissed him that day? He didn't kiss you.

SMALLWOOD: We kissed.

GRIFFIN: You kissed him.

SMALLWOOD: Yes.

The series of questions had been maneuvered purposely by the questioner. Cora had not intended to imply that she only kissed Taggart. They had both kissed. The record would not show it that way if you read back the last question and answer.

And so it went for more than two hours. Laura Griffin asked Cora Smallwood one question after another. She did it deftly. Her voice was measured. There was almost a cadence to the questions, which were designed to almost always elicit a simple response—"Yes."

More than once Liz Kelley stood up to object when it was obvious that the question was framed so that the response would be misleading.

The response would imply something different than that which was intended to be communicated.

The problem was, the objections were not based on legal grounds. Judge Coker repeatedly admonished that Liz would have her opportunity to redirect if she wanted, and with each objection overruled, Laura Griffin would ask the court reporter to read back the last question and response.

The jury got a double dose.

As if timing her finale to correspond with the hourlong break for lunch, at 12:15 p.m., Laura Griffin stopped asking questions. She looked at the judge and with a tired voice said, "Your Honor, I am finished with this witness."

There could be no doubt in the jury's mind that Cora was not a reliable witness. How many times did she confirm that she was a patient in a psychiatric hospital? A smart, manipulative patient who fell in love with her psychologist. The psychologist who had treated her nicely while she was under his care. She had not told anybody at the hospital about their "alleged" relationship.

Cora had agreed that it was her word against his.

After the jury had a full hour and fifteen minutes to dwell on what they had learned during cross-examination, it was Fred Boseman's turn to ask questions. He waited until the courtroom was quiet. He strolled to the podium with a yellow pad; looked the witness in the eye; and paused to get her full attention. Finally, he was ready.

BOSEMAN: Ms. Smallwood, who is David Gobel?

(*Cora smiled. It was as though she had found an ally. Then she responded.*)

SMALLWOOD: He's my boyfriend.

BOSEMAN: Thank you. I have no further questions at this time.

Boseman had acted like a complete gentleman. He strolled to his chair and sat down.

The jury in the jury box adjusted themselves in their seats. Jurors one and four looked over at Forrester's table with piercing eyes that communicated, "How are you going to follow up on that?"

Just as calling Cora had caught the defense off guard, the short cross-examination by Boseman had done the same to the plaintiff. The judge wanted a witness. He did not want the trial to drag.

Forrester asked to approach the bench and explained his problem to the judge. "Our next witness does not plan to be here for another half hour," he said.

"I suggest you have them lined up a little better for the remainder of the trial."

"I can assure you, we will."

Boseman suggested, "Your Honor, I suggest they read a deposition if they intend to put on any of that kind of testimony. There's no reason to waste the jury's time."

He sounded so pleasant. Of course, he wasn't really trying to help anything. He knew Forrester was boxed, and he wanted to take advantage.

After Laura Griffin agreed with Boseman's suggestion, Judge Coker said, "That sounds like an excellent idea. Do you have somebody that you had planned not to call live?"

"Yes, Your Honor. We just hadn't planned on putting that kind of testimony on now."

His Honor replied, "I suggest you put on that kind of testimony now. Who is your next witness going to be?"

You're allowed to read a deposition at trial. After all, the testimony at deposition is

sworn—just as though the person were in the courtroom. If the person is one hundred miles away or is an expert witness, one lawyer takes the witness stand while the other stands behind the podium. The questions are read by the person behind the podium, while the one in the witness stand reads the answers.

There's nothing wrong with that kind of testimony, except it can become monotonous. Boring. Seeing as how the jury had just returned from lunch, such testimony would probably have little impact on the outcome of the trial. The plaintiff's lawyers had no choice.

For the next hour and a half, ninety-three pages of deposition-transcript testimony taken four months earlier was read to the jury. Liz read the questions posed to a psychiatrist who had treated Cora while in the hospital. Bill read Dr. Kennedy Gale's answers.

The second alternate juror slept.

The live testimony of Regina Smallwood Baker took the rest of the day. Of course, she had no firsthand knowledge about what had happened to Cora at the hospital. Her testimony was useful for background information. She explained how she had personally escaped from the Smallwood household. Cora had not been so lucky.

By the time she was finished, the jury knew that Cora had been in and out of hospitals most of her life. She survived on Social Security. Her love-child was now being raised by Regina.

She was allowed to tell the jury that their parents were no longer alive and that their brother was in jail. However, Judge Coker sustained the defendants' objections to the sister giving details of the deaths of their parents. It was while she was on the witness stand that Regina realized for the first time that she, too, was now an orphan.

All eight of the people within the confines of the jury box leaned forward and paid attention when Regina recounted her memories about the abuse Cora survived at the hands of her father. Over the objections of the defendants, she was also allowed to explain her suspicions as they related to the relationship between Cora and her other sibling, Richard. She never cried, but her anger was apparent when she recounted the numerous other dysfunctional relationships that her sister had had with the boys and men in her life.

Finally, Forrester used the witness to demonstrate changes brought about by the hospitalization.

FORRESTER: Do you see your sister often?

BAKER: More often than before she went into the hospital, but not that often.

FORRESTER: Have you had an opportunity to observe your sister both before and after her hospitalization at Greenview Psychiatric Hospital?

BAKER: Yes.

FORRESTER: Is she the same now as she was before?

BAKER: I've seen one major difference.

FORRESTER: Please tell the jury what you have observed since her release from the hospital.

BAKER: Cora used to be a clean freak. She bathed several times a day. I always thought it was because of the way she had been treated and that she was trying to wash away her past. Now, she doesn't bathe. She's not the same Cora as she was before.

With that, Forrester looked to opposing counsel and said, "Your witness."

Unlike Cora, Regina was not misled in cross-examination. She explained her responses, to the chagrin of Laura Griffin and Boseman. When Laura Griffin tried to phrase questions so as to misdirect the responses, Regina firmly pointed out that that was not what she meant to communicate. Once, she exposed Taggart's lawyer for posing a question that she said was like asking, "Have you quit beating your wife?"

Her testimony was remarkable. Better than either Forrester or Kelley had expected or hoped. They knew they needed it after the previous events of the day.

It was during the cross-examination that Boseman had asked, "Have you met your sister's new boyfriend?"

She could not have responded better. She said, "No. I haven't met most of her boyfriends over the years. Cora falls in love easily. She always has. Men take advantage of her. Richard, our brother, took advantage of her. But she still loved him. In a way she named her daughter after him by naming her after the famous tennis player Renee Richards."

Then, without hesitation, she added, "I think that's the reason she fell in love with Mr. Taggart. Isn't his name 'Richard' too?"

Griffin was on her feet. "Your Honor, the last answer was not responsive. We move to strike the witness's testimony about what she 'thinks.'"

Judge Coker complied. He instructed the jury to "disregard Regina Baker's last response." All of the jurors nodded as though agreeing with the judge that they would forget what they had just heard about the "Richards" in Cora's life.

CHAPTER 32

"IF ONLY WE HAD her deposition by video. At least we could've shown it to the jury." It was Bill Forrester back at the office lamenting the fact that Heather Maxwell would be unable to participate at the trial. "Jurors like video. It's like TV, and they're used to it. They would pay attention."

"If only frogs had wings," Rosa responded. "Besides, you never had the opportunity."

If they had found out about her hospitalization sooner, something could have been done. If her psychiatrist had agreed, a video deposition could have been taken and played back in the courtroom. It was too late when, on day one of the trial, Lee told the two lawyers that he had finally located the would-be important witness. Lee didn't tell them that his source turned out to be Laura Griffin's secretary, who frequented a bar where the investigator was also a regular.

Without Heather as a witness, they would probably finish their evidence and rest at the end of the day on Wednesday. There was no reason to dwell on the problem. They had plenty of other work to do in preparation for putting on evidence the next day.

Forrester was sitting behind his desk with papers strewn about. Had several little stacks on the floor and called that organization. He didn't know how long she had been standing there when he looked up and saw Liz just within the doorway.

It was her usual place to stand when they had conversations. There was seldom room on the chairs and couch, which were used as storage places. When Forrester noticed her, she was just looking at him. He knew she had been looking for a while.

Liz kind of smiled. "It's nearly ten o'clock. Why don't we go get something to eat?"

"Where would you like to go?"

"Why don't we go to my house and eat leftovers?"

It was a pleasant thought. There was hardly a better place for the two of them to relax. Talk about anything other than the events of the day. Problem was, if he was going to leave, he needed to get home to his girls.

Before he could decline, the thought was interrupted when the telephone rang. The system had been put on "night ring," so that practically any phone in the firm could be used to answer incoming calls. As usual, Liz and Bill were the only ones still in the building.

On the second ring, Liz stepped out of sight into the hallway.

"Moran, Smith, Forrester and Dees," she answered with a cheerful voice that belied her near exhaustion.

The voice on the other end was foreign-sounding. It was a woman. She said, "Is Mr. William Forrester in?"

"Yes. May I tell him who is calling?"

"This is Ingrid Kline." The voice on the other end was high-spirited.

Liz hesitated a second. Did not want to lose her composure. Finally she said, "One moment, please."

She placed the phone on hold. Paused before stepping into the threshold again. Forrester looked up. "Who was it?" he asked.

Liz was flushed by now. The lower part of her neck where it comes to the chest looked like it was covered in a rash. She said, "It's for you."

With that, Liz disappeared.

"Hello?"

"Bill?"

She didn't have to say anything more. He recognized the accent. He knew the voice. At once he responded with exuberance. He had no thoughts of the woman who had been standing in the doorway.

"Ingrid! Is it you? I can't believe it."

"I can't believe it either."

Ingrid was calling from New York City. She had only just cleared Customs and would be spending the night at the Plaza. She said she knew she should've called and warned him, but it was a spur-of-the-moment thing.

"I've missed you so much, Bill. I can't forget Africa. I can't forget London."

Bill's mind was anywhere but on work. He remembered London and wondered why she had come to America without warning. Neither had called or written the other since London. Was she suddenly ready for a commitment? They both knew that overseas romance could leave them longing and unsatisfied.

"How long are you going to be in America?"

"I can't be here for long. I want to be here forever with you."

He could see Ingrid in his mind's eye. Then he thought of Liz. He had never professed love to Liz, though he probably loved her. He talked about her in his sleep before he even knew Ingrid. He had slept with her since being with Ingrid.

It's strange how love is. We can love different people different ways. Even passionate love can be different.

"So, are you coming to Florida?"

"That's my plan, unless you plan to be in New York tomorrow."

Tomorrow? Tomorrow would be impossible for him. He was in the middle of a trial that he was probably losing. It would be at least three more days before the jury rendered a verdict. It could go into next week. In the meantime, he would be with Liz almost continuously.

"I'm in trial, so I can't be in New York. Of course, I want you to come to Florida, but this trial may last into next week."

Can you imagine what Bill was thinking? Things were getting complicated. Conflicting women problems were not something Bill needed, but Bill had conflicting women problems.

"I know you weren't expecting me. I probably should not have come." Ingrid next heard what she expected to hear.

"Of course, you should have come. I'm dying to see you. We just have to figure out how we're going to accomplish all these things at once."

"Don't you get a little time off?"

Bill said, "You'll never understand this. I'll be working night and day until this trial is over. I can put off anything else after that. Come to Florida, and we'll get together somehow. It just won't be for much time until after the trial is over."

What timing, she thought. Bill was in a jam. She could feel it. She could sense it. The one thing she didn't sense was Liz.

"New York is such a wonderful place. If I come to Florida, I want to be with you constantly. Maybe I'll just stay in New York for a few days. You can call me when you know your plans."

Ingrid was the perfect woman. Bill knew he had been let off the hook on purpose. The two women in his life would not be in Florida at the same time. At least not now. At least not until the trial was over.

After the appropriate protestations, Bill agreed that her plan was probably best. Now they could talk about other things for the next forty minutes.

He hung up the phone and stared blankly at the wall. Then, with both hands, he pushed himself from the chair and walked to Liz's office. The lights were out. He was the only person in the building, and her car was not in the parking lot.

There it was again. The intense sense of loneliness that he felt as he drove the thirty minutes back to his house in Orange Park.

Damn it, he thought.

He was focused on the trial when he got back to the office at 7:45 a.m. Liz was already there. Neither mentioned the night before. They just went to work.

When Bill, Liz, and their client arrived back in the courtroom, Boseman and Griffin were all smiles.

"Juror number four, Ms. Jones, called in." The clerk was telling the plaintiff's lawyers what he had already told the defense. "She's sick, and the judge has excused her for the remainder of the trial."

"So that means the first alternate will take her place." Liz had spoken the obvious. It was just as obvious that the plaintiff was now in a more precarious position.

If any other juror got sick or couldn't show up for some reason, the replacement would be the second alternate. That would mean disaster.

Imagine having an insurance adjuster decide Cora's fate. An insurance adjuster whose position had been molded over the years. He couldn't possibly be fair to the plaintiff, and every lawyer in the courtroom knew it.

On a sheet of paper from a yellow notepad, Boseman passed a hand-written note to Liz. She opened it and then showed it to Bill Forrester. It read, "I've been instructed to withdraw the offer of $350,000. Let me know if your client is willing to take $100,000. I might be able to persuade my client to pay that."

As the judge entered the courtroom with all standing, Forrester folded the note and placed it inside his jacket pocket.

The first witness for the third day of trial was the psychologist who had treated Cora since her release from Greenview Psychiatric Hospital. Frances Dyar, PhD, had been handpicked by Cora's treating psychiatrist, Arlene Silver, MD. Dr. Silver had been hand-picked by Bill Forrester. She would be the second person to testify that day.

Neither of the female doctors were strangers to the courtroom. Both had testified dozens of times.

Dr. Dyar was mostly used in domestic matters. She had impressive credentials as a psychologist who specialized in the treatment of battered and abused women. More than a dozen times, her articles had been published in peer-reviewed journals. She had written a chapter in a textbook used on several college campuses.

Before taking the witness stand, she had been told of Regina's testimony during cross-examination. She would incorporate that testimony into hers. No doubt Dr. Silver would do the same.

First, she recited a litany of credentials, then she was asked about her treatment of Cora Smallwood. After reviewing the medical records that had been gathered, she had spent hours with the plaintiff during visits on fifty-some-odd different days. The records reflected the treatment of Cora's psychological problems for years predating her admission to GPH.

She had also conducted a battery of psychological tests to confirm her own impressions. It was significant that the testing occurred early in the treatment as well as a month ago. The retesting showed little improvement for the patient.

Liz guided the witness through her testimony and laid the foundation for the opinions that only an "expert" is allowed to give.

KELLEY: Dr. Dyar, as a result of your training, experience and education; and as a result of your conversations with Cora Smallwood as well as your treatment of her; and as a result of reviewing her medical records up to the present along with the psychological testing that you have performed; have you formed any opinions as they relate to Cora Smallwood?

DYAR: Yes, I have formed opinions.

KELLEY: Would you please tell the jury the opinions that you have formed?

DYAR: Cora Smallwood had significant psychological problems before her admittance to Greenview Psychiatric Hospital. Because of those problems, she was admitted. While she was a patient at the hospital, she was fragile. Psychologically fragile.

It is not unusual for patients under such circumstances to become enamored with the people who are treating them. After all, the patient has to rely upon the hospital staff for most of her daily requirements. In fact, once she was transferred to the closed unit, she was in total reliance upon the hospital staff, including Mr. Taggart.

Whether it was because Mr. Taggart told her he loved her or she simply had a perception that he was in love, she was totally vulnerable and willing to succumb to sexual advances. When such advances were forthcoming, she willingly relented.

The witness had literally changed her physical position to face the jury as she was answering the questions. There was definite eye contact between those in the jury box and the person on the witness stand. The jury was attentive, as their body language confirmed.

Boseman stood up. "Objection, Your Honor. The witness is not providing opinions; she is merely reciting a story—"

As Boseman had interrupted the witness, the judge interrupted Boseman. "No speaking objections, Mr. Boseman. Come to the sidebar if you want to be heard."

With that, all of the lawyers, along with the court reporter, moved across the courtroom to the usual place out of earshot of the jury.

"Mr. Boseman don't let that happen again. A whole jury panel had to be replaced on day one, and I've since told you that there will be no speaking objections in this courtroom. Do you understand my admonishment?"

Boseman replied, "Yes, Your Honor, but—"

"No buts. State the legal grounds for your objection," the judge demanded.

"She was asked her opinions. She's yet to provide any. She is simply summing up the plaintiff's case the way the plaintiff wants her case to go." Boseman's face was red as he whispered his objection so the jury couldn't hear the side-bar argument.

Laura Griffin chimed in. "Judge, the witness is not being controlled. We join in Mr. Boseman's objection."

With that, the judge whispered, "What do you say, Ms. Kelley?"

"Your Honor, she is expressing her opinions and the basis for them. She's reviewed the records, and she's had opportunity to treat and examine the plaintiff. All opinions do not have to be technical. She will be getting to the technical opinions if the defense does not interrupt and lets her finish. The witness has a right to sum up her opinions, and it's not like she is changing her testimony from when she was deposed before."

"I agree with Ms. Griffin that you are not controlling your witness. I agree with Ms. Kelley that what she is stating is her opinions. The objections are overruled, but, Ms. Kelley, control the witness." The judge had ruled. Unlike some, this judge had control of the courtroom. There would be no further argument.

Back at the podium, Kelley wanted to make certain the jury understood that the judge had not ruled against her. At the same time, she would change her questioning techniques.

KELLEY: Dr. Dyar, have you expressed all of your opinions?

DYAR: No.

KELLEY: Are the recitations that you provided so far to the jury the basis of your ultimate opinions?

DYAR: Yes. They are my opinions but also the basis of my ultimate opinions.

KELLEY: Okay, Dr. Dyar. What other matters form the basis of your ultimate opinions?

(*The diversion of the jury's attention had only been temporary. At this point, the jury was as attentive as ever. They leaned forward as the witness regained eye contact.*)

DYAR: When a person is vulnerable as Ms. Smallwood is, the integrity of the people who provided her treatment is very important. If that integrity is breached, it is analogous to being beaten at the hands of a brute.

(*Kelley had control of the witness. She interrupted and posed another question. She did this while skillfully maintaining the flow of communication between the witness and the jury.*)

KELLEY: Can you provide examples of any breaches in integrity as it relates to the treatment of Ms. Smallwood?

DYAR: Yes. The love affair. The sexual relationship between Mr. Taggart and his patient. That's the sort of thing I mean when I talk about a breach of integrity. It's a breach of trust. In this case, it manifested itself when the relationship ended. When Cora—Ms. Smallwood—learned that Mr. Taggart was married.

Boseman was on his feet again. "Objection, Your Honor."

Judge Coker stared down at Boseman. "State your legal basis for the objection."

Boseman replied, "It assumes facts not in evidence, and it invades the right of a jury to determine the ultimate issues of fact."

Judge Coker looked at Ms. Griffin. "Do you join in the objection, Ms. Griffin?"

"Yes, Your Honor."

Judge Coker straightened back in his chair. Dramatically, he was ready to teach the lawyers a lesson. Unless they had a good basis for an objection, they would not interrupt the testimony. He looked at Elizabeth Kelley and said with a most pleasant tone, "Ms. Kelley, you may proceed. The objections are overruled."

The jurors were impressed. The judge was obviously watching out for them. Maybe these annoying objections would end.

KELLEY: Dr. Dyar, you can proceed. In your opinion, was Cora Smallwood abused?

DYAR: In my opinion, she was. She exhibits every symptom of an abused woman. A battered woman.

KELLEY: And do you have a final diagnosis?

DYAR: Yes, she is suffering from battered woman syndrome. May I explain?

KELLEY: Please explain.

DYAR: Ms. Smallwood entered the hospital needing help. Instead, she developed a love affair. She thought it was treatment, and it made her feel good about herself. The blow came when she learned that her lover was married, and, in this case, her lover was her psychologist. That's different than if it was a boyfriend, husband, or some other relationship. She was seeking a particular treatment.

Each time they had intercourse, it meant something to her. Each time they did anything sexual, it meant something to her, and it was special.

KELLEY: Is there anything to compare it to?

DYAR: Yes. When the trust was breached and the patient knew it, each act that she thought was love became an act of rape.

The skilled lawyer stopped. She looked at the jury and paused. Giving the last response time to sink in. After enough time had passed, she turned to Boseman and Griffin. She said, "Your witness."

Dr. Frances Dyar believed her testimony. It was not contrived, and she was unshakable. If the defense lawyers tried to shake her, Dr. Dyar would make them wish they hadn't.

GRIFFIN: Doctor Dyer, is it your opinion that the plaintiff has been correctly diagnosed with Histrionic Personality Disorder?

DYAR: Yes.

GRIFFIN: That is something that she was born with, correct?

DYAR: Correct. Just like many other patients of the hospital. And she also carries the diagnoses of Post Traumatic Stress Disorder.

GRIFFIN: And the diagnosis of Histrionic Personality Disorder, in her case, is intertwined with the diagnosis of PTSD. Correct?

DYAR: Along with great bouts of depression. The diagnoses are related in this case.

GRIFFIN: And isn't it true that people with Histrionic Personality Disorders often behave in a way to seek special attention and become emotional if they fail to get it?

DYAR: Yes, and that is why it sometimes becomes necessary to admit such patients into hospitals, as in Ms. Smallwood's case.

GRIFFIN: Thank you, doctor, but please just answer the questions.

DYAR: Sure. I just do not want my answers to be misconstrued.

GRIFFIN: Now, doctor, isn't it true that patients with the plaintiff's mental problems can be manipulative?

DYAR: That is often the case, and I would expect it in this case.

GRIFFIN: Okay. What was the plaintiff's diagnosis when she entered the hospital?

DYAR: The same as many other of the hospital's patients, I suppose. Post Traumatic Stress Disorder coupled with Histrionic Personality Disorder and depression.

GRIFFIN: And the same plaintiff who has been diagnosed with those conditions provided you the information that you related to the jury earlier. True?

DYAR: Yes. Along with the medical records and depositions I reviewed.

GRIFFIN: And you believed what she told you. Correct?

DYAR: What she told me seemed truthful and consistent with the records.

GRIFFIN: But she may have been manipulating you, as a person with her diagnosis would do?

DYAR: I don't think so.

GRIFFIN: Well, isn't it true that as to the allegations of this case, it is really Ms. Smallwood's word against Mr. Taggart's

DYAR: Hasn't Head Nurse Robertson testified yet? I read her deposition and it seems to confirm the patient's story.

(*Of course, Nurse Robertson had yet to testify, but the jury now knew that somebody else would be helping the plaintiff. Laura Griffin was zinged again when she continued to try to compromise the doctor's opinions.*)

GRIFFIN: Undoubtedly you are aware, aren't you, Dr. Dyar, that Cora was abused as a child?

DYAR: Yes, I'm aware.

GRIFFIN: And you're aware that she had an incestuous relation-ship with her brother?"

DYAR: Yes.

GRIFFIN: And she had intercourse with her father throughout her childhood. You're aware of that too, aren't you?"

DYAR: Of course.

GRIFFIN: So, she was damaged by her family, by her brother and her father. She's not suing them, but it's the same damages that she's now accusing my client of causing. Correct?

DYAR: Incorrect! Most women in psychiatric hospitals being treat-ed for the condition that Ms. Smallwood was being treated for have been abused by family members. That is not, I emphasize *not*, a license for more abuse.

GRIFFIN: Are you aware that Ms. Smallwood has a boyfriend? David Gobel.

DYAR: I'm not surprised. She'll probably have many boyfriends. Many men may take advantage of her. Hopefully in the future, they won't be her doctors and her health care providers. She lives in a real world. She's in a hospital for the purpose of learning how to cope with it.

GRIFFIN: Then you are saying that it's okay for her to have a boyfriend?

DYAR: It's not the same. The proof is in the medical records. I've reviewed the medical records. Ms. Smallwood is reported to have bathed constantly. In my opinion, such behavior was consistent with a person trying to wash away her past. She was in the hospital for the purpose of trying to wash away her past. Now she's given up. I don't think she ever bathed before she saw me.

When it was Boseman's turn, he left that line of questioning. It was obviously not going too far and obviously wouldn't help. He would wish he had simply declined to ask the witness anything.

BOSEMAN: Isn't it true that if what you think occurred, did oc-cur, the hospital is not responsible unless the hospital had reason to know in advance?

DYAR: "That's a legal question that I can't answer (*and it was, and Boseman knew it*), but I cannot imagine how the hospital could've hid-den from what was going on.

Liz also handled the testimony of Dr. Silver, MD. She had testified literally hundreds of times in criminal cases and dozens of times in civil litigation. She was called upon by both prosecutors and defense lawyers when the psychiatric condition of criminals like Richard Smallwood came into question. She was equally deft at handling questions about psychiatric injuries induced as a result of car wrecks, family deaths, and other trauma. She was an adjunct professor at the University of Florida. She had had her writings published ninety-two times in professional peer-reviewed periodicals as well as a half dozen times in books dealing specifically with sexual dysfunction.

Although she wasn't present during the testimony of Frances Dyar, PhD (witnesses are seldom allowed to be present in courtrooms during the testimony of others), her testimony was consistent. Because she was a medical doctor, however, what she had to say was not totally redundant. She could testify about the "permanent effect" of the damages. She was also allowed to testify on the medical malpractice issue regarding standards of care.

KELLEY: Dr. Silver, based on your training and experience, your examination of the medical records, and your treatment of Cora Smallwood, have you formed an opinion within a reasonable degree of medical probability as to whether Cora Smallwood has suffered a "permanent" injury as a result of her care and treatment at the Greenview Psychiatric Hospital under the care of Richard Taggart?

SILVER: Yes.

KELLEY: Please tell the jury what your opinion is.

SILVER: It is my opinion that she has suffered a permanent psychiatric injury as a result of that treatment. It is my further opinion that the treatment has exacerbated her pre-existing psychiatric condition.

(*With that bit of information, the plaintiff would be allowed to put in the mortality tables that predict her life expectancy. Final arguments could be made for damages for every day of the future expected life. The jury would be told that statistically Cora Smallwood's life expectancy was 46.3 years.*)

KELLEY: And, Doctor, have you formed an opinion within a reasonable degree of medical probability as to whether the care and treatment provided to Cora Smallwood at the Greenview Psychiatric Hospital was within acceptable standards of care?

SILVER: In my opinion, the failure to appropriately supervise Richard Taggart and the actions of Richard Taggart as reported by Cora Smallwood were such that they were below acceptable standards of care.

The cross-examination by the defense was much more guarded than it had been with Dr. Dyar. There were a few obligatory questions.

GRIFFIN: You have to rely on what's in the records and what the patient says. True?

SILVER: Yes.

GRIFFIN: And the patient in this case has a diagnosis of Post Traumatic Stress Disorder and Histrionic Personality Disorder.

SILVER: While she was in the hospital.

GRIFFIN: And that diagnosis means that she was believed to be manipulative.

SILVER: Not necessarily. However, in her case, the records show that she may have been manipulative. That does not mean that there was any license for any employee of the hospital to have anything other than a professional relationship with her. Sex is not professional.

GRIFFIN: Please just answer my questions. Everything will go a lot smoother and faster if you limit your responses to my questions.

SILVER: I thought I was being responsive. I apologize if I gave too much information.

GRIFFIN, *irritated and reticent to keep sparring with the witness*: You would agree that Cora Smallwood's was significantly psychiatrically injured before she was ever admitted to the hospital. True?

SILVER: Yes.

GRIFFIN: And isn't it true that Cora Smallwood would need psychiatric treatment now and in the future even if she had never met Richard Taggart?

SILVER: True.

When it was Boseman's turn, he really wasn't ready for the response he got to his first question.

BOSEMAN: Dr. Silver, your opinion regarding standards of care applies to the hospital only to the extent that Mr. Taggart may have conducted himself inappropriately. That is, you're not saying that any other treatment at the hospital was below acceptable standards of care. Correct?

SILVER: No, that is not correct. Unquestionably, Mr. Taggart's treatment was below acceptable standards. From the depositions I have read, at least one nurse observed misbehavior before Ms. Smallwood was moved into the closed unit. That should've been reported. That was below acceptable standards. *(Boseman tried to interrupt. She stopped him.)*

I'm not finished. Even after the hospital was made aware of what was going on, after it was reported by Ms. Smallwood or her sister, the investigation was a sham. That, too, was below acceptable standards.

Then Ms. Smallwood was told by staff and others that she was not believed. They called her Crazy Cora. Even if she wasn't believed and even if it wasn't true, that was an inappropriate way to treat a patient in a psychiatric hospital.

Cora Smallwood's treatment at Greenview Psychiatric Hospital was wrong, inappropriate, and below acceptable standards of care. She would've been better had she never been admitted for the help that she did not receive.

After several other innocuous questions, the hospital's lawyer made another blunder.

BOSEMAN: You agree, don't you, that under any scenario, whether she's believed or not, Ms. Smallwood was not physically injured?

SILVER: I absolutely disagree. She wasn't a virgin, but the physical contact was made and she was injured. She wasn't scarred on her body. Her brain was scarred. Her mind was scarred. And, in my opinion, the scarring will never heal. She is permanently damaged by the physical contact."

It was a very good morning for the plaintiffs. The case was back on track. The witnesses had held up well, and a directed verdict for the defendants would not be possible. Bill Forrester felt semi-confident that Boseman had lost his battle to convince the jury that the hospital was as much a victim as Cora.

While the hospital was sweating the brutal publicity that was coming from the news media, the insurance company representatives realized that the hospital could be tagged for negligence. If that be the case, it would have to pay.

Still, there was the issue of damages. The defense was controlling that well, and there was still no basis for punitives. There was no evidence of any victim before Cora.

———

Before the day was over, three more witnesses would take the stand. Next, the plaintiff called Raymond Jones, the hospital administrator. Because of Jones's position with the hospital, Forrester was allowed to ask leading questions. He was not asked a single question about the facts of the case. His testimony went like this.

FORRESTER: Mr. Jones, you are the hospital administrator for Greenview Psychiatric?

JONES: Yes.

FORRESTER: And you held that same position while Cora Smallwood was a patient in the hospital?

JONES: Yes.

FORRESTER: In your capacity as hospital administrator, were you the chief executive, so to speak, of the day-to-day operations at the hospital?

JONES: That's correct.

FORRESTER: Therefore, you were ultimately in charge of the hiring and firing of hospital personnel. True?

JONES: Those are some of my responsibilities. I had many others.

FORRESTER: And you are the person who hired Mr. Richard Taggart. Isn't that true?

JONES: There's a committee that hired him. I served on the committee.

FORRESTER: And you also were in the position to require an investigation if you felt one was appropriate?

JONES: I have done that from time to time.

FORRESTER: And you were the person who would monitor any such investigation. True?

JONES: You could probably say that.

FORRESTER: And if you wanted to end an investigation, you could do that as well?

JONES: I don't know what you're getting at. I don't control the investigations once they're started.

FORRESTER: Well, in fact, you controlled the investigation of Mr. Taggart, didn't you?

JONES: Absolutely not.

FORRESTER: Are you telling the jury that after an investigation was finally initiated against Mr. Taggart, you didn't have anything to do with how thorough the investigation was; when it ended; and that sort of thing?

JONES: I didn't do that.

FORRESTER: Mr. Jones, didn't you get to know Mr. Taggart while he was an employee at Greenview Psychiatric Hospital?

JONES: I get to know all of the hospital employees, including Mr. Taggart.

FORRESTER: But as to Mr. Taggart, you also got to know him socially. Didn't you?

JONES: I don't know what you mean by "socially." We've never been out to dinner if that's what you mean.

(*At this point, the witness was red-faced. Obviously angry but under control.*)

FORRESTER: Does hospital business include taking flying lessons?

JONES: Of course not.

(*The witness turned pale. Suddenly he knew where the questioning was going.*)

FORRESTER: Have you ever taken flying lessons?

JONES, *almost inaudibly*: Yes.

FORRESTER: Mr. Jones, please tell the jury who your instructor was. Who provided the flying lessons to you?

(*Boseman was on his feet but before he could interrupt with an objection, the witness answered.*)

JONES: Richard Taggart.

(*Boseman sat down. It was too late.*)

FORRESTER: Do you mean Richard Taggart, the defendant in this case?

(*Forrester was reemphasizing the response. The witness was still pale and was no longer looking the interrogator in the eye.*)

JONES: Yes, sir.

FORRESTER: And would you please tell the jury how much you were charged for the lessons?

JONES: He didn't charge me.

There were no other questions. The jury had gotten the point.

———

Gladys Lake was the person who was in charge of the investigation for the hospital. She testified that she was appointed by the man who had had the free flying lessons. She was appointed after Cora's sister, Regina Baker, complained.

Ms. Lake's job was normally that of a social worker. She had been surprised that it was she who had been chosen to look into the allegations. As part of her investigation, she had talked to Cora, Taggart and all of the medical staff involved in the patient's treatment.

FORRESTER: Did you complete your investigation?

LAKE: I handed in a report, if that's what you mean.

FORRESTER: What I mean is, did you feel that your investigation was complete when you handed in your report?

LAKE: Not really.

FORRESTER: Please explain to the jury what you mean by "not really."

LAKE: I found some inconsistencies. Or, at least they seemed inconsistent to me. For example, Nurse Robertson told me that she had found Mr. Taggart with Ms. Smallwood. So I checked her medical chart. Events like that have got to be charted.

FORRESTER: Was it charted? Did you find anything in the plaintiff's chart about the incident that had been reported to you by Nurse Robertson?

LAKE: No. That's what I found odd. It was my intention to continue the investigation. I went back to Mr. Taggart to ask him about the patient's chart."

FORRESTER: What happened then?

LAKE: He told me that he had heard that the investigation was supposed to be closed. He said that the HRS had completed its investigation and so had the police. He said he wouldn't talk to me any further about it unless Mr. Jones told him to.

FORRESTER: What did you do then?

LAKE: I asked Mr. Jones.

FORRESTER: And did he tell you to do anything?

LAKE: Yes. He told me that I should write a report. He was satisfied with the investigation. He said there was no need to go any further.

FORRESTER: Did you protest?

LAKE: Not really. I wrote my report and closed the file.

On cross-examination Laura Griffin had the witness admit that her report provided no final, definitive conclusions. There were, however, two reports with conclusions. Both HRS and the police found that there was no basis for further investigation.

The witness agreed that there was no reason to believe that the investigators from HRS and the police were hampered in their efforts.

Boseman jumped at the opportunity to cross-examine for the hospital. His questioning was brief but effective.

BOSEMAN: Ms. Lake, did you know Mr. Taggart before these accusations by Cora Smallwood?

LAKE: Yes.

BOSEMAN: Was there ever a time that you considered him a threat to any patient?

LAKE: Never before Ms. Smallwood.

BOSEMAN: Although we are not conceding it, assume that Cora Smallwood's allegations are true.

LAKE: Okay.

BOSEMAN: Was there ever any reason for anybody, including you and including anybody that you interviewed at the hospital, to know or believe that Richard Taggart could be a threat to patients?

LAKE: None.

Boseman felt good about his cross-examination. He had distanced the hospital from Taggart via the plaintiff's own credible witness.

After a break Judge Coker directed his question to the plaintiff's table. "Who is your next witness?"

Forrester stood. "Your Honor, the plaintiff calls Carol Robertson."

Liz watched the jury. The body language confirmed that they recognized the name of the person who had been mentioned so often by other witnesses. Her testimony took a little over two hours, including cross-examination by both defense lawyers. It was beautiful.

Here was this otherwise stern, matter-of-fact type person who still felt pangs of guilt. Although she was not a named defendant, she felt responsible for what had happened to Cora. She had failed to report what she had seen through the window—Cora and Rick's first kiss.

She didn't cry, but her eyes watered throughout her testimony. At one point she looked at Cora and volunteered, "I'm truly sorry, Ms. Smallwood." As with the other witnesses, Cora did not look back.

Her testimony was truthful. She admitted that she had not really seen sexual contact on the night that she had walked into the dark room where Cora and Rick had just completed having sex for the sixth time in five days. Still, she let it be known that the parties were obviously compromised. The judge allowed her conclusion that "it could only mean one thing—they were having, or had just finished having, sex."

After admitting three times that she hadn't immediately reported the event, she told the jury that it was her effort that started the investigation. Got the ball rolling when she called Cora's sister.

Then she blurted out, "The follow-up investigation was a farce. It only accomplished one thing—Cora Smallwood gained a grapevine nickname, Crazy Cora."

Boseman shouldn't have cross-examined. He wished he hadn't when Ms. Robertson turned to the jury and said, "I know I'm as much to blame as Rick Taggart. I should have done something, but I hesitated. It was wrong, and I, as part of the hospital staff, was wrong in failing to do what I knew I should've done."

The plaintiff's lawyers were pleased with themselves as they walked out of the courtroom that evening. Bill Forrester was not quite so pleased after he asked his associate, "Why don't we go have some dinner and then go back to the office and prepare for tomorrow?"

Liz answered, "I don't think so. At least not tonight."

The day ended with neither mentioning the telephone call from Ingrid Kline.

CHAPTER 33

LEE SAID, "I TRIED again. They let me talk to Heather Maxwell, and she is willing to testify. She even sounds lucid. I got a medical release from her and also talked to her psychiatrist. When it comes to leaving the hospital, the shrink said no."

"What is the doctor's name?" Forrester asked as though it made a difference.

"It's in my notes. What does it matter? She tells me it's out of the question. Heather can't leave right now. She wouldn't mind the patient going to a deposition. She just doesn't want her to leave the hospital grounds yet."

"Did you try JoAnne Manchester again?"

"I tried her. That woman is a self-centered bitch. She's emphatic. She isn't going to testify."

The conversation having ended, Forrester and Liz walked to the courthouse, each carrying a briefcase in each hand. This was going to be the fourth day of trial. They were tired. Mentally exhausted.

Without JoAnne Manchester or Heather Maxwell, there were no other witnesses for the plaintiff's case. It would be the defense's turn.

Following the instructions of her lawyers, Cora Smallwood didn't show up. They didn't want her to be called by the defense, which had not placed her under subpoena. Her testimony had been necessary earlier in the trial. There was no reason to suffer through it again.

"The plaintiff rests," Forrester announced to the judge and the jury.

With that, the triers of fact were directed to return to the jury room. The judge had some questions for the lawyers. It was time for the defense lawyers make their separate arguments for directed verdicts. It was fruitless, but it would be malpractice not to make the motions.

"Denied," Judge Coker responded after patiently listening to protracted argument. "Is the defense ready to proceed with witnesses?"

Both lawyers had anticipated the end of the plaintiff's case. Both lawyers acknowledged that they were ready to proceed. The sum total of the defense would take no more than one day.

———

Rick Taggart was the first witness called by his attorney. It needed to be done.

(Remember O. J. Simpson? He was charged with the murder of his wife. Unlike O. J.'s criminal trial, but as with O. J.'s civil trial, the defendant would take the witness stand and deny the horribleness that he had endured listening to for the past several days.)

Mr. Taggart tried to evoke sympathy as he slowly walked toward the clerk. It was hard to tell if he was still suffering from the bullet that Cora's brother had used to knock him off his feet. He looked pale, but that could be nerves. He was definitely thinner than he had been at his deposition.

Before taking the witness stand, he swore "to tell the truth, the whole truth, and nothing but the truth."

Forrester stood. "Your Honor, we would request that this testimony be proffered."

Such a request meant that the lawyer wanted the witness to testify outside the presence of the jury. The idea was to have the judge listen to the witness first to avoid improper remarks from being heard by the jury.

Judge Coker looked impatient as he instructed the bailiff to take the jurors out of the courtroom again. Trial lawyers always wonder why judges have that nasty disposition whenever the rhythm of the trial slows down. They seem to be in a hurry to get it over with. Since all judges don't play golf, what else do they have to do besides judging?

"Okay, Mr. Forrester, what's the problem?"

"Your Honor, we are concerned that the defense will attempt to elicit testimony regarding Mr. Taggart's gunshot wounds. If that is the case, we think it should be proffered first so that you can rule on its admissibility.

"Ms. Griffin, is it your intention to ask those types of questions?"

"Your Honor, we think it's appropriate testimony—"

"I didn't ask you if you thought it was appropriate. I asked if you intend to elicit the testimony about the defendant being shot by the plaintiff's brother. After you answer that question, we can talk about whether or not it would be appropriate."

"Yes, sir. We think that at worst the jury should know why my client looks so pale."

"Ms. Griffin, why would this testimony be relevant?" The judge was grilling her.

As Laura Griffin was thinking of a response, the attorney for the hospital decided to make his position known. Boseman said, "Your Honor, Richard Smallwood, the plaintiff's brother, is a potential witness in this case. We have evidence that he abused his sister. Likewise, he obviously had no problem abusing Mr. Taggart. I think this testimony would be relevant so that the jury would have firsthand knowledge as to the living conditions at the Smallwood house. It also goes to the issue of damages. We think that the jury should know that the damages are less significant or nonexistent because of the plaintiff's home environment."

Taggart's lawyer took over from there.

"We agree, Your Honor, and that is the reason why we plan to simply ask Mr. Taggart a few questions about the events giving rise to his condition in the courtroom today. The jury has a right to know."

His Honor was unconvinced. "Is that the best you can do? I agree with Mr. Forrester that any such testimony would be irrelevant and highly prejudicial. Therefore, I am instructing you not to ask questions that would elicit that type of testimony from this or any other witness." With that, he instructed the bailiff, "Bring the jury in. We need to move this case along."

The preliminary questions were asked and answered. His name, address, education, training, etcetera. He was not asked his present occupation.

GRIFFIN: Do you remember treating Cora Smallwood at Greenview Psychiatric Hospital?

TAGGART: Yes, I remember Cora. (*He couldn't have been more pleasant.*)

GRIFFIN: Have you been in the courtroom throughout this trial and listened to the testimony of Ms. Smallwood and others?

TAGGART: Yes, unfortunately, I have.

GRIFFIN: So you would have heard the testimony of Cora Smallwood and her description of what she described as a love affair?

TAGGART: I heard it.

GRIFFIN: Was she telling the truth?

TAGGART: She probably thinks she's telling the truth, but what she said just isn't true.

GRIFFIN: Can you think of any reason why she would say that you were lovers?

TAGGART: It's not unusual. Patients fall in love with their nurses, their doctors, and, unfortunately, their psychologists. I worked with Cora most of the time she was at the hospital. The explanation is that she is delusional. It's not unusual for a person with her psychiatric problems."

GRIFFIN: Were you ever tempted?

TAGGART: Tempted? Hardly. Cora, like other patients before her, came onto me from time to time. But I was not tempted. It comes with the job.

GRIFFIN: "Came onto you"? What do you mean by that?

TAGGART: You know, like, during sessions she would want to sit next to me. She would put her arm around me. Things like that. In her mind, I'm sure she thought it was romantic. It simply wasn't.

GRIFFIN: Can you think of any specific examples?

(*Taggart was well rehearsed. His responses were smooth. He looked and acted concerned. He paused, for effect, after this question.*)

TAGGART: There were other times. But the situations that Head Nurse Robertson told you about are typical."

GRIFFIN: You mean the kissing episode while she was in the open unit; and the time Nurse Robertson came into Ms. Smallwood's room while you were there?

TAGGART: Yes, those are good examples.

GRIFFIN: Tell the jury what you remember about those situations.

(There was another pause. Taggart deliberately moved so he could look at the jury and so they could look at him. He was sincere as he testified.)

TAGGART: Cora was in the open unit. She was going to be released from the hospital. She asked me to come by, and I did. Actually, I thought she was in pretty good shape—mentally—at that time. I was as surprised as anyone when she put her arms around me. She kissed me. I didn't kiss back. It took me aback. I'm sure that's what Ms. Robertson saw. I don't blame her for the interpretation of what she thought she witnessed.

GRIFFIN: What did you do after that?

TAGGART: I left her room. The next day or the day after, she was in the closed unit. I had heard she had tried to commit suicide. I had no idea.

GRIFFIN: And the other occasion that Nurse Robertson told us about?

TAGGART: I remember that night too. I went to Cora's room because I was told that she had asked for me. I didn't expect anything other than to counsel her. I was told that she was depressed, and when I got there, she was depressed. We talked, and that was it.

GRIFFIN: You didn't kiss her or have sex with her or anything like that?

TAGGART: Of course not. Nurse Robertson didn't say she saw anything like that. She simply saw me in the room sitting on the edge of the bed doing what I do. I was counseling the patient.

When Taggart's lawyer had finished asking questions, Boseman declined to examine. Not so, Forrester. He questioned the defendant for more than an hour. The questions were aggressive, but Taggart was prepared. He was mostly unshakable. Maybe not quite so lovable.

FORRESTER: You admit, sir, that it would be totally improper for a psychologist to have an affair with his patient?

TAGGART: That is true.

FORRESTER: But you do not admit that you had the affair. Right?

TAGGART: There was no affair.

FORRESTER: "But you did, from time to time, have (*and Forrester emphasized the next word*) "urges" to have affairs with female patients?

TAGGART: What?

(*Taggart was a little rattled, and the jury could see it. However, the jury did not exactly know why he would be rattled. Boseman and Griffin were both on their feet. Forrester did not hesitate continuing the cross-examination.*)

FORRESTER: Well, is it your testimony that you've never had an affair with any patient? Never had the "urge" to have an affair with a patient?

(*Before the defense lawyers could object, the witness practically yelled his response.*)

TAGGART: Never!(*He was unnerved. Then, without looking at the jury nor the lawyers, he continued.*) I have never had an affair with any patient. Some of them have tried to have affairs with me. It just goes with the territory.

(*He felt satisfied with his comeback even though he could not know how the lawyers knew about his "urges" (The next question rattled him again.*)

FORRESTER: So it's your testimony that you never had an affair or had sex with a patient named Heather Maxwell nor any other patient. Right?

"Objection!" Both defense lawyers were responding in unison.

"There has been no such testimony. This questioning is improper and without foundation! " Boseman was practically screaming. He added, "We move for a mistrial!"

Judge Coker reacted to calm things down. "Come to the side-bar," he ordered without hesitation.

After the side-bar conference, the judge sustained the objections. He would later consider the defendants' motions for mistrial.

FORRESTER: It's not usual for a patient to come onto you. True?

TAGGART: That's true. It happens.

FORRESTER: And, when you counsel patients, notes are made of such counseling?

TAGGART: Normally.

(*Forrester took the entire stack of medical records concerning his client. There were nine inches of records. He took them up to the witness stand and placed them before the witness.*)

FORRESTER: Show the jury in the records where you reported or made notations of the events reported by Head Nurse Robertson.

(*The witness did not touch the records. He had reviewed them before and he was prepared for this testimony. It was not good testimony, but he was not going to make it worse by searching for something that he knew did not exist.*)

TAGGART: There is no report. That's my fault. Sometimes things get hectic, and we mean to get back to them and just don't.

FORRESTER: So you failed to document Cora Smallwood's medicals on the date that you say she kissed you while she was in the open unit?

TAGGART: I hadn't intended for her to kiss me. There was no counseling. I did not write it down.

FORRESTER: So it's true?

TAGGART: Yes, it's true I didn't chart it.

FORRESTER: And you didn't document the counseling session that you admit took place on her bed and was interrupted by Head Nurse Robertson?"

TAGGART: I should have, but I didn't get around to it. No.

There were no knockout punches through the cross-examination. Things may have been different if JoAnne Manchester or Heather Maxwell had testified. Forrester would have to live with it.

The plaintiff's lawyer said, "One moment, Your Honor." He walked over to the table and whispered to Liz, "Anything else?"

She whispered back before Forrester returned to the podium.

FORRESTER: I just have a few more questions of this witness. You said you were present during Cora Smallwood's testimony.

TAGGART: I heard it.

FORRESTER: And you remember questions about sex and birth control?

TAGGART: I'm not sure what you mean.

FORRESTER: Well, let me get to the point. Isn't it true that you've had a vasectomy?

Lawyers don't like to ask questions they don't know the answer to. The vasectomy issue had been brought out in Cora's testimony about birth control. The lawyer knew that if the witness denied it, there would be no way to prove to the contrary. However, Liz had pointed out that if Taggart admitted the vasectomy, it would prove Cora's veracity. If he denied it now, Forrester could argue during close that Taggart had lied to the patient.

Time passed, and Taggart didn't answer. Forrester had hit upon a question upon which the witness had not been coached.

FORRESTER: Mr. Taggart, have you had a vasectomy or not?

TAGGART (*His voice was irritated and pressing. In reality, the hesitation on the part of the witness had made the question more important than it really was.*): Yes. Yes, I've had a vasectomy.

Forrester took his seat. He would leave it up to the jury to determine how Cora could have possibly known.

———

Attorney Griffin called the next witness, Alice Pierson.

GRIFFIN: Please state your name and address, ma'am.

PIERSON: "My name is Alice Pierson. I live at 9090 Bayberry Downs, Ocala, Florida."

GRIFFIN: Ms. Pierson, have you had occasion to be treated at Greenview Psychiatric Hospital?

PIERSON: Yes, more than once. My life has been saved by the treatment I received there.

GRIFFIN: What have been the circumstances that brought you to that hospital?

With that, Alice went into the sordid details of her family life. The death of her children and her husband that morning when they were on their way to a horse show. She explained how, miraculously, she had suffered practically no injury. Depression had set in, and she had been a regular at GPH.

The defense had the attention of the jury. Alice was a nice lady. Not crazy. She was believable, and her testimony would be believed.

GRIFFIN: And as a patient at Greenview Psychiatric Hospital, did you come under the care and treatment of Richard Taggart, Psychologist?

PIERSON: Oh, yes. I think he's a wonderful man. The last time I was there, he was somewhere else, and I was truly disappointed.

GRIFFIN: On one of those hospitalizations, did you have occasion to have a roommate named Cora Smallwood?

PIERSON: Yes, she was thinner then. Better kept. She was always bathing and brushing her hair.

(*This last response had been an unexpected pleasure for the plaintiffs. Obviously, Laura Griffin hadn't expected any more than a "yes"*)

GRIFFIN: Yes, well…when you were a roommate of Ms. Smallwood, did you have occasions to talk?

PIERSON: Of course. We talked about lots of things. I told her my life story, and she told me hers. I think it's helpful to talk to people about your problems. Don't you?

GRIFFIN: Did you and Cora Smallwood ever talk about Richard Taggart?

PIERSON: Of course. We both were being treated by Richard.

GRIFFIN: Ms. Pierson, cast your mind's eye back. Do you remember Cora Smallwood ever telling you that she and Richard Taggart had an affair?

PIERSON: No.

GRIFFIN: Did she ever tell you she had sex with Richard Taggart?

PIERSON: Oh…oh, no.

GRIFFIN: Thank you. No further questions.

Boseman, making another effort to set himself and the hospital apart from Richard Taggart, told the judge, "We have no questions of this witness, Your Honor."

Forrester walked to the podium. Took his time.

FORRESTER: Ms. Pierson, you and I have never met, have we?

PIERSON: I don't think so.

FORRESTER: Have you ever met with Ms. Griffin before coming into the courtroom today?

PIERSON: Yes. I met with her twice…or, was it three times? That other man was with her this morning just before we came in.

FORRESTER: That other man? You mean Mr. Boseman? The man sitting over there?

PIERSON: Yes. I didn't remember his last name. The man sitting over there at the other table away from Richard.

(*Boseman did not look up as Alice Pierson pointed to him. He acted like he was taking notes and in deep thought.*)

FORRESTER: You met this morning with the lawyer for the hospital and the lawyer for Mr. Taggart?

PIERSON: Yes, sir. This morning.

FORRESTER: Together at the same time, same place, and at the same conference table?

PIERSON: Oh, yes.

(*The point had been made. Forrester paused to let it sink in*)

FORRESTER: You said that you and Cora Smallwood talked about Richard Taggart. Correct?

PIERSON: That's right. Numerous times. (*The next question was a stab in the dark. It couldn't hurt.*)

FORRESTER: Was it you who told her about Mr. Taggart's family?

PIERSON: I don't know. Maybe. I told her about going to his house and that sort of thing. I don't remember if I told her about his family.

(*Forrester had another whisper conference with Liz. He returned to the podium.*)

FORRESTER: When you met with Ms. Griffin and Mr. Boseman this morning, was Mr. Taggart with them?

PIERSON: Yes. He didn't look so good. He says he was shot by Cora's brother. I hope he gets to feeling better."

(*Forrester wished he hadn't asked the question. He had to follow up.*)

FORRESTER: Did he tell you where he's working now?

PIERSON: He says he's working at a middle school in one of those little towns. I think he's a children's counselor. I think he'll be good with children. Don't you?

During the one-hour recess for lunch, Elizabeth Kelley summoned Lee and Rosa. She had an idea that had been approved by Forrester. In fact, Forrester was downright excited. If they could make it work, they would.

Lee would make the arrangements with the hospital. Rosa made the arrangements with Court-View, Inc. On such short notice, it would be expensive. They weren't even sure if the judge would allow it.

They would spend the money and take their chances. It would be like Mohammed and the mountain. If Heather Maxwell couldn't come to the courtroom, maybe they could go to her.

There were no other witnesses to call for the defense of Richard Taggart. The lawyers were convinced that the psychologist was probably not believed.

Boseman for the Greenview Psychiatric Hospital called witnesses all afternoon. He called social workers, nurses and hospital directors. The testimony of each was similar and took less than thirty minutes apiece.

Boseman would ask the name, address, and the occupation of the witness. All worked for the hospital in various and sundry positions. Each knew Richard Taggart and had worked for him both before and after Cora Smallwood was a patient.

The testimony was repetitive but would serve the purpose of showing that the hospital had no prior knowledge of Taggart's behavior. Such behavior was not within the scope and course of employment with the hospital and would not be condoned by the hospital.

Clearly, the idea was to distance the hospital from Taggart and punitive damages. Maybe if they got lucky, the hospital could also avoid compensatory damages.

Here's a typical example:

BOSEMAN: Do you know Richard Taggart?

WITNESS: I knew him at the hospital. I did not know him socially.

BOSEMAN: Was there ever a time that you had reason to believe that Mr. Taggart had an affair or sexual relationship with any patient of Greenview Psychiatric Hospital?

WITNESS: None whatsoever.

BOSEMAN: If you had known of any such behavior, if in fact it occurred at all, and we are not saying that it did, what would you have done?

WITNESS: He would have been reported. He would have been fired.

BOSEMAN: Do you have any reason to believe that Greenview Psychiatric Hospital would condone behavior which would include sexual relationships with a patient?

WITNESS: It would not be tolerated.

The only thing Forrester would do on cross-examination was establish that the witness had no personal knowledge as to whether Taggart did, in fact, have a relationship with the patient, Cora Smallwood. Of course, the witnesses, to a person, agreed that they had no personal knowledge one way or the other.

When Boseman called a "neutral" hospital administrator as an expert witness, his testimony merely summed up GPH employee testimony. At the end, he opined that the hospital could not possibly be held responsible for the irresponsible acts of an employee. Especially since it appeared that if anything bad was going on, nobody knew it. The expert concluded, "My opinion is that the Greenview Psychiatric Hospital's care and treatment of Cora Smallwood was within acceptable standards of care."

Boseman had saved what he thought should be the last thing the jury heard. The zinger.

"Your Honor, the hospital would call one last witness." Boseman was making sure that the jury knew that this was the finale. "We call David Gobel."

It wasn't like Forrester didn't think it was coming. He was planning on it. After Boseman announced the name of the witness, the bailiff dutifully left the courtroom and called the name. The witness was ushered forward.

Forrester was thinking how slick this pudgy guy looked, strutting in all dressed-up, coat and tie, clean-shaven. Another man taking advantage of Cora. Hoping that Cora would get a big verdict and he would get to share in the judgment. It was disgusting, but the lawyer had to live with what had been dealt.

BOSEMAN: Tell the jury your name and where you live.

GOBEL: David Gobel. I live in Starke.

BOSEMAN: Mr. Gobel, do you know Cora Smallwood?

GOBEL: Yes, sir. I should.

BOSEMAN: How long have you known her?

GOBEL: Maybe three or four months.

BOSEMAN: Do you know her through business, or is it social?

GOBEL: I guess you'd say it's social.

BOSEMAN: How often do you see Ms. Smallwood, socially?

GOBEL: I'd say every day.

BOSEMAN: Is it fair to say that you and Ms. Smallwood have a special relationship?

GOBEL: I would say so.

BOSEMAN: Is she your lover?

(*The witness paused. Forrester wished he hadn't. It just gave emphasis to the testimony.*)

GOBEL: I guess you could say we're girlfriend and boyfriend.

With that, Boseman thanked the witness and walked to his seat.

This time, Laura Griffin declined to ask any questions.

The jury looked a little bit uncomfortable. Awarding money to an injured person is one thing. They didn't want to give money to this jerk. None of the jurors sat forward as Forrester took center stage in the courtroom. It was like they were disgusted.

FORRESTER: Mr. Gobel, you said that you are Cora Smallwood's boyfriend, correct?

GOBEL: Yes.

FORRESTER: You said your name is David Gobel?

GOBEL: That's what I said.

FORRESTER: Is "David" your first name?

GOBEL: No.

FORRESTER: Isn't it true that in the phone book you are listed as "R. David Gobel"?

GOBEL: That's right.

(*Forrester stopped. He wanted to get the jury's full attention. He wanted the jury to know that he hated this man as much as they. He leaned forward on the podium to get the maximum effect before asking his next question.*)

FORRESTER: Tell the jury what your first name is. What does *R* stand for?

GOBEL: My first name is Richard.

Forrester turned from the podium so that the jurors could see his face. They could see the look of disgust on his face. They saw him shaking his head as he was walking back to the table where Liz was sitting. Just before he sat down, Forrester looked back toward the witness and said with a voice that did not betray his feelings, "I am finished with you."

It had been a fast-paced day. By the end, both defendants had rested. That was the end of the testimony. They expected no more.

"Any rebuttal from the plaintiff?" Judge Coker asked.

As always, the communication with the judge was formal. He was asking plaintiff's counsel whether there would be any witness to challenge evidence presented by the defense. Evidence not already covered by the plaintiff.

"There may be, Your Honor," Bill Forrester responded.

"What do you mean 'may'? Do you have any rebuttal or not?"

"Yes, Your Honor. One witness. We will be calling one witness in the morning if it meets with your approval."

"If it's not a long witness, I'd just as soon get it over with today."

"I don't know how long she'll take. Certainly no more than an hour or two. There'll be no problem finishing closing arguments tomorrow, and the case can go to the jury by the afternoon at the latest."

Boseman interrupted the two-way colloquy. "Rebuttal to what?" he demanded.

"Rebuttal to your assertion that the hospital had no prior notice of Mr. Taggart's proclivity to have sex with patients," Forrester said.

"Do you mind telling us who you plan to call?"

"Not at all. We will be calling Heather Maxwell. She was on our witness list."

"And how do you expect to do that? The last I heard, she's in a hospital down in South Florida." It was still Boseman asking the questions of Forrester.

The plaintiff's lawyer turned to the judge. "Your Honor, Mr. Boseman is right. We can't call her live. She's a patient in a hospital. I do wonder when Mr. Boseman found out where she was located. He didn't tell us."

"Okay," the judge cut the plaintiff's lawyer short. "Confine your arguments to the issues and direct your arguments to the bench—not to each other. Now, how long do you think it'll take to read her deposition?"

"We don't plan to read her deposition. It wasn't taken. We plan to use Court-View." Forrester was talking as though he had all the authority in the world and the other side could not possibly object. Actually, he had never heard of Court-View being used live at trial in a courtroom.

"Court-View?"

Still responding as though it was an everyday occurrence, Forrester said, "Your Honor, it's video. No different than a video deposition. It's similar to Zoom or Teams, but with only one person appearing on the monitor. Like the way a video deposition looks. Ms. Maxwell has her own monitor. Her doctor has approved it, and the hospital has no objection."

"We haven't approved it!" Bosseman exclaimed.

"Neither have we." Griffin seconded. "We object!"

The judge seemed amused. "What exactly are the grounds for your objection?" he asked. "This is one of the most modern courthouses in the nation. We have multiple built-in monitors for the jury. All of the lawyers have monitors. I have a monitor. The monitors are interconnected. So, what's the problem?"

(Interestingly, the first two all-Zoom, and complete jury trials in the entire nation were tried in the Duval County Courthouse. They were conducted by Judge Bruce Anderson with the assistance of many IT specialists serving as bailiffs, along with multiple lawyers, both defense and plaintiff members of the prestigious American Board of Trial Advocates. Granted, the trials were complicated affairs and very expensive, but binding verdicts were reached. Later, hybrid Zoom trials, where jurors were chosen through use of Zoom while the remainder of the trial was conducted in the courtroom with social distancing, were the norm for a while, during the pandemic of 2020 and 2021.)

"Judge, we are not prepared for Zoom witnesses. It will take at least a day to get the IT people involved." Boseman persisted.

"That is why we are using Court-View. The witness will be visible to us and the jury. It's a direct feed. There is no need for IT," Forrester argued.

"Anyway, between now and the morning, everything will be set up, and the questions can be asked and answered live. It's no different than if the witness were actually present in the courtroom, or if we were showing a video deposition. " Liz and Forrester were double-teaming now.

"Ms. Kelley, I think your counsel can handle this without your help," Judge Coker scolded.

Forrester felt his cell vibrate. The text message was from Rosa. He looked at it, then told the judge, "You Honor, I am advised that if you prefer, we can do all the necessaries within an hour. We can finish the witness today if that's preferable."

Boseman exploded. "Your Honor, we object. There is no authority for this whatsoever. It would be totally prejudicial. We have had no opportunity to prepare for it."

"Are you saying she wasn't on the witness list?" the judge asked.

"Yes she was, but she was in a hospital. There was no way we could take her deposition." Laura Griffin was backing her cohort.

"Did you try to take her deposition?"

"No, sir, but—"

The judge continued. "Do you have any authority against a video exchange within the courtroom? It seems to me that using Zoom is precedent. Agree?"

"No, sir. We hadn't even thought of this—"

"I really don't see anything different between using Court-View or showing a video deposition; or using Zoom, for that matter."

Forrester took his cue. "Your Honor, this is no different, except Your Honor will be present to control the testimony just like you would control any other witness's testimony at trial."

Before the defense lawyers could say anything else, the judge ended the argument. "I've heard enough. Mr. Boseman, Ms. Griffin, unless you can find authority against it, I'm inclined to allow it. I see nothing that would render the evidence unreliable. I'm not persuaded by arguments that you are not prepared to cross-examine a witness who was listed. Apparently you knew that she was in the hospital. You could have taken her deposition. I frankly believe that testimony by a live witness using this Court-View system will be more reliable than deposition testimony taken before trial."

The jury was retrieved from their little room and told to return the next A.M. by eight forty-five.

Locally, the case of *Smallwood v. Taggart; et al.* was a high-profile case. It was the perfect setting for Court-View to strut its stuff. Court-View was willing to work with the lawyers, but it was expensive.

Three thousand dollars to drop everything and do the set up. There would be another one thousand dollars per hour for the technicians—one located in the hospital and the other in the courtroom. The cost would be several times that of a deposition.

As they crossed the street to their office building, Liz asked Bill a follow-up question from a conversation forty-eight hours earlier. "Have you heard anything more from the European lady?"

CHAPTER 34

THE PACE OF THE work had been unrelenting.

Matters had not been helped by the call from Ingrid Kline. He hadn't invited her to Florida, but Bill felt obligated to return her multiple phone calls.

She obviously didn't understand the work of a lawyer. Especially during trial, there is little time for anything other than preparation and presentation of evidence. Maybe that's why the divorce rate of trial lawyers is the highest of any profession.

She had been agreeable enough. Had volunteered to stay out of the way. As the days passed, however, she was not totally pleased that Bill had failed to reject the offer. The conversations grew more tense.

To make matters worse, Liz's change of attitude had not gone unnoticed. She was a professional and continued to work hard. Still, she was a woman scorned—or at least she felt that way.

After four days of trial, Bill lit a Partagas in the solitude of his office. He laid back in his big chair and blew the smoke toward the ceiling. As one puff followed the next, he recounted Rudyard Kipling's poem, "The Betrothed."

His thoughts were interrupted by a tap at the door. Forrester looked over expecting to see Liz, but it wasn't her. It was Lee.

The lawyer sat up. "Uncle Lee. You're just the man I want to see. You and Rosa did an unbelievable job today. Arranging Court-View on such short notice."

"That's what you pay me for. Hopefully it will help. I was just going to ask if there is anything else you want me to do before tomorrow."

Forrester wanted companionship. He didn't feel like being alone and he knew that Liz would not be offering the same kind of company that he could get with the investigator.

Lee obliged and took a seat across the desk. He lit a cigarette and waited for his nephew to speak.

It was really kind of interesting. The nephew was definitely in charge, but there was no envy. Lee enjoyed his job as investigator, confidante and counselor to his driven employer.

Finally, Forrester got around to what he wanted to talk about. He wanted to talk about what he had been thinking about.

"I broke the office rule. My rule, and I broke it."

"What rule is that?" Lee asked.

"Workplace romance. It only causes problems."

Lee sat mute. He knew when not to speak. He'd let the lawyer do the talking.

"It was bound to happen. If Ingrid hadn't called, something else would have occurred."

Lee did not want to comment directly. He said, "You don't need to worry about those things right now. You're in trial. Why don't you just worry about the courtroom right now?"

"You're right. But it's a pain in the ass. When this is over, both of the women in my life are going to hate me."

"So, what's new?"

Bill puffed on his cigar. "You're right again. What's new? Maybe something will work out."

"I wish I had some real advice, nephew." With that, he snuffed out his cigarette and left the lawyer alone.

The next morning Bill didn't have to wait for his alarm clock. It was 6:00 a.m. when the phone rang.

"Bill?"

With a groggy voice, he answered, "This is Bill Forrester." His thoughts weren't clear yet, and he hadn't immediately recognized the accent.

"It is Ingrid, Bill. I wanted to call you before you went to work."

"Ingrid." He was waking up. "Ingrid, this trial will be over in a couple more days. I'm sorry—"

"It is okay, Bill. It was not smart on my part. And I should not have come without planning. I know I caught you at a bad time and you are just too busy right now."

"I am busy, but I'm not too busy for you, Ingrid. There's just nothing I can do right now about this trial. It'll be over in a couple of days."

"I understand. But I have decided to go back home. I am scheduled on a flight this afternoon, and I wanted to call you before I leave."

"Leave? We haven't even seen each other yet."

"True. But I should not have come right now anyway. Things really have not changed. I just miss you. It would have been better if I had left it the way we left it in London. I know that."

"For crying out loud, Ingrid. Don't leave right now. I want to see you. I just haven't had a chance yet. This trial will be over today or Monday. I'm just doing what lawyers have to do."

There was no changing her mind. On the drive to his office, his mind was on anything but the trial. He thought about Ingrid. He thought about Liz.

For the last two days, when he wasn't focused on the trial, he was more than a little bit anxious about the situation. On the one hand, he hadn't created the situation on his own. On the other hand, but for breaking his own rules, there wouldn't be a problem.

When Ingrid had called him, the images of Africa and the passions of London had become imprinted on his mind. Those images were replaced by the anxiety of working with another woman with whom he had fallen in love.

As he reached the office, he realized he felt relieved. He hadn't seen Ingrid, and now she was leaving. That meant he would no longer be at cross terms with Liz. He would have time to work everything out after the trial.

CHAPTER 35

BY THE TIME HE got to the courtroom, Forrester was upbeat. He had told nobody about the news from Ingrid. There was no need to. It was nobody's business.

With the judge's ruling that a simulcast video procedure could be brought into the courtroom, the trial had made a turn for the better. Liz was prepared to ask the right questions, although there had been no opportunity to rehearse with Heather.

The judge wanted the last witness to be finished before noon. The instructions were to be in the courtroom at eight forty-five and to begin putting on evidence at nine. After that, there would be a one or two-hour conference on jury instructions followed by the closing arguments.

Judge Coker wanted the jury to start deliberating as early in the afternoon as possible.

The jurors were not in the jury box when, at exactly nine, Judge Coker entered through the little doorway behind the bench. Those in the courtroom rose until he sat.

"Judge, juror number one hasn't shown up." It was the bailiff talking.

"Has she called in?"

"No, sir."

"How about the alternate? Did he show up?"

The bailiff said, "Everybody else showed up. Yes, sir."

"Then I see no reason not to get on with it. That's why we have alternates."

The lawyers for the defense were delighted. Bill and Liz felt like throwing up.

The alternate juror was the insurance adjuster. The plaintiff's lawyers' nightmare. Now, after the case was going well, things would be ruined because of somebody who had his mind made up before he was ever allowed to sit as a juror.

Forrester stood up. "Your Honor, can't we give her fifteen minutes to show up?" He was practically pleading.

"No. I told you I wanted to get this case over with today. I don't want this to last through the weekend or into Monday."

There would be nothing to do but to proceed. A lawyer lives with bad luck. In a courtroom, he has to act like nothing bothers him while he swallows TUMS or Rolaids. While his sphincter eats a hole in the chair, he just sits there nonchalantly and acts pleasant. That's lawyering. That's the life of a trial lawyer.

"Mr. Forrester, before we call the jury out, is everything in place for your next witness?"

Forrester wanted his answer to last fifteen or twenty minutes. He wanted to delay long enough for the lady juror to show up. All he could say, however, was, "Yes, sir. We're ready to proceed."

"Ms. Griffin, Mr. Boseman, do you have any further argument before we proceed in the manner we discussed last evening?"

Actually, Boseman was prepared to make a lengthy argument. He decided not to. He didn't want to waste time. If one word of evidence could get out before the missing juror showed up, he would be home free. It would be the defense lawyer's dream. He would have an insurance adjuster help decide the fate of a trial that had blown up.

Boseman answered, "No, Your Honor. We'll rely on what we argued yesterday."

"The same is true for us," Laura Griffin said in agreement.

"Okay. Let's go ahead and get started then."

The judge had no more than got the words out of his mouth when the courtroom door opened and a little woman came rushing in, purse in hand and obviously flustered.

"I'm sorry, sir. I had to wait for the train. I hope I'm not too late. I really am sorry."

It was juror number one, and she was talking as she came through the courtroom making a grand entrance beyond the bar.

"Not at all. Take your time. Next time try to leave a little earlier." The stern judge could not have sounded more pleasant and understanding as juror number one was escorted into the secluded area behind the jury box where the jurors would later deliberate.

It was now Fred Boseman's turn to eat a hole in his chair.

Despite his best efforts, smiling all the while, Forrester could not catch the eye of his adversary. He only wanted to wink.

———

At 7:00 a.m., well before the witness had been taken to a conference room at her hospital, an IT guru/technician set up a computer monitor on a ten-foot-long table. The chairs around the table were pushed in, with the exception of the one on the end, where a person conducting a meeting would normally sit. The witness would sit in that chair.

The monitor was placed so that the witness would face its camera. Then the technician tested to make sure that all angles were correct, and that the questioners in the courtroom would be visible to the witness.

The IT lady in the courtroom was just as competent and efficient. A monitor, identical to the one placed before the witness, had been placed on the courtroom podium. The lawyer asking questions would have a perfect view of the person providing testimony.

Likewise, the judge and jury would have the same view on their monitors, which were permanent to the courtroom. The judge's monitor was on the bench. Three monitors were attached to the jury box. The monitors at the lawyers' tables were exactly the same as the judge's. Nothing would be lost on any of the trial participants.

Just to be sure, the technicians remained at their respective venues while being paid by the hour. If Murphy's Law was not thwarted, they would be there to cure any problems.

———

Judge Coker instructed the jury about the purpose of rebuttal, then he said, "Are the parties ready to proceed?"

Perfunctorily all of the lawyers agreed as Elizabeth Kelley took her place behind the podium. She said, "The plaintiff calls Heather Maxwell by Court-View."

The monitors were activated as the judge explained to the jury that they should consider and evaluate this testimony as they would any other testimony, and as if the witness were present in the courtroom.

The picture on the monitors was of a young woman sitting in a chair in front of a mint-colored wall. The wall was bare, and there was nothing to distract the viewer. The witness could see the person behind the podium as the questions were asked.

Heather Maxwell looked to be in her early twenties. Her hair was straight—a kind of ratty brown color. She was thin. Almost skinny. She wore no makeup, and her face was pale. It was a stark contrast to the usual tan of most Florida residents.

Now Elizabeth Kelley asked the witness her name, address and where she was right now. The answers came through the monitor's speakers.

She explained that she was in one of the conference rooms at St. Michael's Hospital. She had been a patient there for more than three weeks.

When asked her history as it related to time spent in psychiatric hospitals, she explained that, like Cora, she had been in and out multiple times starting when she was fourteen. In recent years, she was admitted each time she became too depressed to cope. Right now she was taking Prozac, and that seemed to help.

She, too, had a history of abuse within her family. It was her father who taught her how to "make love" beginning at the age of ten. Her mother had abandoned her and the family a couple of years before that.

She was admitted to a psychiatric hospital for the first time because she was a hell-raising teenager. She was out of control and taking social drugs. She claimed that she was not addicted.

There was a time that she thought she was going to make something of her life. That was during her first admission to Greenview Psychiatric Hospital. It was when she first met Rick Taggart, the psychologist who led the group sessions she was required to attend.

KELLEY: How many times have you been a patient at Greenview Psychiatric Hospital?"

MAXWELL: Three. *(Now she wasn't looking into the monitor. Her face was lowered, the same way that Cora lowered her face when she answered questions. Her voice was quiet, and the IT technician increased the volume on the monitors.)*

KELLEY: You said you met the defendant, Mr. Taggart, the first time you were in that hospital. Tell us how you met him.

MAXWELL: I was in a group session—all of us. After several sessions I felt good. Rick became my friend, and we talked in other places too."

KELLEY: What do you mean by 'other places'?

MAXWELL: You know, we would run into each other in the hall. He would come by my room. We just talked. I felt good.

KELLEY: Did you have any type of relationship with him other than as a patient at that time?

MAXWELL: Not at that time. That was later.

KELLEY: Was there ever a time that you began to have a relationship with this psychologist?

MAXWELL: It was after I was released. He called me at my house.

KELLEY: At your house?

MAXWELL: I guess it was an apartment. I had a job, and I had an apartment. I had a roommate who helped me with the expenses.

KELLEY: Were you expecting him to call you?

MAXWELL: No. Not really. He just called one night, and I answered the phone.

KELLEY: What happened after that?

MAXWELL: He would call sometimes, and we would talk on the phone. One day he asked if I wanted to meet him. We met after work and ate hamburgers.

KELLEY: You didn't go to a bar or anything like that?

MAXWELL: No. We couldn't. I was only seventeen. I'd been in bars before, but it wasn't like that with Rick and me.

KELLEY: This all occurred before the second time you went into Greenview Psychiatric Hospital?

MAXWELL: Yes.

KELLEY: And, before the next time you were a patient at the hospital, did your relationship with the defendant, Mr. Taggart, change?

MAXWELL: If you mean, did we have sex? Yes.

KELLEY: When was the first time you had sex with this man?

MAXWELL: The same night we had hamburgers. He wanted to drive me home. It was my fault.

KELLEY: Why do you say it was your fault?

MAXWELL: It just was. It was in his car.

KELLEY: In his car?

MAXWELL: You know, it wasn't "doing it." It was more like I touched him. You know. *(Heather was obviously uncomfortable, and the jury had caught on. Liz moved on with the questioning.)*

KELLEY: Before you went into Greenview Psychiatric Hospital for a second time, did you ever have intercourse with Richard Taggart?

MAXWELL: Yes. Lots of times after that. Then he didn't want to see me anymore.

KELLEY: Why not?

MAXWELL: I don't know. That's why I went back.

KELLEY: That's why you went back to the hospital?

MAXWELL: Yes. I wanted to see him. I know it was wrong, but I wanted to see him. It was my fault.

KELLEY: Did they just let you in the hospital? For no reason?

MAXWELL: No. I got arrested for stealing things. I knew they'd put me back in. I was a minor.

KELLEY: Did you see Psychologist Taggart after you went back in the hospital?

MAXWELL: Yes. I was in one of his groups. But he wouldn't pay attention to me.

KELLEY: He wouldn't pay attention to you? What does that mean?

MAXWELL: He ignored me. I didn't understand it.

KELLEY: Did he ignore you the whole time you were in the hospital that time?

MAXWELL: No. I found him one day on purpose. I was crying, and I asked him if he would come see me.

KELLEY: Did he come see you?

MAXWELL: He came to my room. I was alone.

KELLEY: Did you have sex?

(*Heather looked up to the monitor for the first time since the beginning of the questioning. Her eyes were red. Tears had welled up and were falling off her cheeks. She stared into the camera and tried to answer. She couldn't. She sniffed and tried again.*)

MAXWELL: I gave him sex while he stood there. He didn't stop me.

KELLEY: Oral sex?

MAXWELL: Yes.

KELLEY: Was that the only time during your second admission to the hospital?

MAXWELL: Yes. He ignored me. He wouldn't see me anymore.

Now for the crucial question. The answer would nail the hospital. Kelley paused and flipped pages in her notebook as though looking for a prepared text which she did not have.

The six jurors and the alternate were glued to their monitors.

KELLEY: Heather, during that second visit, did you ever tell anybody at the hospital what happened? That you had had sex in the hospital with Richard Taggart?

MAXWELL: I told everybody. I told everybody at one time.

KELLEY: What do you mean you told everybody at one time?

MAXWELL: The same day I was discharged. Put out. I screamed it over and over.

KELLEY: What happened?

MAXWELL: I knew I was getting out. I saw Rick—Mr. Taggart— and I told him I was going to be leaving. He ignored me and walked off. I went kind of crazy. I knew it was my fault, but I went kind of crazy.

KELLEY: What happened next?

MAXWELL: He was walking away. I went and pushed him from behind and yelled at him like one of those crazy women in the movies. I yelled at him and told him that it wasn't fair.

KELLEY: What do you mean you told him it wasn't fair?

MAXWELL: I was screaming. I screamed that it was wrong for him to have sex with me and then treat me bad. Ignore me. It wasn't right for him to ignore me. I screamed it. I kept screaming it.

KELLEY: What did you keep screaming?

MAXWELL: I kept screaming that it wasn't fair that he had sex with me and was now ignoring me. They pulled me away.

KELLEY: Who pulled you away?

MAXWELL: Nursers. Orderlies. There were a bunch of them. I don't know how many. Two or three.

KELLEY: What did Richard Taggart do?

MAXWELL: He didn't do nothing. He didn't say a word. He let them pull me off.

Heather was screaming into the camera. She was screaming at the monitor like she had screamed in the hospital. Bawling while she screamed the words.

Liz let her calm down. She waited for more than three minutes. Heather lowered her head like she had at the start.

KELLEY: Did anybody believe what you were saying?

MAXWELL, *quietly now*: No. They said I shouldn't say things like that. They said I should calm down.

KELLEY: Who said that?

MAXWELL: The nurses. The nurses who pulled me off.

KELLEY: After that, was there ever a time that anybody came to you and asked you questions about what you had told them? Was there ever a time when anybody told you that an investigation was being conducted?

MAXWELL: No.

With that answer, the line of questioning changed. Heather had been admitted the third time over her own objections. She had tried to commit suicide two months after the second hospitalization. She took an entire bottle of pain pills but was found by her roommate unconscious. After her stomach was pumped, a judge ordered her back to Greenview Psychiatric Hospital for observation and counseling. This was just seven weeks after she had last gotten out.

During the third admission, she refused to attend group sessions with Taggart. Nevertheless, based on his recommendation, she was released in only eight days.

KELLEY: Heather, do you remember the dates of your admissions at Greenview Psychiatric Hospital?

MAXWELL: Only the second one.

KELLEY: When was that?

MAXWELL: February 14, 2018. I was in three weeks starting on Valentine's Day.

The important thing was that it was three months before Cora Smallwood was admitted.

———

"The Court will be recessed for fifteen minutes," Judge Coker said immediately following the direct examination.

The evidence had been devastating for the defense. Maybe it was even more effective because it was like it was on television. Anyway, the jurors looked exhausted as they were ushered back into the jury room for the short break.

When they were ushered back in, you could feel the mood in the courtroom. Forrester was convinced that Boseman would gladly re-offer the $350,000, previously withdrawn.

Richard Taggart seemed oblivious to the cross-examination. He paid little or no attention. He stared at the table like a beaten man. It was the same way Cora had looked whenever she was in the courtroom. It was the same way Heather looked on video.

Laura Griffin gave up after a few questions. The best she could do was, "Isn't it true that you don't know of anybody who ever saw you have a sexual relationship with Mr. Taggart?"

The witness had simply agreed.

Fred Boseman did little better. When it was his turn to ask questions on behalf of the hospital, he looked directly into the monitor, knowing that Heather was looking back.

BOSEMAN: Ms. Maxwell, please tell me the names of the hospital people that you say pulled you away while you were in hysterics.

MAXWELL: I don't know their names.

There were no further questions.

CHAPTER 36

MAYBE IT'S BECAUSE THEY love the captive audience; or because they love to hear themselves speak. In any event, trial lawyers love to make their closing arguments.

Most experts agree that the case has already been won or lost before that opportunity occurs at the end of the trial. Whatever. It's the ritual, and maybe it does make a difference in some cases.

The way it's set up is that the plaintiff, through her lawyers, has the first opportunity, followed by each of the defense lawyers. The plaintiff's lawyer then has final rebuttal. Even before the trial had begun, Bill Forrester and Elizabeth Kelley had agreed to divide the close. Bill would do the first part, and Liz would follow after the defense.

Each lawyer has his own style. But some things are the same. They all start quietly and thank the jury for spending a week with them. Slowly, they reach a crescendo where they are practically yelling out nouns and verbs to drive home a point that is ever so important. At the end they slow down and thank the jury for a final time.

A main difference this case had from most was the issue of punitive damages. Very few trial lawyers ever have a chance to ask the jury to punish the defendant above and beyond compensating the plaintiff for injuries. Punitive damages simply are not allowed very often—maybe one trial in a couple of hundred. Maybe less.

For emphasis, the verdict form that the jury would use had been blown up and pasted on foam board. Forrester held it in front of the jury in his right hand and pointed with a magic marker that he held in his left. At the end of several questions on the form were the words "yes" and "no." As he argued, he showed the jury which response he thought they should circle; and then demonstrated by marking the blowup.

At the end of all the verdict questions was a long line for the jury to write in the amount of damages necessary to fairly and adequately compensate for the injuries that Forrester argued were "undisputed" in the testimony.

He posed the rhetorical question. "How can I suggest an amount for you to write in on that blank? You decide the damages. That's the tough job for you to do. You have the job to right a wrong. You have the power of the jury. You have the power to determine the amount of a debt created by Richard Taggart and the hospital when they, together, took something from Cora Smallwood.

"Of course, we all know that Cora Smallwood was injured when she went into the hospital. She wouldn't have gone into the hospital if she weren't injured. She left the hospital crippled!

"Now, you have the job of determining the amount of the debt. The amount that has to be paid for the crippling damages imposed on her by Richard Taggart, working for the hospital.

"I don't have the right to tell you how much that debt is. How much those damages are. That is your job.

"One thing you may do is consider the mortality tables that were placed in the evidence. Mortality tables show that she has a life expectancy of forty-six-point-three years. Forty-six-point-three years to live. And, each of those years she will live three hundred and sixty five days as a cripple. And each of those days will have twenty-four hours.

"Twenty-four hours times three hundred and sixty-five days a year times forty-six-point-three years. That's four hundred and five thousand, five hundred and eighty-eight hours that Cora is expected to live." Forester wrote that number on a pad attached to an easel in the courtroom. "How much are her damages worth per hour?"

"You have the power of the jury, and you will decide if each of those hours is worth fifteen dollars. Or ten dollars. On the other hand, you may decide to award minimum wage. Minimum wage for every hour that she is crippled by Richard Taggart and the hospital. It's up to you. You have the power of the jury, and you have the power to right a wrong."

When he got to the last line where a blank needed to be filled in on the verdict form, he gave another speech that he had prepared.

"Most of us drive cars. If we do something wrong, we take our chances. If we're caught speeding or going through a red light or a stop sign, we know that we may get caught. We may get caught just like Richard Taggart and Greenview Psychiatric Hospital got caught doing something wrong to Cora Smallwood.

"If we get caught, we know we're going to get fined because we know we're going to get a ticket, and that's what punitive damages are about. They're a different kind of damages. They're the damages that are assessed not to compensate Cora Smallwood. They're the type of damages that are used to fine the hospital and Richard Taggart and send a message home.

"The message that you have the responsibility to send home is that in the State of Florida, 'we' will not allow hospitals, nor any other institution, to purposely or recklessly injure another citizen. Cora's injuries were not from a mere oversight. The hospital was reckless, and its employee acted with deliberate purpose as he virtually raped a patient who was there begging for help.

"That's why you award punitive damages. The other damages that you award are to compensate her for her injuries and the debt created by the action of the defendants."

Forester paused for emphasis. Now he spoke deliberately. One word at a time. "Only through you can Cora punish those who deliberately and recklessly caused the injuries.

"Now, you know that the hospital has assets. We proved the net worth. The net worth of the corporation that does business as Greenview Psychiatric Hospital is $500,813,568. Does anybody think that the price of a mere traffic ticket would have any effect on an institution with those kind of assets? Does anybody think a ticket for fifty or one hundred or even five hundred dollars would have much of an effect? Does anybody think it would send a message?

"Of course not! Neither would one thousand or ten thousand!

"That's the reason the Judge let us put on the evidence of the assets of the hospital. That's why you get to know the net worth of the hospital."

"And, you have the power of the jury to set a fine of punitive damages strong enough to send a message to the hospital and anybody else in the State of Florida that hears about it that we will not allow this reckless behavior.

"If the hospital had assets of only one thousand dollars, a fine or a punishment of fifty or one hundred dollars may be enough to get its attention. If it only had assets of one thousand dollars, a fine of five or ten percent of its net worth would be fair and shock no one as unreasonable.

"And, I submit to you that when you assess punitive damages and when you look at the assets of the hospital, you will write down an amount that is several times whatever you determine to be the compensatory damages. A fair amount, but an amount substantial enough to send the message that you want to be sent."

No matter what the defendants argued, Liz was prepared to counter.

Laura Griffin told the jury, "It's really one person's word against another's."

Liz countered, "It's not whether you believe Richard Taggart or Cora Smallwood. It's whether you believe Richard Taggart or Head Nurse Robertson, Cora Smallwood, and Heather Maxwell."

Fred Boseman argued, "If Richard Taggart did what he's accused of doing, then it's wrong, and you should punish him, but there's no evidence that what he may have done was done under the training or supervision or on behalf of the hospital. You should not punish the hospital."

Liz countered, "See how they have separate tables in here? From the very beginning, Mr. Boseman obviously wanted to distance himself and his client, the hospital, from Richard Taggart. He wishes that the hospital had distanced itself from Richard Taggart when it had the chance. When they knew that Heather had been injured and other people would be injured after her, they should've done something, but they didn't. They were reckless and a separation of tables in a courtroom does not separate the employee from the employer. Richard Taggart is the hospital and was the hospital for Cora Smallwood."

———

While she made her argument, the last argument of the trial, Bill's mind wandered. There was nothing further for him to do in the case but wait.

He knew he loved her. He admired her as a lawyer and loved her as a woman. Things would have been simple if she didn't work in the office.

Since the first call from Ingrid, she had not acted the same. She was professional all right, but she had lost her passion for them as a couple.

He thought about Ingrid and their conversations of marriage or the impossibility of marriage. He had grown to live with it. Then she had popped back into his life. Even if only briefly. Now she was gone again, but things had changed with Liz.

He would wait until the trial was over. He could figure things out then.

———

"Thank you, Mr. Monroe. We appreciate your having been willing to sit through this entire week of testimony and arguments. Fortunately, or unfortunately, as the alternate juror, it will not be necessary for you to stay here any longer. Of course, you're welcome to stay in the courtroom if that's what you want to do and wait as the jurors deliberate and hopefully come to a verdict. Otherwise, you're free to go. Please see the clerk on the second floor for your final instructions."

As Judge Coker excused the alternate, the other six people behind the rail disappeared through the door marked "Jurors Only." Their instructions had been given, and they were left with the task of considering the evidence; determining the liability; and setting the damages, if any, claimed by Cora Smallwood.

The judge exited through the small door behind his bench.

The lawyers and their clients would wait in and around the courtroom until the jury was ready to announce its judgment. In this case they were kept company by one newspaper reporter, two local television personalities, and their cameraman.

The alternate juror decided that he would at least stick around for a while.

———

Fred Boseman couldn't contain himself. He finally made his way over to the man who had sat for a week with the jury. The alternate who should know best what to expect.

"Mr. Monroe, you don't have to talk to me about the case unless you want to. Based on your experience as an insurance adjuster, I'd be really interested in knowing your thoughts."

The man who would return to his full-time job doling out money to victims on behalf of an insurance company stood up and maneuvered his body so as to shield what he was going to say from anybody else in the courtroom. He didn't want to be heard by anybody other than the defense lawyer.

In a whisper, he said, "Mr. Boseman, I've been in this business a long time. Maybe not as long as you. If it were my company, I'd recommend doing whatever is necessary to settle this case now."

Boseman whispered back, "You wouldn't wait for a verdict?"

"I think you're going to be tagged hard."

Boseman just nodded and then casually walked over to the table where his client's representative had been sitting throughout the trial. He immediately reported what the alternate had told him.

———

After most trials, all lawyers are obliged to tell their opponents what a good job they did. Boseman used that opportunity to shake Forrester's hand, then Liz's. He broached the subject that hurt him most.

"Bill, you two did one helluva job. In fact, you did such a good job, my people want to know if you're still open for negotiations."

Liz let her presence be known. "How much are we talking about?" She was going to be involved with any negotiations surrounding this case.

Forrester stepped back, giving a body language signal that any negotiations from here on would be with her, not him.

"How about five hundred thousand?"

Without hesitation, Liz said, "Our client won't take that. Besides, we wouldn't recommend it. The trial's gone too well."

She had finality in her voice, and Boseman recognized it as such.

Boseman seemed to stroll confidently back to his table and signaled for Laura Griffin to come over. The three of them, Boseman, Griffin and the woman with the money, conferenced in muffled voices.

Only forty-five minutes had passed since the jury had left the courtroom. A buzzer rang, which told everybody present that a verdict had probably been decided. Five minutes later, Judge Coker was back on the bench with the jury still in the Jury Room. Boseman was on his feet. "Your Honor, can we approach the bench?"

The judge nodded, and with that all of the lawyers paraded forward and huddled next to the judge. No court reporter.

"Judge, we think we may be able to settle this case. We don't know what the jury has done, but if the plaintiff is willing, we would like five minutes to see if we can settle this case before the jury comes in with its verdict."

"You can take fifteen minutes," Judge Coker said. As he stood to exit the courtroom again, he instructed the bailiff to tell the jury that they would have to wait a little longer.

For the trial lawyer, there's nothing worse than the time waiting after a jury buzzes to signal that they've reached a verdict, and the time that the verdict is read aloud in the courtroom. Forty-five minutes is usually pretty quick for a verdict. When such a short turnaround happens, every lawyer has an opinion of what it could mean. In reality, nobody really knows.

Although Boseman was still the spokesman with the offers, he was accompanied this time by Taggart's lawyer.

"Liz, you know this has to be our final offer. There's no time to negotiate. I'd offer you a low-ball if I could, and you know it."

"So what are you saying?"

"If your client will take a million dollars, the case is settled."

Her heart jumped, but she looked unfazed. "I'll ask Cora and be right back with you if the offer is two-point-five million."

"Come on. I'm doing the best I can. I worked to get the million-dollar offer."

"Then let's wait for the verdict," Liz replied.

"No, I will go talk to our adjuster. Give me a few minutes.

"So you know, two million will be for Ms. Smallwood. The other five hundred thousand is for Ms. Maxwell."

"Heather Maxwell? The statute of limitations for that woman has run. She doesn't have a claim."

"I know. That's why we're willing to take so little. It's your call, but I would suggest you think about public relations."

The newspaper account was the most accurate in the media. They made multiple stories out of it.

One of the articles rehashed the saga of Richard Smallwood. He was the brother of Cora Smallwood, the plaintiff, in *Smallwood v. Taggary, et al.* The point of his first name being the same as that of the defendant and the plaintiff's new boyfriend was not lost on the reporter. Now, thanks to a plea bargain, he would spend most of his adult life in prison, but he did avoid the death penalty.

It was reported that the Alachua County State Attorney's Office was equivocal as to whether or not criminal charges would be pressed against Taggart, who was still healing from a gunshot wound rendered by the first "Richard" in Cora Smallwood's life.

The major article was about the settlement reached just as the jury was bringing in a verdict. Attorneys William Forrester and Elizabeth Kelley both agreed that no fee would be taken from the portion to be paid to one of the earlier victims of hospital misconduct.

Fred Boseman, speaking on behalf of the hospital, had said that his client wanted to make certain that Heather Maxwell was at least partially compensated even though there was no obligation in light of the running of the statute of limitations. "After all, my client, Greenview

Psychiatric Hospital, wants to help people. Hopefully, the sum of money will help Ms. Maxwell put back a portion of her life."

Three days later the TV personality who had sat through the trial reported his scoop.

"After talking with three different jurors, this reporter confirmed today that the jury had recommended a verdict in favor of the plaintiff in the case of Cora Smallwood—the woman who claimed damages as a result of the love affair she had with her psychologist while she was a patient at Greenview Psychiatric Hospital. You will recall the last-minute settlement for two and a half million dollars that we reported three days ago.

"Marilee Sullivan, one of the jurors, said, 'If they had waited, they would have learned that we had decided she deserved one million dollars for her injuries and three times that amount in punitive damages. The total verdict was four million dollars. Of course, there was nothing in the verdict for the other lady. The other victim—Heather Maxwell.'"

CHAPTER 37

"I TALKED TO INGRID today and yesterday. She's back in Austria and says that it was a mistake; her coming here."

It was the first time that Liz and Bill had been together after work since the second day of the Cora Smallwood trial. They were at the River House sitting on the deck overlooking the St. Johns River. Liz was drinking a twelve-year-old Macallan single malt scotch and water. Bill had a Coke with a squeeze of lime.

"So why are you telling me that?" Liz asked.

"I thought you ought to know. We've never talked about Ingrid."

"I knew who she was. Everybody in the office has heard about her."

"But we never talked about her."

Liz said, "I don't feel like talking about her now, either."

Bill persisted, "I know. I understand. It's just that we agreed again that we'll remember each other, but at this stage in our lives, we'll never be together."

"I told you I don't care."

"She says my life's too hectic right now. If she wanted to come to the United States, she doesn't think we'd ever see each other, and she's probably right. With work, my girls...."

He had hesitated, but Liz didn't jump in. She just sat there looking at him. Never losing eye contact even when she took a sip of the golden-colored liquid.

Bill continued, "I don't have time for her along with my work; the time I want to spend with my girls...and the time I want to spend with you."

Liz flinched, but she still didn't say anything.

"So what do you think, Liz?"

Time passed, and nobody said anything.

Then Liz said, "Love affairs in the office just can't work out. I've thought about it. If you and the other partners agree, I'd rather just work with you."

CHAPTER 38

THE TELEPHONE RANG, AND the receptionist answered, "Moran, Smith, Forrester, Dees and Kelley."

The voice at the other end asked for William Forrester. She was transferred to Rosa, who in turn tried to transfer the call to Bill.

"I told you, Rosa, No more calls today. I've got to get some work done."

He was obviously agitated, with more work than he could hope to finish.

Rosa said, "I know you said that. But you'll want this call. Why don't you take it and see?"

"Okay. Okay. While I'm doing it, how about bringing me the rough draft of the O'Hara brief."

With that, he picked up the phone and recognized the voice on the other end. When he finished, he walked to his new partner's office. He knocked on the door and waited for Liz to motion him to be seated while she finished transcribing something. She saw the wicked smile on his face and cut the dictation short.

"Okay. I recognize that look. What's going on?" she asked.

"You won't believe who I had a call from just now."

"So tell me."

"Do you remember JoAnne Manchester?"

"Do I remember her? It's only been six months since the Smallwood trial. How could I forget her?"

"Do you remember that she wouldn't testify for us?"

"That's what I remember."

"Well, she just called me. She just returned from an extended vacation at a halfway house, where she was drying out from booze and drugs."

"So?"

"So, she said she just heard about the results of the trial, and she wants to make an appointment to see you and me."

"What for?"

"She wants to know if we'll represent her in a case against Rick Taggart and the Greenview Psychiatric Hospital. She wants retribution."